DARK
LIGHT

ALSO BY RANDY WAYNE WHITE

Sanibel Flats
The Heat Islands
The Man Who Invented Florida
Captiva
North of Havana
The Mangrove Coast
Ten Thousand Islands
Shark River
Twelve Mile Limit
Everglades
Tampa Burn
Dead of Night

Nonfiction

Batfishing in the Rainforest
The Sharks of Lake Nicaragua
Last Flight Out
An American Traveler
Tarpon Fishing in Mexico and Florida (An Introduction)

DARK
LIGHT

Randy Wayne White

G. P. PUTNAM'S SONS   New York

G. P. Putnam's Sons
Publishers Since 1838
Published by the Penguin Group
Penguin Group (USA) Inc., 375 Hudson Street, New York, New York 10014, USA • Penguin
Group (Canada), 90 Eglinton Avenue East, Suite 700, Toronto, Ontario M4P ZY3, Canada (a
division of Pearson Penguin Canada Inc.) • Penguin Books Ltd, 80 Strand, London
WC2R 0RL, England • Penguin Group Ireland, 25 St Stephen's Green, Dublin 2, Ireland (a division
of Penguin Books Ltd) • Penguin Group (Australia), 250 Camberwell Road, Camberwell,
Victoria 3124, Australia (a division of Pearson Australia Group Pty Ltd) • Penguin Books India
Pvt Ltd, 11 Community Centre, Panchsheel Park, New Delhi–110 017, India • Penguin Group
(NZ), cnr Airborne and Rosedale Roads, Albany, Auckland 1310, New Zealand (a division of
Pearson New Zealand Ltd) • Penguin Books (South Africa) (Pty) Ltd, 24 Sturdee Avenue,
Rosebank, Johannesburg 2196, South Africa

Penguin Books Ltd, Registered Offices: 80 Strand, London WC2R 0RL, England

"Morning in New York" written by Wendy Webb © 2003 Wendy Webb. Used by permission.
"My Beating Heart" written by Wendy Webb © 2005 Wendy Webb. Used by permission.
"Driving in a Dream" written by Wendy Webb © 2003 Wendy Webb. Used by permission.

Library of Congress Cataloging-in-Publication Data

White, Randy Wayne.
Dark light/Randy Wayne White.
p.   cm.
ISBN 0-399-15336-5
1. Ford, Doc (Fictitious character)—Fiction.   2. Marine biologists—Fiction.
3. Florida—Fiction.   4. Shipwrecks—Fiction.   I. Title.
PS3573.H47473D42   2006   2005058658
813'.54—dc22

Printed in the United States of America
1   3   5   7   9   10   8   6   4   2

BOOK DESIGN BY MEIGHAN CAVANAUGH

This is a work of fiction. Names, characters, places, and incidents either are the product of the author's
imagination or are used fictitiously, and any resemblance to actual persons, living or dead, businesses,
companies, events, or locales is entirely coincidental.

While the author has made every effort to provide accurate telephone numbers and Internet addresses at
the time of publication, neither the publisher nor the author assumes any responsibility for errors, or for
changes that occur after publication. Further, the publisher does not have any control over and does not
assume any responsibility for author or third-party websites or their content.

FOR WENDY

AUTHOR'S NOTE

This book was begun shortly after the eye of a category 4 hurricane dec-
imated the village where I live on the west coast of Florida. Captiva and
Sanibel Island (where I was a fishing guide for many years) were also badly
damaged—but not nearly as badly as portrayed in the national media. I am
pleased to report that the islands are more beautiful than ever, and back to
normal.

Even so, I spent most of the last year homeless, bouncing from place to
place, sometimes country to country, trying to work while also juggling
the details of rebuilding, and the relentless indifference of the insurance industry, and a few local bureaucrats. Happily, much good came from all the
chaos, and I have many people to thank for their kindness and concern.
Many dozens offered me help, even their homes. I will forever be in
their debt.

Much of this book was written in public libraries, and I have become
a great fan of library professionals as a result. I am especially grateful to the
staff at Pine Island Public Library and also Sanibel Library. They were superb, and it was at the Sanibel Library where I found most of my information on the little-known hurricane of 1944. Many of the details in this
novel, although used fictionally, are true, including Cuban fishermen who
washed up on the beach, a man tragically set ablaze at his own moonshine
still . . . and a beachside estate with its own family cemetery. The library
staffs in Holmes Beach, Florida, Key West, Pioneer, Ohio, and Franklin,
Tennessee, were also a great help.

Another favorite place to write was Doc Ford's Sanibel Rum Bar and Grille. I wanted to thank my friends and associates Marty and Brenda Harrity, Mark and Heidi Marinello, Jean Baer, Greg Nelson, Raynauld Bentley, Marita, Brian, Maria, Liz, Jean, and Big Dan Howes. My pal Matt Asen's Sanibel Grill at Timber's Restaurant was another great place to work, as was the Tarpon Lodge on Pine Island.

Others who were generous beyond the expectations of friendship include Ms. Iris Tanner, Gary and Donna Terwilliger, Craig and Renee Johnson, George and Michelle Riggs, Kevin Lollar and Nadine, Moe Mollen, Dr. Amanda Evans, Tony Johnson, David Thompson, Jenny Franks, Bill Wundram, Stu Johnson, Gloria Osburn, Berry Rubel, Capt. Eric Osking, Tom and Sally Petcoff, Capt. Steve Stanley, Dr. Brian and Kristin Hummel, Capt. Craig Skaar, Bill Gutek and his Nokomis pals, the Wells family of Cabbage Key and Pineland, Bill "Spaceman" Lee, Diana, Ginny Amsler, Allan W. Eckert, Jennifer Holloway, and Dr. Corey Malcolm.

This book demanded extensive research in several fields, and I am grateful to the experts who took the time to advise me. Dr. Thaddeus Kostrubala, a brilliant psychopharmacologist, has once again provided behavioral profiles on some truly nasty fictional characters. Dr. James H. Peck, fellow Davenport Central (Iowa) graduate, has compiled exhaustive notes on all the Ford novels, and is due much thanks. Attorneys Tim Bruhl, and Mike McHale, an admiralty law expert provide much needed information.

These people all provided valuable guidance and/or information. All errors, exaggerations, omissions, or fictionalizations are entirely the fault and the responsibility of the author.

I would especially like to thank Wendy Webb for allowing me to reprint lyrics from her original compositions. Ms. Webb was, in no way, the inspiration for the fictional character Mildred Chestra Engle, but she *was* the inspiration for Chestra's haunting voice and lyrics. Ms. Webb, in fact, provided both in her songs, "Morning in New York," "My Beating Heart," and "Driving in a Dream." You may hear Ms. Webb's music on the Internet at: Wendywebbmusic.com.

Finally, I would like to thank my dear sons and buddies, Lee and Rogan White, for once again helping me finish a book.

The loneliness you get by the sea is personal
and alive. It doesn't subdue you and make
you feel abject. It's stimulating loneliness.

—*Anne Morrow Lindbergh*

I had a little Sorrow,
Born of a little Sin,
I found a room all damp with gloom
And shut us all within;
And, "Little Sorrow, weep," said I,
"And, Little Sin, pray God to die,
And I upon the floor will lie
And think how bad I've been!"

—*Edna St. Vincent Millay*

DARK LIGHT

1 Picturing his grandfather's face the last time he'd seen him alive—six years ago?—Bern Heller sat at a table where he'd spread the contents of a briefcase sent by the executor.

There were yellowed photos of a young man, tall, blond.

His grandfather?

No resemblance, but his name was there in faded ink.

A photo of him standing beside a man identified as Henry Ford. Another of him holding a drink tray, a towel over his arm, while Henry Ford and a younger guy—my God, *Charles Lindbergh?*—sat in patio chairs, palm trees in the background.

On the back: Fort Myers, Florida, 1940s.

That was the time to buy property in Florida.

His grandfather had.

Miscellaneous personal items—the attorney had mentioned the briefcase a month ago at the funeral. It arrived today, smelling of nesting rodents. His grandfather had been such a vicious son of a bitch that Heller would've trashed it if he hadn't seen the photos. Henry Ford and Lindbergh—valuable.

Some other interesting stuff, too: Bills of sale for acreage the old man had purchased, handwritten. A passport, German, stamped with swastikas in a couple of places. A nautical map so old the paper flaked in his hands—two sets of numbers, also in ink, near Sanibel Island.

Another old photo, this of an unidentified woman. Glamorous, like a film star from the '40s, a PR shot. The woman in sequins after lighting a cigarette, her eyes staring through smoke into the camera.

God, the face, those full lips. Her body . . .

The thought of it, a woman like this with the old man, was disgusting.

An hour later, Bern checked his watch—time to meet with the red-neck Hoosier he'd hired to run the marina. He stood and looked through his condo window, seeing more palm trees, a bay and mangrove islands beyond.

Moe was telling his boss, Bern Heller, "The guy said he'd be back with a gun. I think he means it. No"—Moe ducked his head into the straw cowboy hat he was holding—"I *know* he means it. It's one of the fishing guides. The spook."

"Spook?"

Moe said, "You know, a colored guy. You don't call them that in Wisconsin?"

Heller gave him a look.

Moe kept going. "You've seen him. Javier Castillo. The black guy with the Spanish accent. He's around here most mornings, getting ice, waiting for his clients."

"Okay . . . the skinny one who goes barefoot. He doesn't look Mexican."

"No, he's Cuban. In Florida, that's what most Mexicans are. Javier owns that boat sitting by the fuel docks. The Pursuit, with twin Yamaha outboards, and the radar. A beauty."

"The greenish-looking one?"

"Yeah. The open fisherman. Blue-green." Moe turned sideways and pointed so his boss could sight down his arm.

Heller ignored him.

Heller was CEO of a company that had built three marina communities on Florida's Gulf coast, most of it on land acquired by his grandfather. This was the newest, Indian Harbor Marina and Resort. Two weeks ago, the eye of a hurricane had spun ashore near Sanibel Island, twenty miles south. Bern had been making rounds since, taking notes, directing cleanup, not saying much.

Their properties hadn't done badly. A couple of condos had lost roofs. Pool screens, ornamental trees, that sort of thing. The worst was right here in front of him, a boat storage barn that had collapsed. Got hit by a tornado, maybe—which is what he was pushing the insurance people to believe.

Heller watched a crane lift a girder from the wreckage as he asked Moe, "What do you think it's worth?"

"The Cuban guy's boat?"

"That's what we're talking about. I'm trying to make a point here."

Moe gave it a few seconds before he named a figure, then added, "It's a well-known brand, less than a year old. We had it on a rack outside the barn. It didn't get a scratch."

Surprised by the value, Heller said, "That's as much I paid for my BMW. How'd a Cuban get that kind of money?"

"The guy's a worker. He came over on a raft and hustled his ass off. He's not a bullshitter, either. That's why we should call the cops now. Javier's gonna pull a gun if we don't let him take his boat. The cops should be here waiting."

Heller had his grandfather's smile. He was smiling now because Moe couldn't keep his voice from catching. The man was scared, even though he acted hard-assed, with that cowboy hat, the redneck nose and chin, the face a triangle of stubble because that's the way movie stars wore their beards. Moe: a hick from French Lick.

"You like that boat?"

"Sure, of course. But—"

"Do you want it?"

"Who wouldn't, but—"

Bern cut him off. "Then we don't want the cops here when the Cuban shows. They'd scare him away. Let him pull the gun and wave it around. *That's* when we want the cops. Let them take him to jail . . . or shoot him." Heller shrugged.

"Either way," Heller said, "the boat's ours."

In fact, all the boats were theirs. They belonged to the salvage company contracted to clear the wreckage. And the salvage company belonged to Heller. But he wasn't going to trust this idiot with *that* little detail.

For more than two weeks, Moe had had to deal with several hundred pissed-off boat owners who paid storage at the marina but hadn't been allowed on the property since the hurricane. Every morning, they gathered at the gate, getting madder and madder—Javier Castillo among them.

As soon as the storm had blown through, Heller had asked the state to declare the marina a hazardous area because of storm damage, so the boat owners hadn't been allowed to step foot on the place. They couldn't move their boats, inspect them, or recover personal items, nothing.

Then, days later, Heller's attorney had sent a letter, registered mail, to the state attorney. It declared that, because the owners had failed to secure their vessels against future storms, the marina considered the boats to be derelict. As derelict vessels, they could be claimed as salvage by a licensed company. Legally, it was edgy—but no one had challenged it so far.

For the Hoosier, Heller summarized, instead. "If these boats go floating off in another storm, we're responsible for damages. A tornado grabs one and drops it in a crowded building? It's our nuts in the wringer. That's why the salvage company has to assume ownership."

When Moe asked, "Yeah, but how can we expect owners to secure their boats when we won't let them on the property?" Heller stared at him until Moe got so nervous he started laughing. "I was *joking,* Bern."

Yeah, Heller was right not to trust this goof with the details.

"It doesn't matter whether a boat is damaged or not," Heller told him. "The salvage company deserves a fair profit for cleaning up the mess. Take me around and tell me what all this crap's worth."

Now the two men were in a golf cart, Moe at the wheel. He would drive a few yards, stop, and tell his boss the resale value of this or that. He'd drive a little ways more, then stop again.

It was weird the way the cart tilted with Heller beside him, the man was so big.

"According to the log, we had three hundred and nine boats in the storage barn. But I think we racked a dozen more the day before the storm hit. Last-minute dumbasses who wanted them out of the water. We were so busy, they didn't get wrote down."

Heller said, "That figures," not mad, but keeping Moe on his toes.

They were on the canal side of the storage barn where wreckage hadn't been cleared. The barn had been the size of a retail warehouse, Sam's Club or Costco, fitted with steel racks six berths' high. The racks had collapsed when the barn imploded, one boat falling on top of another, among the twisted steel; outboard motors, canvas, fiberglass hulls; white, yellow, blue, poking out of the mess; everything jumbled, as if deposited by a glacier.

At least a hundred boats had already been plucked free by the crane. They sat in rows on the shell parking lot, all tilted on their bottoms. Just like the golf cart when Heller sat his weight on the seat, which is why Moe now locked the brake, and stood.

He stretched and popped his back, saying, "Even after all the work we've done, it still looks bad, I know. Like everything in there's completely fucked. But it's not."

His boss replied, "It's okay the way it looks."

"Thanks, Bern. We've been humping it ten, twelve hours a day trying to get it cleaned up."

"That's not what I meant, you schmuck. Another insurance adjustor's coming tomorrow, and I asked some guy from the E-P-A to meet me here tomorrow afternoon. We got hit by a natural disaster, so it's good for them to see it."

Moe thought: *Environmental Protection Agency? Invite those assholes on the property after what you did with the bulldozer?*

He didn't ask. Instead, he stuck to business and talked about the two hundred boats still mixed with the barn's wreckage.

Y ou've got to figure the engines, most of them are fine. Electronics? They've all got fish-finders, radar. Fishing gear, stereo systems, G-P-Ss—it all adds up. Plus, a lot of them, you could stick in the water right now, crank the engines, and they'd run like nothing happened."

"Global Positioning Systems, huh?" Heller said. "I've got one in my car. But a boat's, it's gotta be different, right?"

Moe said, "Yeah, but it's not hard. I can show you now if you're interested."

Heller was interested because he'd copied the numbers from the nautical map he'd found in his grandfather's briefcase. He knew they referred to a latitude and longitude but decided he could wait to find out. "Maybe over the weekend," he said. "We'll have plenty of boats to choose from."

Moe laughed, then became pensive. "I still don't get it. How can a salvage company take a guy's boat even if it's not damaged? Are we sure this is legal?"

Heller began to nod, but his expression said, *Who cares?* "My grandfather figured it out a couple of years ago, before I moved down. A hurricane hit north of Lauderdale, and the smart marinas worked it the same way. The key is the contract we make people sign before we store their boats. There's a clause that covers what's called a 'nonjudicial sale.' If they sign, we can sell their boat for just about any reason we want. There's also a clause that says we're not liable for loss if a hurricane hits."

The lawyers had told Bern neither clause would hold up in court. So far, though, the insurance companies had played along—they were the slimiest con artists on the scene. And the state cops hadn't lifted a finger.

"This was all your grandfather's idea?"

"Basically. I arranged all the details, of course."

"He musta been quite a guy. I think I told you how sorry I was—"

"Yes," Heller said, "he was a wonderful gentleman. The point is, the state cops, and the insurance people, don't care what we do."

Moe began to smile. It was like finding barrels of money in all this wreckage. "I counted forty-five or fifty boats in perfect shape. The biggest—thirty-footers and over—most of those, we stored on cradles outside. Like the Viking diesel, your favorite. Augie's, too."

Augie Heller was Bern's nephew. One of several relatives on the payroll. The little creep had used the boat so much lately that he'd been acting like the Viking was his.

Not a chance.

The Viking was Bern's. Or soon would be.

Who wouldn't like a forty-three-foot yacht with plush staterooms, a Bose entertainment system, and a pilothouse that made him feel like an expert seaman, just sitting at the wheel, even though Bern had never spent a day offshore.

He'd driven the boat several times, but always stuck to the inland waterways. Sometimes he took it down the Intracoastal for dinner at South Seas Plantation, or Grandma Dot's. Man, the boat was *beautiful,* but he was just learning. Getting his confidence up. The pilothouse was loaded with electronics, including a couple of GPSs, so that's what he'd do next—learn how to use the boat's navigation system. Find out what the numbers meant on the old map.

What was today? Tuesday, September 14th. Augie had asked to use the Viking tomorrow—the kid had been taking the boat offshore to fish for grouper. So maybe he'd take a couple of beers, the old map, and figure out the GPS tonight.

Bern was thinking about that as Moe continued, "And the Cuban's boat. There's another one that didn't get a scratch. That's why he's so pissed off."

"Screw 'im. Far as he knows, it got smashed."

"Well . . . I don't know."

"You don't know what?"

Moe said, "Well, the thing is, Javier was a fishing guide on Sanibel before he came here. He knows the business. I tell most of these hicks their boat's totaled, call your insurance agent, they'll say, 'Duh-h-h-h, okay.' Not the fishing guides, though."

Heller began to get suspicious. "There's something you're not telling me."

"Well, Bern, there's kind of a problem . . . Javier *knows* his boat's okay. He waded in that night, after the storm, when no one was here to stop them."

"What do you mean no one was here? What about that old fart you hired as a watchman, what's his name?"

"Arlis Futch. He's lived around here forever. He's a pal of Javier's, so . . . well, I guess Arlis let him have a look."

Heller's face was wide as a box, and his jaw muscles flexed when he was irritated. "I suppose the Cuban came other nights, too. *Did* he?"

The boss was asking if Javier Castillo had seen the bulldozer working in the dark, in the rain, flattening the Indian mounds to fill what had been mangrove swamp.

"It's possible."

Heller's jaw was flexing now. A pit bull on a leash. "Jesus, I tell you to do something, it still doesn't get done."

"I had to evacuate the island. It was mandatory." Moe's tone asking: *What was I supposed to do?*

"The colored guy, though, he stayed here. He didn't run. And the old fart."

Moe said, "I guess. Them and a few others." His tone flat now. "Javier lives south, where the eye came ashore. His house was totaled; now his wife's run off. Javier told me he was coming back with a gun because he had nothing to lose."

"Bullcrap," Heller said. He was picturing the skinny Cuban with a gun, cops yelling *Freeze,* before shooting him.

Good. He hoped it happened.

"Everybody's got something to lose," he told Moe, stealing one of his grandfather's lines. "Find out what it is—and that's how much you can take."

LABORATORY LOG

MARION D. FORD

DINKIN'S BAY, SANIBEL ISLAND, FLORIDA

14 August, Saturday

No sunrise

Returned two days ago, near midnight, 12 hours before a hurricane made landfall. Direct hit on Gulf islands, winds 150 MPH, gusts higher. The marina, my house and lab badly damaged.

When windows imploded, roof began to go, I grabbed a piling, watching whole trees, a canoe, sections of dock, a bicycle tumble skyward, cauldroning like birds.

The storm's northwestern wall was a phalanx of tornadoes. Tornadoes have a signature sound. A diesel scream that ascends on approach . . .

15 August, Sunday

Picking through wreckage, Javier Castillo asked about the stitches in my forehead. I told him I was hit by something during the storm. "God plays with us, sending a hurricane like that," he said in Spanish. I am tired of his shitty jokes.

16 August, Monday
Sunset 19:53 (7:53 P.M.)
Moon waxing
Low tide 7:21 P.M.

Trees are leafless, like nuclear winter. Last night, I watched stars through my open roof, head throbbing, as I replayed the worst of the storm. The wind accelerating past my ears, blowing so hard that it was as if I'd fallen out of a jetliner. No possibility of establishing control, so analysis was pointless. A shadow vanishing into itself. That's how I felt. Released.

19 August, Thursday
Sunset 7:50 P.M.
Low tide 8:18 P.M.

No power or phones. Islanders with million-dollar homes barter in new currency: water, generators, fuel. National Guard has arrived, trailing insurance adjusters, imposters, contractors, politicians in helicopters, lawyers, land speculators with cash. A few marinas are price gouging—or worse.

A hurricane leaves residual odors: bloating fish and trash fires. The scent attracts vultures, human variety. Bloated prices. Con men.

Greed has an odor, too.

WEEK THREE

30 August, Monday
Sunset 7:41 P.M.
Full moon rises 7:32 P.M.
Low tide 6:54 A.M.

Greed . . .

Tomlinson says a hurricane is like a beam of light. It exposes decay, and reveals unexpected strengths. Celestial light—his phrase. Cleansing.

He was stoned, as usual. Behavior even more bizarre. Irritable, too—as if he's been injecting testosterone. Hormones *might* play a role. Most nights, he vanishes to visit a woman he seldom mentions. She lives in a beach estate, an antique gray house that was hidden until the wind stripped the trees away. I discovered it by accident; was unaware the house even existed until the storm.

1 September, Wednesday
Working late in lab

Winds transformed sea bottom, exposing some structures, covering others. Off Key Largo, in 130 feet of water, a sunken Naval vessel, the *Spiegel Grove,* was uprighted by storm currents. Off Key West, an underwater forest of petrified wood was uncovered in an area once sand. The forest dates back to the Pliocene.

Yesterday, Jeth Nichols found an unfamiliar wreck—40 feet of water, 240 degrees off Lighthouse Point. He's been fishing out of another marina where damage was minor. One of those gated condo places, Indian Harbor Resort.

5 September, Sunday
Sunset 7:35 P.M.
Low tide 12:03 P.M.

The hurricane that hit us was the third of the season; more forming in the Caribbean basin. Storms of closed circulation are tropical cyclones. When winds exceed 38 MPH, they are termed "tropical storms" and assigned a name—grating, because a name implies human qualities, intent or malice.

A storm is a mobile dynamic, not a being. Homo sapiens is a mobile being, not a process. The principles of physics and man are diminished by anthropomorphic baloney.

Go to the beach and name waves. Name a lightning bolt. It makes as much sense.

7 September, Tuesday

Sunset 7:34 P.M.

No low tide

Autumn in subtropics: Heat. Jittery wind. Hint of storm darkness even in daylight.

Moon waning; fireflies in mangrove shadow.

Still no phone.

3

16 September, Thursday
Sunset 7:28 P.M.
New moon sets 11:49 P.M.
    Four tropical cyclones developing in Caribbean, one a tropical storm, another hurricane force, winds over 74 mph.

I told Jeth, "Your pal, Augie Heller, makes me regret emptying my shark pen before the hurricane hit."

Jeth Nichols stutters when he's nervous or mad. He was stuttering now. "I know, Doc, I know. Sorry. I was stuh-stupid to ever leave Dinkin's Bay and work for another marina. Javier warned me. I shoulda listened."

Javier Castillo—a Sanibel fishing guide until he moved his family across the bay. Jeth had followed because he was desperate for cash after the hurricane.

I was bending over a tray of salt water, my back turned so it was difficult for Jeth to observe. My left hand was submerged, holding a brooch-sized object encrusted with barnacles. With a surgical probe, I'd removed enough to see that a portion of the object was studded with clear stones.

Diamonds?

With the object cupped, I looked away from the tray. "You said Javier would meet us here."

"That's what he told me. He said he was gonna get his boat this afternoon. He was sure of it."

I pictured a lean man with muscles, a broad African nose. Javier was a good father, a good fisherman. Years ago, he'd floated over from Cuba in an inner tube, which tells you all you need to know about Javier Castillo—he crossed the Florida Straits in a tire.

As if reading my mind, Jeth said, "I wish he'd show up. It'd be nice to see a friendly face."

True. This place was decidedly unfriendly.

Jeth, Tomlinson, and I were off by ourselves, strangers on strange turf—what had once been a fishing village I'd known well but no longer. Developers had transformed it into an overpriced marina community, on the island of Sulphur Wells, twenty-five minutes by boat from our home base, Sanibel Island, Gulf coast of Florida.

Its name was the Indian Harbor Marina and Resort Community, a mall-sized project built by out-of-state investors, with acres of metal buildings, duplexes, condo sites and dockage, most of the new construction intact after the storm.

There was some damage, though. I saw bulldozers and a crane over there bucking twisted metal where the storage barn had collapsed; security guards stopping cars at the marina entrance. Boats that had survived had been dragged to the parking lot, several dozen of them listing on their keels. They were spaced incrementally like cemetery headstones. A hundred or more.

I said, "If Javier doesn't show in the next ten minutes, I think we should stow your gear in my skiff and leave. I can't tolerate much more of this place, or of your pal Augie."

I was using the surgical probe, along with a magnifying glass and forceps, to clean one of several metallic objects Jeth had snagged while fishing a wreck he'd discovered a few days before. That morning, he'd reeled up a section of cable, a couple of pounds of marine growth attached, manmade objects embedded, most he couldn't identify.

There was a U.S. silver dollar, some brass screws, and what now looked to be a diamond brooch. A dozen or so other objects were also attached but too heavily covered with barnacles and goop to make a guess.

A few hours ago, Jeth had called me on VHF radio, asking me to meet him here and have a look.

I hadn't expected to find anything of consequence.

Surprise.

Jeth said now, "Augie isn't my pal, I already told you. I've just got a business arrangement with him and the other guy. They have a boat, I don't. They don't know how to fish, I do. We been catching grouper offshore, sellin' it for top dollar. There's hardly any boats out since the hurricane. But we ain't friends."

Yes, he'd told me. Augie Heller and Oswald, the men who'd offered him a share of the profits to run this marina's forty-three-foot Viking sport diesel. Jeth needed money, so he'd taken the job even though he didn't like the duo and didn't trust them.

My impression exactly. And now Jeth had stumbled onto something important. Valuable, too, depending on the identity of the vessel he'd discovered and what remained on the seafloor.

I hadn't told Jeth that, not yet. I'd seen no reason to risk sharing the information with the two jerks who'd just stomped off to get reinforcements.

I knew they'd be back soon.

I returned my attention to the brooch. The metal filigree was black as gunpowder, scarred with barnacles and worm shell. Silver converts to silver sulfide when immersed in salt water. This object was silver, coated with a black sulfide patina. It had been underwater for a long time, judging from the empty worm casings. Years. Decades. But there was no fresh benthic growth, and the metallic structure was solid.

It had been preserved by something. Sand? Buried and insulated beneath a few feet of sea bottom.

Maybe the same was true of the wreck. Everything cosseted beneath underwater sand dunes until exposed by the recent hurricane.

Thinking about it, I pictured the Sahara desert. Peaks of undiscovered pyramids showing after a wind storm. I pictured the Stony desert and domes of ancient mosques.

As Jeth said, "Even if they weren't such assholes, I don't see how they can claim part of something I found." I touched the object with forceps.

A flake of black patina broke away as if it were a scab. I had my glasses atop my head. I removed the object from the water briefly, holding it close, squinting as nearsighted people do.

If this was a brooch, it was the strangest I'd seen. Staring back at me was a silver skull. It was a military-style skull known as a "death's-head." It had luminous stones for eyes. Several more stones created the upper blade of something . . . a symbol. A portion of leaf cluster framed the symbol.

A . . . swastika?

As I replied, "You discovered the wreck. You're the one who snagged this stuff. The state of Florida may have claims but your partners don't." I took a double-ended mall probe and continued cleaning.

Yes. A swastika.

It was inset with stones, presumably diamonds. Tiny stones, valuable as gems, or maybe not. But part of an insignia from World War II Germany.

Symbols are a form of cipher. This symbol projected a historic energy, dulling the luster of the gems that formed it.

"Then screw 'em," Jeth said. "They've been treating me like some low-life hick since my first day aboard. I ain't sharing nothing with those two." And Javier, the bastards are trying to keep his boat. They're calling everything on their property 'salvage.' "

I replied, "I heard. They should be in jail."

"You remember old man Arlis Futch. He's been working here nights as a security guard. He says he'd quit the damn place if he could afford it."

Arlis had once managed Sulphur Wells Fish Company. I was surprised to hear his name. It had to be embarrassing, him working as a night watchman.

Jeth took his cap off and slapped his leg. "Some of the crap we do for money, huh?"

I said, "It happens to all of us," but was thinking: *What's a Nazi insignia doing in forty feet of water on the bottom of the Gulf of Mexico? Twelve miles off the usually cheerful vacation beaches of Sanibel Island, Florida?*

"Does Augie have the numbers?" I was asking about the GPS numbers, latitude and longitude, that marked the wreck's location. On a forty-three-foot boat, the navigational system would be interfaced. If Heller knew how to use the electronics, the autopilot could steer them back to the wreck. They didn't need Jeth.

Jeth smiled, pleased with himself. "I never showed them how to use the GPS. I ran the boat, all they did was fish. Besides, those lat-long numbers were already in the system."

"What?"

If true, it meant that someone else had found the wreck before Jeth.

"Not the exact numbers," he said. "It was a waypoint left by the boat's previous owner, that's my guess. No way in hell was there a wreck down there before the storm, so maybe they punched in rough numbers for a pod of tarpon. Or a bale of grass."

Jeth was grinning as he added, "I erased the numbers after I wrote 'em down." He patted the pocket of his cargo shorts. "Got them here."

"Smart," I said. "I should've guessed."

Jeth is the quiet type. Like most introverted people, he knows how to be aggressive without making a fuss.

My magnifying glass has a 4-power wide-angle lens with a quarter-sized 9-power inset.

Amplified details: I was looking at an elite military decoration. A death's-head made of silver, impressionistic design, lower jaw replaced by the upper blade of a swastika. The top of the skull sat upon the blade like a head on a platter.

The eyes were oversized and empty, the diamonds bending prismatic light on this pale September afternoon. The elemental combination—silver, fresh sunlight through crystallized carbon—seemed conflicted and obscene. Use natural pigments to create pornography, you might achieve the same effect.

Not pure silver. The galvanic pores indicated it was a ferrous amalgam. The pores were filled with salt that had crystallized when exposed to air.

Some metals absorb salt water, and deteriorate from within after long submersion. Which is why everything Jeth found was now soaking in a bucket of salt water, and why I was using this saltwater tray to keep items submerged while doing a preliminary cleaning.

From what I'd seen so far, the items warranted care.

I'd already removed a calcareous shell that covered an insignia of similar size, this one of forged bronze. It was an eagle that held part of a circular wreath in its talons. Most of the wreath had corroded away.

Tomlinson had come along out of curiosity. He'd seen the thing. Jeth had not.

Because of the death's-head, I felt more certain that Tomlinson had correctly identified the bronze eagle. Anyone who's read a little history could have made a good guess. It was an icon of the Third Reich, a German eagle, square-winged, industrial looking, as if designed by an architect who worked only with cement. The missing wreath had probably encircled a swastika.

Tomlinson had reached his finger toward the insignia reluctantly, as if it might be hot. "I don't want to hold the thing," he'd said. "Just a quick impression to confirm it's the real deal. As you know, only crystals preserve human vibrations better than metal does."

No. I didn't know, and I doubted that it was true. But I'd stood patiently as he touched an index finger to the beak of the eagle, then pulled his hand away.

"God Aw'mighty," he said. "I can't be around that for more than a few minutes at a time. I'll be wrestling with demons all night."

It was authentic, he told me. It had a history. Then he jogged away.

Crystals and metal. Diamonds and silver. Tomlinson would have been even more unsettled by this death's-head.

Two artifacts of similar derivation, each suggesting the authenticity of the other.

A pattern was emerging . . . and there were several more clumps of objects attached to the cable. It had looked like a tangle of garbage when they'd first dumped it at my feet, and that's the way Jeth's partners had treated it until I'd told him to hurry and get me a bucket of salt water before it all disintegrated. The two men had suddenly become interested because I was interested.

It was a mistake on my part. It's not uncommon for me to make mistakes, but this particular screwup had spawned an argument about who owned the salvage if the salvage turned out to be marketable.

Salvage law. Augie talked as if he were an expert, which was unlikely. I'm familiar enough with the subject to know that admiralty law is ancient and complicated. It's impossible to live near a Florida marina without meeting a random cast of treasure hunters and similar dreamers who believe the myth that anything lost at sea instantly becomes the property of the next person to come along and find it.

"Salvage" is a word, but it's also a precise legal term, and people around Indian Harbor Marina were misusing it like a weapon.

Heller was no attorney, and he was certainly no expert. So it had been dumb of me to be so obvious when they'd first dumped the clutter of cable at my feet.

We'd argued. They'd threatened. Jeth has the size and hands of a country boy fullback, I am not a small man, and probably look less bookish than usual because of stitches in my forehead, so finally they'd stomped off to get help.

Yes, it had been dumb, and disturbing, too. Since the storm, I'd felt upbeat, full of energy. I'd felt a letting-go sensation; freedom from all circumstances impossible to control.

Falling from high altitude—a suitable metaphor for much of life.

The headaches were still with me, though. I'd noticed that my balance and timing were off, and that my coordination—never great—was shaky.

Lately, I'd been making more mistakes than normal.

4 "A skull with diamonds. Weird." Jeth had moved to get a look at the death's-head. He stood in his fishing shorts, heavy legs apart, tattered boat shoes on a man raised barefoot. "Motorcycle gangs wear those sorts of badges, don't they?"

"Um-huh," I replied. "The gang that made this, though, preferred tanks and planes."

"Tanks? Oh . . . *Real* Nazis. Are you sure?"

"No. But I don't have another explanation."

"It's gotta be worth some money."

"You'd think. How much, a collector could tell you. Maybe a lot. The rest of this stuff will take a few days to clean, so we'll see." I gestured to the five-gallon bucket at my feet. It contained a soup of salt water, cable, and more encrusted artifacts. "I'm wondering what kind of wreck you found. A German war medal this close to Sanibel?"

Jeth pursed his lips, an idea forming. "You've heard the rumors there's a sunken German submarine out there. That it's filled with mercury, so it floats around underwater. Or that it's booby-trapped, and that's why divers who found it won't tell where it was."

Yes, I'd heard the rumors, and didn't believe them. Not after doing some research. U-boat activity in the Gulf of Mexico was brisk during World War II. German subs sank merchant ships, and they came close enough to Florida's shore to deliver, and probably pick up, Nazi spies. But there was only one recorded sinking of a U-boat in the Gulf—off New Orleans.

It wasn't impossible that a second U-boat was out there, but it was improbable. The Germans kept exacting records.

I told Jeth what I knew, adding, "Let's assume it's not a sub. Then what's down there? The silver's well preserved—why? Considering where you found it, and how long it was down there, it's in good shape. After fifty, sixty years underwater—I'm guessing metal this delicate would have crumbled. Maybe the wreck was buried, then uncovered by the storm."

"Meaning, it was protected. Kinda insulated?"

"Yeah. You know what the bottom's like off Sanibel, it's all sand. Hurricane wind—what'd we have, gusts of over a hundred and seventy miles an hour? Underwater currents had to be pumping like fire hoses. They eroded the sand away."

Jeth was picturing it, nodding. "Makes sense, or we'd of found the wreck a long time ago. Two-forty heading off Lighthouse Point. I've been over that bottom a hundred times, never saw a thing, but last week I was running along, watching my fish-finder, when those GPS numbers popped up on the Viking. I slowed—I knew there wasn't no structure in the area but figured, what the hell."

Fish-finder—a common term for a device that pings sound waves off the sea bottom and produces a digital likeness of what lies beneath.

Jeth said he'd begun to do a search pattern watching the screen of his fish-finder. He was about to give up when there it was—something on the bottom.

"The wreck was sticking up where nothin' had ever been before," Jeth said. "The fish-finder marked it sharp as looking at TV, so I figured it was a new wreck. The storm caught a boat out there and sunk her. But then I reeled up this old stuff."

I said, "Makes me wonder what else is there. What'd it look like on your sonar screen?"

"There's a main structure, fifteen, twenty feet long, then a bunch of scattered junk. Comes up three, maybe four feet off the bottom."

"That's all?"

"At the most, maybe five feet."

"If it's a boat, and the hull's intact, then the rest of it's still buried. Or . . . it could be a plane."

"Yeah, I hadn't thought of that. There used to be a military air base around here during the second war. Fighters and bombers, all prop planes. They used Captiva Island, and some of the other islands, for target practice. But why would an American plane have a German war medal aboard?"

I said, "Maybe one of the instructors brought it back from Europe as a trophy. Or twenty years later, some private collector packed it aboard a Cessna that had to ditch in the Gulf. No telling until you take a look for yourself."

"You mean *we* take a look?"

"It's your wreck. Your call."

"We need to dive it, Doc."

"I'm willing. I was hoping you'd ask."

"You were the first one I called because that's what I was already thinking. Javier, too. Maybe we can use his boat—if the damn marina lets him have it back."

I said, "Sure. Does he dive?"

Jeth said, "I don't know if he's certified, but, yeah, he's got tanks and stuff. Thing is, the visibility's so bad now we wouldn't be able to see the end of our nose. And the water won't clear up for weeks, maybe a couple months, she's so stirred up."

He reminded me that there were two more hurricanes down by Cuba, one of them maybe headed this way.

Actually, both were now on track to hit Florida's Gulf coast. I'd listened to VHF weather on the boat ride here. Statistically, there wasn't much chance we'd get another direct hit. But even if the storms passed within a few hundred miles, it'd be too rough to anchor offshore.

I said, "Then either we use the small window we have, tomorrow or the next day, or we wait a month or more. Even if it's murky, I wouldn't mind giving it a try."

"I don't know, man. The water out there's thick as motor oil. We won't be able to see nothing. Just feel around with our hands. Us bumpin' into stuff, crap bumping into us. Doesn't sound like much fun to me. Javier's not gonna be too wild about it, either."

I was holding the death's-head in my hand. It seemed too light, too fragile, to support the history it represented.

I said, "Nobody likes diving in murky water. If those storms hit close, though, they could bury your wreck again. We wouldn't get another chance."

"Crap . . . I hadn't thought of that. Geez"—the big man made a face of distaste—"we've both seen the size of sharks out there. Big ol' lemons, and tigers and hammerheads. Bull sharks, too. Big as canoes, and they're always on the feed. If the water's clear, I don't worry about them when I'm diving. But, if the viz is crappy—"

"Sharks see better in the dark than we see in daylight," I interrupted. "They're the least of our worries. I think we should go if weather allows."

Jeth made a low sound, close to a groan. It told me he would dive in the murk but hated the idea.

"Then we can't show this Nazi thing to Augie?"

I said, "Augie Heller? No. I don't even know the man, but I do know one thing about him: He'd try to beat us to the wreck."

I refilled the pan with salt water, then used the forceps to remove a final layer of barnacle. The entire swastika was now visible. Twenty-six diamonds, counting the eyes.

Jeth took a closer look before straightening, gazing around, head moving slowly, trying not to show that he was nervous. "That thing's gotta bad feel to it. Sorta like this marina."

I knew what he meant. The Indian Harbor Marina and Resort had once been a village of tin-roofed cottages built on shell mounds, called Gumbo Limbo, plus docks and a commercial warehouse. I'd had friends here, crabbers and mullet fishermen. Among them was a long-legged woman with skinny, countrified hips and denim-colored eyes. A woman who wore boots and jeans, who owned her own boat, and lived an edgy, independent life of her own design. She was a powerful lady, Hannah Smith.

Like the village she'd once called home, Hannah was gone.

Florida's most destructive storms have been developmental, not environmental. I'd read about the village's transformation in the newspaper, heard about it from locals. I hadn't relished the idea of coming back. I'd done it for Jeth, no other reason. Now I was eager to leave.

Jeth was right. Indian Harbor Marina and Resort had a bad feel.

I'd wrapped the bronze eagle in a towel soaked in salt water. I now did the same with the death's-head, as I said "We've given Javier enough time. Let's get out of here. There's a better way to clean this stuff, anyway. When we get back to Sanibel, I'll call an archaeologist pal of mine and we can do it in my lab."

What was left of my lab, anyway.

I glanced toward the bay. "Where's Tomlinson?"

"Huh?"

I repeated myself as I squatted, placed both towels in the five-gallon bucket, and nodded toward the docks where my boat was tied: a new twenty-one-foot Maverick with a ghost blue hull and a high-powered Yamaha engine on the back. Just looking at it gave me pleasure.

The boat was empty.

"Where'd he go?"

Tomlinson had witnessed our confrontation with Heller and Oswald. I'd told him to go back to my skiff and stay there in case we had to leave in a hurry. But giving an order to Tomlinson was another mistake. Counterculture visionaries have an aversion to authority. Ordering him to do something was a guarantee he'd do the opposite.

Jeth said, "Tomlinson's about as predictable as a fart in a forest fire. He coulda wandered off anywhere, that bonehead. If it wasn't for Javier, we shoulda left the moment I realized there was gonna be trouble . . ." He was looking over my shoulder, his face registering surprise, then tension. "Probably should of . . . buh-but it's too late now. Here they come."

Augie Heller and Oswald. And they had someone with them.

"Jesus, that's the head guy, the owner," Jeth said. "That smile of his . . . He sounds like the nicest Yankee in the world, but he looks at you like a bug he'd squash, give him a chance. I won't even talk to him, he makes me so nervous. Which tah–tuh–tells you something."

5 Augie and Oswald were walking fast toward us, an older man leading the way. He was NFL-sized, bald, late forties, with a monk's dark wreath of hair. He was wearing shorts, TopSiders, a green polo shirt with marina logo. No one was smiling. They were pushing a hard-assed attitude ahead of them like an energy wave, the way they leaned, fists pumping.

Augie: Stocky, short, in his midtwenties, midwestern vowels; big-city volume. He had a swagger that comes with money and inherited power. His buddy Oswald was older by a decade. He was pudgy, with a bubble-shaped butt, but had the same attitude of tough-guy indifference. Another guess: He worked for Augie's family.

As they got closer, I decided that the older guy *was* Augie's family, a dad or an uncle. He was twice the size, but there were genetic similarities. The same elongated earlobes, Scandinavian chin, and slaughterhouse forearms, the same big square head and hands. The expressions on the faces of all three men pointed, territorial.

I got a glimpse of the smile Jeth mentioned. Jolly, but fixed in place, worn like a warning. It told you something about the owner. He was a handler; he knew how to deal with people and the smile was part of his technique. He was showing it to me, letting me know that he was nobody's fool—if I was smart enough to read it.

I fitted the top onto the bucket. I used my eyes to motion toward the marina's southern boundary, where I'd finally picked out Tomlinson. "There he is. It looks like he's already irritating the hell out of everyone."

Tomlinson was on the far side of the property, much of it still flooded, standing by a green boat on a trailer, talking to men who wore hard hats and orange vests. He'd wandered off shirtless, wearing baggy khaki shorts—"Bombay Bloomers," he called them. Very British, with pleats, pockets, and a fly that buttoned. He'd bought knee-length socks to match. He was wearing them now with Birkenstock sandals—his "hurricane kit," he called it.

Goggles, too. They were strapped around his neck like an RAF pilot, loose and ready—old-fashioned, with a leather strap and thick green lenses. "Kilner goggles," Tomlinson had said they were, made in the early 1900s by a London physician. The special lenses, he claimed, revealed human auras and energy fields.

They were among the newest in Tomlinson's long list of weird interests.

When I'd showed him the bronze eagle, he'd put the goggles to his eyes briefly. Bizarre.

Jeth said, "I don't see him. Where?"

I pointed, watching as Tomlinson became animated, using his hands to converse with the men wearing hard hats. He gestured toward the green boat, angry for some reason. Why?

Jeth stared toward the parking lot for a moment. "Hey—that's Javier's boat. The green Pursuit, with twin Yamahas. What's Tomlinson doing?"

What it looked like he was doing was climbing onto the boat. Maybe with reason: For the first time, I noticed Javier Castillo in the distance, walking like a man on a mission.

But why was Javier walking away from Tomlinson?

From a hundred yards, I watched two of the hard hats reach, grab Tomlinson by the belt, and haul him off the trailer as he tried to swing a lanky leg aboard the boat. One of the men wagged a finger in his face while another held him. A warning.

Three marina employees stood nearby, hands on hips, a classic aggressive posture intended to broaden a man's shoulders.

I pointed at Javier, who had now reached the marina's access road. Jeth and I both watched as he vaulted a fence rather than use the main entrance where a security truck was parked next to the gate. A clot of people were gathered outside the gate, no one getting in.

Jeth said, "Geez, the owner of this place really looks pissed off," now gazing in the direction of the three men striding toward us. "He's a big'un, huh?"

Yes, he was a big one. Coming to claim what we had taken from little Augie.

I lifted the bucket that contained the artifacts and said, "Time to leave. Go get Tomlinson. He'll listen to you—put him in a headlock if he doesn't. I'll bring the skiff and meet you at that little clearing in the mangroves. Once we're off marina property, there's nothing they can do."

Jeth tried to downplay his surprise. "You want to run?"

"Yes, I want to run."

"I don't know, Doc. You know how fishermen gossip. What'll people say?"

"They'll say we're not in jail. Jeth . . . ?" I glanced and saw that the men were closing. "Let's *move*."

He did, grabbing his fishing gear and striding away from me, his eyes fixed, which caused the owner to pause, Augie and Oswald stumbling to a halt behind.

I waved at the three men. Gave the group a smile of my own, and pointed toward Tomlinson, who was still arguing with the hard hats. *Meet me there.*

Angry little mobs are unsettled by people who respond cheerfully. It added to their confusion.

When I got to my skiff, I set the bucket on the casting deck, then ignored it. I ignored the men, too. I knew they were watching as I waded through the flotsam toward the boat's console. I got aboard and flicked a toggle switch beneath the wheel. There's a built-in fiberglass tank astern plumbed to circulate salt water—a well for keeping live fish.

As water hissed into the tank, I behaved as if I'd lost something, it didn't matter what as long as it bought enough time for Jeth to drag Tomlinson to the mangrove clearing, where I'd meet them.

As I hunted through compartments, I noticed a raft of dead fish floating in the trash line. The fish were bug-eyed from the pressure of internal gases.

I snuck a look at the bucket that contained the artifacts. Glanced again at the fish. Mullet, spadefish, a couple of snook, several sheepshead, their color leached gray.

Folklore credits animals with knowing in advance when a killer storm is coming. It suggests they escape to a safe place.

Folklore is often wistful.

From Tomlinson's direction, I heard a muted shout. I turned and saw a white truck similar to the truck parked at the marina gate. Big tires, windows open, SECURITY on the door. Inside were two men, their expressions cop-serious as they accelerated toward Javier's boat, where Tomlinson was still arguing.

Augie Heller's group was watching, too, reading body language, no longer focused on me. The owner said something. He watched a moment longer, then decided that's where he was needed. They headed off at an angle to intercept Jeth, who was walking faster now.

In a rush, I freed my boat's bowline, and grabbed the bucket from the casting deck. It was heavy. I popped the plastic top, the smell of organic rot and metal blooming. Looked to make certain I wasn't being watched, then poured the contents into the flooded live well.

The artifacts I had cleaned sank to the bottom, still wrapped in their towels.

Had Jeth mentioned the owner's name?

Whoever he was, I knew he wouldn't settle for half of nothing. He wouldn't give me his special smile—not if I handed him an empty bucket.

Javier's boat was on the far edge of the clearing near a hill-sized mound of dirt. The hill was backdropped by wreckage of uprooted trees where shoreline changed from shell to asphalt. The shell was bone gray against the wet asphalt, the survey stakes the same shade of yellow as a backhoe parked on that raw space.

It was land being prepped for a parking lot. Or more condos.

The boat's trailer, I now noticed, was hitched to a hydraulic handcart. Maybe Javier had been muling his boat toward the ramp when Tomlinson came along.

Which didn't explain why Tomlinson was still trying to climb aboard the damn thing. I watched him attempt to vault himself onto Javier's boat again . . . watched the hard hats pull him to the ground.

There were a half dozen of them, different sizes, and ages. They wore their helmets straight like derbies, no scratches showing, new safety gear worn by novices not old construction hands. They looked like school-crossing guards confronting a homeless person, this shirtless outsider with hippie hair and baggy shorts.

Amusing. But not to Tomlinson, who was furious. His chin was thrust forward, fists clenched as if he might take a swing at somebody. Also amusing. Tomlinson, the Rienzi Zen Master. The passive, nonviolent hemp smoker. Tomlinson the Gandhi devotee. The worst he might do was give them a stern lecture, or a forgiving hug.

I stood at the wheel of my skiff, idling toward the clearing. I was in a hurry, but going slow in this shallow water, protecting my new propeller, which was attached to my new engine, which was mounted on the transom of my new skiff. It gave me time to allow my eyes to drift along the shoreline. As I did, I felt the same emotional jolt as when I'd arrived an hour earlier, seeing the place as it had been, unchanged. Not as it was.

What had been subtropical forest was now a hollow geometric; a rectangular space that had been bulldozed flat, surveyed, and graded—the precursors of high-rise construction so obvious that the sky seemed already darkened by stucco.

PRECONSTRUCTION PRICES. PENTHOUSE SUITES. GATED WATERFRONT, ASSOCIATION DUES, ASSIGNED DOCKAGE.

There should be standardized billboards, the destiny of commercial waterfront in Florida is so predictable. There probably *were* similar billboards on the road into this place: a village that was now a commercial venture to be split up, repackaged, and sold like berths on a cruise ship.

Pre-Death Chambers. A Tomlinson phrase.

There had once been a fishing village here . . .

I pictured a woman I'd lost only a few years ago standing on the porch of a house that no longer existed. Yellow house of pine, a tin roof. The woman had Deep South eyes that hinted how the weight of her body would feel, her footsteps resonate on wood, leading me to a cooler and darker place, her skin burning beneath my fingers.

I could hear the woman's woodwind voice in fragmented sentences, the oboe notes of her laughter:

"Way I'm built, when it gets cold? You could see my nipples through a raincoat . . .

"I'm a Gemini born on the cusp. But with Leo rising. Like two people in one body, both of us bossy . . .

"We can have separate lives, Ford. We'll be like secret partners."

The voice of a woman I'd liked and admired, Hannah Smith. Maybe even loved, though I've never settled on a comfortable definition for that overused word. I stood at the wheel, imagining the sound and shape of her, feeling nostalgic . . .

Irritated, I caught myself. There's a long list of self-indulgent emotions, and nostalgia is as pointless as—

"Doc! Get over here."

Jeth's voice.

Startled, I refocused.

Now what?

Tomlinson's confrontation was no longer amusing. There was Jeth, striding up behind the hard hats, giving the situation some gravity because of his size. Arriving at the same time was Augie Heller's group, the oversized boss man already elbowing his way in. Nearby was the security truck, doors open, two men keeping an eye on things from striking distance. The tallest of them wore a cowboy hat. White straw.

"Doc?"

Jeth called again as I watched Tomlinson step toward the marina manager. He was overexcited, and moved too far into the big man's space, bumping him accidentally. Immediately, though, he declared a truce with his hands, eager to talk.

That's not the way the owner read it. He stepped aside as if dodging a bull, dwarfing Tomlinson. Then he reached and caught Tomlinson's hair in his fist. He did a competent trip-step, and jerked my friend's head backward as his knees hit the ground. The man yanked hard a couple more times to demonstrate his control, Tomlinson's neck snapping puppetlike.

"Doc!"

I leaned on the throttle, throwing a geyser of muddy water astern, hull shuddering as my boat plowed shoreward. Before the Maverick grounded itself, I bailed into water calf-deep, and ran . . .

6 The hard hats had formed a screen to keep Jeth back. Nearby, men from the security truck were stirring. Jeth was their main concern . . . until they spotted me coming.

I ran into the clearing where there were mounds of gravel and survey stakes all around, slipping my glasses into my shorts, my eyes adjusting to a world that blurred, the security guys watching.

I was near enough to hear: "All I wanted to do was talk, man! My buddy owns the damn boat, so what's the big deal?"

Tomlinson was yelling, not pleading, but pain inserted exclamation points. The manager was hurting him.

"Let go . . . you are really blowing your cool, man. That's not hair. You're pulling my *flag,* man!"

The manager telling him, "You come charging at me, what do you expect?" Smiling as he talked. The accent was Minnesota or Wisconsin, only a generation or two removed from migration.

As I sprinted, the hard hats turned from Jeth to me, realizing that they'd have to intercept. Nervous men sometimes use body language to anchor an alibi. These guys were already telegraphing excuses: This wasn't *their* fight. For the money they were making?

It gave them a reason to get out of my way.

I slowed to a walk. "Let him up," I told the big man. "Get your hands off him."

Augie pointed. "He's the one I told you about, Uncle Bern. With the big mouth. I'd be happy to shut it, if you want."

Showing off his tough-guy attitude for the uncle who was also his boss. Augie and Uncle Bern, a pair.

Near us, an engine started, and the security truck spun away toward the marina entrance, Oswald now inside beside the driver. An emergency of some sort, judging from the warble of sirens in the distance. And getting louder.

The man with the white cowboy hat had stayed behind. He was putting the hat on now, ducking his head into it like he'd maybe seen rodeo riders do. Showing forearms that were colored with script and decorations, a guy who was no stranger to passing out in tattoo parlors.

"Mr. Heller? This is important." His tone was urgent.

The owner still had his fingers knotted in Tomlinson's hair, but he shifted his attention to cowboy.

"The fella who said he'd be back with a gun? The front gate just radioed—they spotted his truck parked down the road. The cops are on their way."

That got the big man's attention. He straightened, holding Tomlinson's head off the ground like a trophy. "Just the truck or did they see him?"

Behind me, one of the hard hats said, "If you're talking about Javier Castillo, he was just here. We caught him and the hippie moving the boat."

"Javier's got a gun?" Jeth looked unconvinced but concerned.

The owner spoke to Tomlinson, but he was studying me. "What were you doing, helping him steal our boat? You fellas don't care what you steal, huh?"

Meaning the contents of the bucket.

Uncle Bern was evaluating. Apparently, he decided that I was the threat so he shook his hand free of Tomlinson's hair and stepped in my direction. He glanced at his nephew, who was approaching from the right. "I'll take care of this, Augie. But stick close. Moe?"

Cowboy hat, who was edging closer, stopped.

"The same goes for you. We don't want the Cuban's friends getting in the way."

What the hell did that mean?

Moe understood, though. He touched a finger to the brim of his hat.

I stopped an arm's length away, looking up at the man's box-shaped face, his fake smile, the jaw muscles flexing as he said, "I hope you're not thinking of doing something stupid, Mr. . . . ?"

"His name's Ford. *Doctor* Ford, according to Stuttering Jeth."

Jeth said to Augie, "Hey, you can kuh-kuh-kiss my butt," as Heller said, "Doctor! Well, we should be able to talk this out."

The smile broadened, telling me he was a reasonable guy, but I could see the menace. He wasn't nervous. Seemed right at home in nose-to-nose confrontations, this one just beginning, both of us aware. Wondering how far the other would take it.

He took a moment to check over his shoulder as two sheriff's cruisers lurched to a stop, light bars strobing. The cars scattered people who'd been massed at the gate. He waited for a third cruiser to appear before saying, "Augie claims you've got something that belongs to us." The man let that hang for a moment before asking, "What's in the bucket, Dr. Ford?"

"It's none of Augie's business. Or yours."

"They were using my boat and my gear. That makes it my business. Whatever they bring back belongs to my marina. Rules of salvage, my lawyers say."

Smiling, I said, "Really?" I looked at Javier's boat, the barn wreckage, the boats in the background. "Maybe your lawyers will get a chance to catch up on their admiralty law. While you're in jail."

I turned, intending to tell Tomlinson and Jeth to get aboard my skiff. Once we were away from marina property, we could hike to the road, and find Javier. Before I could speak, though, Heller reached and clamped his hand on my shoulder.

"Whoa there, Ford. You're not going anywhere until I see what's in the bucket." He seemed more interested, though, in what was going on now at the entrance: Deputies moving along the inside of the fence, hands on their weapons.

Moe said, "I'll get the bucket, Bern. And anything else I think belongs to the marina." Moe began to walk toward the shoreline, but he was watching the deputies, too, who were now fanning out near the section of fence Javier had vaulted earlier.

I had tolerated Bern Heller—barely. But no way was I going to let some stranger go clomping around on my skiff. I said, "Heller?" then rolled my arm under his, and slapped his hand off my shoulder. I got him hard beneath the bicep, then turned immediately and started after the man in the straw cowboy hat.

I could feel Heller behind me, walking too close. I expected him to say something, or grab me again. But I didn't expect to hear Jeth say, "Oh shit. We need to get over there. They'll kill him!"

I stopped, and turned. In the far distance, I could see Javier, cops crouched on one side of the fence, Javier on the other, as he ducked through a mangrove thicket, no idea he was being watched. He was wearing shorts and a red T-shirt, carrying something in his hand that was hammer-sized. He held it beside his face, pointed skyward.

I hurried to find my glasses.

A gun.

7

"Augie! Stop them!"

Jeth and Tomlinson were hurrying toward the fence, yelling at Javier, trying to stop him from climbing over the fence onto marina property. I watched Augie and three of the hard hats move after them, but that's all I saw because Bern Heller grabbed me by the shoulder again, and spun me around.

Showing me his pasted smile, he said, "You think you can steal from me?" He reached his right hand toward the stitches on my forehead. "That the problem? Someone hit you with an ax? The way farmers do to get a jackass's attention?"

The natural reaction when a stranger's fingers stray within a few inches of your eyes is to flinch. That's what I did . . . and Heller used his left hand to slap my face, open-palmed. I saw the hand move, a gunslinger blur, and didn't have time to react. Then he slapped me with his right hand a micromoment later. A boxer's technique: fake right, then attack with a left-right combination.

Both caught me square.

Too stunned to respond, I stood and let it happen, hearing the same raw sound as when I'd slapped his arm away. Skin on skin, but louder because he banged my left ear hard. It caused an instant ringing in my head.

Even so, I heard a jumble of voices, Jeth, Tomlinson, Augie, all reacting simultaneously, their words vague and faraway. Vague, because I was furious—a fast chemical transformation. My concentration imploded in an emotional burst. Vision and concentration narrowed as adrenaline spiked, so it was like staring down a tunnel, or the bore of a gun. I felt an ether chill move up my neck, a chemical blooming.

I looked hard at Bern Heller. Saw him in shades of black and white beneath a tropic sky that had been drained of color.

"Look at this. The guy's kind of mild lookin' until he gets mad. Are you mad, Dr. Ford?"

I saw the blurred movement of Heller's right hand as he swung to slap me again. I crossed with my right to block. Wanted to catch his wrist because, once I got his hands under control, this obnoxious bastard was going to the ground no matter how big he was . . . then maybe into an ambulance.

Or maybe not. Uncle Bern, jumbo-sized and rubbery, was also quick. Quicker than me—since my concussion, anyway.

I didn't get my hand up in time, and he connected on the left side of my face. Hit me hard enough with his palm to create starburst colors behind my eyes. Then slapped me with his left.

"Don't let him do that to you! *Doc?* Do something!"

Jeth's voice? Tomlinson? I couldn't sort it out. In some faraway synapse, I realized that Heller had found this clever way to keep both of them from warning Javier.

"Well, *Doctor.* Why *don't* you do something?"

Whap. He slapped me again, then once more. I threw my hands up, expecting him to hit me again. Instead, he pivoted to the side, and kicked me, a boat shoe in the butt. Not hard—it was a message. It demonstrated contempt.

I lost it. Which is what he expected. I ducked and charged, my vision blurry. As easily as the man dodged Tomlinson, he dodged me, pivoting like a matador. My hair wasn't long enough to get a handhold, but he did the same quick trip-step, turning my body as he drove me hard, back first, onto the limestone.

Then . . . I was looking up into the September sky, colors returning, Bern Heller's face hanging over mine. He was close enough so details weren't blurry. The man had an oversized head like a robot: forehead, cheeks, and chin. His jaw mandible was a structure of interlocking cordage covered with skin.

Something I hadn't noticed before: no beard stubble. Heller's face was wiener smooth, his small blue eyes looking out. He'd managed to pin my right arm with his knee; had his forearm on my throat. The jugular vein side, shutting off the blood to my brain.

I struggled to move. Couldn't. Tried to speak. Couldn't.

He leaned his nose near mine, and whispered so only I could hear. "You snobby-assed motherfucker, if we was alone, I'd strip those pants off you and stick a broom up your butt just to see you wiggle. I've done it to pigs, and some of them *like* it. What about you? If you ever come back here, I'll give it a try. Stick it right up your ass."

The man was giving me a private glimpse of the craziness inside him. Delighted with his secret profanities, the control he wielded. It was a glimpse of the demonic little boy who lived behind those blue eyes.

Not quite blue, though. Up close, the intensity of his eyes, altered their color a few shades to cobalt. They were glassy receptors, hunting probes that I associated with reptiles and certain birds. Animals accustomed to dampness and night.

Somehow, I got my left arm free. Formed a fist and hit him with a couple of weak shots to the kidneys. He responded by driving his forehead into my nose. Head butt. Almost got me square, but I turned my face in time. Still, I felt a dizzying explosion in my brain, then warm rivulets of blood.

"That's enough, goddamn you. You're hurting him. Let 'im up!"

A familiar voice. Whose?

It seemed to come from miles away, a voice that was energized with the rage of a victim who'd snapped after being cornered.

I'd never before heard this man enraged.

Tomlinson's voice.

In the hazy, graying world of unconsciousness, I considered hitting Heller in the kidneys one more time. Decided no. Paybacks were hell with this guy, as the weight of Heller's forearm on my throat, anvil heavy, squashed me into a blackness.

"Get off him!"

Tomlinson again. My weird friend. "Heller, I'm not going to tell you again!"

Rage and violence. Strange. Hard to associate those emotions with Tomlinson.

"Goddamn it, I warned you—"

Through the darkness, I heard a *whooping* sound. Felt a jolt . . . and, suddenly, the weight was gone from my throat. Light gathered beyond my eyelids. I opened them to see a storm blue sky, Heller no longer hanging over me like a vulture.

I rolled to my side, then sat, fingers exploring esophageal cartilage for damage. I was aware of men shoving, Tomlinson in the middle. Grunting sounds, strained voices swearing. Noises men make when fighting.

I turned. Focused. Could this be real?

Tomlinson had his big, bony hands around Bern Heller's throat. Had his fingers locked deep in neck tissue, and he was backing the larger man toward the water. He didn't seem to feel Heller's fists pounding at his shoulders and ribs. Ignored Jeth, who was alternately shoving Augie and trying to separate Tomlinson from Uncle Bern.

"Jesus, Tomlinson, you're gonna kill the asshole if you don't stop!"

The absurd grin remained fixed on Heller's face. He made gurgling noises, trying to talk. He didn't take Tomlinson seriously, despite what was happening.

His attitude: *I'll end this when it stops being funny.*

Tomlinson's face had turned a mottled gray, his expression grotesque, as he continued to push Heller toward the bay—Heller's grin beginning to fade now. Suffocation is the first of primal horrors, and he realized that Tomlinson wasn't going to quit.

"Let go of his throat! Damn it, they're going to shoot Javier!"

I glanced toward the fence, seeing that Javier was now on marina property, still holding the gun but that it was pointed at the ground. He appeared stricken, the central figure in a shrinking circle as deputies moved into position.

Something else I saw: Cowboy was headed our way carrying the five-gallon bucket he'd taken from my boat. The bucket, plus the jumble of cable dragging it behind, and a couple of wet towels under his arm—the Nazi artifacts.

"Javier!" Jeth shouted, and ran toward the fence. His voice finally registered with Tomlinson, who had the confused expression of a man trying to disentangle reality from a bad dream. He looked into Heller's plumbright face for a moment, then slowly removed his hands from the man's neck. He stared at his fingers as if they were strangers.

Before Heller could recover, I had Tomlinson by the arm, pulling him. "This guy *wants* them to shoot Javier. Let's get over there."

Javier appeared dazed by what was going on around him, a man who'd paddled an inner tube across a hundred miles of ocean but who now looked as indecisive as a child, standing motionless in his red T-shirt and ball cap.

He was encircled by uniformed deputies who were using whatever they could find for cover—a fifty-gallon drum, abandoned pontoons, trees—as they kept their guns trained on the man, leapfrogging into position. More than once they'd told him to drop the weapon, get down on the ground, don't make them shoot.

Javier just stood there.

But the cops were taking it slow, which told me Javier had gotten lucky. These were pros who'd read the signs correctly: The man was frozen; immobilized by emotional overload, the same way some kids freeze when they get to the highest limb on the tree.

"Javier! Don't move."

Jeth's voice. Magic today because it was like watching Tomlinson again, the way Javier's face changed: puzzled, then aware but confused.

He focused; saw Jeth and Tomlinson running toward him, me not far behind. His face came alive. Javier smiled wanly, and shrugged his shoulders: *See the stupid thing I've done?*

The cops were not reassured. They wanted Javier to remain catatonic, not suddenly alert and maybe thinking of doing something stupid to impress his friends. They also didn't want civilians running toward them, screwing up their lines of fire—something made clear when a pair of deputies faced us, one of them yelling, "Stop! Get on the ground!" Pointing a left index finger at us but his weapon drawn.

We were close enough to hear Javier call out, "Hey, those are my friends. Don't shoot my friends, okay? They didn't do nothin'. If you want, I'll drop my pistol. Okay? *Watch*. That's what I'm doing. I'm dropping my pistol"—the deputies had Javier's chest centered above their gunsights, leaning as he let the pistol roll off his finger to the ground—"See? I tell you something, I *do* it. My friends, though, they just want to help—"

Which is as far as he got before he was tackled from behind. Other deputies charged in, one of them kneeling to take Javier's pistol.

"It's not even loaded, man, 'cause I couldn't find the bullets." Javier, now being handcuffed, sounded apologetic. "That storm, the *cabrone,* Carlos. Everything in my house is wet, piled up like garbage. But I don't want to shoot nobody anyway. I just want my boat."

They had him on his feet, frisking him again. "See the pretty green boat over there? That's mine, man."

A deputy checked the cuffs as he told Javier that he was under arrest, then began to recite his Miranda rights.

As they were leading him away, Javier called to Jeth, "I didn't tell you but I shoulda. Anita, she left me, and the girls, too. The storm took them, it was the same thing. That *cabrone,* the hurricane. That fishing client of mine who's an attorney, call him, okay? You know his name."

Javier's bemused look again: *God's shitty jokes!*

Behind me, I could hear Bern Heller yelling, "That's it? That's all? The guy's obviously crazy, comes on my property with a *gun,* and all you do is *talk* to him?" His throat was hoarse. His voice was shaking, he was so mad.

"Mr. Castillo is on his way to jail. What did you want us to do, Mr. Heller? Shoot him?"

Heller nearly said, *Yes,* but caught himself. Instead, he pointed at us. "What about these three jerks? They're not only trespassing, we caught them stealing. We already recovered our things from their boat."

I turned to see the deputy rip a sheet of paper from his clipboard at the same instant he lifted his head, seeing me. He spent a moment looking at my bloody shirt, at the gash on my face caused by the head butt.

"Whose boat?"

"The guy wearing glasses. His boat."

"The man who's bleeding, you mean."

"Yeah, that's right. He stole from me and wouldn't give the stuff back, so I detained him."

The deputy said slowly, "Your employees removed property from a private vessel?"

"Because we saw them stash it in his boat. They stole it from us!"

The officer moved his eyes to Jeth, then to Moe, who was on his knees trying to wipe the fish stink off his hands having already tried the towels. The deputy looked at Tomlinson, with his hippie hair, wearing the magic green goggles around his neck.

"I'm going to get my tape recorder," the officer told us. "A couple more deputies, too, to take statements." His tone saying: *This is going to take awhile.*

8 Bern looked forward to telling Moe that he was fired, then slapping the man stupid. *Stupider.* The loser: he'd just stood there and admitted to the cops that he'd taken the stuff from that jerk's boat. Moe had time, he could have made up a story.

When they unfolded the towels and saw the Nazi badges, even the cops didn't say anything for a while, all of them breathing through their noses as they moved closer to look. A diamond swastika. Silver skull with diamond eyes. A German eagle on metal that might have been brass, it was so black.

In Milwaukee, by the airport, there was a shop that sold stuff like that. On the south side, near the nudie bars Bern frequented whenever he was in town, always staying at the best hotel in the world, the Pfister, down by the convention center.

The store called itself a war museum, but was really a place that sold retail. Japanese samurai swords, uniforms, old medals, a German Luger pistol engraved with SS lightning bolts—Bern had bought a working replica for his collection—and similar things. Expensive.

Nothing in the place, though, as impressive as the diamond swastika. Probably nothing as valuable, either.

"Who knows what else was in that glob of stuff?" Bern had said to Moe as the cops pulled away, the lunatic Cuban handcuffed in back of a squad car. "Damn it, we may never know now!"

Which was true because the cops had made Moe give back everything he'd taken from Ford's boat.

Ford, being a smart aleck even with his swollen face, had thanked the cops for the diamond swastika, and offered to let Heller keep the bucket, which the jerk had filled with rotten fish. His tone had been so easygoing, eager to be fair, that the deputies had actually said, "There you go, Mr. Heller. Dr. Ford's not filing charges, and he's willing to compromise."

Redneck Cracker jerks, sticking together, even though the cops pretended to be impartial—they'd as good as *told* Ford he should press charges. They probably bowled together on weekends. Belonged to the same lodge.

He'd like to get Ford alone. The man thought he'd taken a beating? Bern hadn't even gotten *started* good. On his grandfather's farm outside Baraboo, what they'd done to pigs to get a laugh before slaughtering them—that's what he wanted to do to Ford. No . . . the hippie first, *then* Ford. Catch them someplace in the middle of nowhere, nobody around to hear.

Moe had it coming, too. Slap him a few times, then use elbows on his kidneys. Let him piss blood for a week to remind him how stupid he was. That's what Bern *wanted* to do.

Problem was, he couldn't fire Moe. Not now. Moe knew how to scuba dive. In fact, he'd taken Augie and his chubby butt-buddy, Trippe Oswald, to the same instructor, Korzeps, in Fort Myers, where they both took the course, while Moe completed some kind of higher certification.

Bern needed the man's scuba skills. Maybe there were more diamond-studded badges out there in the Gulf.

Another small problem: Moe knew things that could cause Bern trouble, maybe even put him in jail. The boat barn that had collapsed—he'd bribed the building inspector, so it wasn't up to code. Also, Moe had been on site when Bern had bulldozed the mangroves, then used the Indian burial mounds for fill—which added a couple more acres of waterfront property but was a felony.

Hurricane damage could explain everything. Unless someone like Moe started talking.

Bern needed something on the man. Something that could put him in jail. Let Moe use his scuba skills until they didn't need him anymore, *then* fire that loser's butt.

Bern gave it some thought, and came up with an idea, the sort of thing his grandfather had pulled on his employees all the time. Relatives included.

But Bern couldn't trust himself to talk to Moe right away. He was too mad. So he waited a couple of hours, then called Moe to tell him they had to load diving gear on the Viking tonight because they were diving tomorrow.

"We need to go looking for the place where they found those diamonds," Bern told him. "Get out on the water before those Sanibel jerks do. Can you get back to the marina by nine?"

Bern also mentioned that, in an unrelated matter, they had something important to discuss.

Moe was suspicious. "Unrelated to what?"

Unrelated to your being choked to death, Bern wanted to say. "Don't worry. It's good news." *Good news for me, anyway.*

He turned his thoughts to Augie. Another idiot. But at least Augie had told Bern what he needed to know.

Right after the confrontation, he'd dragged Augie inside the Viking, insisting he remember where they'd found the artifacts. Augie had just played dumb, pissing him off, and further pissing him off because Augie had seen the hippie and Ford make him look like a fool. Worse, Augie would tell the rest of the family. By Christmas, when nearly a hundred Roths, Pittmans, and Hellers gathered in Appleton, every branch of the family would know that a hippie had beat his ass, and a dork had made him look dumb.

Finally, Augie had mouthed off just one time too many.

In a tone that was supposed to show he was an adult, not a kid anymore—like that was possible—Augie had told him, "Out there on the Gulf of Mexico, all you see is waves, and every wave looks the same. It's

not like driving the boat ten miles down the channel for dinner at South
Seas. Next time, maybe I'll take spray paint and make an *X* on the fucking water."

Jesus, that did it. Bern was punching buttons on the GPS one moment,
next Augie was on the floor after being slapped so hard that his vision was
blurry. Then Bern was grabbing Augie's belt. He lifted him one-handed
and slammed him against the cabin wall.

"You worthless little punk, you've been tit fed all your life. Never smart-
mouth, *ever.*"

"Sorry, Uncle Bern. I mean it, I really am."

"Grandy's dead, so you can't go tattling to him. I'm God, as far as
you're concerned."

Grandy—Augie's great-grandfather, Bern's grandfather. Augie had been
the old man's favorite.

"I don't know what I was thinking. It'll never happen again."

His uncle had nodded toward the boat's controls as he lowered Augie
to the floor. "Maybe there's something you *can* tell me. Yesterday, I put some
numbers in that GPS, just messing around. Today, you and stuttering what's
his face used the boat. Now I can't find those numbers. Someone erased
them from the memory."

Augie had shrugged, afraid to speak.

"Did you or your butt-buddy, Oswald, screw with the machine while
you were fishing?"

Augie shook his head. "No. Just Jeth."

"When you stopped to fish, did he say anything about the GPS? That
the spot was already marked . . . was he *surprised*?"

"Well, the first time we found the wreck, we did slow down kind of
sudden-like. He mentioned something about a 'waypoint,' then we started
going back and forth, back and forth, like plowing a field. He was watching the fish-finder, looking for something."

"You didn't find it right away?"

"No."

Bern had begun to smile, feeling better about things, more like his old
self. That explained why someone had erased the coordinates Bern had

punched in three nights ago—the numbers he'd copied from the old man's map. Turned out Stuttering Jeth wasn't such an idiot after all.

Bern had thought: *I know where the wreck is.*

B ut first, he had to create a way to control Moe.

By ten that night, with Bern supervising, Moe had finished loading scuba gear onto the Viking, including the old nautical map with the latitude/longitude coordinates in his grandfather's writing. Then it was time to carry out his plan.

He said, "Let's go for a walk. We have important stuff to discuss."

Bern practically had to shove the man to get him moving. That's how suspicious Moe was.

Now it was 10:35 P.M., the two of them walking toward the canal that was cement seawall on one side, mangroves on the other. The rubble of the boat barn was to their right, the fuel docks brightly lit ahead, as Bern said, "I've been discussing your progress with some of the people in the organization."

Moe said, "Your family back in Wisconsin?"

It was irritating, the way he said it, but Bern remained pleasant. "The company employs hundreds of people, not just relatives. Don't *ever* think that some of us get ahead just because we're related. Hard work, that's all that counts. And talent. Just like in the NFL."

Moe nodded. His boss had played two seasons of professional football, and liked to drop it in whenever possible.

"Anyway, we've been talking. We like your initiative, your organizational skills. We've been thinking maybe it's time for the next step. Like maybe it's time you were *director* of a place like this."

Moe kept his lips pursed, sometimes nodding, as if he somehow had a brain that analyzed information.

"As director of a resort community," Moe asked, speaking thoughtfully, "are you saying I'd be doing, existentially, what your job is now?"

Existentially. Did the idiot mean *essentially?*

Bern put his hand on Moe's shoulder, moving him along. "Exactly right. I'll keep my condo here, of course. But we'd find something just as nice for you."

"Housing, too?"

"One of the perks of being an executive. Expense account, too. You've got to make nice with people, after all. It's what we do."

"Dealing with the public," Moe said, relaxing enough to make a chuckling sound, "I do it every day."

Moe had been so jumpy when he'd arrived that, if Bern moved a hand to swat a mosquito, or to wipe his bald head, the man had flinched. He was calmer now as they walked along the seawall beneath the sodium lights that made the boats and fuel pumps look yellow, the water black.

"Funny thing is, Bern, I thought you were mad at me because of this afternoon." That laugh of his, it was as disgusting as his tattoos, both arms looking like he'd dipped them in Easter egg dye.

"Mad because you told the cops the *truth*? No, no, it was a tough situation. You and me, we didn't have time to discuss what you found on the boat, to agree on a story. If it wasn't for you, we wouldn't have had the stuff back in the first place."

They were almost there.

They had crossed the parking lot, all the empty boats making it seem quieter, and were nearly to the bay where there was more seawall and a boat ramp. Security lights were bright along the water, showing docks, and the gravel area where Bern had parked the bulldozer.

Nearby, spaced along the seawall, were a dozen fifty-gallon drums in various colors. They stored dirty oil from boat engines in black drums. The yellow drums held insecticides. The green drums were for fertilizers, used mostly on the golf course.

When Moe noticed the barrels, he said, "What are those doing there?"

Bern said, "I mentioned that someone from the EPA was coming, right? I requested an inspection so they could test our water quality, take soil samples, that sort of thing."

Which was craziness, but Moe listened. Listened to Bern tell him that, when the state had declared the marina a hazardous area, it was only good for a month. The month was up in a few days, which meant that boat owners would be allowed to come onto the property. Bern said they needed more time to move the boats to a secure area where they could be auctioned before the owners knew if their vessels had been damaged or not.

A few more weeks, they'd be ready.

"I told the EPA we were missing drums of oil, poisons, and stuff because of the hurricane. The feds could close this place for another month if our water's so polluted it's dangerous." Bern used his smile. "They pay for cleanup, plus reimburse us for lost business—and the public won't be allowed within a mile of the place."

"FEMA, because it's a disaster area. Right?"

Bern gave Moe a nudge toward the bulldozer. "You've got a brain. That's what we like about you."

For the next ten minutes, Bern used a digital camera to film what Moe was doing under the security lights. He was intentionally dumping petroleum products and pesticides into the bay, which also happened to be a federal wildlife preserve.

Lots of close-ups of the face: Moe beneath his cowboy hat, oblivious at the controls.

The only time Bern got nervous about Moe using the bulldozer was when the retard made a beeline toward a mound of fill dirt on the far edge of the property. Nobody was supposed to disturb that, Bern had told everybody.

Moe remembered in time, and swung the bulldozer around.

Enough. Moe's ass was his anytime he wanted it. Bern switched off the camera and headed back to the condo.

His thoughts swung back to that dork, Ford. *Just let him get the man alone . . .*

I was in my laboratory, leaning over a shallow tray of sodium hydroxide that I'd just prepared by mixing distilled water with laboratory grade NaOH pellets. A weak solution, into which I'd placed the silver death's-head, with its diamond eyes and swastika. The bronze eagle, too.

I'd done a clumsy job of butterflying my split cheek but it felt okay, and my headache, which had become chronic, had eased. Work can be an enjoyable distraction. I was enjoying this.

I'd separated a couple more interesting objects from the cluster Jeth had found, and they were also in the tray: a cigarette lighter, barely recognizable, and two silver coins. Both coins were German five-mark pieces, eagles and swastikas on the back, a man's bust on the front indistinguishable because of ridges of calcium carbonate.

One coin was dated 1938, the other 1943.

More and more, it was looking as if the wreck was circa World War II, not the detritus of some unlucky modern collector whose plane, or boat, had gone down.

I straightened and braced a hand on the stainless table, testing and discarding explanations.

Was it possible that local stories about a sunken U-boat were based on fact? It'd been several years since I'd researched the subject, but I remembered reading that there were three, maybe four German subs unaccounted for *after* the war. A theory was that one of the missing subs had been used by high ranking Nazis to escape before the Reich fell. The others had been scuttled, or stolen by the Soviets.

A U-boat off Sanibel? No . . . the scenario was implausible. Islanders would have known if a vessel that size had been attacked so close to shore. In forty feet of water? For a submarine, that was rendezvous depth, not battle depth. Even a small submarine needed one hundred feet of water to submerge.

There were dozens of people living on Sanibel and Captiva who had lived on the islands during the Second World War. Details of a sunken U-boat would have been anchored in oral history. Fact, not legend.

It was nearly 7 P.M. I went out a screen door, exiting my lab, and crossed a breezeway to another screen door, which is the entrance to my home.

An unusual structure, for an unusual lifestyle.

I live in a house built on stilts over water, connected to land by fifty feet of boardwalk. Dinkin's Bay Marina, with its ship's store, take-out restaurant, and docks, is just along the shore, a quick walk through the mangroves. Tomlinson, nonconformist that he is, lives on the other side of the channel, aboard *No Mas,* the sailboat that has been his home for years.

I'd had to rebuild the boardwalk after the hurricane. Felt lucky that any of it survived. Same with my house. It had been built in the early 1900s by a thriving fish company that constructed similar piling houses all along the coast. They'd built them to house fishermen and also as storage depots where fish could be iced.

The design of the buildings varied but not much: there's a lower platform for mooring boats and an upper platform with two small cottages under a single tin roof. One cottage served as a bunkhouse large enough to sleep a dozen men. The other was used for storing ice, so the walls are triple thick.

These structures—fish houses, they're called—had to be as well built as any seagoing vessel, so the company had used cypress, or Miami yellow pine, which, when cured, is so rock hard you can't drive a nail in it.

So, yes, I felt lucky my house and lab had survived. There was a lot of damage—I'd had to gut the place because a tornado took the roof off. On a laboratory wall, I've tacked photos of the way it had looked the day after the storm, even though the details were vivid in my memory: the tin roof shredded, lower decking gone, pilings and lamp poles all leaning at the same precise angle, still pointing toward the hurricane's exit path—northeast. There was something accusatory in their uniformity; the impression that my home had been violated.

It *had* been violated. I'm not a sentimental person, but it was painful to look at the mess. Stare at my damaged property too long, and the image became penetrating, like staring at a strobe light.

As Tomlinson said when he came to check on me after the storm, "Looks like she collided with an iceberg. Which is kinda far-out, if you think about it. Your place has always seemed more like a ship than a house, anyway."

I replied, "Iceberg. Interesting metaphor, this close to the equator."

"She almost sunk but didn't. That's what I'm telling you. You'll get her fixed up fast, though. People say things'll never be the same? Dude, I am *glad*. It's exciting. Your place will be better than ever."

Hard to believe at the time, but it was turning out to be true. No, I wasn't surprised that my ship of a house was standing.

My kitchen, appropriately, is the size of a ship's galley. There's a two-burner propane stove, and copper-bottomed pots and stainless pans hanging from the ceiling. My office desk is across the room near the reading chair, and the wooden RCA shortwave radio I sometimes use. I went to the desk now and rummaged through it until I found an unused notebook. In pencil, I labeled the notebook, NAZI ARTIFACTS, and returned to my lab.

Through the north window, storm clouds leaned westward toward a harsh and angular light. The sunlight fired distant mangroves, transforming gray trees to silver, dark limbs to copper. I could see a pod of bottlenose dolphins cruising along the oyster bar that edges the channel. Their skin was luminous as sealskin.

I watched them for a while—fluke tails slapping; herding mullet into the shallows—before returning to work. I placed the new notebook beside the tray of sodium hydroxide, and snapped on fresh rubber gloves.

Beside the tray was a smaller basin that contained a ten percent solution of nitric acid. I'd already dipped the artifacts in the acid bath, and rinsed with freshwater. All but the cigarette lighter were cleaning up nicely.

I was wearing rubber gloves because the artifacts, I decided, were too delicate to risk tongs. So I was using my hands—taking all the precautions, because archaeological restoration is not my field.

I'm a biologist. That's my business: collecting, and selling, marine specimens. Vertebrates, invertebrates, sharks, rays, sea urchins, mollusks, and plants. I sell them live, mounted, or preserved to schools and labs around the country. Sanibel Biological Supply, Inc. I also do consulting work, which pays most of the bills, as well as my own research—a passion.

These artifacts were becoming another passion.

The silver death's-head now lay on the bottom of the tray, diamond eyes focused upward through the lens of sodium hydroxide. I couldn't keep my own eyes off it. Each time I came near the thing, I paused to stare. Couldn't quite define why.

The cigarette lighter drew my interest, too. It had been engraved with a person's initials, which added a sense of intimacy. Some long-gone man or woman had carried it, held it, leaned their face to it in darkness. I wouldn't know what the initials were until the barnacle scars were removed, but the etching was unmistakable. A portion of an N showing? Or an M. Possibly a V, or a K.

The lighter was personal.

I paused to look at the lighter now. Tried to project what the initials might be. Stopped, though, when I heard the engine of Tomlinson's dinghy start in the distance. Checked my watch: an hour or so before sunset. That's when he usually came ashore.

I returned to the window and there he was: yellow shirt adorned with bright hibiscus flowers, his hair stuffed under a Boston Red Sox cap. On the bow of the red dinghy was a ditty bag—he always carried it when he planned to shower at my place. A long, warm-water shower instead of a sponge bath aboard *No Mas*. Ladies, he told me, appreciated the extra effort.

Which meant that he was stopping by the lab for a beer, a shower, and then to stroll the docks until after dark. After that, he'd vanish. Him on his bicycle, sometimes for hours. Occasionally, most of the night. Presumably, he was with his new love interest. Washed and fresh for the woman he seldom mentioned and we'd yet to meet. Tomlinson's "mystery woman," the guides called her.

I'd never met her, but I knew where his mystery woman lived.

A week or so after the hurricane, I'd gone for a late jog. The moon was full, it was impossible to sleep, so I'd run toward the Gulf along Tarpon Bay Road to the beach. Continued running on a ridge of firm sand when I happened to notice Tomlinson's bike in the moonlight. It was chained to a boardwalk that led into bare trees.

Unmistakable, Tomlinson's bike: a fat tire cruiser, peace signs painted on the fenders, and a plastic basket on the handlebars that reads: FAUSTO'S KEY WEST.

On my way back, the bike was still there, and I heard music coming through the trees. A piano played elegantly. I recognized the melody but couldn't name it. Something from the 1930s or '40s, not big band. Torchy, with smoky subtleties.

I stopped to enjoy the music, my shadow huge on the white sand. Among the trees was a two-story house I hadn't known existed, the foliage had once been so dense along that stretch of beach. The storm had taken most of the trees, though, so the house was now exposed, a Cape Cod–sized place with gables and an upstairs balcony. It appeared solitary on its own grounds, a moneyed estate that had once been hidden—an indignity to be endured.

I felt like a voyeur. Which is what I was, in fact. The music stopped a couple of minutes after I did, yet I stood looking at the house, oddly pleased that I'd never suspected the house was there.

Something else that pleased me was that I could also see the rhythmic flare of Sanibel Lighthouse, far, far down the beach. The lighthouse had been built in the 1880s during the era of train barons: a tower of steel rails, one hundred feet high, and capped with a crystal lens.

Until the storm, it hadn't been visible from this section of beach.

As the music was ending, Tomlinson appeared on the balcony. He wore a white linen jacket, and slacks he'd bought at the consignment store on Palm Ridge Road, his favorites. There was a last alto flourish on the piano, and then a woman appeared, her hair silver in the moonlight.

His mystery woman. Finally.

The woman was thin as a reed in her sequined gown. She moved elegantly, like her music. Elegantly . . . but with a measured slowness that I associate with injury, or old age. It was incongruous with the way the gown hung on her body, the sleek contours, and also incongruous with what happened next: the woman stopped, held her hands up, palms outward—an invitation to Tomlinson. There was no music, but she wanted to dance.

For a few seconds longer, I watched as they joined and began to sway, dancing to the cadence of storm waves and a pulsing lighthouse beacon.

Their shadows were a single vertical stripe on the house's gray shingles, elongated by moonlight.

I crossed the lab to get a rack of test tubes. Returned to the artifacts, and, once again, found myself staring at the death's-head.

Why?

I thought about it for a moment, trying to pinpoint the allure. It seemed important that the attraction be defined—another compunction not easily understood.

Part of the fascination was the historical linkage: days that would live in infamy; boogie-woogie bugle boys who battled their way to the gates of gas chamber horrors.

There was an underlying component, though. A more intimate association.

What?

I leaned to focus, letting the nearby cigarette lighter, and bronze eagle blur. I'm not a fanciful person. I had to consciously will my imagination to wander.

Was it the design?

Yes. The medal's design had something to do with it. The skull had a hint of smile showing above the diamond swastika. Smiling as it screamed. It was a design that celebrated the killing of one's enemies. It seemed to encourage the action while depersonalizing the act. It hinted that, to participate, was to be part of a joyous brotherhood.

There was a wink in the death's-head's smile. A secret shared by few.

That secret; the brotherhood—I know both. Knew them better than I could admit. I *am* a marine biologist. But I've done other work in my life, too. Clandestine work in South America, Indonesia, Southeast Asia. In the world's most dangerous places, a man who studies fish does not invite suspicion.

I have traveled the world. I still do.

The death-head's secret, and its brotherhood—I was more than aware. I was a colleague.

The association with the Third Reich was unsettling until I reminded myself of a core precept: I belonged to a *just* brotherhood. There was a moral partition.

Or was there?

I felt a gathering uneasiness. The association was repellent; the connection stronger than I cared to explore.

Instead, I chose to focus on detail: twenty-six diamonds. Silver filigree.

Presumably, a man awarded such a thing was an exalted member of the brotherhood and good at it. Good at killing. Or delegating. As I'd told Jeth, this wasn't an ornament worn by pretenders. It was real. It was murder's totem.

I pictured the badge pinned to the chest of a German officer. The bronze eagle, too. An award ceremony with drums. Black boots goose-stepping, a Nazi war hero at attention, insulated by ritual as his homeland self-destructed . . .

My imagination faltered. The allure, though, remained.

What else was on that wreck?

What had Jeth found, out there in the Gulf?

I went to the VHF marine radio mounted on the wall. Locals communicated on channel 68 and that's where I keep the dial, squelch low. Now, though, I switched to the weather channel, then knelt to open storage cabinets. From a shelf, I took a low-voltage transformer. It was book-sized, with a meter, a rheostat, and alligator clips, red and black, similar to jumper cables.

Near the tray of sodium hydroxide, I plugged the transformer into the wall and tested it. Most of my electronics hadn't survived the storm. The transformer worked fine.

I messed with the transformer's rheostat as I listened to the mutant, computerized voice of the weather channel:

From Cedar Key to Cape Sable, and fifty miles off shore: Small craft advisory issued, small craft warnings anticipated. Tomorrow, winds out of the southeast, twenty to twenty-five knots, decreasing after sunset, and calming to twenty knots on Saturday.

For the lower keys and Florida Bay, a hurricane watch is in effect . . .

Tomorrow would not be a good day to dive Jeth's wreck. The next day, Saturday, would be better. With hurricanes building in the Caribbean, though, the weather would soon worsen. It would probably remain windy and rough for the next several weeks. Off Grand Cayman Island, there was a hurricane gaining strength. Another was headed for the western tip of Cuba, and a third storm, off Nicaragua, was forming.

Should we dive tomorrow, or Saturday? We could. Twenty-knot winds weren't dangerous, but it would be miserable in open water. Bang our way out to the wreck at first light, twelve miles of salt spray and abuse, then anchor in heavy seas. Get the hell knocked out of us just to explore a wreck by touch, feeling around in the murk?

Exasperating.

I'd left a phone message for a Key West friend who's a marine archaeologist. He works with the late, great Mel Fisher's treasure salvage organization, restoring artifacts brought up from two of the richest galleons ever discovered—the *Atocha,* and the *Ana Maria.*

Mel and his team had spent years looking for those wrecks. Finally found the *Atocha*'s brass cannon forty miles from Key West, in the shallows of a World War II bombing range called the Quicksands. He'd taken great delight in showing friends bars of silver that had been snagged by impatient fishermen. The fishermen had broken off fish hooks and lures, indifferent to what lay below.

Jeth had not been impatient. He'd finessed the treasure he'd snagged to the surface.

If anyone knew the best way to preserve delicate metals, it was my friend Dr. Corey.

Rather than wait for his call, though, I had decided to move ahead with the cleaning procedure on my own. I told myself it wasn't because I couldn't rush out to the wreck and explore. Told myself I wasn't behaving like some overeager kid; that I was willing to wait patiently until my archaeologist pal offered his advice.

The artifacts, though, couldn't wait—I told myself that, too. The unknown objects, still clustered on the cable, required immediate attention. Minute by minute, they were deteriorating.

Partial truths make the most palatable lies.

The cleaning process is called electrolytic reduction. It sounds complicated, but it's not. It's based on the same galvanic principle used to make flashlight batteries: Dissimilar metals interact electrically. It also explains why outboard motors disintegrate unless protected by zinc plates.

To continue, I needed a couple of stainless steel rods, a roll of copper wire, a six-volt battery, and . . . what else?

I was rummaging through the storage cupboards when I felt the pilings of my fish house resonate. Realized a boat was docking outside.

Looked and there he was. Tomlinson.

10 Tomlinson was in one of his moods. It rarely happens, but it happens. The joy goes out of him and shadows flood in.

Upon his arrival, I'd counted his foot-slap cadence as he came barefoot up the steps to the lab: three steps to the stairway, seven steps to the upper platform. He'd rapped on the lab's screen door. *"Beer?"* Sufficiently at home to offer me a drink from my own refrigerator.

I'd told him, "No thanks. A bottle of water—if you have it."

He was on a second beer now, his Adam's apple bobbing like an oscilloscope, graphing flow from a bottle that was already half empty. He lowered the bottle, and wiped his mouth with the back of his hand, making the sound men make when they're thirsty and need a drink.

"That's better," he said, sounding relieved.

He noticed the tray of sodium hydroxide for the first time, and went to it. "Hey—you cleaned up some more stuff. Jeth's going to be psyched. The cash monkey is climbing all over the poor boy's back. He's broke."

"I know."

"Old German coins, huh? Pieces of silver—eighteen pieces short . . . get it? Sell these bastards, let Caesar choke. Oh . . . and a cigarette lighter?" There was an odd inflection in his voice. Not surprised . . . but *surprise.*

"With engraved initials," I said. "We should be able to read them in a few days, maybe a few weeks. I'm not sure. Here, I'll show you how it works."

The transformer, with its meter and jumper cable clips, was on a shelf above the artifacts. I took a strip of stainless steel, attached an alligator clip, then placed the strip into the tray that held the artifacts. To the other clip, I secured copper wire that had several more clips attached. One by one, I connected the clips to the death's-head, the eagle, the cigarette lighter, and coins, everything submerged in sodium hydroxide, now connected in series.

I touched a finger to the transformer's rheostat, watching the meter, as I told Tomlinson, "Different metals have different electrical potentials, high to very low. Stainless steel has a low potential. Silver and bronze, they're higher. The sodium solution completes the circuit, so electricity flows from the artifacts to the stainless plate, carrying molecules of metal. Tarnished metal."

Tomlinson said, "Ah."

"Electrolysis," I told him. "It's why we bolt zinc plates to outboard motors, and driveshafts. Zinc has a high electrical potential, so it gives up its molecules—*deteriorates*—instead of the aluminum. Zinc becomes the sacrificial anode. It's a term engineers use: a sacrificial pole."

Tomlinson was listening, but his mind was somewhere else. "Sacrificial pole. I like that. Like yellow leaves on mangrove trees. They absorb salt, and drop off so green leaves can survive. Sacrificial leaves."

"Similar, I guess. Yeah . . . I guess it fits."

"Sacrifice—powerful, man. A dynamic." Looking at me, he touched a finger to his forehead. "Is that what you were doing when you split your head open? Risking your butt to pay my tab, ol' buddy. Protecting me?"

I raised my hand to interrupt, but he didn't stop.

"I *know* that you got the concussion before the hurricane. Before you got back to Sanibel, but that's not what you've been telling people. You didn't get hit by something during the storm. You were off on another of your so-called research trips—this is the fourth time you've dodged the subject."

I raised my voice. "*Enough.* Okay?"

The beer hadn't buoyed his spirits, and the man wasn't buoying mine with his serious similes and dark questions. It was true that I'd been injured before the storm. But it was no one's business but my own. I wasn't going to tell Tomlinson, even though personal history was involved. Ours. His past, my past; two life forces, in opposition, that had finally intersected. I was dealing with it, but I wasn't going to discuss it. Not today.

Probably never.

Tomlinson was as subdued now as he'd been earlier in the afternoon, on the boat trip from Indian Harbor to Dinkin's Bay. He'd sat alone on the forward cushion, legs intertwined in full lotus position. Eyes glazed, staring at a gray horizon that melded into gray mangroves.

Violence creates chemical and emotional by-products. Depressants that, hours afterward, permeate the veins with a poison that sometimes scars for years. Tomlinson had felt the poison. He'd sat himself up there in the wind, perhaps thinking it would cleanse him.

I knew better.

He was still feeling the poison now. It was obvious from the way he'd mutter to himself, arguing internally, his attention scattered. Earlier, when he'd tried to apologize to me for his behavior, I'd told him it wasn't necessary.

He'd replied, "Are you kidding? What I did makes all my so-called spiritual convictions a joke, man. Have you ever seen me lose my temper before?"

"You've come close a few times, but . . . no."

"I didn't just lose my temper. I went nuts. Snapped like a dry twig. Like some country club–Republican psycho. Rush Limbaugh on a very nasty acid binge—that's the way I acted. Doc, I wanted to slap the smirk off that overbearing jerk's face . . . no, I wanted to *kill* him. There, I said it! I wanted to choke him until those sick blue eyes of his bulged like muscat grapes." Tomlinson touched a finger to his chest, his expression posing a question: *Me?* Like he still couldn't believe it. "Hatred, man. I was boiling with it. It came out of nowhere, like something evil slipped into my head when I wasn't paying attention. That old expression: My blood ran cold. I experienced it, man. A chemical change. Like there was Freon in my veins."

Once again, I was tempted to say, *I know the feeling,* but didn't.

He felt hatred, and poisonous regret. Oddly, I *didn't.* Maybe I should've. I'd been bloodied by an oversized bully. My friends had seen me slapped, kicked, and humiliated. But I didn't feel scarred by what he'd done to me. The poison wasn't there.

A concussion can cause unexplained highs and lows—maybe that had something to do with it. Or maybe it was because I'd been beaten by better men than him. I'd wrestled in high school, won a couple of titles at state. In a national tournament, had even made it to the quarterfinals, which is when the seeded stars from Iowa, Pennsylvania, and New York began to appear.

Wrestling's a sport, but it's also a sort of monkish apprenticeship. The learning curve is trial by fire, and Heller's ugly face wasn't the first to hang over mine in victory.

Jeth, though, had felt the humiliation I didn't feel. On the boat, he'd said, "Hell, next time you meet that jelly-assed bastard?" His bark of laughter was as forced as his words. "He won't have a chance."

I had replied, "If I'm lucky, there'll never be a next time," but didn't mean it. I'd told him that mild lie because it was unwise to tell him the truth: There *would* be a next time. I would make certain it happened.

When Heller had kicked me—is that when I'd decided? No . . . it was when I'd realized he wanted the police to shoot Javier. That kind of murderous indifference could only be assigned to a sociopath. It required a second, and more private, meeting.

I'm a professional. I have been beaten by better men. But I have also disposed of better men than Bern Heller.

I swam back out of my thoughts. Something in Tomlinson's tone had caught my attention. "I have someone who'd like to talk to you," he was saying. "A lady friend, she's got a place off the beach."

He was on his third beer, still sitting on a lab stool, watching me work. Finally, he was getting to it.

"Oh? And when would this be?"

"Tonight, if you don't have plans."

I said, "Have we met?," knowing we hadn't, picturing the woman in a sequin gown dancing on the balcony.

"Not in this karma. But on a previous lap or two, yes. I'd bet money."

I smiled.

"It has to do with Jeth's wreck. She's interested. I told her what he found . . . I hope that's okay."

The crew at Indian Harbor Marina had seen the artifacts, as well as half a dozen deputies. By tomorrow, people would be talking about the diamond swastika from Key West to Tampa.

"Perfectly fine. Your girlfriend, why's she interested?"

"No, not a girlfriend. I'm open about my girlfriends . . . not in an ungentlemanly way, of course. Neither of us are that damn crass. But her, well . . . she's different. You probably noticed I haven't said much."

"We're discreet," I said agreeably.

It was true. Morally, Tomlinson has the sensibilities of a Zen Buddhist monk—which he is—but he's also as randy as a rabbit. He loves women. Loves them without apology, without device. His girlfriends know he's not monogamous, and they don't seem to care. The only guy I've ever met who can pull that off.

One of them tried to explain it to me. "When it comes to sex, most men are hunters. They plot, use camouflage, set up traps to get what they want. Not Tomlinson. He gives sex. Makes it a present. You receive his absolute, complete attention, so you feel like the most beautiful, desirable woman on earth. With him, sex isn't a biological function, it's ceremony. He's fun."

Sounding serious now, not fun, Tomlinson told me, "The lady you're going to meet, she's a woman." Meaning, not a girl.

Once again, I asked why she was interested in the wreck.

Shaking his head, he replied, "She wants to tell you herself. There's personal history involved, I'm sure. Hers. Maybe hers and yours. Even for me, this lady's a tough one to read."

There it was again: personal history. I smiled. The only time Tomlinson says he can't read someone is when he doesn't want to tell you what he thinks they're thinking.

"This isn't the first time she's asked to meet you." He paused. "She's extraordinary, man, trust me. One of the most beautiful women I've met in . . . well, name a time. Forever."

That was an odd way to put it.

I made a gesture of consent.

"Around nine? She's a night person. I told her it would have to be after sunset anyway, because we do drinks at the marina. And Doc? She's . . . classy. The way she dresses, especially—"

I caught his meaning. "I will try to remember to remove my lab coat, and rubber gloves, and wear clothing that doesn't smell of fish. Are shorts okay? The way my face looks, she's not going to notice anyway."

"Shorts, well . . ."

"Slacks and a jacket, then."

Tomlinson was silent for a moment. He had been staring at the tray of sodium hydroxide for a while. The liquid's surface convexity magnified the objects slightly. "The cigarette lighter," he said, "it's not in great shape."

"No. It may be silver coated, but it's cheap ferrous metal beneath."

"Someone cared enough about it to have it engraved. Any guess what the first initial is?"

I said, "Too early to tell. Speaking of initials, you didn't tell me her name. Your lady friend."

Tomlinson replied, "Mildred. I love that name—old, for an old soul. Mildred Engle. But she goes by her middle name, Chestra. Chessie, if she likes you."

11 At 8:40 P.M., I turned down the drive to Mildred
Engle's home, the lights of my old pickup sweeping
across a mailbox, a nameplate—SOUTHWIND—then
trees, patches of cactus, a gazebo, and, to my left, what looked to be
a rock garden.

Rock gardens are not common on Sanibel, an island composed of sand.
Particularly gardens of symmetrical, knee-high stones.

I was early. I left the truck running, and got out to have a look.

Through stripped trees, I could see the shape of the house silhouetted
against a spacious darkness that I knew marked the Gulf of Mexico. There
would be a rind of white beach between, the Yucatán beyond.

Stars, too. They were immobile above clouds that sailed a twenty-knot
wind toward Cuba.

Weather was deteriorating.

I placed my hand on the first stone I came to. Gray marble, but not a
solitary stone. It was a slab of marble that had been fitted atop a marble
box. I explored with my fingers. There was an inscription.

This wasn't a rock garden. It was a small cemetery—not unusual on the
islands. The bridge to the mainland hadn't been built until the early '60s
and bodies don't store well in the subtropics.

I knelt and removed my glasses, attempting to read the inscription in
the peripheral light from my truck.

"The name on the grave is 'Nellie Kay Dorn,' Dr. Ford," said a woman's voice from behind me. "She was born in eighteen . . . eighteen fifty-eight? She died in the early nineteen thirties. Am I right? My memory has gotten so spotty. I hope the dead will forgive me."

My headlights shot a golden tunnel through the trees. Moths orbited through incandescent patterns of dust. A black figure stood at the tunnel's edge.

"It's a family cemetery. Dorn and Engle, some Brusthoffs, too. Fourteen of us in all. I doubt if the local government will ever let it become fifteen. Modern times. That's what they tell me, anyway."

Her tone was ironic; her voice a note lower than most women, with a hint of accent—Scandinavian?

I stood. "Ms. Engle?"

"Chestra." The figure dipped—a slight curtsy that somehow mocked its own formality. "I hope I didn't scare you, Dr. Ford. I'm a sucker when it comes to long walks at night. Please . . . come inside. Ladies shouldn't introduce themselves to men in bars . . . or in graveyards, I suppose. And I at least *try* to be a lady. Now I've gone a made a mess of things."

The figure turned. For an instant, I saw a face in profile—a nose . . . section of cheek . . . an eye—the face whiter than the new moon visible through the trees.

"Not at all," I said. "I prefer women to ladies."

Laughter.

"Come to the house, then, while I change. The door's open."

The figure moved away.

Chestra Engle wasn't wearing sequins, as when I'd watched her from the beach. She was wearing a black chemise, ankle-length, with a pearl appliqué on the bodice that, at first, I thought was a brooch, the lighting was so poor. I had followed her through a hall, up a stairway, into this room of antique furniture where Tiffany lamps were soft, and candles flamed on the fireplace mantle.

Seen from behind, she was a lean-hipped woman with silver hair, in a dress that clung. Nice.

"I hope you don't mind, but I keep the lights dim this time of year. It's because of turtles nesting. From May to October, they bury their eggs on the beach, and if the baby turtles see lights they crawl away from the ocean and die—" She stopped, catching herself. I heard her alto laughter once again. "Listen to me—telling a marine biologist his business. It would be like telling Charles LaBuff, someone who's studied turtles forever."

"Not quite the same. I'm a fish guy, mostly." I was looking around the room, seeing the kitchen to my left, photos on walls and mantelpiece, a grand piano in the next room, its lid a glossy black ramp beneath the crystal chandelier. On a nearby desk, a single framed photo was visible, black-and-white. A woman.

I said, "You didn't get much storm damage. You're lucky."

"Lucky, and good. This house, anyway. It was built by one of my relatives, Victor Dorn, in the late eighteen hundreds. How many hurricanes do you think it's weathered in a century? I hope I'm as solid as this old dame when I'm a hundred." She bent to dim a lamp, then stood, and turned.

For the first time, I got a clear look at her face. Tomlinson had described her as extraordinarily beautiful. She undoubtedly had been—two or more decades ago. Skin looses elasticity as we age, desiccated wrinkles multiply, and it hangs from our bones as we shrink.

The disappointment I felt was immediately replaced by guilt. Dismissing a person because of age? I'm not so shallow that I don't recognize my own shallowness.

If Chestra Engle noticed, she was amused, not hurt. "Don't you look dapper tonight. Here—let me turn the light brighter, so I can get a better look."

She did. I stood there in my khaki slacks and black sport coat, face bandaged, and watched the woman age another five years.

"May I get you something to drink, Dr. Ford?"

"Please, Ms. Engle, just Ford. Or Marion."

"Our friend Tomlinson always refers to you as Doc."

I nodded. *Fine.*

"In that case, I'm Chess, or Chessie, short for Chestra. It's an old family name that has something to do with music in one of those silly Norse languages no one understands anymore. As in or*chestra?*"

I smiled at her self-deprecating manner. "All right, Chess, I'd like a beer, if you have it."

"A beer? Just a beer?" Her disappointment was sincere. "I so rarely get a chance to make a drink for a man. A *real* drink. May I? Scotch on the rocks? A highball?"

I hadn't heard the term in years; didn't know what it was, so I said, "A highball. That sounds good." It seemed like the right thing to do: Please this nice lady who was eager to do what she'd done for men when she was younger.

She had a dated, jazzy way of talking: "this old dame" . . . "guys and gals" . . . "we had a ball" . . . "this takes the cake!" Mostly, it was in her intonation—"*That's* enchanting"—and sentence patterns that shifted abruptly from formal to Hollywood wiseguy—"A delightful man, but I told him, 'Hey, kiddo, shake a leg.' "

Irony and amusement were there, too, a consistent subtext from a person who paid attention, had seen some places . . . her sharp eyes still saying, *Show me. Prove it.* A young woman, drop dead gorgeous, was still alive inside Chestra Engle, looking out.

For the first ten minutes, it was a struggle not to check my watch. There were more interesting things to do than spend an evening with a woman her age. The highball helped. Turned out to be whiskey and ginger ale. I don't drink either one, but I drank this. Gradually, her speech patterns began to sound stylish. The accent was Austrian, she told me, and she had a fun, straightforward view of the world that was charming.

I liked her. Understood why Tomlinson—Tommy, she called him—had been spending time here, but I didn't understand why he'd been reluctant to discuss her. The age difference, maybe? No one has ever called the man shallow.

"Would you like another highball, Doc?"

"No, thanks. Water's fine." I'd mentioned the wreck a couple of times, thinking she'd want to discuss it. So far, no luck, and I tried again. "Chessie, I'm still not clear about your interest in the artifacts our pal found."

My impatience received a wave of dismissal, and a smoky chuckle. "There's time for that. Do you mind? I'd like to get to know each other better."

It struck me that she was eager for company and didn't want to let me go. I found it mildly irritating: She'd invited me to discuss a specific subject, but was behaving as if I'd accepted a social invitation. We seemed to perceive time differently.

The age difference maybe?

We were on the balcony, now, where I'd watched her dance with Tomlinson. She stood at the rail. I sat in a deck chair, listening to the Gulf of Mexico pound the beach below. Clouds scudded overhead, reflecting pale starbursts from Sanibel Lighthouse.

Heavy seas out there in the darkness. We would not be diving tomorrow.

"I was dying to ask before but didn't. What happened to your face?"

"I'm surprised you waited this long."

"It would have been impolite. We didn't know each other. *Indelicate*— it's a word one seldom hears these days."

I said, "During the hurricane, I got hit by something. Debris— something in the wind."

The woman replied, "Really." Not a question. She didn't believe me, and it took me aback.

We'd exchanged the sort of information people trade when they've met. Her family had owned this house forever—called Southwind because that's the direction it faced. Some of her happiest childhood memories had been here. She'd been in her Manhattan apartment when the hurricane hit. October was when she normally returned to Florida, but she came early because of the storm. Yes, the damage was terrible, and the aftereffects: homeless people; islanders out of work. Tomlinson? She met him on the beach a few days after the storm.

"Another lost soul wandering," she told me. "It's unusual for me to talk to anyone because I go out only at night. Even on an island like Sanibel, I suppose it's dangerous for a woman alone. But . . . the storm was a reason to be friendlier, somehow. Or am I being a sap?"

She couldn't go out during the day, she told me, because of a skin condition. Doctor's orders. First she freckled, and then the freckles quickly turned to skin cancers. She didn't say it, but I suspected the malady was xeroderma, a condition first documented in Guatemala, where I've spent a fair amount of time.

"You're not a sap," I told her. Then I glanced at my watch for the first time. She noticed.

"The wreck your friend found," she said immediately, "how far offshore is it?"

It took me a moment to react. "Shouldn't you first tell me why you're interested? I don't have a lot of experience, but I've heard that treasure hunters try to keep their secrets *secret*."

The woman turned, saying, "Fair enough," her voice a forbearing smile. Above her shoulder, I could see the new moon magnified by the horizon's curvature. It was huge, an orange scimitar, as pointed as a cat's pupil.

"Tommy described some of the things you found. German war medals, one with diamonds, I think he said."

"Nazi war medals, yes. That's right."

"Do you think there's more to be found?"

"I have no idea. There's wreckage. We plan to dive it and have a look."

"When?"

"We wanted to go tomorrow, but—"I nodded as the wind stirred the bare tree canopy, and motioned toward the beach where collapsing waves made a waterfall rumble—"the weather's terrible, so maybe the day after. It's supposed to be calmer on Saturday, then it's going to get bad again."

She used both hands to hold her glass, a heavy crystal tumbler. She lifted it to her lips. "Do you really believe the wreck was buried by a hurricane?"

"I think you misunderstood Tomlinson. I believe it's possible that it was *uncovered* by the recent hurricane. In this area, the Gulf of Mexico is sand bottom. Picture a desert hidden by water."

She smiled, head tilted, thinking about it. "What a lovely image. Sand dunes. Sheiks riding sea horses. Turtles paddling around the Sphinx."

"You're right about the sand dunes," I said, trying not to show my impatience. "Wind creates underwater currents that are proportional in strength. Dunes shift; the bottom changes."

"Then your wreck could have also been *buried* by a hurricane."

"Yes," I said. I stood and looked at my watch again. "I suppose so."

"Dr. Ford"—her tone was instantly businesslike—"I have a proposition to make you. You and your friends. I would like to finance your . . . ? What would you call it—your 'recovery expedition'? You yourself told me that the man who found the wreck is out of work. And what you're proposing to do—excavate and salvage—sounds as if it could take weeks, even months, to finish properly."

She was facing me. There was a percussion flare of lighthouse and clouds behind her, as she continued, "I would pay him a salary—whatever you say is fair—plus all related expenses. There was another man you mentioned, a fishing guide."

"Javier Castillo."

"That's right. We could hire him, too. You put in your time and expertise, organize a team, and I'll fund it . . . within reasonable limits, of course. Would you also expect a salary?"

"No. I have my own work, but I find this interesting."

"Wonderful! An even better deal for me."

I was looking into her face, lips still full, those dark eyes, thinking: *Yes, at one time an extraordinary beauty.* I asked, "What would you expect in return, Chestra? Odds are slim we'll find anything else valuable."

Her laughter was unexpectedly theatrical. "Are you asking what share of the profit I expect? I don't know . . . whatever's fair, I suppose. But that's not why I want to be involved. It's so exciting—shipwrecks and treasure.

I want to be part of it. Show me what you've found; what you *find*. Stories to take back to New York—that's what I'll get in return. I want to finance stories that will keep me warm all winter."

Theatrical. Yes, that described her.

I said slowly, as a statement: "You don't want anything in return? No matter what we find, it's ours?"

"Well," she said, turning away, "I would expect to at least see what you brought up. There might be one or two small items that I'd want to keep . . . as mementos."

"The diamond war medal, for instance?"

"No," she replied immediately. "Not that. You and your team can sell it, split the money, I don't care. One or two small things . . ." Her voice drifted for a moment before she caught herself, and smiled. "I wouldn't take anything of value. Just mementos. And the fun of it!"

Theatrical—my impression hadn't changed. I placed my glass on a table, looked at her, and said, *"Really."* Using the same word, the same tone that she had before, to let her know I thought she was lying.

I checked my watch: 11:25 P.M. I told her I had to leave.

12 It was nearly midnight. Bern Heller could still hear the bulldozer as he sat in his condo. He was going through his grandfather's papers, taking a few at a time from the briefcase, then moving them to a file, or the trash.

The photo of the unidentified woman, though, remained on the table. The woman with her film-star face, full lips, hair brushed glossy onto her shoulder, dark eyes smoldering through cigarette smoke.

Idiotic, to keep the picture out. The woman had to be—what?—in her late sixties. Maybe seventies. An old hag, if she wasn't already dead.

Even so . . .

Her eyes. Mostly, it was her face and eyes. Beautiful, that wasn't the word. Sexy—she *was,* but that didn't say it, either. Looking at her gave Bern a strange feeling. It was a swelling sort of feeling, but an emptiness, too. Like there were things he could want and work for all his life, it didn't matter because they would never, ever be his.

This woman—just another example.

It created an emptiness. Anger, too.

He left her photo at his elbow, and turned his attention to the briefcase.

There were three passports—not one—he'd discovered. One German, one U.S., both issued to Bern's grandfather, the same young man in the photos with Henry Ford and Charles Lindbergh.

The third was also U.S. but newer, issued July 1956. The photo was nearly twenty years older, and it at least resembled the old man. The blond hair almost gone, but the vicious smile unmistakable.

Bern had the passports on the table, comparing them, the woman's photo nearby, Moe and the bulldozer still out there rumbling and beeping, forward and reverse.

His grandfather's German passport had a green cover. Bern took it into his hand. There was a Nazi eagle embossed on the front, the eagle holding a swastika in its talons.

It was the same eagle he'd seen on the medal that Moe had handed over to the cops.

Bern wiggled in his chair. He opened the passport, finally getting somewhere.

The inside pages were yellowish. His grandfather's photo—in his late teens—was on the right, his signature beneath, written with an old-timey flourish.

On the left was the Nazi eagle again, and REISPASS printed in bold script. Next to the eagle, but twice its size, was a faded red *J*. The *J* had been stamped over words in German, a language that Bern never bothered to learn because so many people in his family spoke it it was the best way to ignore their constant bickering.

What did the *J* mean?

He leafed through the passport, seeing that the old man had done some traveling. France, Switzerland, Denmark, some other countries with names that Bern didn't recognize. Probably places that no longer existed. The Nazi swastika was stamped in black upon each return.

The last stamp, though, was U.S. customs, New York. It was dated February 1939.

The pages were empty after that.

Bern opened his grandfather's first U.S. passport. It had a blue cover, and had been issued five years later, 1944—his grandfather a citizen by then, already a nickel-dime hoarder, and owner of several thousand acres of Florida land that was supposedly worthless, sometimes a buck an acre.

Not a customs stamp in the book.

Hmmm . . .

Bern opened the third passport, also U.S., issued in '56, Miami. There were trips to South America, Europe, Africa documented, the late 1950s being a fun time to travel, apparently. Or maybe it was a way for the old man to avoid his daughter, and the oversized baby she never stopped bitching about—Bern. Even in his teens, she'd say to him, "I've never been the same, you tore up my insides so bad." Or: "You know why you hate Grandy so much? 'Cause you two're alike. You even look alike."

The thought of that made Bern want to spew.

Was it true?

He opened the German passport, then the newest American passport. Bern held the photos side by side, trying to imagine himself at similar ages. Studied his grandfather nose, the eyes, the shape of the jaw and head . . . then stopped, puzzled, as he compared one photo with the other.

There were similarities: the hair, the prominent nose, the light colored eyes. But could age change a jawline? The width of a forehead?

These are photos of the same person?

In a little more than a decade, the old man had changed from a decent-looking guy into a pig.

Was that possible?

Bern imagined himself as a football player, five years college, two and a half in the NFL. They'd taken tons of pictures. He'd never been great looking, but, yeah, his face had changed over the years. Maybe a lot.

It scared him. One day, he'd be as nasty looking as his grandfather?

The photo of the woman was at his elbow.

Hard to a believe, a girl this pretty. She'd let the old pig touch her?

Bern touched his huge index finger to the woman's photo. He looked into her face, feeling her eyes.

In the photo, there were details he'd missed. Each time he looked, he noticed something different. It was fun.

The lighting was fancy. It took awhile to figure it out. The photographer had set up the shot so that woman's eyes were shaded, staring through smoke from shadows, but her hair was glossy blond. There had to be lights to her left, but also behind her because the smoke from her cigarette was backlit, a translucent curling haze.

Bern smiled. There was more.

In the sequined dress, the woman's hip was canted because she was leaning against a grand piano, a black one. There was a silver cigarette case in her left hand. The silver case was partially hidden because the hand was on her hip. Her right hand was at ear level, cigarette between her fingers, nails polished but clear.

The cigarette case, that was interesting.

Were those engraved initials showing above her fingers?

He wished he had a magnifying glass; decided he'd get one. Maybe take this picture to one of those camera places, and have it blown up. Why not?

Had he had even touched a woman as beautiful as this? Or *seen* a woman who came close? In movies, sure. A few. But not in person. Not where he could reach out and put his fingers on her flesh.

The woman's face. She had the fullest, most sensual lips. Those eyes . . .

Bern stared until he began to experience the strange swelling sort of feeling that had become familiar over the years. The feeling that there were things in life that were out of his reach, no matter how badly he wanted them. It created an emptiness in him . . . then anger. A woman who looked like this would never come to him willingly. Was that fair? No. Did he have a right to resent it? Yes.

One way to deal with the feeling was to go ahead and *take* what he wanted. It was something Bern had done before. Never around home, but if he was on a trip . . . Meet a woman who lived alone, don't give her a name, but follow her. Or spot someone attractive in a parking lot, walk up and smile.

It was justifiable, as long as he didn't overdo it—which had happened only twice, both mistakes recent, both here in Florida. Both times, buying garbage bags at convenience stores afterward, then driving half the night to a place he knew was safe.

For an instant, images moved through Bern's mind: a white hand sinking into a fifty-gallon drum, a small shape in fetal position, the diesel machinations of burying an object beneath fill dirt. A redhead was next, only a month later . . .

He shook himself. *Get over it!*

Think positive.

He replaced the image with another, and immediately felt better because picking a woman, getting her alone, and taking her was okay. *Healthy,* when the feeling got too strong, or the timing was right, or he met someone he considered especially beautiful, and got the hots for. Then it was worth planning.

Planning was good. Exactly what he *hadn't* done both times he overdid it, and had to buy garbage bags, bleach, rubber gloves. All because he hadn't planned, and got a little carried away.

There was a word for *that*. The word made him nervous, too, when he heard it.

None of his women had the haunting, gaunt beauty of this one.

Her lips, God. In those days, the lips had to be real, not all shot up with plastic crap. Full lips, so sensual.

The feeling the woman in the photograph gave him . . .

Okay . . . so what if she was an old hag by now? If she wasn't already dead, it didn't matter. A woman like this, even in her seventies, he'd do it. Just to touch her . . . check out where things used to be, get his skin on her—like visiting a museum!

Plan it. That's what he should do. Somewhere in the briefcase, there had to be a clue to her identity. The old man didn't do anything by accident. He'd put her photo on top of the pile for a reason.

There were lots of papers, most in German. Maybe she was mentioned. Or in the old man's leather-bound journal, handwritten, the last entry dated October 18, 1944, also in German. Augie spoke the language. He could get Augie to translate, maybe—the kid was scared shitless of him now.

Or . . . he could call his grandfather's personal assistant, Jason Goddard. The man smelled of mothballs, but he had a brain that filed details away like evidence. Jason might know the woman's name, if she was still alive. Even if he didn't, what the hell?

Just trying to find out who she was made her seem more real when he imagined how it would be: Putting his hands on her. Taking her. Covering those amazing lips with his mouth as he stripped her clothes off. Do it better than his grandfather ever could've, much better, harder, too.

Make her old body bounce like a young girl!—punishment for allowing an animal like the old man to touch her.

Punish. That was another word that fit. In Bern, it helped the swelling sort of feeling last.

17 September, Friday
Sunset 7:28 P.M.
New moon + 1 sets 12:02 A.M.
Low tide −0.4 6:03 A.M.
     SE wind freshening. Excellent day for collecting . . .

Because Tomlinson was in a happier mood, and because he asked, I told him, "I'm supposed to see Chestra again tonight. She lied about why she's interested in the wreck. I called her on it. I thought she'd be offended; instead, she got a kick out of it. She said she'd tell me the real story, if I came back."

"She lied?"

"Well . . . she didn't actually lie, she just didn't tell the truth. I was going to leave—it was after eleven. I wasn't mad—what do I care?—but then she offered to play something on the piano."

We were on the lower deck of my stilt house, standing near a five-hundred-gallon wooden tank made from a cistern similar to the one I use for showering. I'd sawed it in half, sealed the wooden staves, then added pumps and a complicated filtration system. The tank is roomy, the water deep and clear, so it's a good place to keep fish, delicate tunicates, sea urchins, sea stars, bivalves, and other marine creatures I gather during collecting trips.

I was transferring specimens now, using a dip net, taking them from my boat's live well. I'd been on the flats, collecting, taking advantage of the

powerful new moon low tide to restock my aquaria. The wind was howling, but there were protected places in the backcountry to anchor, and
wade with a bucket and cast net.

Tomlinson watched as I returned to my boat, saying, "I told her I'd drop
by after nine, no special time. Have a drink, listen to what she has to say,
then I'm out of there. Are you okay with that?"

"Okay with what?"

I said, "You know. No matter what a guy says, it's poison to spend time
alone with his girlfriend."

"Chessie and I, we're not a boyfriend-girlfriend thing, man. I already
told you. We talk, we dance. That's all. Go as long as you want, stay as late
as you want."

Boyfriend, girlfriend—talking as if we were in high school.

I said, "I'm not going there as her date, I want to be clear about that.
It's about the wreck—she's offered to pay Jeth and Javier. A woman her age?
It should be obvious that it's just not . . . It would be nutty."

Tomlinson grinned. "Whoa there, daddy-o, you thought *I* was dating
her. It's okay if I'm nuts? Besides, age should have nothing to do with it."

I was tempted to tell him, Yeah, but you're not as shallow as me. Instead, I said, "Daddy-o?"

He continued to grin, and made a calming motion with his hands.
"Chill, man, because it's cool, very cool. She played some tunes for you?
She sang? I dig listening to the lady weave her spell."

Yes, Chessie Engle had played. When she offered, I'd agreed out of po-
liteness. At a party, when someone comes into the room with a guitar, or
sits at the piano, I bolt for the nearest door. I dread that feeling of being
trapped by social protocol. I'd heard her music from the beach. It was elo-
quent and professional, but it was nearly midnight, and I wanted to get back
to the marina.

I figured I would stay for one song.

I didn't get home until after one.

I told Tomlinson, Yes, she performed, and then tried to describe the experience. "I had no idea. At the piano, she's . . . And her *voice* . . ."

I couldn't find the words, so he provided them. "She's a superb musician. She has the tonal confidence of a young woman, but a very old soul. Her vocals go right through the heart into bone—haunting. Chestra is haunting."

I agreed, but additional praise seemed pointless. I didn't expect her to be that good. I don't expect *anyone* to be that good. I said, "How could a woman with that much talent remain an unknown? Most of the songs she performed, she composed herself. But no records or CDs."

It puzzled Tomlinson, too. His tone was guarded. "It's interesting, man, the way you phrased that: How could a woman with that much talent remain unknown? *Exactly.*

"The first time I heard her play, I did what everyone does when they stumble on a genuinely gifted artist. I searched for comparisons. Laura Nyro, Norah Jones, Joni Mitchell before cigarettes destroyed that beautiful instrument of hers. She's their equal in every way, but comparisons don't work because they're all originals, Chessie included."

He was thoughtful for a moment. "I haven't figured it out, man, and I've worked in the music industry. Chessie is smart, and classy, but she also has a weird vibe. Powerful; she's a force. Especially when she's at the piano. Her voice isn't audio—it's chemical. So watch yourself, man. Watch yourself. Hear?"

Was that some kind of warning?

Tomlinson was wearing his baggy British shorts, and a tie-dyed tank top that read: WEIRDNESS IS ONLY WEIRD IF YOU FIGHT IT. He also had the Kilner goggles strapped around his neck. He touched the goggles now. "It has to do with her aura. Chessie's different. When I use these to look at you"— he fitted them over his eyes—"I should be able to see three auric layers. The etheric, the astral, the mental."

I said, "Oh, please," and continued working.

"This is science, man. Read the Bible, those halos weren't made of plastic. The brain and body put out thermal energy and electromagnetic waves. I've recoated these lenses with dicyanin dye, which makes them . . . well, imagine that it's an auric prism."

I had a net full of thrashing grunts and pinfish. I lowered them gently into the tank. "I'm imagining."

"When I look at you . . . I see all three energy layers. Hmm. Yes, a sort of cloaking effect. Lots of blue and violet in your ethereal layer today. Light blue, which is good. Means your creative side is growing. Green, that's the dominant color. Far out. Doc, you're entering a period of growth and change you've never experienced. Normally, there's a lot of red in your aura—no offense."

I said, "None taken. We were talking about the old lady."

"You think of her as old?" His surprise was genuine. He removed the goggles. "Maybe I did, too, at first. I'm trying to think. Well . . . if I did, she seemed younger every time I saw her—because she's fun, so full of life. Until you came along, anyway."

I looked at him. *Huh?*

"We had some fun. The friendly type. Discussed old movies; she'd play the piano. Dance, like I mentioned. Then she shut the door on me. Emotionally, I mean. I think it was because I was trying too hard to figure out her act. The karmic story. You know, the big picture? Then you came along." He made an open-palmed gesture, telling me it was no big deal.

"A week ago, I took these to her house." He tapped the goggles. "I think it scared her."

"That's enough to scare anybody."

"No. It's because I can see what other people can't."

I said, "There are some who doubt?"

He was oblivious to the sarcasm. "She doesn't have a normal aura. The energy pattern she gives off, it's black and white. Evil and good, nothing else. Weird, compadre. Spooky. I'm not convinced she's *real*."

I said, "Terrifying," thinking: *The man has been up for a while, meditating, conversing with God, smoking dope like there's no tomorrow.* I changed the subject, saying, "Hand me that bucket, would you?"

Many people lost boats in the storm, Jeth included. Which is why he was now in the starboard seat beside me after asking if I'd give him a ride to St. James City on Pine Island.

By car, it was an hour-and-a-half drive. By boat, even in this crummy weather, it was twenty minutes.

We were taking my boat.

"I'm done fishing out of Indian Harbor Marina," he said. "So I've got to do something to make money. I just talked to Mack. He's pissed I quit, and won't hire me back."

"What?"

"Even though I'm a guide, he still thinks of me as a marina handyman. There was a ton of crap needed doing, but I took off for Indian Harbor. So, hell . . . I don't know what I'll do. Maybe a water taxi business. Cast-net mullet—anything. There's a guy in St. James who's got a Mako he says Javier and I can use in exchange for a cut of what we make."

"Javier's still in jail?"

"Nope. One of his fishing clients is an attorney, Steve Carta. Steve got him out already. I've been through that drill, man. It sucks."

I wasn't certain that Chessie Engle and I would come to an agreement about salvaging the wreck, so I didn't mention that he might already have a job. I drove the boat and listened.

I was glad Tomlinson wasn't along to tell Jeth how dark his aura looked. He was glum; under a lot of pressure. Jeth had finally married Janet Mueller, his on-again, off-again lover. She was a great lady who'd endured too much tragedy, including the loss of a child. Janet was now three months pregnant, and didn't need the additional worry of how they would pay bills.

Even when I told him about the German coins, he didn't smile. "Coins, huh? If we find a million of them, maybe I can make the last two house payments, then buy my own boat."

It's the randomness of life that's at the root of two delusions: good luck, and bad.

I was one of the lucky ones. I didn't lose my boat because I didn't have a boat to lose. I'd ruined my much-abused Maverick months before by running it over a ski jump—*intentionally*—on a black, black night.

Big loss. To me, a boat's a tool that I also use socially. All along the coast of Southwest Florida, there are islands to visit. I use a boat the way most people use a car.

I spent weeks researching what boat to buy next. I thought seriously about one of the rigid hull inflatables used by the military and Coast Guard. Also considered catamaran hulls. The design makes a lot of sense.

But when it came time to put down money, I bought a newer version of the boat I'd trusted for years. Ordered the twenty-one-foot Maverick with a 225 horsepower Yamaha. A ghostly gray-blue hull, jack plate, and poling platform. The Maverick is an open boat classic that'll run sixty miles an hour in a foot of water, handles like a Lexus, and rides smooth and dry even in weather.

I'd taken delivery one week after the storm. Lucky.

Dinkin's Bay is a brackish lake that opens through mangroves into a water space of islands called Pine Island Sound. Seventy miles to the north is Sarasota. Fifty miles south is Naples. Marco's next, then the Everglades littoral, and the Florida Keys.

Hundreds of islands lie between, some inhabited, most not. St. James City is to the east of Dinkin's Bay, a couple miles away.

I told Jeth, "Hold on," and leaned on the throttle, feeling the hull lighten beneath me as it popped friction-free from the surface, then settled on plane—"plane" meaning the boat had partially escaped the wave system beneath, and was displacing less than her own weight.

Nice.

It was after 3 P.M. Tide was up but ebbing. Wind: twenty knots, east-southeast; bay choppy, even though we were in the mangrove lee. I crossed the flat to Green Point, running forty miles an hour in knee-deep water, then cut behind the ruins of an abandoned fish house, spooking pelicans and cormorants off roosts, their wings creaking in the volatile air.

At Woodring Point, I found the cut, slowing long enough to wave at my cousin, Ransom Gatrell, who was sitting on the porch of her little Cracker house, reading—a financial report, most likely. A blue tarp, government issue, covered her roof, and the roofs of neighboring houses. Trees were down, dumped in splintered circles by tornadoes.

She blew me a kiss. I saluted in return, and continued on.

My engine was new, still going through its break-in period, so I varied speeds, accelerating, then decelerating, taking it easy as we slipped into the larger waves of Pine Island Sound.

Jeth had ridden in silence, but brightened now that we were away from land. "She rides nice."

"Yeah."

"Solid, like she's got a keel with ballast. Quiet, too."

"Yeah."

"I haven't felt a drop of water. Is she trimmed much?"

"No, just a tad."

I smiled, and got a fraternal smile from Jeth in return. There are few things as freeing as being on open water, in a boat that's solid and fast.

Not everyone, though, felt as we did on this blustery, choppy day.

A mile from St. James City, as we approached the Intracoastal Waterway, Jeth lifted his head, and said, "I'll be damned, it can't be. But, by God . . . *it is.*"

To our right, traveling north in the channel, was a white sportfishing diesel. The person driving the boat was either cruel or a novice, because the vessel was plowing along at the worst possible speed: banging hard on waves, and throwing a mountainous wake.

"That's the Viking from Indian Harbor Marina," Jeth said.

"Are you sure?"

"Guarantee it. See—" He pointed. "That's that fatass, Oswald, and Augie on the flybridge. The little creep. He's so dang stupid, he probably tried to go offshore in this weather and fish. Either that, or—" Jeth's expression became serious. "Hey! Either that, or they were outside trying to find my wreck. Damn it, Doc, I bet that's what they were dah-dah-doing! Trying to steal from me. As if I don't already have enough problems. Damn it, you think they could've found it? It's *possible.*"

I put my hand on his shoulder. "We don't know that for sure."

"Why else would the idiot be out on a day like this? Waves offshore gotta be five or six feet. I thought I erased those GPS numbers, but maybe I didn't. Something *else* I managed to screw up." He took off his ball cap and slapped his leg. "And it's not like they're gonna tell us if we ask."

I thought about it for a moment. "Maybe they will tell us. Let's find out."

I turned toward the Viking, running with the wind. Used the trim tabs to flatten the bow solidly on track, then pushed the throttle forward.

"You're not going to try and talk to them, are you?"

I shook my head, feeling the wind, focused on the white boat that looked whiter because of the gray water. "Augie's got ego problems. He might tell us without saying a word."

Now Jeth's expression said, *Huh?*

I ran a parallel course as if to pass the much larger boat port to port, which is how it's supposed to be done. Once the Viking was beside me, though, I turned sharply, and nudged the throttle forward, increasing speed as I steered as if to ram them. Held the course steady, seeing the boat's size inflate . . . seeing Augie's profile up there high above us on the flybridge, Oswald, too . . . seeing Augie turn, finally noticing us . . . watched Augie begin to wave both hands frantically . . .

"Doc?"

I said, "Just wanted to get his attention," as I turned hard to the right, plenty of room to spare, then banked left toward the Viking's stern. I backed the throttle, slowing for the seven-foot wake rolling toward us . . . powered up one side of the wave, then surfed down the other. Turned hard to port once again . . . so that we were directly behind the slow-moving Viking, matching her speed.

We followed for less than a minute before Jeth said, "Don't you wish Javier could see this? Man, I wish I had a camera." A smile in his voice for the first time in weeks.

Yes, Javier Castillo would have enjoyed seeing what we were seeing.

Bern Heller and Moe were both aboard, sitting miserably in twin fighting chairs on the stern. Both of them seasick—their pallid, glazed faces unmistakable. Too sick to notice us right away.

Jeth said, "Maybe you should sound the horn to get their attention. We gotta let them know we're seeing this."

"Wait. Let's see what happens."

A lot happened. Very soon.

We watched as Moe's cheeks bulged suddenly. His expression was a combination of surprise and confusion. What should he do? He lunged for the transom but not in time—unfortunate for Heller, who was downwind.

Moe vomited. Wind caught it.

It took Bern a confused moment to realize what had happened. He touched fingertips to his face, sniffed . . . then shot Moe a murderous look before he, too, lunged for the transom.

On the flybridge, Augie was motioning for us to go away, leave them alone. He looked pissed off, frustrated.

I told Jeth, "See? There's your answer." Then explained that a guy with Augie's ego, if he'd found the wreck, would have been pumping his fist, a knee raised. Or giving us the finger, at the very least. No matter how sick his crew was, Augie would have done something to tell us he'd won.

"They may have looked for your wreck, but they didn't find it," I told him.

"It kinda makes sense," Jeth said. "But I'll bet they were looking for it. Doc? We need to get out there. Soon."

We didn't linger in the Viking's wake. Bern finally noticed us. Eyes wide, he stumbled into the main cabin where his gear must have been stowed, and came out waving something . . . Jesus, a long-barreled pistol. He gave us the same look of rage he'd flashed Moe—murderous.

"That guy's crazy," Jeth said.

I said, "Oh yeah, certifiable. He's got demons."

I pointed the Maverick's bow toward St. James City.

14 Returning alone from St. James City, I slowed to an idle as I approached the marina basin. Because his dinghy was tied off the stern, I knew Tomlinson had returned to *No Mas,* the Morgan sailboat that's been his home for years. It floated water light on the bay, a gray shell attached to its own mirror reflection, a mesa of bare mangroves behind.

No Mas was a safe, familiar presence among the storm wreckage. Tomlinson had just rigged a new mooring anchor—a buoy chained to a submerged engine block not far from the docks. The storm had taken the previous one, and it was good to see the boat near her old spot.

People who live on boats tend to be nonconformists, often weird—especially sailors—and Tomlinson's about as unusual as they come. He's one of those rare beings who can wear bizarre clothes, say outlandish things, roam the docks with blazing van Gogh eyes while conversing with imaginary spirits, yet he still exudes a bedrock dependability and decency. He's commonly described as "genuine" by people who love him but can't figure out why.

The word applies. Normalcy requires varying degrees of pretense. We all create façades of one type or another. I have built my own walls high. But Tomlinson's incapable. Genuine. That's him.

The man wasn't wearing bizarre clothing now—except for the Kilner goggles. Otherwise, he was naked, sitting on the cabin roof. Singing, too, judging from the way his head was tilted, mouth wide. He looked like an animated skeleton, skin over bones, gaunt, like something lost too long in the desert. His Woodstock hair, salt-bleached, was given form by the goggles' strap. The boat's white fiberglass hull darkened his tan.

He saw me and waved me over. I wondered if he'd noticed that my aura had a little more spring in it after witnessing Bern Heller being seasick.

I waved and shook my head. *I'll stop later.* There was something I wanted to do while it was fresh in my mind.

It is understandable that sudden change—change visited by a hurricane, for instance—causes us to reflect upon more subtle changes that give texture to our daily lives. As I approached the boat basin, I thought about friends who'd been scattered by the storm, and other friends who'd rallied because of it.

Captain Alex had taken the storm as an omen, left the charter boat business, and moved to Virginia to look after his aging parents. Sally Carmel sold her palatial home near Miami, and moved to Coconut, where she'd grown up, and where my uncle Tucker Gatrell once owned a ranch. Greg Nelson gave up his fishing schools, married Laurie, and was concentrating on being a chef. Gene LaMont, one of baseball's managerial greats, postponed buying a new Sea Ray because of all the cleanup work, and also because his daughter Melissa was about to marry her sweetie, Clay.

The list was long, I realized, perhaps because the change was profound: A young lady I'd helped not so long ago, Shanay Money, had entered University of Florida law school, leaving her trashy father and family behind. The nephew of a man I admired very much, the late Frank DeAntonio, had called Mack out of the blue after the storm, said he'd won the New Jersey lottery, and wanted to visit Dinkin's Bay on his new boat.

Eddie DeAntonio had asked Mack if the "freakin' island" had blown away, and said his late uncle mentioned a guy name Ford, and "some weirdo named Tinkerbelle."

Eddie was expected to arrive around Christmas.

In the month since the storm, three friends had been were hospitalized, one acquaintance had died, there were two marriages to attend, and my cousin Ransom had fallen in and out of love.

Small events and intimacies seemed more important now. I didn't understand why.

Standing behind the marina's pole barn, which serves as a maintenance shed and warehouse, I told Mack, "The marina's not the same without Jeth around. And now that Janet's pregnant—"

Mack made a shushing motion with his hand. "I'm trying to count, darn it, Doc. Every time I get to twenty, you say something and I've gotta start over."

Mack is Graeme MacKinlay, owner and operator of Dinkin's Bay Marina. Mack, the transplanted New Zealander who is partial to white Panama hats and fine Cuban cigars.

He had a clipboard in his hand, checking inventory. Pawing through boxes of T-shirts, boxes of shell ornaments, rubber alligators, hats, and pink plastic flamingos. Pausing to write numbers on a sheet.

The storm had ripped away the barn's roof, so there'd been water damage. He'd lost thousands in merchandise, along with part of his dock system, plus all the damage to the buildings.

Insurance agencies, we were all learning, bill promptly, but pay off reluctantly, and at their own pace—if they pay at all.

Jeth had asked him for his old job back a few hours earlier. Since then, Mack had showered, changed into fresh clothes, and he'd lit a new cigar. His mood hadn't improved, though.

"I let Jeth live here, paid him decent wages even in the slow times when I didn't need him. September, October? Might as well close the place. But I still paid him. So what's he do after we get the guts kicked out of us by a hurricane? Goes north to a marina that didn't get much damage. It's business, Doc. Money. It's got nothing to do with Janet being pregnant."

Mack takes many things seriously, but nothing quite so seriously as money. He keeps a big wad of hundreds in a money clip, and likes to count it when he thinks no one is looking. He still has an old-fashioned cash register in the ship's store because the ringing sound of a sale makes him smile.

Mentioning Janet, though, caused him to soften a little.

I said, "You know the story about her first child. Before she moved here from Ohio? Then that nightmare she went through when the boat sank, and those divers were lost."

He made the shushing motion, then grimaced. "Damn it all, you made me lose count again. Besides"—he tossed the clipboard onto a table—"I don't have enough business now to justify putting Jeth back on the payroll. Even with the docks we lost, I still have more empty slips than I want to think about. Every boat that sunk, or got blown away, I lost a customer. Lost the fuel sale, the bait and beer. Everything. Not to mention the tourists who aren't coming because of all the baloney they see on the news.

"The storm was bad. But what happens after a hurricane, it's worse. No one tells you that."

The pressure was getting to Mack. It was the same with all who were dependent on the economic interlinkings of tourism. Resorts, restaurants, hotels, and retail shops were suffering, but surviving. So far. Other small business operators—fishing guides, tour operators—were already broke. There were no tourists, so cash flow was zero. Most had to borrow against their boats or property to pay bills. Which meant they had no money for new roofs, or windows, or whatever else they needed to stem damage done by rain and mold. So they stood helplessly, watching their homes disintegrate around them, as the rains continued.

In a disaster area, cash is king. Contractors have so much work, there's no reason to do a job on the gamble that insurance will pay off months later. And the federal emergency agency, FEMA, had been more trouble than help. With its reams of forms, it leached valuable time from those who had no time, and provided nothing in return.

There were a lot of desperate people who, as weeks passed, were becoming more desperate.

Javier was one. Jeth another.

Mack added, "There's a rage growing in people. Have you noticed? Not everyone. Just the ones who had property that got a direct hit. It's been over a month, most of the state's already recovered, but folks in this area are still fighting for their lives. It's like they feel targeted. Shit on by God, by nature, the government, insurance agencies, everything. They're snappy, like dogs, ready to bite. But bite who?"

I'd noticed. The bands of a hurricane may extend hundreds of miles, but the eye is narrow. If you're not in the eye, a hurricane is just bad weather; sometimes, *very* bad weather. But the eye is different. The eye of a hurricane is a sustained and mobile explosion. It is an immense tornado, miles wide, preceded by a cavalry of smaller tornadoes.

Shit on by God, by nature, by the government, and insurance agencies. As analysis, it was as accurate as any I'd heard.

A wooden fence separates the marina parking lot from the area that lies behind the maintenance shed. We stood among junked outboards, boats on trailers, marine litter all around, Styrofoam, kapok, and trash hanging in the trees, blown there by the storm. To the northeast, I could see a patchwork of blue tarps. They covered damaged roofs: Mack's home, the marina store, and the gift shop.

All across South Florida, blue tarps designated homes that had been in the storm's path, thousands of them. They were government-issue, fifteen-by-fifteen-foot polyethylene. The tarps stunk of plastic, and similar materials that are transitory and disposable. Which is why I'd ripped my tarp off the second night, and used bits of scavenged tin and wood to plug my roof.

Something else I could see beyond the fence: Tomlinson in his dinghy, steering toward my house. Far behind, just poking through the westward opening into Dinkin's Bay, was a green mullet skiff. It was locally made, marine plywood. A small man stood alone at the controls.

The man looked familiar, and so did the boat. Arlis Futch? Jeth had said he was working at Indian Harbor Marina as a night watchman.

What was Arlis doing in Dinkin's Bay?

To Mack, I said, "You know what you can afford, and can't. I hope you don't mind me making a pitch for Jeth."

"Don't worry about it. Hell, Doc, I miss the kid, too. He's been hanging around here since he was in high school. And Janet—she finally has a chance to have a baby . . ." He sighed, his smiled weary. "See ya, Doc."

As I opened the gate, Mack looked up from his clipboard. "Tell Jeth to call me, okay? Who knows. I might be able to find something. He really is a hell of a nice kid."

15 "It's been four weeks since the storm," Tomlinson told me, "and I've decided that man's greatest structural flaw is that we can't use our dicks as snorkels. Who's had time to come up for air? It's even worse for women. They're all pent up, like overinflated balloons."

I stood at the north window of my lab, looking out. Yes, it was Arlis Futch. A short man with huge forearms and hands from pulling nets, wearing a big Bing Crosby hat. But Arlis wanted time alone before he came ashore. That's the way I read it, the old man drifting a hundred yards from my stilt house, engine off, in a boat designed for netting mullet, but which was now obsolete because of a net ban that had taken his livelihood away. Not only his, but the livelihoods of several thousand Florida commercial fishermen, most of them competent, responsible people; a few, redneck trash.

The good and the bad, it didn't matter. They'd vanished not long after their promises to fight back had been dismissed.

Arlis was one of the good ones. He'd been close friends with Hannah Smith. *Very* close friends, which was still a source of uneasiness for me. Hannah had lived and behaved as she pleased, which included sometimes offering herself as comfort to a lonely old man she care about and respected.

I turned from the window, and listened to Tomlinson tell me that fluctuating barometric pressure—because of all the hurricanes—was having a major effect on Florida's female population.

"On the clitoral scale, barometric pressure's been seesawing like a teaser pony in heat. That's why every women on these islands looks flushed, nervous. You've noticed? They're all static charged from that storm. Every single one. And they'll all need grounding very soon. *Safely* grounded. Or they could blow up like the damn *Hindenburg*."

I rolled my eyes as I interrupted, "I hope you're not referring to Mildred Engle; trying to give me a subliminal suggestion for some reason—"

"No, of course not. But you never know, Doc. A woman with Chessie's aura?"

Yes, I told him, sometimes I *did* know.

He'd come to use the shower again, Friday night being traditional party night at the marina. In the first weeks after the storm, I was among the few to have a generator; also had my own water, the big wooden cistern full and clean. I'd gotten used to locals stopping by to cook something or wash, but Tomlinson has always been a regular.

"I'm talking about women in general," he continued. "That's why you can't miss the party. Women are counting on all of us. They've been sending unmistakable vibes. And don't think for a minute *you're* not expected to contribute something to the cause."

I nodded, playing along. "Yeoman's work. Probably a couple dozen females will be here tonight."

He was pulling clothing from his ditty bag—tie-dyed shirts, a sarong. "Yes, and most of them over forty. Older women are the world's best lovers, as you possibly know. It is because they go at it like they may never get another chance. However, they also sap more energy. Caloric output, in medical terms. So you need to be back from Chessie's in time for a little nap and a few vitamins before the party really gets going."

It was obvious but I asked, anyway. "What time did you start drinking this afternoon?"

The question offended him. "Why? Because I'm cheerful? I'm almost always cheerful. The fact that I occasionally have a few breakfast beers has nothing to do with it."

"Cheerful, yeah. But you seem damn near giddy. Or maybe you've been smoking already—"

His head began to bob, interrupting me to demonstrate that he felt no shame. "Just a couple of tokes with my morning tea. Opening the brain receptors, telling the gods I'm still down here, awaiting instructions. But giddy?" He was mulling it over. "Hmm . . . you *could* be right. I purchased some amazing weed off a Key West chum. Grown somewhere off Marathon. Really great shit."

I said, "Apparently."

"They call the stuff Seven Mile Bridge, because it's about as close as you can get to walking on water. Plus, it gets you over the hump." His tone changed, taking a chance. "You want to try some? You've got the green aura thing going, which mean's you're open to new experiences."

I never smoke. Ever. But heard myself say, "Maybe. Let me think it over."

Someone had told me marijuana mitigated chronic headaches. The words were out before I'd even thought about it.

Tomlinson's reaction was a combination of surprise and concern. But it pleased him, too.

"Sure, man! Maybe tonight after the party. Hang out, pass the pipe, and get weird. I've *always* wanted to see you stoned. Find out what my buddy's like without all the shields in place. All the redundancy defense systems, weapons locked and loaded."

"Don't get carried away," I told him. "It's just an idea. Something I haven't tried."

I was separating more man-made objects from the cable. I now had two trays of sodium hydroxide going, artifacts in each. I told him, "Go take your shower."

**16**

Arlis came up the stairs, bent and slow, at the pace of an old man in a rest home. But became momentarily younger when he said, "I probably don't have to tell you there's a naked woman out back'a your place washing her hair. If she's your girl, I apologize for lookin' but I couldn't hardly not look. She's standing out there naked for anyone to see."

He shuffled through the door, into the lab, adding, "I didn't stare, though. I averted my eyes. But even a quick look at something like that makes me wish I was twenty years younger."

Arlis stopped, rested a hand on the lab station's marble counter. He was wearing coveralls, rubber boots, a Bing Crosby hat over his thick glasses, his eyes moving around the room. Taking in details—the pine beams, the thick walls—appreciating the craftsmanship, before he asked, "Where's your hippie friend?"

I said, "That was him. Tomlinson."

"What?"

The person showering. It's not a woman; it's Tomlinson."

Arlis's rheumy gray eyes stared at me, letting the words register. Then he made a face as if he'd just stepped in something nasty. "That's a *man* out there?"

"By all reports, he's a man. Yes."

Arlis shuddered. He thought about it a moment longer, then shuddered again. "Gad! I was havin' . . . *thoughts.*" He asked it again, not wanting to believe. "The naked woman out there's really a man?"

"Um-huh. You must of seen him from the back," I said. "Otherwise, it's obvious. At least, that's what the ladies say."

Arlis groaned and shook himself. "God Aw'mighty, I've just about had it with this getting old shit. One minute, I'm damn happy my body's showin' it's still got some perk. Next minute, I got the heebie-jeebies 'cause these worthless eyes a' mine got me lusting after some dope-smoking hippie, thinking he's got a good ass."

The old man hacked as if to spit. "You got anything to drink around here, Doc?

"Beer," I said. "All I've got's beer."

Arlis said beer would do.

Twenty minutes later, keeping some distance between himself and Tomlinson, who was toweling his hair, Arlis said, "It's some kinda Kraut badge. A fancy one. That eagle, too, with the square head. They both come from WW II. When we whupped the Nazis."

In his nasal, Cracker accent, he said the letters—double-u double-u two—and pronounced Nazis *Knot-says.*

Arlis was leaning over the tray of sodium hydroxide, inspecting the medals, telling us what we might not know because his generation had done it, not ours. He looked like he wanted to reach and touch the things. The space of all those years now separated only by a few inches of clear water.

"They operated around Florida, you know. Nazi subs—U-boats, we called 'em. They sunk a lot of our freighters." He looked to confirm that we were interested. "Sanibel, Captiva, and the barrier islands off Sarasota. We had coastal patrols, by boat and on foot. Coast Watchers, they called themselves, all volunteers. I did a few of them beach walks myself before the Army finally let me enlist at sixteen.

"People who lived near the Gulf couldn't burn lights at night for fear they'd silhouette merchant vessels, and U-boats would sink 'em. So we had to black out our windows or the Coast Guard would come along and shoot the damn things out."

It was a relief for him to be talking history now, something he was strong and sure about because, only a few minutes before, he'd nearly broken down when he told us how ashamed he was to have ever worked for a snake like Bern Heller, and he was glad they'd fired him yesterday after what happened to Javier.

"Getting old and dumber is about the most surprising thing that ever happened to me," he said. "I was a strong man for so long, it takes some getting used to, being weak."

This was the way Arlis was dealing with it: getting in his boat, burning energy by taking his apology from island to island, meeting friends.

Being on the water would help.

Arlis said he'd been in my house once before, long ago, just after the war, when it was still being used to store ice and fish, and to house fishermen.

"It smells the same, a good smell," he said. "Pine lumber, and creosote. I can smell the bay coming through the floor. Same as I remember when I come back from the Army."

The war—that was something the old man was comfortable talking about. The war, and how it had changed Florida. Arlis had lived it, and he'd done some reading. The subject served to reestablish him as the man he once was. It also distanced him from the breakdown we'd witnessed.

I'd asked him to take a look at the Nazi medals lying in the sodium solution and tell me what he thought. Any ideas about how they'd ended up in forty feet of water, twelve miles off Sanibel Lighthouse?

That got him started; gave him a reason to stick around and finish the second beer Tomlinson poured. Also, the medals were right there to be seen, artifacts from another era. Like him.

Arlis's gray eyes were huge through his glasses when he leaned to study detail. Hypnotic, that was the effect.

Tomlinson and I left him alone for a while so he could get himself under control. We retreated to the lower deck, where I chipped away four dollar-sized objects from the cable. I selected them randomly—there was no telling what lay beneath the armor work of calcium carbonate and barnacle scars.

As I worked, Tomlinson had glanced at the upper deck—*empty*—before he said, "It still bothers you, doesn't it? I immediately picked up on the vibe. Because Arlis and Hannah were once lovers."

I'd made the mistake of admitting my uneasiness about their relationship years before, and I was still paying the price. "Doesn't bother me a bit. Besides, they weren't *lovers*. Hannah was just . . . extrafriendly to the guy because he's old. It was more like a therapeutic sort of deal."

Among Tomlinson's catalog of facial expressions is a superior all-knowing smile that, more than once, I've been tempted to slap off his face. I was tempted now. "Oh, *great*. Sure, that explains it, then. *Therapy*. So there's no reason for you to make silly judgments about Hannah being with a man his age. Seems like I remember you saying it was . . . disgusting?"

Before he could find the right word—I'd said *distasteful*—I held up a warning finger. *No lectures!* Then handed him the four barnacle-coated objects, sharing their black sulfide stain now that he was freshly showered.

A few minutes later, the objects were soaking in sodium hydroxide as I prepared a third electrolytic reduction system. Hannah was a valued memory. I wouldn't allow my own petty feelings about her relationship with Arlis Futch to impose on that memory.

Well, I'd try, anyway . . .

I readied copper wire, and another steel plate, as we listened to Arlis tell us how World War II had transformed Florida. Changed it more than any state in the union, he'd bet money. Florida had so much coastline, lots of deepwater ports, and we're so close to Cuba, the Panama Canal—"Strategic location, understand?"—it made sense for the military to build a hundred new bases between Key West and Jacksonville, and order tens of thousands of personnel south.

Florida's population nearly doubled in six years, he told us.

"South Florida used to be *Southern*. The war brought in Yankees from New York to Colorado. That's why it's Northern-like today."

And the weather? There was another attraction. Troops could train here all year. Mess halls had fresh produce, even in January. And, in an era when coal and oil were rationed, buildings didn't need to be heated. Which is why, Arlis told us, the government also built POW camps in Florida.

Arlis had a know-it-all manner that was irritating, but I paused when he mentioned prisoner of war camps.

"POWs in Florida? I never heard that before."

Arlis said, "Hell, 'most no one knows it, 'cause no one really gives a tinker's damn, these days. There was twenty or thirty POW camps in Florida; nearly a hundred thousand German prisoners. I should know, I worked at the camp in Fort Myers. You didn't know about that? It was at Page Field, one of the smallish ones. Two hundred and seventy-one POWs, we had— I did the head count lots of nights."

I listened to him tell us that his brother, Lexter, had served in Europe two years before the Army finally took Arlis, so Arlis did what he could for the war effort as a civilian.

"Some of them prisoners were pretty decent guys. They were off U-boats, the African Tank Corps, pilots in the Luftwaffe. Some of them, though, were bastard Kraut Nazis. Superior acting, like their shit wouldn't draw a fly. So I wish't they'd given me something other than a club to carry, but I was civilian staff."

Page Field was on the mainland, fifteen miles from Sanibel. The county's population has exploding southward, so the little transit airport was now a snag of open space in a flood of shopping malls and traffic.

"The camp was active all four years of the war?"

"Longer. All the camps stayed active. The earliest POWs came off U-boats that the Brits killed before Pearl Harbor got us into it. I didn't leave for Army boot camp 'til late in the war, and when I come home on leave in '46 we still had the POW camps.

"Some people said it was because the Krauts didn't want to leave Florida. But I also heard we kept 'em around for cheap labor. We used them in the fields, picking citrus and such stuff, for eighty cents a day plus meals. Everyone needed workers because our men were away at war. Like the mess left by the hurricane of '44—who else was gonna deal with it? The POWs were a hell of a big help, cleaning up the mess."

Tomlinson said, "The hurricane of '44? I've never heard of that one."

"That's because the war was still going on, so it didn't make much news. Not like the hurricanes of '28 and 1931—they're the ones you read about. But bad? You want to talk about a *bad* hurricane? The '44 hurricane was a hell of a lot worse than what just hit us. Worse than the storm that hit the Keys awhile back. It flooded Sanibel, a direct hit. Almost washed the lighthouse away. Three hundred and some people were killed. Check the history books. It came late—October 19th—ask anyone who lived through it. We didn't get no early warnings then.

"Boys," Arlis continued, "you have never *seen* a hurricane if you didn't live through the storm of '44. It reminds me of some of the stuff that went on in them war years . . ."

I turned away.

Jesus, the old know-it-all was feeling his beer already. Chattering along, no longer bothering to confirm we were listening. He was in the early stages of a talking jag, and it wasn't going to be easy to get him out the door if we kept feeding him beer.

Next, he'd be talking about the good old days if we didn't find a way to stop him. What it meant to be a native Floridian, fifth or sixth generation. How good the fishing used to be before everything went to hell.

I heard Arlis saying, ". . . we'd catch so many mullet in a single strike, you couldn't even pull the damn net in . . ."

Here we go.

The man was already into it, talking nonstop, and now also looking at his empty glass so that Tomlinson would notice.

I interrupted, "Tomlinson, what time is that party supposed to start? Shouldn't we be . . ."

Too late. Tomlinson was already crossing to the galley. Came back with a quart bottle, saying, "Our pal here's getting thirsty."

He filled Arlis's glass with beer, and kept the rest for himself.

17   Still irritated, I listened to Arlis awhile longer, exaggerating my attentiveness, hoping Tomlinson would get the hint and realize it was time for the old man to move along.

No luck. Tomlinson, who was perceptive in elevated ways, could also be obtuse. Now, for instance. Sitting there guzzling my beer, straddling a lab stool as if he were in some Key Largo bar instead of a working laboratory. Goading Arlis to drone on and on via the intensity of his interest. Mr. Sensitive showing respect for oral history.

Or maybe he was encouraging the old man to talk because he knew it aggravated me.

Um–huh, Mr. Sensitive. Sensitive as a damn anvil.

"Well," I said finally, "some of us have to work." And moved away.

My headache had returned. Arlis's nasal twang had found the rhythm of blood throbbing in my temples and every word had a serrated edge. I made an effort to tune him out. Fragments of sentences registered, though. They caught my attention on a level of consciousness that stays alert for useful information.

I checked the transformer's voltage meter, adjusted the rheostat, then retrieved several more encrusted objects. His voice wasn't as penetrating from the other side of the room, where I began chipping away at barnacle growth with a stainless pick.

"Bunch of Cuban fishermen washed up afterward, and we buried them right there on the beach, close to the lighthouse. Bloated, but no vultures around 'cause even the birds had been killed . . .

". . . we didn't get no warning, so people rode out the hurricane of '44. Some *famous* people, too—or just missed being here. This was a sleepy part of Florida, but some of the world's biggest names, they *knew* about these islands . . .

". . . beautiful women? We had film actresses. I saw a woman on the beach, she'd make you ache. Still can see her face, if I close my eyes . . .

"The night the storm hit, one of our Coast Watch cruisers was out. Got a report someone saw lights. Maybe a U-boat, they said, but it was probably them Cubans. The Coast Watch boat—I can't remember her name. Anyway, she never came back . . .

"Thomas Edison lived here, but was dead by then. Charles Lindbergh, though, I saw him many a time. And his wife, Anne . . . ? I think she was *here*. Staying at her cottage on Captiva, where she wrote books.

". . . John L. Lewis, too. He was almost as powerful as FDR in them war years. The great labor man; the coal miners' union. Mr. Lewis, he loved to fish. He had a place at Pineland, up on the Indian mounds. You could see it from Captiva . . .

"Henry Ford, his house was on the river, and his family used it. You know the place, the mansion next to Edison's where they have tourist trolleys now . . ."

I paused, as my attention vectored, drawn by the association of names. It was an eclectic list. Worth remembering, I decided.

Consciously, I summarized details: In the fall of 1944, four of America's most famous and influential people, and/or their family members, had ties to the Sanibel area: The inventor of the automobile, the president of the United Mine Workers, the first man to fly the Atlantic solo, and his literary wife.

Yes, impressive.

Arlis was now saying, "I think there was a famous poem writer here, too. She had a hard name to remember. Saint-something. Edna . . . Saint-something, that's close. She came almost every year."

The name came into my mind as Tomlinson said it. "Edna St. Vincent Millay? She was an amazing poet; one of our first great feminists."

"That's the one," Arlis said. "When the Sanibel Palms Hotel burned, the book she was writing got burned up with it. It made the newspapers, how sad she was about losing all those pages. But that was a few years before the storm, as I remember . . ."

Five powerful people, not four. Both women Pulitzer Prize winners.

Somewhere in the past, I'd heard that Millay had stayed on Sanibel. She'd written one of my favorite stanzas: "Whether or not we find what we are seeking/Is idle, biologically speaking."

I was also aware that Ford, Edison, and the Lindberghs had lived in the area, and were friends, but I'd never heard their names connected in this way.

I listened to Arlis tell us, "I met Mrs. Millay. She was nice. Smart, too, and she knew it, which wasn't considered polite for women in those days. That's probably why some folks gossiped about her. Not the locals—it was always outsiders. She liked her whiskey, that's what I heard." Arlis lowered his voice. "She liked men, too. Young ones. And *girls*. What they mostly talked about, though, was her being a Commie."

I glanced at Tomlinson to see his reaction. "She was a socialist, that was no secret. Most intellectuals of that period were. Still *are,* as far as I'm concerned. She wrote some very heavy stuff about the movement."

"Well," Arlis said, "in the war years, because of all the censorship, the only way to get news was to talk to outsiders. That's what we did, so you never knew what to believe. People said Mr. Lewis was a Commie, too. And you shoulda heard some of the stories that went around about Henry Ford.

"They said that Mr. Ford went to Germany and built a car factory for Hitler. That Ford and Colonel Lindbergh was both secret supporters of Hitler. They were all close friends, you know, Mr. Ford, Colonel Lindbergh, and Thomas Edison."

Tomlinson was nodding, aware.

"At Mr. Ford's house, there was a German employee or two—that kept the rumors going. He had a bunch of them working for him in Detroit. Germans, I'm saying.

"People worried they was spies. Who knows? The first time we marched our POWs to Mr. Ford's mansion to work, those Germans pretended like they weren't happy to see more Krauts. But they were, I could tell."

I was listening again, interested. "You took POWs to Ford's home more than once?"

"Not me. The captain in charge of the Page Field camp. In '44, there was a big storm in August, too. Not a hurricane, but enough to knock down trees. We liked to keep them Krauts busy.

"One thing I do know for certain," Arlis added, "is that Hitler gave Mr. Ford a medal. Check the history books, there's photos of Ford wearing it on his chest. A cross of some kind, a famous award, but the name of it's gone from my memory now."

I watched Arlis turn to lean toward the reduction tray. The sodium hydroxide was bubbling as the old man's reflection colored the surface. "Mr. Ford's medal wasn't as fancy as this one, though. Bigger, maybe, but not as fancy." He meant the silver death's-head.

The lenses of his glasses caught the light. "You figure those are real diamonds?"

I'd looked at the stones under a microscope. No visible scratches. I said, "I think they are," then asked for his opinion again: How did Nazi medals end up on a wreck off Sanibel?

Arlis shrugged, and used the back of his hand to wipe his face. "Hard to say. There's a story about a sunken a U-boat, but it's bullshit—us old-timers would've known. They can't be off a German warship or freighter, neither. We'd a blowed the bastards out of the water before they made the Florida Straits."

He thought about it for a while, then impressed me, saying, "A plane, maybe? I've read that some of the Nazi big shots, the really bad ones—the ones who did experiments on people? I read some of them escaped before the war ended. They had new identities, the routes all planned. They left Europe on a U-boat headed for South America, or even the U.S. Once they got ashore, they could've switched to a plane. In those days, planes crashed a lot more often than they do now."

He was silent for a few moments more, then impressed me again. "Know what, Doc? A medal as fancy as this, it's the sort of thing generals wear. Except for all those diamonds. The diamonds, they just don't fit. Think about it. Who would you give a medal that's covered with diamonds?"

I was still processing the question when Arlis and Tomlinson both spoke at the same time. They said: "A woman."

18 After sunset, east of Dinkin's Bay, the peaks of storm clouds were neon pink but water swollen at their anvil bases.

More rain coming.

I was at the marina, moving from pod to pod of partygoers, drinking iced tea from a plastic cup. The crowd was sufficiently relaxed and fun, there was no need to drink anything stronger. I was dressed for my visit with the stylish Chessie Engle, wearing a white Cuban guayabera tonight with khaki slacks. Me, a guy whose standard uniform is fishing shorts and a pullover shirt, so I got some comments: *Who you all dressed up for? Gotta new one on the line, Doc?*

Most of the liveaboards were present. JoAnn Smallwood and Rhonda Lister were holding court from the stern of *Tiger Lilly*. They had the music turned loud, blasting Capt. Buffett's tales of sharks and motel maids across the bay. Dieter Rasmussen and his exotic-looking new girlfriend were serving drinks to visitors aboard his forty-six-foot Grand Banks trawler, *Das Stasi*. Several off-duty restaurant employees were there, too, along with Mack and his marina staff.

Mack had mellowed. In fact, Mack was at his cheery best, as were Ozzie and Doug Fischer, Alex, Dave Case, Neville, and the other fishing guides. It was because Bill Gutek, who'd been sent to Baileys for potato chips, re-turned with a dozen attractive, active women in tow. The women had stopped their bachelorette limo to ask Bill if he knew a place they could all dance, and maybe go for a late swim.

He'd led them through the marina gates, into Dinkin's Bay, and then locked the gates behind him. Which is why all the men were cheerful, and why Bill Gutek was enjoying celebrity status that exceeded the status of owning a beautifully refurbished thirty-two-foot Island Gypsy trawler that had a massage table installed in the master cabin.

I was content to drink tea because the party had all the required elements for a long and memorable evening. It would still be going when I returned from Chestra's, and timing was an important consideration. When I saw rain clouds, though, I threw my cup in the trash, and went to get my first beer.

More rain?

I've been a water person all my life. It's my work, and also a refuge. It represents safety. More than once over the years, locating water, escaping into water, has saved my life.

When the hurricane hit, though, water became a new enemy. The earth, the sky, even dust molecules were saturated with the stuff. It was inescapable, seeping into every dry and precious space. Each day, I battled a leaking roof, leaky windows, footpath quagmires, sinking boats, the water-enraged tempers of friends, and temperamental pumps, all the while aware that the incursion of freshwater into salt water was also killing the bay on which I live.

In comparison, the ten days prior to the storm, which I had spent in a foreign land, had seemed undemanding despite tumbling off a rock, and cracking my head open.

Almost undemanding.

At incremental spots around the docks, Mack's crew had placed buckets filled with ice and bottles of beer. They'd added rock salt to the ice— a trick I'd taught them—because salt water freezes at thirty degrees, not thirty-two degrees, so bottles floated in an Arctic slush.

I plucked a bottle of Coors from a bucket, popped the top, and drank until I felt the first hint of brain freeze—refreshing on this wind-hot September night. Then I walked to a corner of dock where a shepherd's crook lamp illuminated water.

The water was green beneath the yellow light, with just enough clarity so that I could see the head and jagged teeth of an alligator gar protruding from under the dock. The fish was as long as my arm. Alligator gars are commonly found in the Everglades. Strictly a freshwater animal, but here it was.

The gar was here because inland Florida and Lake Okeechobee were flooded. The Army Corps of Engineers was opening locks, dumping metric tons of storm offal, a chemical soup of fertilizers and poisons. Now the polluted mess had reached the sea, carrying freshwater exotics with it.

Usually, the Corps dumped the offal into canals that carried it to three different regions of the state. Lately, though, they'd been routing the entire mess to the west coast of Florida.

Criminal.

Because the water was murky, I couldn't see a killing blue algae smothering sea grasses, but I knew it was there. I couldn't see the oil-based pesticides and insecticides used by Florida's sugar industry, and its thousands of golf courses, but I knew they were there, too.

Laws regulating the use of such chemicals, and the treatment of water, don't anticipate catastrophe. Nor do they address the unyielding adhesive properties of three elemental atoms in union: H_2O. Once joined, they will transport poisons as dependably as they transport surfers.

I remembered Tomlinson saying that a great storm was cleansing. Something about it exposing decay.

This water was the definition of decay. The contaminants it contained were killing the bay's own natural filtration system.

Buffett was now singing about an over-forty pirate as I took a long, slow swallow of beer, and watched the gar. The fish was a few inches below the surface, in the shadow of the dock. I considered its armor work of scales, the reptilian head and lateral fins. It was pterodactyl-like. A primitive sniper, I decided, balanced on the edge of light, waiting for a target to appear.

The imagery became less fanciful as my thoughts transitioned to fresh memory: a lone figure beneath a desert sky, clothes acidic with the odor of horse and sweat. The weight of a rifle . . . the weight of elbow on rock. The firefly luminescence of a night-vision scope as the figure knelt at the

edge of darkness—me, the lone figure, waiting for a target. Me, holding a weapon's scope to my eye hoping to see a human profile appear from . . .

"Doc! Did you hear me?"

I was so deep in thought that I fumbled my beer and dropped the bottle. When the bottle hit, there was a suctioning sound created by the sudden displacement of water.

The fish spooked, its mouth wide in the yellow light. It displayed its teeth to discourage pursuit . . .

I turned. Jeth was standing in the shadows where the dock T-ed. Tomlinson was gliding up behind him, both men barefoot, their voices easy to hear now because the music had stopped.

From the distance, as Rhonda called, "What do you beach bums wanna hear next?," Jeth told me, "I want to dive the wreck tomorrow; Javier, too. We don't care what the weather is. Tomlinson agrees."

I glanced to see my bottle do a cobralike descent into the murk. Normally, I'd have found a net and retrieved the litter. After riding out a category 4 storm, though, I watched the thing sink. I pictured it as a good habitat for some lucky octopus or lizard fish.

I looked at the streaming clouds above us, then at the thunderheads—lightning flashing in them now. "What about a boat? *No Mas* is too slow, mine's not big enough, and that Mako you borrowed—"

No need to finish. The boat from St. James City was so old, its deck was springy as a trampoline. Javier had begged off, so Jeth had nursed the thing back to Dinkin's Bay alone. We couldn't take it.

"Bill said we could use his Island Gypsy. He's not going to be in any condition for rough water tomorrow because of the girls he met, and I've let him use my boat lots of times. Javier's looking for a boat, too, but we *know* the Island Gypsy. It's a sure thing."

I asked, "Javier's looking for a boat to borrow? I hope so, because if he goes back to Indian Harbor he'll be in jail again."

"I'm sure he meant borrow," Jeth said, but he didn't sound certain.

Borrowing another person's boat, I wasn't wild about the idea. Both men were looking at me. I shrugged, and said, "The last I heard, it's supposed to blow fifteen, twenty tomorrow out of the southeast. Anchor in that slop, then get in the water?"

"We don't care, Doc. It's better then letting someone else get out there first."

That was true. I agreed to go, adding, "Here's why—"

I explained what I planned to tell Jeth, anyway: my archaeologist pal from Key West had called. It was a brief conversation—he was en route to Madrid.

"In his opinion," I said, "the state of Florida has no claim on your wreck because it's twelve miles offshore—outside state boundary waters. There's a federal statute, though, called the Abandoned Shipwreck Act. If we dive the wreck, draw some diagrams, and fill out the right forms, we can file a claim in federal court. That doesn't mean we'll own what we find. We'll have to deal with the boat's previous owner, or an insurance company, and try to come to some agreement."

Tomlinson added, "If it turns out the boat's owned by someone we can contact and get to agree to let us salvage the things, it's not complicated." He'd been in the lab when I got the call, Arlis Futch still jabbering away, and had agreed to do some research on admiralty laws. "Either way, it's important we're the first to dive it and bring up something, in case we need to file a claim. Salvage isn't finders keepers. But that's the way we need to approach it."

"If someone else doesn't dive it first," Jeth said, meaning Heller's bunch. "Maybe they'll smarten up and use seasick medicine next time."

I'd also told Jeth I'd done preliminary cleaning on several more pieces. It wasn't encouraging news, but I told him, anyway: There were some brass screws and a brass bolt. Nothing spectacular. There was also a bullet, a live round, which could be interesting once I got the brass clean enough to read the manufacturer's stamp.

"Why's that interesting?" Jeth asked, sounding disappointed. A couple of brass screws and a bullet?

"Because it's a nine-millimeter cartridge. German Lugers fired nine-millimeter parabellums. That's the pistol the Nazis used."

"Oh, I get it. There could be some guns down there."

"Well, if there's ammunition . . ." I gestured with my hands: *Could be.* "Weapons from that era are valuable to collectors. But what kind of shape they'll be in if we do find them?" *Who knows?*

Jeth looked in the direction of the marina store. His bride was there, Janet Mueller Nichols. She was waiting in the glow of security lights, the parking lot behind her. Even at that distance, Janet looked glossy and ripe in her pale maternity blouse. Judging from the way she shifted from one foot to the other, she was also impatient, ready to drive to their rental apartment in Iona.

Jeth noticed, too. "Well," he said, "maybe we'll have some luck for a change and the weather will break tomorrow. Doc? About the stuff you've already got cleaned—that diamond Nazi thing, the coins? Can I try and sell them now?"

Before we found out the boat's identity? I told him it was risky. Also, the metal might disintegrate if we removed objects from the sodium solution too soon.

He shook his head, frustrated, and I watched him glance toward his wife again. After only two months of marriage, he already knew the importance of body language. "I wish we could make it faster because . . . well, with the baby coming and all. Janet, she's worried . . . and, hell, I don't blame her. What I'm saying is—"

Tomlinson decided to help. "Money's tight, and Janet's thinking it might be smart to move back to Ohio to be with her family. Jeth's asking you for a timetable. When you think he'll start seeing some cash."

I said, "You two separating during a pregnancy," then paused, realizing how judgmental I sounded. I tried again. "I wouldn't do anything drastic until you talk to Mack. And until we get a look at what's on your wreck."

Jeth didn't brighten much when Tomlinson tried to change the mood. "Tomorrow morning, we'll pack ourselves a nice lunch, throw beer in the cooler, and have some fun. Maybe water visibility will be better when we get near the bottom. Hell, compadre, you could be a rich man and don't even know it."

I had another beer, but dumped the remainder into the water—no late-night drinking for me if we were diving in the morning—then looked up, checking weather: Stars were hazy with smoke from trash fires. In the jet stream, thirty miles above Sanibel, bands of stratus clouds filed southward. Wind currents were volatile up there on the rim of weightlessness, reacting to hurricanes now gathering power off Cuba. The precise arc of clouds reminded me of the incremental lines of magnetic power.

I listened to Jeth tell me he'd have the boat fueled, loaded, and ready to go by late morning, while also thinking about Chestra's offer to pay him and Javier a salary. It would take a lot of pressure off two very good men, but what was her angle?

I checked my watch: 9:30. Time to find out.

 **19** I'd misjudged the woman's age, possibly because of the tricky lighting on the second floor, with its Tiffany lamps dimmed and candle shadows flickering in the wind that had drifted through the open balcony doors.

The doors were open now.

Chestra Engle was younger by a decade. Or more. Soft light is supposed to be kind. Instead, it had contributed to yesterday's misimpression—my *first* impression, which is why the snapshot had imprinted so convincingly: wrinkled face on the shrinking scaffolding of Mildred Chestra Engle.

Tomlinson had been surprised when I called her an old woman. I now understood why, sitting in the same room, with the same candles and lamps, but seeing her clearly for the first time. The woman had wrinkles— smile furrows; a sagging area beneath the chin—but her skin wasn't a tragedy of lines, and she wasn't old.

No. My amended guess: she was a few years beyond what some call middle age; a mature woman who, when the light was right, was still attractive. *Handsome* is a word commonly used to describe women her age. Lean, fit—some curves evident beneath the gold lamé gown she wore tonight. You didn't need an imagination to know that she'd once been extraordinarily beautiful.

Chessie's facial bones had the classic structure: cheeks that created shadow, large eyes staring out, a jawline that curved into hairline on a delicate stem of a neck . . .

I was thinking about that—facial subtleties, the structural dimensions of beauty—when I heard Chestra ask me, "When you disappear from the room, Dr. Ford, is someone special with you? Or are you all alone?"

"Sorry, Chess. What did you say?"

She repeated herself, laughing as she added, "Please be a dear and tell me I'm not boring you. I won't be offended if it's true. Why, at times I find myself a dreadful bore—"

"Not at all. I apologize." I realized I'd been staring at her face, something that was impolite in her world. No . . . it was an *indelicacy.* Her word. I reached for my glass of soda water, lime twist. "I was thinking about tomorrow's dive, wondering if I'd forgotten something."

She looked at me for a moment, enjoying my dishonesty, before saying, *"Really."* Said it with the familiar flat tone. Sat facing me, eyes searching mine, a woman who'd been stared at by men all her life, I realized, in exactly the same way I'd been staring, so knew when men were lying.

She seemed oddly pleased by my discomfort but didn't press. The polite thing to do was change the subject. She did the polite thing.

Conversation is no longer considered a skill, but it is. Chestra was expert. Talking with her was effortless. She had the knack of asking questions that probed, but that also made me feel important. My opinion was valuable to her—she listened. I was interesting; the topics fascinating: sharks, water pollution, the dynamics of storms and open sea.

She didn't insult me by playing the role of the hopelessly ditzy female to reassure my male insecurities. She wasn't cutesy, she didn't chatter, she didn't flirt, she didn't ramble, and didn't use double entendres to test what she, at least, considered tasteful boundaries. When I asked her a personal question, she was sometimes so shockingly frank that I felt it was safe to be honest in return. An example: "Men are pack animals, like wolves. That's why I've learned never to show fear, and how to use a gun!"

She had a wiseguy cynical side that I liked, especially when discussing relationships and marriage:

"I think the reason most women marry, Doc, is they fear being alone more than they fear having a keeper.

"I married once, never again. I don't have the patience it takes to fall in love with a man I'm marrying for money . . ."

When I told her no, I'd never been married, she said, "Good for you. You're smart. Too many women treat husbands like horses. They use love like a bridle to steer and control—or to punish them when they misbehave."

She was funny, too. Didn't mind being the butt of her own jokes. One of her gambits was to ask some cliché rhetorical question—"*What* is life?"—but flip the emphasis so that she hinted at her own goofball mistakes. "What *is* life?" Use the profound cliché to illustrate life's silliness. Endearing.

Good conversation was as important to her as being a hostess who made good drinks, real drinks, and who served excellent hors d'oeuvres, such as the shrimp, black bread, and Feta cheese now on the table before us. Conversation was ceremonial, something that shouldn't be rushed by business.

So I didn't press. She led, I followed. The woman was insightful, and entertaining.

Even so, I still had to get home and plan what could be a difficult dive, and it was already ten-thirty . . .

"Doc? Can you at least have of glass of wine? I have a very nice Riesling . . . or a Syrah from South Africa. I want to walk you around the houses, and show you why I want to be involved with salvaging that wreck."

"Show me?"

"Photographs. They'll make it easier for me to explain."

The woman's instincts were excellent.

Chestra believed that her great-aunt was aboard the vessel that Jeth had discovered, the night it went down in a storm.

"She was from the Dorn branch of the family. Marlissa Dorn." The woman searched my face briefly—had I heard the name?—before she continued. "The story's become part of our family legend. I grew up hearing it, and now I want to know the truth. What happened that night? Was Marlissa the only one aboard who drowned? Those questions have never been answered. I've. wondered about it for years. Fantasized, in fact, the story's so romantic—I'm a sap for stuff like that."

The woman gave me a look that was, at once, tolerant and scolding. "I didn't lie to you last night. I *will* get fabulous stories from this. But I don't expect you to find anything valuable. If you do, we'll split the profit, whatever way you think is fair. But I'd want to keep a memento or two, that's all. Some small thing to remind me of Marlissa."

We were upstairs, standing at a wall that was a museum of photos. Nearly all black-and-whites. They documented the vacation activities of the three family branches—Dorn, Engle, and Brusthoff—who shared this beach house, Southwind.

"Marlissa was my godmother," Chestra said. "I was an infant when she died, but she's remained an important figure in my life. Why shouldn't I get involved now? I can afford it. I'm not the kind of gal who sits back and expects the world to come to me. At this stage of life?" She left that out there, but didn't seem to be fishing for compliments.

I said, "There're a lot of wrecks in the Gulf of Mexico. What makes you think this is the one? Why would you associate your godmother with Nazi artifacts—"

"I'm not certain, of course. I don't know . . . it's a feeling I have. Legends invite all sorts of theories, from the silly to the possible. I'll show you one possible explanation." She had a scarf in her hand, and motioned for me to follow. We crossed before the open balcony to another section of wall, where she pointed to a photo of two men. One was dark-haired, with a pointed, ferret face. Beside him was a younger man, tall and blond, with a prominent jaw and nose.

Chestra touched her finger to a second photo: the same dark-haired man was there; the blond man behind him, a drink tray in one hand, a towel draped over his arm. The dark-haired man was sitting next to a good-looking guy wearing jodhpurs and a leather flight jacket.

Surprised, I said, "That's Charles Lindbergh," having already realized who the dark-haired man was.

Chestra said, "That's right, and Henry Ford's beside him. I live in Manhattan, so it isn't snobbery when I say I don't consider this area to be, well . . . metropolitan. In those years, though—these photos are from the 1930s and '40s, I think—Sanibel, Naples, Sarasota were all small towns. Everyone knew each other. The famous and the not-so-famous. Saw each other in stores; went to the same dances."

I almost asked, but stopped myself. She interpreted my uneasiness correctly, though, and answered. "No, I'm not telling you this stuff from memory. Kiddo, I'm well aware I'm not a girl anymore, but I'm not so blasted old that I was attending dances in nineteen forty."

She touched her hand to my chest, silencing my apology. "I inherited Marlissa's diaries. She was a marvelous writer, and I've read them all many times.

"That's how I know that the handsome young blond gentleman in the photo worked as a jack-of-all-trades in the area, including some part-time jobs for the Ford estate. You've seen Henry Ford's house, of course, next to Edison's estate, on the river in Fort Myers."

This was like listening to Arlis, but without the irritating jabber.

"The blond gentleman was German. From Munich, I think. His name was Frederick Roth."

"I see."

"He was also my aunt Marlissa's lover—not something she revealed anywhere but in her diary. This was during an era, of course, when it wasn't proper for young ladies to have lovers.

"Marlissa and Frederick met coincidentally aboard the ocean liner *Normandie*. They were both making the transatlantic crossing to America to start new lives. He worked in the ship's kitchen; Marlissa was in a first-class cabin.

"The crossing took several nights in those days, if the weather was bad. And the weather was bad." Chestra's expression was dreamy and distant. "Have you seen photographs of the *Normandie*? She was the most luxurious ship of her time. Marble floors and rare wood; formal dances in halls with orchestras and ice sculptures. My godmother had a sly way of writing. Certain letters meant certain words. It took me years to figure out her . . . code, would you call it?" The woman smiled. "I gather that Frederick was a very good dancer . . . and a wonderful lover."

She added, "The night my aunt was killed, when her boat sank off Sanibel, Frederick was aboard with her. That's how the story goes, anyway. Marlissa's body washed up on the beach. His body was never found."

The woman looked toward the open balcony, hearing storm waves rumble ashore. Her smile became bittersweet: *See? Isn't it romantic?*

I still didn't know why she felt there was some connection with the artifacts. I also wanted to hear why her godmother and lover were twelve miles offshore at night, during a storm. It was a nice story, but it didn't make sense.

"You're saying that the Nazi medals we found belonged to Frederick Roth?" I found it improbable. Diamonds weren't the sort of thing awarded even for combat heroics, and the man in the photograph was too young to earn medals for anything else.

"No. I'm not saying that at all. Frederick and Marlissa came to America a couple of years *before* the war started."

"Then I don't see the connection. He didn't return to Germany?"

"They both remained in America. He worked, sometimes at the Ford estate, and Marlissa wintered on Sanibel. Sometimes spent the entire year. Here, in this house. They wanted to be married.

"According to Marlissa's diary, Freddy—that's the way she referred to him sometimes, 'Freddy'—he was determined to make a fortune so her family would accept him." Chestra's tone became sardonic. "Money is the great unifier, is it not? It's the only religion that offers heaven on earth."

Roth believed that Florida real estate was the fastest way to get rich, she told me. During those years, fishing and farming were the main sources of income in the area, supplemented by tourism. Farmland was valuable, bay frontage less so, but it was still much preferred to beachfront.

Because I knew it was true, I nodded as she said, "Apparently, locals thought beach frontage was worthless. It was sandy, hot, buggy. A garden won't grow near a beach, and you can't dock a boat because of the waves."

Tourists liked beaches, though, which is why Roth began to buy up inexpensive beachfront anywhere in Florida he could find it.

"In her diary, Marlissa wrote that Freddy owned 'miles and miles of the stuff.' He bought waterfront for as little as ten dollars an acre, and seldom more than fifty dollars an acre. Marlissa kept very accurate records."

I said, "I don't understand."

"Marlissa wanted Frederick to become rich so they could marry. So she loaned him the money. That's why she kept records. She had an inheritance, and our families have always been . . . comfortable. Fifty dollars for an acre of beach may not sound like much now, but Frederick was hired help. He made a buck a day.

"I see. He was a hardworking guy in love with an heiress. I still don't understand, though, why you think there's a link between the artifacts we found and your godmother's lover?"

The woman shrugged, and swept her scarf through the air, frustrated. "Oh . . . I don't know. Wistful thinking, I guess. Silly hopes? They *are* from the same era." She looked toward the balcony again where wind moved the curtains, bare trees visible out there in the darkness.

Theatrical? Once again, I got that impression. The woman could be frank at times, but she also maintained a distance. Drama was an effective shield.

Chestra wasn't telling me everything. Why? She seemed to lead me close to the truth in the hope I'd provide my own answers. Or that I would discover information that she possessed but didn't want to share.

I provided her with a possible explanation now. "The fact that Frederick Roth lived in Florida during the war doesn't mean he wasn't a Nazi. He could have been a sympathizer. Or an operative sent to gather intelligence for the German regime." I was referring to the brotherhood I know so well.

I looked at the photo again: an athletic young man serving drinks to two of the most powerful men in America. Add to the mix the famous names Arlis had mentioned: John L. Lewis, Anne Morrow Lindbergh, Edna

St. Vincent Millay—all of them living or vacationing on the same rural coastline, in the relaxed atmosphere of palms and surf.

Why hadn't I thought of it before? During that era, Sanibel was an ideal location to drop an intelligence officer. Infiltrate the local social structure, find the sort of job that allowed him to eavesdrop on conversations. Rifle personal papers and appointment calendars while his powerful employers swam or fished. Perfect. A smart operative could blend in for years, generating a quality of intelligence worthy of a diamond pin. How the German military got the medal into the agent's hand was problematic. But not impossible.

Chestra was silent for a moment, her expression troubled—her godmother's lover was a Nazi?

"I've always thought it was extremely unlikely that Frederick worked for the Germans. Quite the opposite, in fact, from what Marlissa wrote about him. Which is why I never gave it serious consideration until . . . now. Until Tommy told me what you'd found. Medals and diamonds and coins, all from that time period. It's too coincidental."

I asked, "What did you read in your godmother's diary that made you believe he wasn't a Nazi sympathizer?"

Chestra gave me a sadder version of her *I told you, it's romantic* look. "Because Marlissa was doing something else that wasn't considered proper during the time. Particularly for a wealthy young woman of her class. Frederick Roth was a Jew. He didn't advertise it—working for Henry Ford? But it's there in her writings."

Bern Heller sat in the marina's business office, still queasy from being seasick, looking at a computer screen in the late-night quiet, his condition not improved by what he had just read:

> At the request of Swiss authorities, Nazi Adolf Eichmann required that all Jewish passports must be stamped with a large red letter "J." It was not only to restrict Jews from emigrating to Switzerland. The infamous red "J" was also a way of identifying Jews who wanted to leave Germany, so they could then be diverted to death camps . . .

Bern couldn't believe it. Didn't want to believe. He read the same paragraph several times.

He'd brought a few items from the briefcase, including the old man's earliest passport, the one with the swastika embossed on its green cover. He had Googled a few key words, then opened an Internet article that included a photo of a German passport that also had a swastika embossed on its cover.

The passport was identical to his grandfather's: Nazi eagle, and the word REISPASS on the inside cover. Stamped on the word was an oversized *J. J* for *Jew.* The passport had been issued to a woman, but everything else was the same.

Bern opened his grandfather's passport and checked again. There it was, a big red letter *J* on the page opposite the old man's name and photograph. Frederick B. Roth, issued 1938, Berlin. Just like the passport on the computer screen. Hard to believe that the *J* didn't stand for *jerk,* knowing his grandfather. But Bern couldn't argue with history, which was right here staring him in the face.

A Jew? My grandfather was a Jew?

Bern thought: *Perfect. I spend the day puking, wanting to die. Now this.*

Shock and self-pity, his first reaction. A dizzy unreal feeling. Then he began to think about it.

His grandfather was a Jew? No way. There had to be another explanation.

The Internet article contained more photos—peasant faces with graveyard eyes; skeletons covered with skin. There was also an article. Bern reread portions of it now, hoping to find something that would hint at another explanation. Had to be one: Nobody hated Jews more than Grandpa Freddy.

. . . Hitler was determined to solve what he called the "Jewish problem" (Judenfrage), and put Eichmann in charge of Zionist Affairs. On August 17, 1938, legislation forced German Jews to adopt the middle name of either "Israel" or "Sarah" if the bearer did not already have a very distinct Jewish name—

Bern paused to look inside the passport again, seeing Frederick B. Roth written there, signature below. He didn't know what the *B* stood for, but at least it wasn't *Israel.* Was there a distinctive Jewish name that began with *B?*

Bern sat thinking about it. There could be hundreds of them, for all he knew. He'd never had reason to keep track.

He said it again, whispering: "The old man was a *Jew.*" Thinking: Finally, *something* that explains why he was such a world-class asshole.

He spun the passport onto the desk, as if the thing was poison, and stood. He ran a hand over his bald head, and looked out the office window toward the bay where, for no reason he could think of, someone had started the bulldozer. He could hear the irritating *bleep-bleep-bleep* the machine made in reverse. Probably that retard Moe out there doing extra work to make up for puking all over his boss who had every right to rip the Hoosier's head off—and he *would,* when the time was right.

Not now, though. Bern was dealing with something a lot worse. He felt dazed. This was about the most shocking thing he'd ever experienced. It was right up there with the first time he went a little too far; felt a woman— a stranger—go limp in his arms, breathing stopped, heart silent . . . which he wasn't going to think about . . . no, he wasn't going to revisit that nightmare again. Not right now.

He shifted thoughts to a more pleasant shocker, the Packers sudden death win against Chicago, tied 6–6, at Lambeau Field, when the Bears blocked a field goal attempt. But their kicker, this little Polack rocket, recovered the ball and somehow managed to run twenty-five yards without tripping or stopping for a cigarette. Packers win one for Bart, 12–6.

No . . . this was far more serious and shocking because it meant that if his grandfather was Jewish, then . . . then his mother was Jewish, too, and . . . *Wait a minute.*

Damn.

How'd he missed that? *Bern* began with a *B.*

Was Bern a distinctive Jewish name? Or *Bernard,* which he was sometimes called. He'd never been told that it was Jewish, but think about it: Who in their right might was going to walk up to a guy his size and say, "Hey, what's the deal with the Hebe name?"

Evidence was stacking up.

Son of a bitch.

Some situations, profanity was appropriate, and this was one of them because there was no dodging the implications.

Bern spoke aloud again, not whispering: "Shit!, this means I'm a Jew, too. A *Jew?*"

Talk about a brain zap. Meant that as a kid, that's what he was, even though he didn't know. Riding his bicycle, giving punks a pounding when he felt like it, working around the farm—*pigs?* Playing college ball, then two years in the pros, same thing. The whole time, he was a Jew but acted normal like anyone else because his grandfather had hidden it from them all these years.

Bern felt as unsteady as he had that morning banging out into the Gulf of Mexico, Sanibel Lighthouse off to the right, into waves as high and gray as March snowdrifts back in Wisconsin. Who would know about this stuff? A doctor? Maybe there was a test you could take to find out for sure . . .

On the computer, a timeline from that era was included. Bern took the time to read it, thinking he might be able to think better if he was calmer.

1938

- April 26: Mandatory registration of property owned by Jews inside the Reich.
- August 1: Adolf Eichmann establishes the Office of Jewish Emigration and increases forced emigration.
- August 3: Italy enacts anti–Semitic laws.
- August 8: Concentration camps open in Austria.
- October 28: 17,000 Polish Jews expelled from Germany, 8,000 stranded.
- November 9–10: Night of Broken Glass: Anti-Jewish demonstrations destroy 200 synagogues; 7,500 Jewish shops looted; 30,000 male Jews sent to concentration camps (Dachau, Buchenwald, Sachsenhausen).
- November 12: Jews forced to transfer retail businesses to Aryans.
- November 15: All Jewish pupils expelled from German schools.
- January: Hitler in Reichstag speech vows that if war erupts, it will mean the extermination (*Vernichtung*) of all European Jews.

Whew—talk about yanking the welcome mat out from under a whole tribe of people. Jerk or not, he had to admit that his grandfather showed brains getting out of Germany when he still could, 1938 obviously not a good year for the Hebes . . .

Careful.

. . . for people of Hebrew extraction.

"Solve the Jewish problem?" He'd done the six-year redshirt program at Badger U, and knew what that meant. Truck innocent people off to the gas chambers or burn them alive. What kind of scum did that sort of thing to their fellow human beings?

Bern spent a moment picturing himself in Germany, 1938, a group of soldiers dressed in gray approaching him, but each one scared crapless because Bern wasn't about to run from a bunch of cowardly Nazis. Grab one by the throat, that was the way to start, then kick the legs out . . .

Enough, *enough* . . .

He wanted to be damn certain of this before he started casting Nazis as bad guys.

Thing was—and this still made no sense—Bern couldn't think of anyone who hated Jews more than his grandfather. Of course, the old man hated every shade of colored person, too, plus Catholics. People from the South—rednecks or white trash. Florida? They were retard Crackers, and who could blame the man, frankly. California Commies, same thing. The Wegian Legion from Minnesota, don't get Grandy started on them. The Wegian weenie whiners. But why would his grandfather, Frederick Roth, hate Jews if he *was* one?

Or . . . maybe this was all bullshit. Everything in the briefcase fake.

His grandfather had done some bizarre things in the twenty months he lived after being diagnosed with prostate cancer. He'd changed his will umpteen times, depending on who in the family had pissed him off most recently. Bern, who he despised, was suddenly made chief executive officer of all the old man's holdings in Florida. A shocker—apparently forgetting that Bern had spent three weeks in a teenage psych ward for braining the old bastard with a ball-peen hammer. Also forgetting the feud the assault had signaled, grandfather and grandson trying to top the other's vicious attempts to get even.

Another shocker: Augie, the old man's pet, had been demoted from his cushy executive job in Oshkosh and transferred to Florida to be Bern's assistant.

Behavior that was as weird as the old man leaving a briefcase that contained passports and other stuff—and Bern had to admit this—that were sucking the joy right out of knowing the old bastard was rotting in his grave. Which probably was the *intent.*

How could he fake the briefcase's odor, though, the smell of rodents' nesting? And why the photo of the glamorous woman with the smoldering eyes?

Bern wished now he'd brought all the passports with him so he could compare the photographs again. The young blond Jewish guy was actually his Hebrew-hating grandfather?

Wanting to question whether that was true was something that seemed less and less weird.

B ern signed off from the computer, picked up the passport and other stuff he'd brought—a bottle of Pepto-Bismol because he still felt seasick, a garbage bag just in case—and went outside into the sodium daylight of a marina after 10 P.M.

Yes, there was Moe out there by the docks, riding the dinosaur-sized dozer, cowboy hat tilted forward on his head as if he were on a mechanical bull. What was the retard doing this time of night? Outside, with a storm forming, too, light flashing in mountainous clouds to the east. The sort of day Bern was having, he'd probably be struck by lightning. Maybe for the best.

Bern walked toward the bulldozer. What he wanted to do was take the Luger replica he'd bought in Milwaukee and shoot the man between the eyes. Same one he'd used to scare the dork Ford, and stuttering what's his name following behind the Viking so close Bern could hear them laughing their butts off whenever he stopped puking long enough to catch a breath.

To Moe, Bern had said, "You could've spewed on them but chose me instead?" The two of them finally on the dock; Bern on his knees, running cold water over his head. He'd wanted to say, "That shows questionable business judgment . . . a decision an executive *probably* wouldn't make. Like handing the cops several thousand dollars' worth of stuff that's rightfully mine. A death wish, *motherfucker,* that's what it shows!"

Another situation in which profanity would have been appropriate.

Take the Luger, stick the skinny barrel in the Hoosier's ear, and squeeze off two or three from the eight-round clip. No . . . better yet, use Cowboy Moe's own weapon, the chrome .357 six-shooter he carried in his truck. Afterward, turn himself in, and tell the jury exactly what had happened: I'm sitting there, minding my own business, so sick I wanted to die. Seriously—*die*. On the back of a boat, trying to breathe air that didn't taste like diesel fumes. Finally, getting a little better—dozing, I'm pretty sure—when I feel what I think is salt water hit me in the face. But guess what . . . ?"

Not guilty. Even if only one of the jurors had experienced a hell trip like today with his idiot nephew. First time in his life Bern could actually *smell* colors. Reds, blues, greens—each with its own unique diesel stink, and they all triggered the gag reflex.

Bern was determined to keep his temper, though. He needed Moe. Couldn't fire him yet because no way was Bern going out in rough weather again, no matter how much he loved the Viking. So Moe's scuba and boating skills would be needed. Bern didn't care anymore about profit, but he still wanted to find the wreck. For one thing, he wasn't going to let the nerd laugh at him, then steal what rightfully belonged to him. Something else: His grandfather knew the wreck's location. Why?

Bern had a lot on his mind—the Jewish thing drifting in and out between thoughts of holding a gun to the Hoosier's head . . . of wondering what the old man's real motives were . . . also seeing the glamorous woman, imagining her photo, hoping she was still around with those smoldering eyes. She *had* to have been some beauty queen the old man was wild about—why else the photo?

Forgiveness, as the old man used to say, was for people who didn't have the balls for revenge.

That's how Bern *planned* to spend the evening: sit in his condo, and leaf through the leather-bound journal, hoping a woman's name jumped out at him from all that faded writing. The other papers, too, most of them in

German, which he didn't understand, but a name, at least, might point him in the right direction. Tell him the woman's identity.

How would the old man feel if he knew Bern ripped the clothes off his old sweetheart?

Go insane, that's what he'd do. Touch the sacred flesh was the best way to screw his grandfather.

Tomorrow, he'd put a call in to Jason Goddard, the old man's personal assistant. Leave a message, because it was Saturday, then try a cell phone number that might still be good. Also, he was thinking of asking Augie to contribute his expertise, the little brownnoser who'd learned to speak and read German to get in good with the old man.

Trust him with the old man's journal? He'd give some thought to that.

Now, though, Bern had to make nice with the redneck Hoosier—and do it in a hurry, too, with that thunderstorm coming. Moe was working overtime, trying to make up for what he'd done that afternoon.

Not a chance in hell.

21 I'd been wondering about it for a while but told Chestra, "I just realized something. There have to be twenty, twenty-five photographs in this room. But your godmother, Marlissa Dorn, isn't in any of them. I find that surprising." I waited for a moment, deciding if I should add, "There are none of you, either." Then did.

The woman was standing with her back to me in the gold lamé gown, her shoulders wider than her hips, silver-blond hair piled atop her head, a pearl necklace visible beneath wisps of hair and delicate ears. Without turning, she said, "You're not the first to notice. Tommy asked the same thing."

Meaning Tomlinson.

Outside, there was a flash of blue light, then another. Lightning. It illuminated the balcony's wrought-iron railing, trees beyond. A cell of cool wind blew through the doors as Chestra said, "Storms. I just adore them. Don't you?" Then turned in synch with the movement of curtains as if she, too, had been levitated by wind.

"There's a reason there so few photos of Marlissa and me," she said. "For Marlissa, the explanation is fascinating, but sad, too. For me, though, it's just ego plain and simple. I'm a proud old broad who can't stand the way she looks, especially when compared to the way I used to look. Ego, pride." She wagged her eyebrows and took a sip of her drink—chartreuse and soda, an exotic liqueur unfamiliar to me. "Name a conceit. I delude my-self that it's okay because I admit that I'm vain. I haven't reached the age where my body only embarrasses others. Why advertise what you've lost and can never recover?"

I said, "I'm looking at a very handsome woman; one I find charming. I like her. Don't be so hard on the lady, okay?"

"Handsome." Her tone was dry, acknowledging the euphemism. "I guess I should be content with that. I have a photograph of my god-mother, which I'll show you—it'll help you understand why I'm such a goose about photos. You'll fall in love with Marlissa. Every man does. But wouldn't you rather hear her story first? You asked the question: Why were Marlissa and Frederick several miles offshore in a storm?

"It's possible, Doc, that you'll be the first to see that boat in many, many years. What remains of it, anyway. You deserve an answer."

I said, "I'd like to do both. And see pictures of you, too—there've got to be some around."

Outside, there was another strobe of light. Thunder is noise created by a shock wave of air set in motion by an abrupt electrical discharge. This shock wave vibrated through the floor of the old house, rumbling as it rolled toward open sea.

Chestra listened for a moment, then was suddenly in a hurry. "You're a dear man. But forgive me"—she touched her fingers to my cheek as she swept past, heels clicking on tile. I got a whiff of perfume, faint vanilla and musk—"I have to change."

"What?"

"I can't go to the beach dressed like this, and I never miss a storm. I feed on them. The energy. To see a big one come pounding off the Gulf—" She was already taking off jewelry—a bracelet, the pearls—as she headed for the stairs, her bedroom below. Over her shoulder, she called, "I won't be a minute. Will you join me?"

I checked my watch. Nearly eleven. "I guess. But I still have a lot of work—"

"I'll holler when I'm ready." She put her tongue against her teeth and whistled—a wolf whistle. In Manhattan, it's the way people would've hailed a cab to a Dempsey fight. "This one's going to be a doozy, Doc!"

A photo of Marlissa Dorn. I was eager to have a look—although I expected to be disappointed. Chestra Engle was sharing a family legend, not talking about a real person. Legends never disappoint, people often do. Her godmother's photo most likely would be the rule, not be an exception.

Even so . . . there *were* some exceptional photos in this museum of a house. As I waited, I poured a glass of wine—the woman had no beer—then moved from wall to wall as if touring an art gallery.

All three branches of Chestra's family exhibited the physical characteristics that I've come to associate with wealth, particularly from the previous century: tall, confident smiles, good teeth, glossy hair, athleticism, and bone structure that contained at least some of the elements we associate with health and beauty.

Women in the Dorn branch possessed more of the classic attributes than most. They were uncommonly attractive. Nellie Kay Dorn was among the most beautiful of all. I'd recently touched my fingers to her headstone: BORN 1868, DIED 1934.

It could be a social maxim: beautiful people attract power, power attracts the beautiful and powerful. I wasn't surprised, therefore, to find photographs of celebrities Arlis Futch had mentioned while describing the small, sociable place that was the Sanibel area in earlier times.

There were several photos of the poet Edna St. Vincent Millay. In one, she wore a flapper's hat, her intelligent eyes aware of the incongruity. Another was labeled: *Edna two days after fire, Palms Hotel.* She looked exhausted—I remembered Arlis saying a manuscript she'd been working on had been lost. Marlissa's blond lover, I noticed, was in the background of a third photograph. The poet was smoking a cigarette. He was holding a beach towel.

In separate photos, I found two celebrities whom Arlis hadn't mentioned. One was New York playwright and novelist Mary Roberts Rinehart. The writer was posed in front of the house she and her son had built on nearby Cabbage Key; another was taken on a beach with members of the Engle and Dorn families.

The second celebrity was industrialist Harvey Firestone, the tire millionaire. I'd read that Firestone, Ford, Edison, and Lindbergh had all been friends, and remembered something about them collaborating on a search for synthetic rubber. Prior to World War II, most natural rubber came from the Pacific Rim, controlled by Japan, so the project was vital. Many of the plants Edison had tested in his Fort Myers laboratory were grown or collected locally—some from barrier islands, including Sanibel.

Rinehart and Firestone. Add two more powerful names to the mix.

There were more shots of Charles Lindbergh, some with his wife, Anne, both showing congenial smiles, their hands always linked in some way, like two islands that had joined as one. Celebrity was a weight. So was tragedy. They had experienced both—their eyes were armor-plated.

Union boss John L. Lewis was on the wall. With his bushy eyebrows, he resembled the crabby old guy on *60 Minutes,* and looked about as much fun. There were other celebrities: Clark Gable, the boxer Max Baer, Danny Kaye, Raymond Burr, actress Patricia Neal—not unexpected in an exclusive hideaway like Sanibel Island. There was a photo of a tough-looking guy in a flight suit posing with several Dorn and Engle girls, all beauties. It was captioned: *Gen. Jimmy Doolittle, Page Field, 1941, before bombing Tokyo.*

Page Field was where Arlis had worked guarding POWs. Doolittle had trained there?

Marlissa Dorn's German lover wasn't in the background of this photo. But he was in several others—usually a vague figure, part of the scenery, but always aware of the camera's presence.

Sanibel Island, World War II. The perfect place to seed a Nazi intelligence agent.

We crossed the porch into a chorus of wind and surf, the tree canopy writhing above us. It was a black night, but the sand trail was luminous through bare trees. The trail glowed white in the darkness as if saturated with sunlight from years in the tropics.

"I have only one flashlight. I'm sorry." Chestra had changed into slacks, and a white blouse that snapped like a sail until she got her jacket on. She'd handed me a rain slicker as we went out the door and I was carrying it under my arm as I followed.

"Do you do this often?"

"*What?*"

I had to yell to be heard above the wind. "Do you . . . do you have some kind of shelter? Is that where we're headed?"

"Shelter . . . *Why?*" It was impossible to hear so close to the beach, and she laughed the question away.

Chestra may have had a flashlight, but she didn't use it. She seemed to know exactly where she wanted to be and was in a rush to get there. The storm was rolling in from the mainland—cumulus towers flickering to the east—as clouds sumped cooler air off the water, fueling volcanic updrafts with a black Gulf wind. It's not unusual for sea and storm to interact in opposition. The woman had to lean toward the beach as she walked, one hand out to steady herself against the wind.

The trail narrowed as we crossed a dune of sea oats and cactus, trees behind us, ocean ahead. There were no stars, no horizon. The sea was a vague, unsettled darkness. Shoreline was defined by sound; whitecaps by the faint fluorescence of breakers as waves sailed shoreward, ridge after slow-rolling ridge. They made a keening *hiss,* accelerating as they bottom-shoaled, and then imploded—*boom*—before their mass was suctioned seaward, a formless volume reforming.

The rhythm was respiratory: flowing, then ebbing. Implosions were steady as heartbeats. It was as if something was alive out there, a huge and breathing darkness inhabiting a void that was the Gulf of Mexico.

"This is why I usually come in October!"

"What?"

Chestra waited for me to draw closer. "This is why I come to Sanibel during hurricane season. I have the beach to myself, and the storms are magnificent!"

We were on the beach, walking toward Sanibel Lighthouse, waves to the right, trees and a boardwalk on our left. On the horizon, storm clouds were mountainous lanterns that flared internally, discharging in random disorder. Ahead, the lighthouse turret strobed as precisely as a metronome: *flash . . . flash*—ten second pause—*flash . . . flash*. Each frail burst was absorbed by darkness, diffused by wind.

"Do you feel that? Wait!" The woman held her hand up, and stopped. She tilted her head as if trying to identify an unfamiliar sound.

"Feel what?"

"The wind off the ocean. It's dying."

Darkness seemed to slow its respirations as my senses tested.

She hooked her arm into mine, a gesture so natural I didn't notice for a moment. "The storm," she said. "It's nearly here."

A squall cell moving seaward siphons air from the Gulf until just before it hits. The transition is prefaced by a momentary calm, then a gust of cold air as wind direction reverses. That period of calm is a dangerous time to linger in an open area because the storm, only minutes away, is preceded by a low-pressure wall that's supercharged with electricity.

She was right. The sea breeze had calmed. We were standing on a base of silicone, within spray's reach of a saltwater conductor. Hard to imagine a more precarious place. "It's coming, all right," I yelled. "We need to find cover."

She was facing the storm. "Not yet. Just a little longer. Please?"

"Chessie"—a balloon of chilled air enveloped us—"this is crazy. We have to go now."

I winced as a searing light bleached the world of color. A simultaneous explosion darkened it. A wall of wind followed, gusting cold from the east, and I felt the first fat drops of rain.

"Go ahead, Doc. I'm fine. This is what I love to do!"

In another cannon burst of electricity, I saw her face—she was smiling, skin pale as snow, and her eyes were closed.

Our arms were still linked. I tugged and stepped away, hoping she would follow. She didn't. It was pouring now.

"Chess!"

"I'm okay. It's what I want!"

Air molecules sizzle when torn from adhesion by electricity. Their glow is a zigzag schematic of the voltage that obliterates them. Air sizzled now as lightning bracketed us, positive and negative ions rejoining in thunderous strokes. A lightning bolt, when grounded through human tissue, is five times hotter than the surface of the sun. It cauterizes as it wounds—in one side, out another. The hole is darkened by exploded blood cells.

"We can't stay here. I'm serious. This is insane."

"Isn't it! It's exquisite!" She was laughing, her formal hairdo sodden ringlets in slow collapse.

I couldn't leave her to the storm. A woman her age? For a moment, only a moment, I felt the same strange sense of freedom that I'd experienced during the worst of the hurricane. I was powerless against the random physics of earth and sky. Analysis was pointless, so why waste energy thinking about what might happen? A shadow vanishing into itself—that was the sensation. Release . . .

Above my head, there was a molecular crackle as a bolt touched the beach so near I smelled the smoke of incinerated sand. Another exploded in the canopy of a distant palm—fronds twirled like feathers through a fog of rain.

This was worse than insane, it was stupid. This wasn't an unavoidable hurricane, it was a common squall. I squatted, swept Chestra Engle into my arms, and carried her through the rain toward Southwind.

D oc?"

Rain was rivering down the small of my back, my boat shoes were sodden. In my arms, the woman was a source of warmth, not a weight.

"Doc?"

"Chess."

"Is . . . there something wrong?"

No, there was nothing wrong. Because it was the shortest distance, I'd carried her cross-country, angling into Chestra's estate from the beach. With her still in my arms, I'd stopped just outside the picnic gazebo, the nearest structure, warm rain sluicing down. She was asking why we were standing in the rain when we could be inside. Why didn't I carry her an additional few steps to the dry chairs that sat upon the dry floor next to the drink cart and hammock, all sheltered by the gazebo's screens and shingled roof.

Behind us, there was a rumble of thunder . . . a flash. Then another. I used each micromoment of illumination to study the woman's face. I'd been doing it since first noticing an aberration created by the brief and dazzling light—nothing else explained it. It was the illusion that Chestra's appearance changed slightly with each incandescent blast. She'd made a remark about storms—"I get energy from them!"—that sounded offhand at the time but now seemed weirdly applicable.

"Doc? You're a big strong guy, and I won't pretend I don't like being carried like some sultan's jewel, but I think it's time to put me down." She laughed, and placed her palm warm against my face, tracing its shape. I'd lost my bandage in the rain, and her stroke was tender. "I promise I won't go galloping back to the beach. Cross my heart."

She did, touching a finger to her breast as I watched. Her white blouse was soaked, translucent in storm light, her body visible beneath. I waited for another lightning burst . . . then one more, my eyes now staring into hers.

The illusion wasn't imaginary, yet it was still an illusion. *Had* to be an illusion. With each bloom of electricity, the woman appeared fuller, younger. I could see the way she'd looked in her fifties . . . now her forties. She was as beautiful as any woman in her family. Chestra was as beautiful as an woman I'd ever held.

Because of storm light? There could be no other reason. The human eye is sensitive; retina cones can numb. Stare at a star for more than a minute and it will vanish—an illusion.

Still . . .

No—it *did* make sense. Our perception of reality is visually based. Change the light and our reality is changed. We are a photosensitive species. There are certain processes in chemistry in which light alters not only the appearance of a substance but also its molecular configuration. In a laboratory, mammalian cells mutate if grown in a room with fluorescent lighting. Light absorbed through the eye affects our pineal gland's production of serotonin. Red light penetrates more deeply into our tissues than blue light. Our DNA is coded to repair some—but not all—cellular damage caused by ultraviolet light. It's an omission that defines the aging process more accurately than the clumsy prop we invented to measure age: time.

Illusion or reality, the storm was indifferent.

I ducked through the gazebo's doorway, let Chestra's feet swing to the floor, then stepped back and watched as she flipped water from her hair and hands. "My God, I haven't had that much excitement since . . . since"—her voice was energized—"since . . . well, I think it would be indelicate for me to confess."

"Sounds interesting."

"Doesn't it? I so wish it were *true*."

"Don't give up hope. I like indelicate women. Confessions, too."

She was there again, alive behind those eyes: a younger woman inside, staring out, saying, *Show me. Prove it.*

I answered aloud. "Okay, I will." I stepped closer, unsure of my own intent. I touched my fingers to Chestra's face as gently as she'd touched mine. She held my gaze a moment longer before looking at the ground—a retreat. Or submission?

"I'm a mess, Doc. My hair, and my clothes are soaked."

"So I see." The blouse was pasted against her skin, and I cupped my hand around her warm ribs. "This material, when it's wet—I like the color better."

The color of her skin, I meant.

She did not look up as she said, "We should get back to the house, and find towels. We'll catch our death."

I placed an index finger beneath her chin and lifted. Her face was dark, then abruptly illuminated as lightning crackled in the treetops. For an instant, her eyes incandesced blue as a welder's torch . . . then vanished into shadow as the gazebo vibrated beneath us, our ears ringing.

"My God, that was *close*! What a peach of a storm, though, Doc, huh?" She turned away, instantly changed, her voice friendly, conversational—herself again.

The air was a mix of ozone and smoke. I'd felt a tingling through my wet shoes. Storm light had, once again, transformed perception, and all the potential it implied.

In a similar conversational tone, I replied, "That was too close," as I, too, attempted to return to normal. "Do you know how many people a year are killed by lightning in Florida? Chessie, it's not safe to be on the beach when a storm is so close . . ."

I continued talking, listening to myself as if removed from the room. Something unexpected had happened between us. What? *Why?* Tomlinson's ridiculous theory about sexuality and seesawing barometric pressure came into my head, and was dismissed just as quickly.

I'd held a woman in my arms. My body had reacted. My eyes and modern brain had cooperated by creating a preferred reality. As an explanation, it was . . . rational.

There are certain rare people, however, who are born with a pheromone signature so potent that, even in a crowded room, every member of the opposite sex is aware when they enter, or exit. Maybe it came down to that. Sensuality is more subtle than sexuality; beauty is more complicated than bone structure, elastic skin, and an assemblage of hydrated cells. With certain women, I realized, age did not matter. Mildred Chestra Engle was one.

". . . Chess, when you feel that blast of cold air? You should head for cover fast. Weather's volatile around salt water. When unequal pressure systems collide, it's more like an explosion than a storm."

Jesus, was I as stuffy and bland as I sounded?

Chestra's smile said *Yes,* but it was okay. She was the good hostess once again, ever polite. She had her arms folded modestly across her chest, hiding herself, but freed a hand long enough to motion me toward the door. "I know about dangerous storms. I made you a proposition, remember? A business proposition concerning a boat that was lost in a storm a long time ago. Come on, I'll show you."

It was an excuse not to be alone in our sodden clothes. We both knew but played along. The gazebo was already filling with the scent of her. The September air was body-heated.

She led, I followed. I thought we were going to the house. Instead, she led me to the family cemetery where I'd first heard her voice. Chestra knelt by a marble crypt that I recognized as the grave of Nellie Kay Dorn. She used the flashlight to illuminate the headstone next to it.

"This is my godmother," she said and placed her hand upon the stone, an affectionate, familiar gesture. I got the impression Chestra came here often.

She held the flashlight steady. In the harsh light, I read what the stonecutter had engraved:

MARLISSA ARKHAM DORN
BORN FEBRUARY 7, 1923, VARGUS, AUSTRIA
DIED OCTOBER 19, 1944, SANIBEL ISLAND, FLORIDA
WHOM THE SEA GIVES UP, GOD EMBRACES

October 19—she'd died in the hurricane Arlis had told us about.

Chessie stood. "It's an old line, but I mean it: Let's get out of these wet things and into a dry martini. What a night! I'll show you Marlissa's picture."

I checked my watch: 11:20.

I told her, "Just one."

There were two photos on the piano, black-and-white glossies, and I looked from one to the other as Chestra played softly. She'd changed into a lime satin robe and heeled slippers. I stood barefoot on a towel; another wrapped around my neck.

Coincidentally, she was playing the melody I'd heard while eavesdropping from the beach—a song I recognized but had yet to ask its name.

One photo was of the boat that had sunk on the night of 19 October 1944. It was a beauty—a thirty-eight-foot Matthews, according to information on the back. From the data that was noted, I would've known a man had written it even if I hadn't seen the precise masculine hand.

Built 1939, Port Clinton, Ohio. Oak keel, double oak frame, Philippine mahogany planking. Master cabin and crew quarters bunks six. Twin gas engines, Chrysler straight-8s. Top speed, 25 knots, range 400 miles.

Yes, a beauty. A vessel that had been much loved, judging from the number of times it was a backdrop for family photos. But this was the first full shot of it I'd seen—taken from the beach, probably, because the aspect was from the vessel's port side, forward of the bow.

The photo showed the boat under way, a white wake breaking beneath bow stringers, yacht pennants flying from the wooden radio mast and bow pulpit, all indicators of speed. It was a classic design from that era: low, roomy wheelhouse, three portholes forward, a stern deck that was open. Lashed to the stern was a wooden dinghy; an American flag on the transom above it, catching the wind.

The boat's hull and wheelhouse roof were painted black or midnight blue. The decking and cabin frame were amber-stained mahogany; the wheelhouse roof was painted white.

The vessel's name was *Dark Light*. It's rare when a boat is christened with a name that fits. Most suffer cutesy double entendres, or names that are saccharine sweet attempts at poetry. I've never named a boat for the simple reason that I lack the imagination. *Dark Light* was perfect for this vessel. It celebrated her hull color, and also her quickness—twenty-five knots was lightning fast in those times. Even now, it's fast for a boat her size. The name was subtle and esoteric, like her understated design.

It had been a tragedy to lose a craft so articulately made to a storm. But *Dark Light* hadn't fallen to just any storm. Arlis had seeded the date in my memory: 19 October 1944. A hurricane had flooded Sanibel on that date. It was a storm that had killed several hundred people. Among the dead were Cuban fishermen who were buried on the same beach where the body of another victim was found: Marlissa Dorn.

I'd just visited the woman's grave. Now I picked up her photo and looked at it closely for the first time.

I expected to be disappointed by this "extraordinary beauty," as she was described by Chestra.

I wasn't.

The photograph was a black-and-white glossy, eight-by-ten, framed and glassed. It was a Hollywood-style glamour shot that I associate with film stars from the 1930s and '40s. Full length, professional lighting.

Marlissa Dorn wore a black gown that accentuated how she would look if a man were lucky enough to see her naked: long legs, sensual symmetry of hips, breasts full and firm enough to resume their natural curvature once free of the garment's constraints.

The gown was black but glittered with sequins. She stood with hip canted to one side, her opposite hand held at eye level, a cigarette between her fingers. The woman was leaning against a black grand piano as if taking a break from performing.

I glanced at Chestra and studied her face for a moment as she sat at the piano and continued to play. I returned my attention to the photo.

Marlissa's cigarette was freshly lit. The smoke formed a lucent arc with the same curvilinear contour as her hips and breasts. She was staring through cigarette smoke at the camera, her hair combed full and glossy to her shoulder, head tilted in a way that emphasized the intensity of her gaze and the dimensions of her perfect face.

Her eyes were shadowed, I noticed. It added an exotic, smoldering effect.

The photo had been lighted and composed by a superb craftsman. The photographer also had an extraordinary subject to work with.

There were photographs in this house of several women who resembled Marlissa Dorn—the delicacy of chin, the swollen weight of lips, her body, her eyes. But the genetic pool had found a separate and elevated balance in this woman.

"Isn't she the most exquisite thing you've ever seen?" Chestra spoke without looking up from the keys.

A few faces came into my mind—film stars from the same era. Rita Hayworth. Lauren Bacall. Veronica Lake. Women who were signature beauties of their generation. I prefer women whose beauty requires time to assemble. The appeal is more private. But there was no denying that Marlissa Dorn was among the rarest of the rare.

"Yes. She's very pretty." Once again, my eyes moved from the photograph to Chestra. There were startling family similarities. I noted the shape of Marlissa's chin, the wide full lips, the eye spacing . . .

"Please don't flatter me by saying I look like Marlissa. Tommy did the same thing. I'm all too aware that she was in an entirely different league."

I paused a moment to inspect her intonation. There was subtext of some kind. Drama. Or was it jealousy? I find beautiful women intimidating. Most men do—the cliché of the prettiest girl in school who can't get a date is experientially based. Women are intimidated as well. Beauty is *supposed* to be only skin-deep but it's not. Beauty is power. Its facial components can be described mathematically, but emotionally it is nature's prime currency. We attempt to trivialize beauty's power because it makes us uneasy, even as we covet it.

I shrugged. The woman was commenting on a family legend, so I let it go. "Your godmother was gorgeous, no question. This looks like a PR shot. I'm surprised movie producers didn't mob her."

The woman stopped playing, but the piano's sustain pedal let the melody echo. "Oh, but they did. Not mob her—that came *later*. By the time Marlissa was fifteen, she'd been offered several modeling and film contracts. At sixteen, she starred in her first film. Her talent was considered quite remarkable."

I asked, "Hollywood let her keep her real name?" It was the most tactful way of saying I'd never heard of Marlissa or her films.

Chestra resumed playing, but more softly. "Hollywood wasn't the only place in the world where films were being made. My godmother was wooed by Europe's greatest directors of the period—Max Ophuls, René Clair . . . even Alfred Hitchcock before he came to the States.

"Her first film was a critical success. Her second film would still be considered a classic today if the war hadn't come along"—Chestra was playing the melody's moody refrain, her fingers lingering on the notes—"or so I've been told. The only existing prints were destroyed during the fire-bombing of Berlin."

It was after Marlissa's second film, Chestra told me, that Hollywood producers took notice.

"They offered her a huge contract for those times. Money, furs, first-class accommodations if she would come to Hollywood. I still have copies of those contracts, if you're ever interested. I inherited them along with her journals and a few other things. I was her only heir."

I said, "You told me that she made the transatlantic crossing in 1938 aboard the *Normandie*. She came because of Hollywood."

"Yes, and also the fact that she had family here. But two things happened while she was aboard the *Normandie* that changed my godmother's life forever. One of them ruined her career as an actress, the other caused her death."

If Marlissa and Frederick Roth hadn't fallen in love, Chestra said, neither of them would have been aboard *Dark Light* the night that the thirty-eight-foot Matthews went down.

The woman's film career had already ended by that time.

"Marlissa's dreams of being a film star were destroyed years earlier. That makes her death less sad somehow, don't you think? To go on living after your dream has died? I don't see the point."

It was while she was aboard the *Normandie* that a newsreel featuring the chancellor of Germany was released. It had been shot months earlier and showed him sitting next to an actress he'd already acknowledged as his favorite—a Russian named Olga Chekhova. He was a film addict, and in 1936 he'd honored her as Germany's *Schauspielrern,* or "Actress of the State."

"There are a couple of books that mention Chekhova," Chestra said. "She was a habitual liar, they say . . . and also a spy. In one of the books, there's a photo that was taken of their little group the night the newsreel was made. I'll show it to you someday, if you like."

Also seated at the table, flanked by Hermann Goering and Joseph Goebbels, was a young woman of extraordinary gifts. Her table mates had just enjoyed the premiere of her newest film—her last before leaving the Reich, as only she knew.

Chestra told me, "With the newsreel cameras rolling, Adolf Hitler leaned and put his hand on Marlissa's shoulder. Then he looked into the lens and announced to a million moviegoers that she was his Aryan ideal and the most beautiful woman on earth."

He was wearing a prissy white dinner jacket, she added.

"The expression on his face was disgusting, and the way his fingers moved on her shoulder—like a spider's legs."

It was a death sentence in Hollywood, Chestra said. The most evil man on earth had put his mark on Marlissa. It was a curse.

"As my godmother disembarked in New York, she couldn't understand why there were so many paparazzi. Dozens of them—*that's* when she was mobbed. They nearly crushed her. She was hospitalized."

Marlissa Dorn never allowed another photograph of herself to be taken.

I said, "That song you're playing. What is it? I've heard it before but the title won't come to me."

Chestra reaction was unexpected—dubious but interested. She said, "You know this melody?," and played the last few notes of the refrain.

"Sure. It's one of those classics from . . ."—I looked at Marlissa Dorn's photo as I placed it on the piano—". . . from your godmother's era."

"What *should* have been her era, you mean. She never got her chance."

I was about to say, "It's a tragic story," but she cut me off by transitioning to a different melody, playing louder. "There are some wonderful classics from that period. Written by people who *lived*. People who knew about love, and about pain. Not that terrible, computer-generated junk they hammer us with in hotels and malls. Those aren't songs. They're video games for the ears."

She said, "'In the Still of the Night,'" and played a few bars before smiling. "Cole Porter."

It wasn't the doo-wop song that I associated with the title. It was dark, distinctive. Nor was it the song that I'd first heard while eavesdropping from the beach.

She said, "'Isn't It Romantic,'" and played a little of that classic before melding into "Night and Day," then "For Sentimental Reasons," then "As Time Goes By."

None were the melody that I recognized but couldn't name.

Chestra stood, done playing. She closed the keyboard and touched her fingers to the instrument's curvature, letting it guide her to where I stood, photos on the piano. Because her hair was still damp, she had wrapped it in a blue scarf.

"My godmother played. In fact, this was her piano. A Mason and Hamlin, handmade in New York. She preferred it to a Steinway."

I said, "Oh." I was done with Marlissa Dorn and now concentrating on the photo of the Matthews motor yacht. If Jeth had found *Dark Light*'s remains, I wanted a blowup of this picture. Better yet, a schematic of the design. And I'd need all the data I could gather about the hurricane of 19 October 1944. If we found the vessel's engine and drivetrain, lighter objects would have been spread by directional currents.

The woman and I had come to a general agreement about the money she would invest and what she expected in return. Contingent on their approval, Chestra said she would pay Jeth's and Javier's standard daily charter fee for a week, guaranteed, and up to ten days if there was evidence that we'd found *Dark Light*'s remains. At that point, we would renegotiate.

When I asked if she thought that we might also find the remains of Frederick Roth, she said yes, it was possible, his body was never recovered. Chestra then explained why he'd been at the vessel's helm the night she went down.

"People who lived in the area were naturally suspicious of Frederick—there was no disguising his German accent. The war was on, news was often censored, so the local rumor mills ran nonstop. In Marlissa's journals, she wrote about some of the rumors—she was hurt by them."

Chestra wasn't certain whose idea it was, but Frederick signed up as a civil defense volunteer to demonstrate that a German could also be pro-American. On the Gulf coast of Florida, the work consisted of running Coast Watch patrols—looking for unauthorized aircraft, foreign vessels, or suspicious activity.

Arlis had mentioned the Coast Watch organization, but I let the woman talk.

Marlissa didn't need to volunteer the family boat, Chestra said, because it had already been conscripted by the military for Civil Defense duty. *Dark Light* was the fastest cruiser in the meager fleet.

"The last entry in Marlissa's journal was dated the afternoon of October 19, 1944. She wrote that the weather was bad and she was worried about Frederick because he was taking the boat offshore, alone for some reason. She even knew the course heading: 240 degrees."

Chestra removed the towel from my shoulders and began to fold it, her expression thoughtful. "Until Tommy told me about the Nazi medals you found, I assumed that Marlissa's trust in her lover was deserved. Now, though . . . I'm more open-minded. You can understand why I'm eager to find out the truth."

I remembered Arlis mentioning that on the night of the storm, suspicious lights were reported off Lighthouse Point. Maybe a U-boat, but Arlis thought it was more likely Cuban fisherman who were later found dead, bloated, on the beach. The Coast Watch lost a boat that night, he'd told us. He didn't mention the boat's name.

Dark Light? I would ask him.

I also remembered Arlis describing a woman he'd seen earlier on the beach—did he refer to her as an actress? A woman who was so beautiful that he could still picture her face. In the small, small town this area had once been, trivial details might remain etched deep in an old man's memory.

I shared none of this with Chestra.

"Do you have any idea why Frederick Roth was taking the boat off-shore in bad weather?"

"No. I guess it was his duty. I can't imagine another reason." I watched her flick the towel as I'd once seen her use a scarf for effect.

"You assume that your godmother went with him because she was worried about him going alone. Did anyone see her get aboard?"

"I think someone did see her. I'm *certain* of it—that's part of the family story, anyway. Their names, though, are long gone."

"Would you mind if I looked through your godmother's journal? I've spent a lifetime around boats. Maybe I'll see something you missed."

It surprised her and she took a moment to think. "It's very private, of course, a diary. When does a person give up rights to their secrets? I don't see anything wrong with it, I suppose . . . but a lot of the writing's in her own peculiar code. I *mentioned* that to you. I don't think you'd make much sense of it . . . or have patience for all her girlish babble."

I didn't say it but was thinking, *Right.*

The woman was lying.

Before I left, Chestra asked me to look at Marlissa Dorn's photograph one more time.

"Do you see what she's holding in her left hand?"

I used the damp towel to clean my glasses, and, for the first time, noticed a silver cigarette case. The case was partially hidden beneath Marlissa's hand, which was on her hip. I tilted my glasses and held the picture closer. Was that an engraved initial on the cigarette case near her finger? I needed my magnifying glass.

"That's the sort of memento I'm talking about. Something she held and carried, that was part of her life. *Personal*—I don't care about the value. Find this for me, or something similar, and I'll consider every penny well spent."

I lowered the photo. "Do you know if your godmother had a matching silver lighter? A silver cigarette case and a lighter. They'd go together." I paid close attention to her reaction.

Chestra was puzzled, nothing more. "I suppose it's possible. In those days, everyone carried cigarettes, although I know she rarely smoked. A lighter, yes—it's likely she had one."

It was evident that Tomlinson hadn't told her about the cigarette lighter Jeth had found. I was pleased. There had to be a reason Chestra Engle was withholding information from me. Until I found out why, I would reserve a few secrets of my own.

As I was going out the door, the woman placed her hand on my shoulder, then pulled it away. The gesture was spontaneous, her expression pained—she wanted to tell me more but couldn't. That was my impression. It was the most subtle of apologies.

"Doc?"

I waited.

"The story I told you about my godmother. And the newsreel. Do you scientific types believe that there's such thing as good and evil? That there are people in the world who are truly *evil?* Or do you think it's all a bunch of silly hobgoblin nonsense?"

This was not one of her mock profundities. She was referring to the tyrant who she believed had put his mark, and a curse, on Marlissa Dorn.

I said, "I've met my share of men capable of evil deeds."

"So have I, Doc. So have I." Chestra touched a finger to her lips, then touched it to my cheek. "But I'm talking about something very different."

When I didn't respond, she said, "Let me know how the dive goes tomorrow," then stood watching from the doorway as I walked down the steps toward my pickup truck, lightning still flickering to the northeast.

At 10:15 P.M., Bern Heller was standing near the marina's boat ramp watching a thunderstorm dump rain on distant islands—Captiva and Sanibel both smudges beneath mountainous blue clouds—and thinking: *The perfect ending to a perfect day: I get struck dead by lightning after finding out the old man's Jewish, and being so seasick I wanted to die.*

There. He could get his wish—but a day late and a dollar short, as usual.

Moe, the goof, had finally noticed that he was standing there like an idiot, wanting to ask him why he was charging around on the bulldozer this late at night, long after everyone else had gone. Was it maybe, just *maybe,* an effort to make up for tossing his cookies on Bern that afternoon?

The Hoosier looked at him, did a double take, waved, and put the bulldozer in neutral. He left the machine idling and scrambled over the armored tread to the ground, removing his hat to let his boss see how hot it was up there pushing levers two hours before midnight.

"Thought you'd be asleep by now, Bern. Pretty rough day we had ourselves out there on the water. But what's done is done, thank God . . ."

Bern gave him a look, and Moe changed subjects without taking a breath. "So you're probably wondering why I'm out here instead of home gettin' some z's. Guess I'm a workaholic. You give me a job to do, I can't sleep until it's done right."

"A workaholic, huh?"

"Yep, always have been. Guess it's in my genes." The man was using his jeans right now to wipe his dirty hands.

Bern half listened as Moe explained that he was working late because the EPA people had postponed their tests until Monday, so he'd decided to make sure the water and soil samples they gathered didn't leave any doubts about the pollution caused by hurricane damage. That way, the marina would be guaranteed the extra month they needed to process and sell all those boats.

". . . a government job, like working for the EPA, wouldn't that be nice? Show up anytime you damn well please, sit on your ass, with all those benefits."

Bern tuned in long enough to interrupt. "I thought I told you to dump the barrels and all that crap last night. Workaholic, my ass. Alcoholic, is more like it." Bern swatted at a mosquito, and saw the Hoosier flinch.

"I did dump that stuff, Bern. But I thought I'd do a little extra"—Moe had a wink in his voice—"I figured, while I was out here, on a nice dark night like this? I might as well make a little more of that mangrove swamp disappear."

Bern said cautiously, "Okay. But where're you getting the extra fill?"

He was beginning to feel uneasy.

For the first time, Bern focused on what there was to see around him: dark night, lightning still dumping rain on distant islands, a slash of moon to the west. Docks, dark water glistening in the security lights, the boat ramp only a few yards from where he stood. The fifty-gallon drums he'd lined along the seawall were gone, just as Moe had said. Rows of boats in the parking lot far to his left . . . then an open space with survey stakes. It was where he planned to build more condominiums.

Everything looked normal. Except for . . .

. . . except for that green boat with the twin outboards. It was the Cuban's boat. The crazy black guy the cops hauled off. It was still on its trailer, but now much closer to the boat ramp. Why? He started to ask Moe but stopped midsentence, feeling a chill.

Beyond the Hoosier's shoulder, Bern could see the bulldozer, a couple tons of yellow metal and hydraulic hoses, CATERPILLAR in black on the side. The machine's blade was elevated higher than its cab, the bucket holding several hundred pounds of dirt and limbs. Bern noticed, for the first time, a fifty-gallon drum beneath the limbs, enough of the metal showing for him to see that the barrel was capped but leaking oil.

The oil was black as blood in the machine's headlights, a steady *drip-drip-drip* dripping off the blade's cutting edge.

Below, the fresh fill dirt was stained a dirty, petroleum brown.

Where had the barrel come from? This one had been buried somewhere, judging from the amount of dirt atop it. Bern knew where there were two barrels on marina property that he wanted to *stay* buried.

He looked beyond the green boat, seeing fresh bulldozer tracks disappear into the darkness toward the little hill he'd created; built it himself, he told people, to remind him of Wisconsin.

Bern was thinking, *Dear God, no. Don't let this be happening.*

Bern spoke slowly, forcing himself to sound calm. He said, "Moe? I don't think you heard me. I asked a question." Bern was also trying to breathe slowly, not wanting to show the sick feeling in his stomach or the pulsing cold chemical sensation now creating pressure on his brain. "I'll ask you again—where'd you get the extra fill dirt?"

Moe began to fidget, twitch, was messing with his hat.

"Moe? The fill you used. Where'd it come from?"

Moe wanted to run because of the look on his boss's face—but he couldn't run, couldn't even manage to form words right now. He turned his eyes slowly toward the darkness beyond the green boat where the clouds were filled with lightning. It was also where Bern had built his own hill because Florida didn't have any hills. He'd told the staff not to touch it.

Bern focused on the bulldozer once again, the fifty-gallon drum still *drip-drip-drip*ping from fifteen-feet above. "You took the dirt from my hill, didn't you?"

The man nodded but didn't reply.

"*Didn't* you?"

"Yeah, I think so." Moe was looking his boots.

"That's where the oil drum came from, too. You dug it up."

"Um-huh, yeah, I found it there. Which made me think it was a good idea. There's *another* barrel buried out there, too. I figured, while I was at it, with them EPA people coming—"

Much louder, Bern said, "Without my permission, you excavated the hill. Took all this stuff from where I planned to build my house."

"Your house? You never told me—"

"I told you not to touch it!" It was impossible to stay calm now.

"I didn't take much dirt, Bern. Honest. Fifteen, maybe twenty yards of fill. Enough to make another buildable lot, and you know how much a buildable lot's worth. I'm trying to think, just the way you told me. Like an executive. I wanna be more around this place than just some big lazy buck, working for beer money who doesn't give a damn—"

Buck? The Hoosier racist probably hated Jews, too.

Bern lunged at the man as Moe scrambled backward, scared shitless, seeing his huge boss coming at him. Moe high-stepped onto the bulldozer and swung himself into the cab.

"I'll put it all back, Bern. Just the way I found it. Promise!" Moe was hurrying, aware that the bulldozer's cab was his only refuge. It was caged with steel, and the machine was intimidating, the way the blade could lift and turn.

"Get off that thing, goddamn you! Come down here right now!"

Moe yelled, "This won't take but a few minutes. Watch!" The transmission lever was on Moe's left and he slapped it, throwing the machine into reverse, foot on the accelerator, using the steering sticks to spin the machine around, smelling the stink of diesel exhaust.

What he didn't want to do was run over his boss, so he pivoted in his seat to look over his right shoulder . . . which is when his elbow accidentally hit the lever that operates the dozer's cutting blade and bucket. With robotic precision, the bucket rotated downward, dumping a quarter ton of dirt and debris, including the fifty-gallon drum, the entire load coming *this* close to crushing Bern Heller, who jumped out of the way.

For a moment, Moe's boss looked at the sky. *I haven't suffered enough? What next?!*

The steel drum, that's what was next. On impact, the lid shot off like a volcano blowing, spewing a geyser of oil as the drum tumbled toward the boat ramp, steel on gravel causing a terrible clatter that was abruptly muted by the shock of seeing something else slide out of the barrel—a broken-bird-looking creature, but human-sized, its wings folded at grotesque angles.

No . . . not a bird.

Human.

Moe's eyes were locked onto a detail. He watched a tiny pale object become buoyant in the sludge pouring out of the barrel. The pale object was shaped like an autumn leaf . . . a *maple* leaf. Slowly . . . slowly the autumn leaf ascended, oil pouring off it, and finally breached the pool's surface.

No . . . not a maple leaf. It was flesh. It was human. It was a pale white hand.

Moe had switched off the bulldozer's engine. He sat in the steel cage, staring, then swung down from the dozer, moving slowly as if the abrupt silence had weight.

"This is terrible. Who could have done such a thing?" At first, Moe didn't recognize Bern's voice. It sounded mechanical, like a robot, saying words that were emotional, but with no emotion to them, as if his boss had been programmed with a computer chip.

"God only knows," Bern said, "how long she's been in there. Years, maybe. Someone probably killed her, and stuck her in that barrel, before we built the place."

Moe couldn't take his eyes of the delicate white hand—a child's?—but was aware that something else was going on now. Something not associated with the broken-bird-looking creature that appeared to have been melted, stored in petroleum.

Nearby, there was an unexpected sound . . . unexpected movement.

The green boat. Bern was now staring at the green boat.

In his robot voice, the boss was saying, "Drug smugglers, I've heard they used to smuggle in marijuana. At this dock, right here where we're standing. Cocaine. Illegal substances." Bern was walking toward the green boat now, his movements also mechanical. "If this poor dead girl was involved with those sorts of people . . . drug smugglers? Pimps, maybe. I hate to say this, but she probably got what she deserved."

There was someone in the boat, Moe realized. That's what Bern had noticed. A shadowy figure . . . a man, just his forehead and eyes showing over the side of the boat, watching what was happening.

Didn't think he'd been spotted. But now . . . ?

Bern continued talking, probably to cover the sound of his footsteps on gravel. "A real stroke of luck, Moe, you almost dropping that barrel on me. The poor woman. She could've been in there for decades, and maybe has family still wondering what happened to her. That's if her family's still alive or cares anything about a girl who hung out with drug filth like she must've . . ."

It was the colored guy hiding in the boat. The Cuban who'd gone nuts and got arrested—Javier, who Moe had always enjoyed talking with, sometimes standing on the dock drinking coffee together before the man's fishing clients arrived.

Javier was standing now, realizing he'd been spotted. He seemed undecided about whether to run or not as Bern continued toward him, walking slower now so as not to scare the man, a sick-looking smile trying to form on Bern's face. "Javier? Is that you? Javier! How you doin'? It's okay. No need to be scared. You think you've had a bad day? Personally, I've had a heck of a day. Climb down out of there and I'll tell you about Augie taking us out in the Viking—you'll get a laugh out of this one."

In his mind, Moe was yelling at the Cuban, telling him: *Run! Get the hell out of here, you idiot! You can't see why he's being so nice?*

Moe wanted to run, too. He wanted to get in his truck, leave the marina, leave Florida, go back to Indiana and get a factory job; dump his fiancée who never stopped badgering him to get a better job, make more money, move up the ladder. Join the Kiwanis? He told her he'd do it, and it still wasn't enough.

But he couldn't run. Not now. Not after witnessing what had come out of that barrel.

In Moe's mind, a question kept cycling over and over: *How did Bern Heller know that the bird-looking creature with the human hand was a woman?*

Something else: *How much would it be worth to Bern if Moe didn't ask?*

18 September, Saturday
Sunset 7:27 P.M.
Low tide 7:28 P.M.
    Two more tropical cyclones designated; weather deteriorating in Gulf.

At noon, two hours later than planned, we freed the lines of the thirty-two-foot Island Gypsy after Jeth came aboard and told us, "I give up. Javier doesn't answer his cell phone, and his home phone hasn't worked since the hurricane. We'll have to dive the wreck without him."

We motored out the channel toward Pine Island Sound. Jeth was at the wheel, his mood as glum as the weather. His attitude: *Javier's desperate for money, but the bonehead doesn't show up for a paying job?* Even so, he provided a steady flow of excuses in his pal's defense.

"Maybe he and his wife got back together—that would explain why he didn't call. Or maybe one of his daughters got hurt or sick . . ."

He was irritated. Understandable. He'd wasted most of the morning making phone calls, hailing other skippers on the VHF, trying to track down his buddy. Javier had not only stood us up, he'd made us late—intolerable, in the world of charter boat captains.

"Or maybe Javier fell off the dock with the phone in his pocket, I've done that plenty of times . . ."

Aggravated and protective both. Worried, too. We all were. What we knew about Javier Castillo was this: The man was a professional. To miss a charter and not notify us? Something serious had happened.

Wind had swung from the southwest, fifteen to twenty knots, seas six to eight feet, according to the VHF radio mounted above the Island Gypsy's stainless wheel, clutch levers to the left, chrome throttles on the right. The vessel had twin Volvo diesels, so it was fast for a trawler—thirteen knots cruising speed, if the weather was right. Her control console was mahogany, gauges mounted flush: fuel, oil pressure, water temp, twin tachometers. Electronics were in Plexiglas cabinets—sonar, GPS, and radar—all screens easy to read without having to look away from the vessel's huge windshield.

Looking through the windshield now, I could see the foredeck begin to lift and fall, Picnic Island and Punta Rassa in the distance, gray waves bigger as we turned south toward the causeway, already lots of car traffic lined up on this Saturday afternoon—because of storm damage, the bridge was closed every other hour for repairs.

Sanibel Lighthouse lay beyond, and the Gulf of Mexico.

"Last time I was in a boat this big, I was still managing the fish co-op at Gumbo Limbo. Before the Yankee bastards tore the place down and named it Indian Harbor. It was a big ol' Hatteras, and Hannah Smith was aboard. She'd never seen the Tortugas."

Arlis Futch was talking, standing next to Tomlinson, who was at the chart table reviewing my dive plan. Tomlinson shot me a quick look when Arlis mentioned Hannah Smith. I'm not sure what my reaction was, but it seemed to amuse him.

As far as I was concerned, Arlis was good news. He'd heard Jeth hailing skippers on the radio and offered to check Javier's house, see if the man was there.

He wasn't. Neither was his truck.

Arlis showed up at Dinkin's Bay in his mullet boat half an hour later and offered to fill in.

The old man liked to talk, but that was okay. Maybe I was a little uncomfortable when he discussed Hannah, but I could endure that for a while, too. We needed another person who was good with boats and who had enough experience on the water that he could be trusted in a tight spot. This was going to be a difficult dive and I was glad he was along. Besides, I had questions to ask Arlis.

He was answering one now, which is why he was on the subject of women.

"Hannah Smith—now, there was a woman. Not beautiful in a flashy way. Not like that actress I told you about. Close my eyes, I can still picture her face, not all the details, of course—what was that, fifty-some years ago? I'm dang glad that she didn't live to see what happened to her little yellow house on the Indian mound."

Meaning Hannah, not the actress. He already told me that the name Marlissa Dorn didn't ring any bells.

"I knowed there was some Dorns that vacationed on the islands. There was another family, too, and they was all part of the same clan by the name of . . . I can't remember. You want to talk about beautiful women, though? Those women were all pretty as pictures, every single one. They come from money—of course, most people with mansions do."

I asked, "Was the other name Engle, or Brusthoff?"

He said, Maybe.

A few minutes later, though, he said, "Marlissa . . . Marlissa. Hmm. Maybe I did hear that name a time or two before. Brusthoff, I *know* I heard that name."

He remembered the boat—a good-sized Matthews with a black hull, and lightning fast for the times. It *could've* been the Coast Watch boat that went down the night of 19 October 1944. The name, though, hadn't stuck with him.

"*Dark Light,*" he said, thinking about it. I watched him tilt his head upward and his eyes drift to the left. People commonly do that, I've noticed, when they're trying to recall visual images. Numbers and hard facts, though, the reaction's different. They often look downward or to the right. Arlis was trying to picture the boat.

"The name would make sense with that black hull. Thing is, I was working at the P-O-W camp in Fort Myers by then. So I'd lost touch with all the little details about what was going on on these islands.

"I hadn't been on Sanibel for eight, ten months until a week or so before that dang storm hit. Talk about bad timing. That's the only reason I know someone reported seeing what was maybe a U-boat but was probably a couple of Cuban fishing smacks.

"A Coast Watch boat went out that night," he said, "and it never came back. I didn't know the men who was aboard her, either. *That* I would remember."

I asked, "Men?"

Arlis replied, "Aboard the Coast Watch boat, you mean? That's the way it usually worked. The crews were civil defense volunteers, and they'd take turns. Alternate shifts, but they 'most always worked in teams of two or three men. I don't think women was ever assigned to boat crews. Maybe beach patrols but not boats."

Beach patrols, he added, consisted of watching for suspicious activity and maintaining an island blackout, but also the more hazardous duty of regular sweeps of Bowman's beach and Captiva, confirming they were deserted. Nearby military bases used the islands for target practice. Live fire— .50 caliber machine guns and bombs.

"Nobody knows how many tons of bombs they dropped on North Captiva. Cayo Costa, too. Volunteers weren't always locals, neither—so it was dangerous. They shifted around the state, depending on what was needed. They could get lost, or stranded."

I listened to him tell Jeth about the Cuban fishermen washing up on the beach but no vultures being around because the storm was so bad, before he told me, "There mighta been a woman drowned, too. Seems like there was . . ."

I'd asked about that, and also if he remembered a German named Frederick.

"What you've got to keep in mind, Doc, is a lot of people died in the fall of 1944. A couple hundred folks killed by a storm was minor compared to the number dying in Europe and the Pacific. I guess we got used to it. Death. It's something we dealt with every day. Back then, it was personal and sad, but it wasn't news. You see what I mean? Families took care of their own. We buried our own. There wasn't all the forms and crap there is now. Someone died? You said words and put 'em in the ground."

We were coming around Lighthouse Point. The trawler began to lunge and fall in cement silver waves that rolled toward us at wheelhouse level. I was standing at the galley's stainless sink, making sandwiches and storing them in plastic bags for later—a good thing I'd started early, because it was too rough now to do much besides hold on, and try to talk above the noise of creaking hull, and the pots-and-pans clatter of a small boat struggling in big sea.

The chart table was on the starboard side. Tomlinson and Arlis were both seated there now. I watched Arlis lean toward the cabin window, pull the curtain aside, and look toward the island. We were only a few hundred yards off the beach. "Right there's where we buried those Cuban fishermen. They had no family, so we did it for 'em."

He was pointing at Sanibel Lighthouse, and two white clapboard houses on pilings that were visible above the surf line. The houses were old, and looked vaguely Polynesian with their pitched roofs and cupolas. The lighthouse resembled an oil derrick, except for the glass lantern room at the top.

"The Coast Guard had three or four men stationed in those very houses when the storm hit. They said the lighthouse swayed back and forth like a tree in the wind. The military built a separate tower nearby, and the wind blowed that thing away. They built it especially so they could climb up high and watch for German submarines."

Arlis added, "Funny, huh? The night someone reports a U-boat out there, the tower gets blown away."

I was about to nudge the old man back onto the subject of Frederick Roth when Jeth interrupted, saying, "Doc, the visibility down here sucks. Do you mind taking the wheel until I get up on the flybridge? Probably would be best if there were two of us—a buddy system kinda deal."

We were quartering waves on the port side, and every sixth or seventh roller broke over the bow, causing the Island Gypsy to shudder as her propellers cavitated. The foredeck was awash; wheelhouse Plexiglas streamed with water. Jeth had the windshield wipers on, and they provided frail, pyramid-framed glimpses of the horizon ahead.

Jeth waited until I was at the helm before zipping his foul weather jacket, then tightrope-walked to the cabin door and stuck his head out. Disgusted, he said, "Hell, I think it's raining, too." At the same instant, Arlis surprised me, saying something unexpected: "And right there's where we captured the prisoner who escaped." He was still looking through his thick glasses out the starboard window.

Standing with the wheel in my hands, I said, *"What?"*

Arlis repeated himself and pointed toward shore.

We were running parallel the beach, scrawny-looking casuarina trees and coconut palms visible from the peak of each freighting wave. Through the trawler's windshield, I could see houses, hotels, and condos, too, most of them patched with blue tarps.

I said, "You captured a German prisoner? Or was he an escaped prisoner of war?" I was confused.

The cabin door banged shut as Jeth went out into the weather.

Arlis's tone became impatient—wasn't I following along? Or was I dense? "Of course it was an escaped POW. We got the whole Atlantic Ocean between Florida and Germany, how was a Nazi gonna get here if he wasn't *already* a prisoner?

"That's why the Army captain sent me back to Sanibel even with the weather bad as it was. Three Kraut prisoners escaped the camp at Belle Glade. We got a tip at least one of them was hiding out somewhere on the islands and nobody knowed the area better than me. Plus, I had my own boat, and the ferry wasn't running."

Above me, I heard Jeth bang twice on the cabin roof. He wanted me up there. An extra set of eyes in foul weather.

"You caught the German?"

"What did I just tell you?" That irritable tone again. "Me and a couple of them big island boys, the Naves and Woodrings. I don't know what happened to the other two Krauts. Ours, though, he went back to prison and hung himself. Good thing, too, 'cause he was as bad as they come.

"It was during that time Oscar Jefferson's daddy got burned up at a moonshine still. Somebody poured corn liquor on him and lit a match. We figured it was the Nazi. Peter, that was his name. We caught him right *there.*"

I said, "The escaped POW was Peter?"

Arlis looked at me like I was an idiot. "No. Oscar Jefferson's *daddy* was Peter. The Nazi, he's the one we caught right there by that old house." He banged his index finger on the cabin window, pointing to the spot, but then got a brief cheerful look on his face, a light going on inside his head. "You *asked* me about those people. Mr. Brusthoff, and the Dorn girls. That's their place right there.

"Hell, I thought that house was torn down long ago. But that's where we found him. What I remember is, there was a rumor one of those Dorn girls was being especially nice to that German. Maybe Oscar Jefferson's daddy, too. People loved to talk in those days."

Above me, Jeth kicked the cabin roof twice more.

My squall jacket is green, made of waxed cotton. I put it on after making eye contact with Tomlinson, who'd been listening to Arlis as carefully as I. No need to talk—he would pay attention and take the wheel if I called. Next to Tomlinson's arm, I noticed, was a file he was assembling. The folder was labeled: ADMIRALTY LAW.

To Arlis I said, "You're not your normal sweet self today. Have a sandwich—I think your blood sugar's low," then went out the cabin door, into a wind that was dense with rain and diesel fumes. I climbed the flybridge ladder and took the companion swivel seat on Jeth's left.

From the vantage point of the flybridge, it was easier to see Sanibel Island and the area where Arlis said they'd captured the German POW. We were near enough to the beach that I could see a few solitary strollers and a familiar boardwalk—this is where I often jogged. The boardwalk and the beach disappeared briefly as each wave peaked and slammed ashore.

There were hotels and condos down the beach, but here the only structure was visible through leafless trees: a Cape Cod–style house and gazebo, all sided with gray shingles. *Southwind.*

Through the rain, I could also see a tiny lone figure on the balcony bundled in a blanket. Chestra Engle held up her hand—a wave?

No . . . more like an invitation to dance.

26 Jeth is not quick to use profanity—it's risky with his stutter—but he used profanity now. "*Sonuvabitch.* We got company. And guess who?"

I was so busy going over our scuba gear, double-checking gauges, regulators, flashlights, strobe lights, and safety lines, that I hadn't noticed the forty-three-foot Viking sportfisherman dolphining over the horizon toward us.

It was the boat from Indian Harbor Marina. I didn't want to believe it. Bern Heller was giving it another shot after being so sick the day before?

No . . . it was Augie up there on the high flybridge. It looked like his buddy Oswald was beside him. Both wearing yellow rain jackets—Augie shaped like a brick, Oswald pudgy enough to resemble a squash.

Jeth was furious. "If they think they can come out here and chase us off this wreck, they can by God kiss my ass on the county square. Not after what we've been through already!"

Our day had not gone smoothly. Javier had failed to show, and then we couldn't find the wreck. Not at first, anyway. We'd banged, yawed, and surfed toward the horizon for more than an hour in the burly trawler before our electronic navigation equipment told us that we were 12.1 miles off Sanibel Lighthouse.

"We should be right on it," Jeth had said, then scampered below to use the GPS and a better sonar unit.

He'd programmed the computer with the lat-long numbers and we all focused on the sonar screen as the GPS directed us the last few yards to our destination. For an instant, the wreck appeared on the screen: a geometric shape etched in red sitting on a white digital line that represented sand bottom—soft sand, because the line was thin.

An instant later, the wreck was gone.

Jeth swung the trawler around and tried again. Same thing happened.

Problem was, waves and tidal current were pushing us with such force that it was impossible to stay over the wreck for more than a few seconds. Even with twin diesels, the Island Gypsy wasn't nimble. It was built for open water cruising, not sharpshooting bottom structure in heavy seas.

After a half-dozen failed attempts to hover above the wreck, Jeth hinted that maybe I'd have to change the dive plan. I told him yes, I could do that, but it would take time, which meant we'd have to come back another day. This kind of sea was no place to experiment with a haphazard underwater attack.

I had a plan. We were going to stick with it.

We'd made marker buoys—used the noodle-shaped Styrofoam floats you see at the beach and a hundred feet of fishing leader to attach them to concrete blocks. The Styrofoam noodles were six feet long, red or orange, which would make them easier to see in big water.

My plan was to idle back and forth, watching the sonar, and to drop buoys to create a rough outline of the wreck that would be visible on the surface. Anchoring was going to be tough enough in this mess without a visual reference.

When I told Jeth that I'd scrub the dive before changing the plan, he made a couple more tries and got lucky. He held the sonar's transducer over the wreck long enough for us to get a buoy out.

After that, it was easier to get the other markers positioned, but things still didn't go smoothly. Two of the buoys drifted away because they were weighted with only half blocks of cement.

It took me several attempts to swim the boat's big Danforth to the bottom and get the anchor buried where we wanted it. The sand was soft, which is why the anchor pulled free on the first two tries.

Then one of our three safety lines got fouled in the starboard prop. Bobbing around beneath a brass propeller sawing at a rope wasn't fun. The prop's blades were sharp and the propeller dropped like a guillotine as each wave swept past. As I was cutting the rope, I swung my head to avoid the prop and the driveshaft caught me on the side of the head.

Great. Blood in the water and a new scar.

It was after 3 P.M. by the time the boat was positioned and our gear was ready. Everyone aboard had a copy of the dive plan; presumably, they'd gone over it. Even so, I risked offending my pals by insisting on a meeting to review. The maxim sounds as stuffy as a spinster teacher: Plan your dive and dive your plan.

I don't care if I did seem officious. The term *recreational dive* is one of those fun misnomers, like *recreational sex*. Both, if approached recklessly, will put you in the hospital with something penicillin can't cure. Or in the grave.

Under the covers, spontaneity is good. Underwater, spontaneity is usually bad.

Tomlinson, Jeth, and I would dive. Safety was our only imperative. Salvaging items from the bottom was secondary, I told them.

Along with standard dive systems—inflatable BC vests, gauges, weight belts, regulators, and tanks—each of us would wear heavy gloves, carry a waterproof light, an inflatable six-foot distress buoy, and also a strobe light attached to our BCs. We could activate the strobes below or above the surface by screwing the lens cap tight.

I didn't have to tell Jeth and Tomlinson that I am aware of at least six people—divers and fishermen—who'd still be alive if they'd carried little pocket-sized strobe lights with them. Both men knew. They'd lived it.

The wreck wasn't deep, only forty feet. Jeth and Tomlinson were using standard tanks and air, so their maximum safe bottom time at that depth—three atmospheres, for the sake of calculating—was eighty minutes. They could expect their air supply to last around an hour or so but, to be on the safe side, we'd stay down for no longer that forty minutes.

An extra safety cushion was that I was using an Azimuth rebreather system with a nitrox gas mix. If needed, I had a maximum safe bottom time of more than three hours.

Arlis would remain aboard the Island Gypsy, standing by with the additional tank and regulator I'd rigged to a safety line clipped to a big red rubber buoy. If he needed to communicate with us, he would start both engines. The sound of rumbling engines is unmistakable underwater.

The most likely emergency was that our anchor would pull free—the signal for that was to rev the engines at steady three- or four-second intervals, like blowing a whistle. The signal meant: Grab a line and prepare to be dragged along the bottom. Surface slowly.

The emergency signal—or diver recall—would be several short staccato revs of the engine.

Arlis bristled when I told him he had to wear a safety line and a life jacket while we were underwater. "I ain't never worn that crap, and I never will."

I was tempted to tell him to stop behaving like an irritable old asshole . . . and realized I was getting a little irritable myself.

Instead, I reminded him what we all knew but seldom stopped to think about: In rough seas, if we got separated from the boat the odds were against survival. In all likelihood, we'd probably never be found. If Arlis fell overboard and we surfaced one minute later? No more Arlis. If he fell overboard and the boat pulled anchor? We would all die.

The water was warm—eighty-three degrees. Even so, tropical hypothermia, a little-known phenomenon, gradually slows the heart until it stops. Hypothermia wasn't the primary danger, though. It was the size of the waves and the water color. Under these conditions, it would be unlikely to find a lone swimmer.

I'd tossed a sixty-foot safety line off the stern, a six-foot Styrofoam noodle attached. I pointed at it now. "Have a look." The noodle was orange, but it was invisible except for a microsecond when it was buoyed to the peak of a wave.

In these seas? For a swimmer, the fatal edge of visibility was thirty yards. Even from the top of a wave. Any farther and the boat would vanish, probably never to be seen again. Nor would a swimmer be visible from the boat.

Thirty yards of separation—that was the distance to the abyss.

"You are wearing the damn safety line," Jeth told Arlis. "And a life jacket, too."

A moment later, Jeth saw the Viking hounding toward us, and added, "Sonuvabitch."

It was Augie and Oswald all alone in the big white boat with the fly-bridge tower, bright chrome and red canvas, and outriggers swaying. Half a million dollars of fiberglass, electronics, five-star amenities, and serious naval architecture.

"The guy is such an asshole!"

Not unusual to find one aboard a vessel like the Viking.

"What pisses me off most," Jeth added, "is that we spent—what, more than two hours?—rigging for this dive, and they don't have to do a damn thing but anchor, put on their tanks, and swim down to the wreck."

That seemed to be their plan. As dive plans go, though, it was a bad one.

Tomlinson, Jeth, and I were suited, tanks on, fins in hand, ready to roll off the stern. But we waited, watching the Viking rocket toward us, throwing geysers of white spray. The boat came in much too close and fast, Augie backing the throttles at the last moment and sledding away. The wake he created hit us like a freight train. It nearly tossed Arlis over the transom.

"You low-life Yankee 'bagger! I'll gaff you like a fish if I see you at the marina!"

Arlis was in a mood.

The Viking's flybridge towered above us; Augie appeared smug and professional up there, looking down. The boat was equipped with a PA system for communicating with dockhands, and we watched him put the microphone to his mouth. "You're anchored on my wreck and this is the last time I'm warning you. The wreck my boat found and we're claiming it. Legally." His voice boomed over waves; his Wisconsin accent magnified, as he added, "You people will learn not to mess with us. One of you already found out."

I assumed he meant me. But why the nasty, knowing slyness?

When Arlis replied with his middle finger, Augie looked pleased. "My uncle talked to our lawyers this morning and that's what he said to say if you were here. Admiralty law. Look it up. The laws of marine salvage and a thing called the law of finders. Which means you're trespassing . . . dumbasses."

I looked at Tomlinson who was smiling and shaking his head as he spit into his face mask. "It's called the law of finds, not finders," he said quietly. "Nothing to worry about. The wreck's ours, if we do this right. I've got the whole business scoped; all this deal needs is for us to add water."

He glanced up at Augie and tried to lighten the mood. "Cheeseheads," he said. "It'll take evolution another three hundred years before they should be allowed to mate south of Chicago."

I was watching Augie maneuver the sportfisherman into the wind, preparing to anchor. Oswald had disappeared belowdecks and reappeared carrying two BC dive systems, as Augie hit a button and their anchor plummeted into the water. Immediately, he killed the vessel's engines and hurried down the ladder to his pile of scuba gear.

Augie hadn't set the anchor by hand; he didn't wait until his boat swung tight on its line, an indicator that the anchor would hold—temporarily, anyway.

It looked like they were both going in the water. No one above to make sure the boat was still there when they surfaced.

I looked from Jeth to Tomlinson, then Arlis. Even the old man managed a bitter smile.

"Augie doesn't have a clue what he's doing, does he?"

Jeth said, "He's dangerous in a way that gets other people hurt." His tone suggesting that we should get moving before Augie had a chance to hurt us.

We got in the water, Jeth, then Tomlinson following me on the surface as I pulled myself along the safety line toward the red and orange buoys that outlined the wreck below.

I'd just found something interesting when, above, Arlis fired the engines and gave the emergency recall signal.

The object I had found was metallic looking, heavy, and shiny. It was buried in the sand, only a rectangular edge showing. Hard to say with confidence because of the murky water, but it appeared to be golden in color. No barnacles, no benthic growth, and it hadn't tarnished.

Gold is one of a very few metals that retains its pure color after long submersion in salt water. What else could it be?

Gold.

I had made a couple of attempts to dig the object free when I heard the diesels start. The staccato bursts were jolting.

Emergency. Arlis repeated the pattern, revving the engines. Unmistakable.

The visibility was so poor that I had to hold my dive watch against my face mask to see the luminous numbers. We'd been on the bottom less than twenty minutes.

I touched my hand to the bottom. We weren't dragging.

I gave two sharp tugs on the rope that was our search line. Tomlinson and Jeth both gave two sharp tugs in reply. They were okay.

What could be wrong?

So far, the dive had gone without a hitch, even though conditions were awful. We were only six feet apart, spaced incrementally along the rope, yet I couldn't see anything but the yellow cones of my partners' flashlights through the murk.

Which was okay. The plan was still workable because we were using a keep-it-simple-stupid search technique.

The search line was connected to the anchor line. Kick slowly over the bottom and the rope would rotate us in an circular pattern, like pencils in a protractor or spokes on a wheel. Complete a circle, then move farther out toward the circle's perimeter. Gradually, we'd progress to the end of the rope, covering the wreck site in orderly six-foot swaths.

Easy.

It was the best way I knew to explore a wreck in near-zero visibility. And we were *on* a wreck, there was no doubt about that now—the remains of a boat, not a plane.

Our signal for *Come look* was three sharp tugs on the rope. Jeth had been the first to call. He was on the inside lane of the perimeter, holding his flashlight close to something he wanted us to see. Frozen in a swirl of lucent silt was the boat's propellers, both still connected to driveshafts. There were a few barnacles on the props and some new benthic growth—but not much, considering the pitting done by electrolysis.

This wreck had been insulated by sand. Buried, then uncovered by the recent hurricane. I had no doubt about it now. *Anaerobic*: the word for an environment that has no oxygen so cannot support the crawling, boring, sessile creatures that destroy wood and bone and scar metal.

The gilded rectangle of metal I'd just discovered also had no barnacle scars. I'd used my left hand to dig around it, but sand collapsed into the hole. Tried again using my blunt-tipped dive knife. Contact with the object made a distinctive soft *tink*.

It was definitely metal. Soft metal.

The thought came into my mind again: *Gold?*

Silly. Scuba divers don't find gold lying on the bottom of the seabed. That's fairy-tale stuff. Except, of course, for Mel Fisher, and Kip Wagner, and Alan Eckert, and . . .

I had found a couple of old-style bottles. They were in my mesh dive sack. And a corroded blob that was handgun-sized.

But gold?

Jeth had found German coins here, so why not? I used my knife and dug faster around the object, trying to expose enough to get a grip on the thing before the sand collapsed once again.

That's when Arlis started the engine and gave the emergency signal. Diver's recall—we had to surface immediately.

I had no way to mark the object. An inflatable buoy would've been swept away by waves. So I left it. I gave a sharp tug on the rope followed by a steady pull—time to surface—then followed the rope, hand over hand,

toward the pale pulsing strobe light that marked where our search line and the anchor line intersected.

I was on the outside perimeter of our search wheel. I moved slowly over the bottom, aware that Tomlinson was only a body length in front of me; Jeth a body length ahead of him. I stopped for a moment and jettisoned a squirt of residual air from my BC to maintain negative buoyancy. I wanted to make certain I didn't ram Tomlinson from behind.

That's when something big came out of the gloom and rammed me. Hit me high near the shoulder, knocked the mask crooked on my face. I could feel a slight suctioning draft as whatever it was sped by.

A few minutes earlier, I had felt an unexpected bump on my thigh. Thought it was Tomlinson's fin.

Ahead, I could see the foggy corona of two flashlights.

The thing that had hit me wasn't Tomlinson.

I came into my mind that it might be Augie and his squash-shaped friend, Oswald. They might be dumb enough to charge around forty feet beneath daylight. But did they have the courage?

I doubted it.

I straightened my mask, tilted it, and exhaled through my nose to clear the mask. When the water was gone, I shined my light to the left, then the right. The color of invisibility was a silted gold that began and ended at my faceplate.

Nothing.

But something was out there. Something big. Circling, maybe. Or turning right now, building speed to hit me again.

I told myself not to panic, stick with the plan. This was like being on a beach in a lightning storm. There was nothing I could do to prevent from being struck, so why worry?

All true, but I didn't experience a feeling of untethered freedom, as I had during the hurricane. I was scared. Something was out there in the gloom. Something that could see me with sensory precision. Something that had probably already noted the accelerated pounding of my mammalian heart. The fresh cut on my forehead would leave an unambiguous trail of blood.

As I followed my partners up the anchor line, I expected to be hit again. I wasn't.

On the surface, as I allowed waves to sweep me along the safety line toward the dive platform on the stern, I expected to be hit from below. I wasn't.

As I hurried to vault myself out of the water, pulling my legs up into a fetal position, I decided that maybe it *was* that idiot Augie who'd crashed into me.

It wasn't.

The forty-three-foot Viking sportfisherman had broken free of its anchor and was adrift. That was why Arlis had sounded the emergency recall. It had happened only a minute or so after Augie and Oswald, wearing scuba gear, had entered the water, Arlis told us.

"They never even submerged," he said. "When they saw the boat drifting, they took off swimming after it. But there's not a chance in hell they caught up with that thing."

I had my rebreather system off by then, standing on the dive platform. The Viking was a pendulous splash of white in the distance shrinking fast.

Arlis was on the flybridge, already motoring toward our anchor, using the automatic wench to retrieve it, while Tomlinson, Jeth, and I stripped off our gear on the stern. I felt the Island Gypsy swing her beam to the waves and knew that we were free.

"One of you boys get on the radio and raise Fort Myers Beach Coast Guard. Tell 'em to stand by. You other two, get up here. I need you as spotters. Whoa! *First,* pull the safety lines in, dummies! Do I gotta tell you everything?"

Arlis wasn't old and feeble now. He was his acerbic, irritable self—taking charge, which is exactly what he was supposed to do.

When he realized that the Viking had pulled anchor and her two divers were adrift, Arlis had done something very smart. He'd reacted as only a person with his water experience would have. I had rigged a backup dive system—tank, regulator, and BC vest—and clipped it to a safety line. The safety line was tied to a red mooring-sized rubber buoy. If one of us had gotten tangled in rubble below, an emergency air supply was ready.

Because the Viking was drifting faster than Augie and Oswald could swim, Arlis expected the two to turn toward our boat. Maybe they did—he wasn't sure. He lost sight of them within seconds. When the two men didn't reappear swimming toward our vessel, he realized the waves and current had taken them. They were adrift.

Immediately, Arlis inflated the spare BC and tossed the backup dive system overboard. It was still attached to forty feet of rope and a rubber buoy. When the two divers realized they were in trouble, it was likely that they would inflate their BC vests. Their drift pattern would be similar to that of the backup air system. The red buoy gave us something visible to follow.

We were following it now.

"I'll give you the wheel, if you want."

Jeth shook his head, and told Arlis, "You're doing just fine." He spoke without turning his head to look at the old man because he didn't want to take his eyes off the water.

Arlis nodded. "You made the right decision." Sure of himself, his ego coming back to life out here in big water.

That was fine with me. I liked his confidence. We needed it.

We'd already divvied up search quadrants: I was on Arlis's left, scanning the area ahead, and abeam the trawler's port side. Jeth was to Arlis's right, responsible for the right side. All three of us kept track of the red buoy ahead as it bucked from wave to wave.

With each set of breakers, though, it seemed less and less likely that we would find the two men.

I'd checked my watch when I felt us break free of our anchor: 4:27 P.M. By 4:40, I was losing hope. It seemed improbable that we hadn't caught up with them in ten minutes. By 4:50, I was beginning to second-guess: Was following the buoy still the smartest thing to do? Augie and his partner would've stopped chasing the Viking after only a few minutes. They would have then turned into the waves and tried to swim in the direction where they hoped our trawler was anchored.

Neither of them looked like long-distance swimmers. They would have soon tired. They had no other choice but to inflate their vests and resign themselves to the hope that someone would come searching for them.

Their maneuvers would have changed the course of their drift. If our course was off by only a few yards, we'd already passed them. We needed to turn back and make another try.

Below, Tomlinson was on the VHF with Fort Myers Beach Coast Guard. He'd stuck his head above the ladder long enough to tell us that a search-and-rescue helicopter was being scrambled at the St. Petersburg base, seventy miles north. I'd tried to get him to change places with me—his eyesight is perfect; I wear glasses—but he insisted that he stay below.

"Maybe I'll see something down there that you can't see from the flybridge."

In a search that seemed increasingly futile and random, it made as much sense as anything else.

We had closed on the Viking. It drifted beam to the sea, only a few hundred yards away now. I entertained the mild hope that the two men had somehow caught up with their boat. Perhaps they were drifting with it, hanging onto the anchor line.

Unlikely, but we'd soon find out.

To my left was a thin charcoal smudge that I knew was Sanibel Island. Ahead, it was raining over Fort Myers Beach. I could see squall clouds dragging tendrils of rain across the water, sunlight oscillating through rain mist, the streaming light interrupted by clouds.

I checked my watch: 5:03 P.M. We'd been searching for half an hour. The wind had a silver edge to it, blowing steadily from the southwest. It glazed the waves with icy light. I looked at Jeth, who simultaneously looked at me. Arlis remained steadfast at the wheel—still wearing his Bing Crosby hat; the orange life jacket we'd forced on him, an absurd touch.

Jeth's expression said, *This is hopeless.*

I nodded. Hopeless.

I knew Augie only well enough to dislike him. The other guy, Oswald, we had never exchanged a word. But to be adrift, alone, in a wind-glazed sea . . . night coming soon, and death soon after—I didn't wish that hell on anyone . . .

From below, I heard a unexpected banging sound.

"Hey! Why's he doing that?"

Then we heard it again: a panicked banging on the pilothouse roof, Tomlinson signaling from below. Arlis backed the throttles and shifted to neutral, all of us turning as one. We heard the cabin door slam, then Tomlinson's voice. "Stop! Turn around. They're behind us!"

He came charging up the flybridge ladder, still wearing the pirate's bandanna that he always wore when diving. He turned and pointed, yelling, "See them, they're right there! Don't take your eye off them. *Nobody* take your eye off them."

Off what? I saw nothing but rolling waves.

"Arlis! Give her some throttle, I'm losing them. Here—" Arlis stepped aside as Tomlinson jumped to the wheel. He popped the throttles forward and the trawler lunged into the next wave.

Then I saw it: one of the six-foot-long Styrofoam noodles that had drifted slowly away from our wreck site because it was weighted with only half a cement block.

How had I missed it? We'd passed it on our port side. *My* side.

Clinging to the orange buoy were Augie and Oswald, waving frantically. They were wearing black wet suits and black BC vests—Tomlinson would've never seen them if it weren't for the orange marker.

"Okay, okay, I got 'em. I'll steer." Arlis was at the wheel again. "You boys find a boat hook. I'll bring us alongside and you can pluck 'em out—and watch those two don't piss all over you 'cause they're gonna be happy as drowned dogs that we found them."

I started to suggest to Arlis that the safest way to approach the swimmers was with our beam to the sea—get upwind and we might drift down and crush them. But he cut me short, saying, "When I want your advice on how to pick up contraband in a big sea, I'll send a telegram. Until then, you just shut your hole and do what I say."

Jesus. We'd left with Santiago, but it was Captain Bligh taking us home.

Tomlinson wasn't empathetic. "Contraband?" he said, very interested. "Mind if I ask—"

"Mary-juana," Arlis replied. "You know any other that pays as well? Back in the 1970s and '80s, my pot-haulin' business associates would drop bales from a plane and I'd fetch 'em out of the water. A'course, that was a hell of a lot harder than this. It was at night. Couldn't use lights. More than once there was other boats out there, too, wantin' to steal what was ours. Got so I could shoot pretty good in rough seas."

"No kiddin'," said Tomlinson, impressed.

The old man cackled and said, "Made enough money to buy Miami," giddy enough to quote a fellow pirate. "Some of it really good shit, too."

Augie Heller and Trippe Oswald—the guy had a first name—were so grateful to be pulled from the water that they probably did pee down their own legs.

Oswald was bawling and Augie's eyes were glassy—shock. Sledding up and down those waves, they'd gotten a glimpse of the abyss. There was something worse than death. It was a dark and random indifference. They'd given up. Been reduced by their own terror, and the two men couldn't immediately resume their old façades.

Both were shivering as they peeled off their wet suits despite the warm storm wind blowing across the Gulf from Yucatán. We gave them blankets, bottled water, and sandwiches. Put them at the settee table inside the pilothouse, while Tomlinson cancelled the Coast Guard search and Arlis swung the trawler around hoping to catch up with the red buoy and recover our backup dive system.

Oswald was a chatterbox nonstop talker: "Couldn't swim another stroke, dude. My legs were like fucking cramping, and I even started praying, man. Promised God if He'd help me just this once that, no shit, I would like do anything He asked. Next thing I see is this beautiful fucking boat, almost on top of us . . ."

I tuned him out within a minute.

It was Oswald's way of discharging fear. Humiliation, too. We were the assholes Augie had told not to dive his wreck. We were the dumbasses who knew nothing about maritime law. Bern Heller's lawyers had warned us—the same lawyers, presumably, who'd figured out how to steal boats under the guise of admiralty salvage laws.

It is humiliating to be saved by an adversary. And we'd saved them.

Augie and Oswald were grateful—at first. Thanked us over and over;

made weak, ingratiating jokes. They were in our debt because we'd saved their lives. *Forever, man.* Was there something they could do for us? Name it.

Forever didn't last, nor did their gratitude. It began to erode when the two men made their first experimental stabs at manipulating the other guy's recollection of what they'd just experienced. The gradual process of reinvention also required that they distance their association with witnesses they couldn't manipulate: us.

Augie Heller was a man who was uneasy in anyone's debt. Especially ours. He rallied quickly.

"Know what I think? I'm glad you found us, but we would've made it. How long were Trippe and I swimming, only an hour or so?"

I told him, "It probably seemed like an hour," anticipating what was coming next.

"Okay, so we were taking a break when you came along. We would've rested for a little bit, then swam another hour. Rest, swim, rest, swim. And we had the vests on. No way we could drown. What do you think, Trippe?"

Oswald said eagerly, "You're no quitter, Augie. No shit, when I started to lose it I thought you were gonna slap the crap out of me. And when you started to lose it, dude, no way was I gonna go off and leave you—"

"I never lost it," Augie interrupted, an edge to his voice.

"Well . . . yeah, I guess now that I think about it . . . you didn't really *lose* it—"

"Neither one of us lost it. We stayed pretty cool out there."

"Yeah. I guess you're right. We handled it pretty good."

Augie said, "What I was asking was, you how long do you think it would've taken us before we made it to Sanibel? Doing what we were doing: swim, then rest, then swim some more. We'd of made it around eight or nine o'clock? It would be easier at night because we could have swam toward the lights. Climb up the beach and hitch a ride. Or call Moe with his pickup truck. We'd of had a couple of hours to spare before closing time." Augie had a nasty laugh.

I was thinking: *By 9 P.M., they would have been off Fort Myers Beach, bobbing toward open ocean and the Dry Tortugas, a long hellish night to endure before tropical hypothermia provided relief. Death would have arrived not long after their last dawn.*

"How drunk you think we're gonna get tonight, Trippe? We'll take the Viking back to the marina, hose her down, then you and me are hitting the bars, man! We'll get Moe, too—can you imagine how that cowboy would've freaked if he'd been with us today? He'd of been taking shots at the damn waves."

Shooting at the waves? The two men exchanged looks, sharing an inside joke that I didn't get.

I sat listening as Augie switched subjects, eager to dismantle, then rebuild, the most painful facts before he had to face his uncle.

"That shitty anchor on the Viking? How many times did I say we needed a new anchor?"

"At least once, Aug. Maybe twice. That's the way I remember—"

"Twice, my ass. I told you umpteen times. I mentioned it coming out, but you probably didn't hear. 'We gotta get a decent anchor for this boat.' That's exactly what I said . . ."

I was thinking: *We gave up life in the trees, the ability to hang by our toes and scratch our own backs, for this?*

28 Arlis and Jeth were above on the flybridge. We'd pulled astern the forty-three-foot sportfisherman. Had been drifting along with it, presumably while they discussed the best way to put one of us aboard—dangerous in a running sea—or how to snatch the Viking's anchor line and take her in tow. I considered going topside to find out, but decided Captain Bligh could make the decision on his own.

Tomlinson, Jeth, and I still hadn't had a chance to talk about what we'd seen or found on the wreck and we couldn't talk now because we didn't want to share information with the two guys from Indian Harbor Marina. Tomlinson had found something interesting, though. Sizable, too, judging from the shape of his dive bag, which was on the stern deck. When I'd asked about it, he'd whispered, "Later. After we get rid of these two."

For the last ten minutes, he'd been standing at the pilothouse console, using the VHF radio to keep Fort Myers Beach Coast Guard updated on our progress. Emergency distress calls are treated seriously; they require a follow-up interview before an incident report can be closed. Tomlinson had cleared his throat a couple of times before I realized he was trying to get my attention. His way of communicating privately while Augie and Oswald chattered away.

I turned. He was shirtless, the pirate's bandanna tied around his head, wearing navy blue polyester dive pants called dive skins. He held up a warning index finger: *Pay attention.*

I listened as Tomlinson interrupted Augie. "Hey, guys, we're about to take your boat in tow, so there's some stuff we need to get straight first—for the Coast Guard. Which of you is the legal owner?"

Augie's expression said: *Why are you bothering me with this crap?* "Our marina owns it, I guess. It's corporate property. So that makes me captain. Is that what you're asking?"

Tomlinson had found the trawler's papers in a black leather portfolio that was zipped inside a waterproof case. He was leafing through documents that looked like service records, warranties, documentation, a registration. Owner Bill Gutek ran a tight ship.

Tomlinson said, "The same information I've got to give them about this boat"—he held the sheath of papers as an example—"they're going to want for the Viking. And the Coast Guard has ways of checking if you give them wrong info. Are you *sure* the vessel's registered in your marina's name?"

No, it wasn't registered to Indian Harbor Marina. I could see it on Augie's face. But he said, "Yeah, I'm sure. That's how it's down. Under the exact same name as the marina, tell them that. We're the owners." Augie's tone saying, *Whatever.* He didn't care that we knew he was lying.

Tomlinson held his hands apart, palms up—sorry he was being such a pain in the butt. "The Coast Guard's waiting for this stuff, man. If they go aboard the Viking, they'll find the ship's papers. They gotta match what you tell 'em. Or they'll keep you at the Coast Guard station all night."

Augie's expression: *Shit, now we've got to deal with this?*

Tomlinson offered, "Or maybe . . . I'm just guessing here, but it's *okay* to tell them if you've not the owners. If your marina claimed it as salvage after the hurricane—the same way you got Javier's boat?—then maybe you have a right to use it. It's no big deal, man, if that's how you got the Viking. But it's gotta be the truth."

Augie was confused. "Javier?"

"The colored guy who showed up with the gun," Oswald said. He was chewing on his third sandwich. "That Pursuit with the twin Yamahas is his. Was his, I mean. *Javier.*"

"Oh yeah, the green boat with the radar," Augie said slowly. "I'd forgotten that part of it. Moe loves that boat."

"Oh yeah. Moe *does* . . ." Oswald left that hanging as he continued eating.

They were exchanging private information.

I said, "Is there something about Javier Castillo that we don't know?"

I got a shrug, and an indifferent shake of the head, before Augie looked at Tomlinson and said, "Okay, sure. If the Coast Guard has to know, our marina . . . no, the salvage company we contracted *claimed* those boats, all perfectly legal, and they can talk to our lawyers if they have any more questions. We just want to get the boat home, wash her down, and get a drink."

Tomlinson plays the role of the dope-addled hipster flawlessly because he is so often dope-addled. But he also possesses an extraordinary intellect. That big brain of his was working on something now. I sensed it. His low-key manner, playing the role: a burned-out flunky who was harmless, embarrassed because he had to ask questions.

"Good. I'll let the Coast Guard know. Doc? Arlis might need help topside. A couple extra hands to get a vessel that size under control."

Did he want me to keep Augie and Oswald busy while he spoke to the Coast Guard?

In reply to my look, I received the slightest of nods. *Yes.*

Augie and Oswald followed me up the flybridge ladder in time to hear Arlis tell Jeth, ". . . that's what I'm trying to get through that thick head of yours. If you're ever on a boat that sinks—you can be five thousand miles offshore, it don't matter—and if that boat happens to be carrying livestock, the first thing you do is find the pigs. You can drop a pig in the middle of an ocean at midnight and he'll swim straight for shore. It's a gift that a hog's born with. Only the Good Lord knows why."

When Jeth saw me, his expression read: *Help.*

"A horse? Don't waste your time messin' with a damn horse. Sheep and goats are almost as bad. Now, a dog, hell, a dog will chase seagulls, it don't matter to him. A dog could swim forty miles of open water and just be touching the beach, but if a seagull flies over? A damn dog will head right back out to sea.

"That's why you always should open their pens quick on a sinking ship. These days, a lot of sailors aren't aware of that information. A cat, now there's an animal that's *aware*. A cat is smart. Know how you can tell? That's right—a cat will already be *in* the water, waiting to climb on the first pig that swims along—"

Arlis knew that we were listening and couldn't ignore us any longer. He paused and glared at me. "I suppose you come up here to tell me how to tie a knot. Or maybe you want to take the wheel and show me how to bow up to that vessel's stern quarter gentle as a baby's butt so one of you snotnoses can step aboard—"

I interrupted, "Nope, you've got the helm, Arlis. But you don't own that boat." I pushed my chin toward the nearby sportfisherman. "This guy says he's captain of the Viking, and he's the one best qualified to say how we take her in tow. Augie's going to stay up here and tell you how he wants it done." I put my hand on Augie's shoulder and pushed him a step closer to Arlis. "Go ahead. Tell Arlis what to do next."

I looked at Jeth—*Let's go*—and followed him down the ladder. As we left, I lingered long enough to hear Arlis saying, "Hey, I recognize you now. You're that spawn from Indian Harbor Marina. 'Member me? The night watchman you called Old Dude? *You're* supposed to tell *me* how to handle a boat?

"Why . . . you little penis-nosed twerp, you about knocked me overboard an hour ago. Just before I saved your ass—which I wouldn't do again in a million years. Augie? I wouldn't name a damn goat Augie, nor a horse neither, which is an even dumber animal, doesn't come close to having the brains of a pig . . ."

Tomlinson was talking on the VHF when Jeth and I came into the pilothouse. He motioned for us to hurry, and pointed to a paper at his elbow as he said, "Thanks very much, Marine Operator. Go ahead and put that call through."

From the radio's speaker came the sound of a ringing phone.

Tomlinson was cheerful. Clear-eyed, too—unusual for this late in the day. He said, "I just finished talking to the Coast Guard. I told them the Viking was adrift, no one aboard, and that she was going to kill herself ashore in less than an hour—if she didn't hit a bridge or another boat first. Does that seem accurate?"

Through the trawler's windows, I could see the sky bridge that connected the mainland to Estero Island and Fort Myers Beach, the horizon lifting and falling as we drifted. I nodded, and said, "Yes," as Jeth said, "No doubt about it," both of us aware of why he'd asked a question that had an obvious answer. Legalities were involved, and our responses might become part of the public record.

Jeth and I hold the same commercial Coast Guard licenses: 100-ton ocean operators, unlimited range. In a court of law—federal admiralty court, for instance—the opinion of three licensed professionals would have weight.

"Here." Tomlinson tapped the printout he'd made at Sanibel Library while doing research on admiralty law. "I gave the Coast Guard the Viking's documentation numbers and they found an emergency number for the company that owns her. Something called Boston Camera and Lexicon Software Analysis."

As I moved to look, I heard a man's voice say through the radio speaker, "This is John MacNeal. The Coast Guard says you have information about a boat my company owns. I'm president and CEO, so I have full authority . . ."

Jeth and I stood shoulder to shoulder listening but also reading:

. . . a ship abandoned in peril is not without proprietorship. Those on board, if forced to relinquish control of their vessel, do not give up title. However, if a crippled ship is at risk of wrecking or sinking, it may be rightfully assumed that the vessel's value to its owner has been significantly diminished . . .

For this reason, Admiralty Law permits great latitude in the common

law of salvage to encourage salvers to rescue a vessel in peril from otherwise total loss . . .

From the radio, I heard the voice of John MacNeal say, "If you have
any connection whatsoever with those *people* at Indian Harbor Marina, this
will be a very brief conversation, Mr. Tomlinson. My attorneys are dealing with them."

I heard Tomlinson reply, "Our only association with them is adversar-
ial. They took a boat that a friend of ours owns—stole it, as far as I'm concerned. Maybe you had a similar experience."

There was a moment of static, then silence, before MacNeal responded.
"Maybe. Whether it's true or not, would you mind if my attorney listens
in? We'd also like to record this for our records."

Tomlinson said, "It won't be the first time my conversations have been
taped. You're in the Boston area? I attended university there. I can give you
the names of some local people who can vouch for my character. Call
them, but make it quick. Your boat's adrift, no one aboard, and pretty soon
she's going to beach herself or hit a bridge."

Tomlinson gave the man names: Dr. Kenneth Kern, Massachusetts Lab-
oratories; William Martin, naval historian; Dr. Musashi Rinmon Niigata . . .

Musashi? That was a surprise. Musashi was Tomlinson's ex-wife and
mother of their daughter, Nicola. They were back on speaking terms?

Tomlinson talked, as I continued to read:

. . . Admiralty Law understands that a salver assumes risks, and is entitled
to recoup expenses plus fair profit, but only upon successful completion of
the task.

However, just because a vessel has sunk does not transfer title of either
the ship or its cargo to a salver. A salver who removes ship's cargo or
equipage when the vessel is no longer in peril is wrongfully relieving another of his property, unless that vessel or property can be proved abandoned. In the navigable waters of the United States, this period is 30 days.

A ship's misfortune does not license immorality. Theft is theft, no matter the water's depth. Therefore, a vessel's owner may negotiate the cost of proposed salvage, or refuse a salver's assistance. The owner has the right to decline all salvage benefits, unless the derelict vessel threatens the public safety and well being.

Tomlinson had underlined the last sentence.

I heard John MacNeal say, "You say there's a chance our boat may drift into a bridge?"

Tomlinson replied, squinting at the GPS, "There's a chance, yes. But I think it's unlikely. I'm looking at a chart right now, and the way we're setting it's more likely she'll go aground on the shoals off Fort Myers Beach. Damage shouldn't be bad: props and driveshafts. Vandalism while she's there, that's your biggest concern."

I wasn't surprised by his honesty. Nor was I surprised when he added: "Mr. MacNeal?"

"Yes?"

"I don't want you to feel pressured. We're going to try and save your boat no matter what. Rest easy, man. Whether or not you decide to negotiate a salvage fee with us"—Tomlinson looked at me and tapped his finger on another series of paragraphs that he'd underlined—"it doesn't matter. We'll still do what we can. I want you to know that before you make a decision—"

I began to read again, as MacNeal interrupted, "Hold on. I've got another one of our attorneys on the phone. This may take a few minutes."

In keeping with Admiralty Law, a claim for a salvage award requires that three criteria can be demonstrated:

(1) Maritime peril from which the vessel or her cargo could not have been rescued without the salver's intervention.

(2) A voluntary act by the salver. The salver must be under no official or legal duty to render the assistance.

(3) The salver must have success in saving, or in helping to save at least part of the property at risk, and be able to substantiate the worth of his assistance.

Tomlinson had put a check mark beside each paragraph. My guess was, he'd gone through the list one by one as he described the Viking's situation to the Coast Guard. It was now part of the official record.

After a long silence, MacNeal returned, saying, "I just spoke with an old acquaintance of yours, Dr. Ken Kern. My company does some work with Mass Labs. Because we told him how serious the situation is, he had no choice but to tell us the truth. He told us that when we checked your record, we'd find seven arrests for possession of illegal substances."

I was thinking, *We can say good-bye to a salvage fee,* as Tomlinson replied cheerfully, "That's correct, seven. I'd like to think it shows how generous I was in those days; eager to share my goodies even with undercover cops. Trying to spread enlightenment among the Boston pigs."

"You sound proud to be a convicted drug user." MacNeal seemed to be throwing things out, then standing back, judging Tomlinson's reaction.

"If you mean 'convicted' as in someone who has convictions, I am proud. *Very* proud."

A careful sociability came into MacNeal's voice. "Dr. Kern told me that one of those arrests was because you took the rap for a friend. A student who was a few weeks away from graduating. My guess is, that student's now a highly respected Boston geneticist."

Tomlinson looked at me, his innocent expression saying, *What, me worry?* "I don't remember if that's true, or who the friend was, but why not? Seven's such a lucky number, man. How could I resist?"

There was another silent conferral before John MacNeal, president and CEO of Boston Camera and Lexicon Software Analysis, began to speak in sentence fragments that were sometimes quickly amended—he had attorneys whispering in his ear.

MacNeal told Tomlinson that he advised us *not* to attempt to save the company's boat. It was too dangerous, his company would assume no liability. However, if we went against his advice and made an attempt anyway we had his permission to board the Viking. If we considered her derelict and a potential danger, we also had his permission to take reasonable measures to bring the boat to a safe port. Tomlinson could assume a role of custodial responsibility, pending negotiations for a salvage award.

Yes, paraphrasing his lawyers, that was clear.

MacNeal said, "I guess that means I'm washing my hands of it. You assume all responsibilities and liabilities, and the boat stays in your possession until we reach a fair settlement. Whatever you do, though, don't let those *people* at Indian Harbor get their hands on it again. I'd rather let the boat sink."

Tomlinson signed off from the marine operator, and looked at Jeth, who was still processing what he'd heard. Jeth said slowly, "You mean the Viking's not Augie's anymore?"

"That's right. It's *especially* not Augie's. Not his marina's, either."

"The guy doesn't even know us and he's letting us borrow it?"

Tomlinson said. "No. It's more like we've adopted it—for now. MacNeal's a nice guy, but he and his lawyer knew they didn't have a choice. Risk a multimillion-dollar liability suit if the boat hits a bridge? It's ours to keep until we settle. You and Javier suddenly have a very cool boat on your hands. And the timing couldn't be better." He held up an index finger: *Wait here.*

There was something he'd been wanting to show us. He went out the cabin door and returned with all three dive bags. Inside were objects that we'd gathered while surveying the wreck. The objects had a few long-dead barnacles on them, but not many—an indication they'd been buried in an anaerobic environment.

I'd found a rum bottle with raised lettering—RON BACARDI, HAVANA—plus the gun-sized glob. Jeth had recovered a flask-sized chunk of black-encrusted metal, and a couple of smaller chunks—silver?

As I held one of the pieces, I realized it was the first opportunity I'd had to tell them about the metallic rectangle I'd been trying to dig out of the sand. Could it have been gold? More likely, it was something golden looking in that silted light.

I hadn't mentioned that I was knocked sideways by an unidentified animal, either—probably a shark, though it could have been a giant grouper. That feeling of shock, then dread, was something I would have to process on my own. My profession was beneath the water's surface. I'd be going back into that murky water very soon.

I said nothing, as I inspected the encrusted chunk.

Jeth and I then watched as Tomlinson reached into his bag and pulled out a 1940ish dwarf-sized Coca-Cola bottle, then a broken phonograph record that was made of unexpectedly thick plastic.

"It's an old 78," he said. "I'd love to find out what's on it."

He saved the best for last: a wooden plaque. He placed it on the galley cabinet so we could inspect it.

"We'll have to get that in salt water right away," I told him, leaning close. "The stuff Jeth found, too."

"Of course."

The plaque was made of teak, most likely, swollen and black from years of being underwater, and covered with sand. It was the carved nameplate from a boat, a portion of it broken away long ago.

Touch a finger to the letters, and it was easier to read:

ARK LIGHT.

Jeth said, "*Dark Light.* It's the wreck your friend said she'd pay us to salvage."

Tomlinson replied, "Now we've got the boat to do it. Even in bad weather. Since Javier's not here to do the honors, why don't you go up and tell Augie the good news?"

That morning, watching from his condo window as Augie and Oswald pulled away in the Viking, Bern Heller experimented with the idea of using the boat to escape to some foreign country that had islands with palm trees, and straw huts and women who poured coconut milk over their hair and bodies to keep themselves feeling smooth . . .

Were there islands like that anymore? Were there ever?

Didn't matter. He could still think about it.

. . . escape to an island that belonged to a country not interested in a few mistakes a man might make while living in Florida. Not if the man had money, and a yacht as classy looking as the Viking, where he could take the women with their coconut-smelling hair. Keep the air conditioner in the master suite going; make drinks for them while they took care of his laundry, his cooking . . . his other needs, while they were at it.

Bern pictured himself alone on the flybridge, all his belongings packed below, a trunkload of cash and certified checks hidden somewhere safe after cleaning out the corporation's accounts. Pictured himself heading out across the Gulf of Mexico . . .

No, not the Gulf of Mexico. The water had to be calm. It had to *stay* calm.

. . . he pictured himself alone on the flybridge, keeping the boat close to the beach where there wasn't any wind. Ride along nice and smooth, no more worries. He could follow the shoreline around to Mexico, or even Colombia—a favorite hangout of his grandfather's judging from the passports that were still scattered on the nearby desk along with the leatherbound journal, the photo of the glamorous woman who was now probably an old hag, and documents mostly written in German.

Something new was on the desk, too. A registered letter from the old man's personal assistant, Jason Goddard. And a package. They'd been sent overnight mail, but they couldn't have anything to do with the message he'd left on Goddard's machine: "I was wondering about the woman in the black-and-white picture . . ."

Or could they? Goddard was prompt. Known for being a step ahead. His grandfather referred to him as "my point man," as if they were in a war. Or: "My personal son of a bitch," because Goddard's the one who did the old man's dirty work.

But send an overnight package in reply to Bern's phone message? Nobody responded that fast, not even Goddard. Besides, the envelope had a thick feel—there was a lot more than information about a woman inside.

Nothing good ever came in a thick envelope, that was Bern's experience. Which is why he still hadn't opened it. The way his luck was going? The damn thing could wait until tonight. Or tomorrow. He didn't care.

Bern just wasn't up to dealing with another shock. There'd been too many, way too fast. Last night was yet another example: The redneck dumping a barrel that contained the body of a woman who'd been quietly buried . . . nine months?

Yes, about that long. The girl Bern had spotted in a Gainesville parking lot, drop-dead gorgeous, with eyes that were way too good to waste time on him, so he had followed her. Got a little carried away when he dragged her out of the trunk, into a field, because the little bitch was a fighter—a mistake on her part, but his mistake, too, which he could admit to himself.

How long, though, was he going to have to pay for one or two stupid mistakes? Fair was fair, but he'd suffered enough.

The thing that tumbled out of the barrel *probably* was the girl from Gainesville, though he couldn't swear to it. Hard to recognize what it was after being packed in a petroleum product for that long—dirty two-cycle motor oil in this instance. Which is what saved Moe's Hoosier ass.

Very calm and cool, Moe had looked at Bern and said, "Girl? I don't see any girl." This, with the girl's body only a few feet away, all folded up like a paper angel, oil streaming off it. And just after hearing Bern say that the girl looked so tiny, she almost had to be the sort of person no one would care about, or come looking for.

"A crack whore, most likely," Bern had said.

And Moe had replied, "Girl," like: *What are you talking about? That thing's not human.* Which was a big relief that got better when Moe suggested it was probably an animal of some sort that fell into the barrel then couldn't get out. And added, still very cool, "Do you want me to bury that mess where I found it, boss? Or do you want to take care of it yourself?"

At the time, Bern had his hands full. Full, because of the Cuban he'd spotted watching them from the twin-engine boat that was green in daylight but looked bluish in the yellow sodium lights.

The Cuban had tried to run. Jumped out of the boat and scampered, Bern on his heels, the Hoosier lagging far behind. When Bern caught the Cuban, he'd looked as surprised as some of the wide receivers Bern had played against, a white guy his size dragging them down from behind.

He had the Cuban's arm levered up, and his knee on the guy's throat so he couldn't cry out, which is when Moe revisited the subject: "Girl? I don't know why you keep saying that, boss, I'd *swear* it was some kind of animal. We can use the bulldozer and bury it where it belongs."

Which saved him.

It didn't save the Cuban, who was listening.

The phone on the desk of his condo was ringing. Bern didn't notice right away because his ears were also ringing. They'd been ringing since about 1 A.M. that morning, when Moe's unexpected gunshot had temporarily deafened him.

Bern looked at the caller ID, seeing: PRIVATE NUMBER.

There was a trick his wife back in Madison had learned, how to program her phone in a way so her own number was shielded from the person she was calling. She didn't do often do it, though. More likely, it was Jason Goddard, who was also an attorney and did tricky stuff all the time.

Bern answered.

Damn. His wife.

Even though impaired, he had no trouble hearing: "Bernard, you said you'd call me last night. I tried three times and you never answered—the last time was ten minutes after midnight!"

At ten minutes after midnight, he and the Hoosier were trying to decide what to do with the Cuban. Call the cops and let them deal with him? Or take care of the situation themselves.

". . . which is thoughtlessness, plain and simple. I swear, you haven't been the same since you took that Florida job. What's got into you? The money's *nice,* I'm not saying I want you to *quit,* but try and be a little more thoughtful. It's like Florida has taken all the sweetness out of you, Bernie . . ."

Sweetness? The woman was still loud and clueless, something that *might* change about a month after they sealed her coffin and got a few feet of dirt on it.

". . . so I'm just gonna come right out and tell you what's got me so upset. It's that Augie. I was talking to your sister-in-law yesterday, and Augie told her that you got yourself into another brawl. But this time with some hippie who nearly killed you. Is that true, Bernard? Did he hurt you? You never said a doggone word . . ."

Augie, the little fucking snitch. If he'd told his motormouthed mother, half of Wisconsin would know by next week. A really shitty thing to do to a former pro lineman in a state where fans worshipped their football players. Spread a rumor about him getting his ass kicked by some pansy doper.

Bern interrupted his wife long enough to say, "A hippie choked *me?* Geez, honey, that's so crazy it's funny. The guys at the Cadillac dealership are gonna laugh their tails off when they hear it. No . . . of course it didn't happen. Augie wants my job, honey. The whole family knows . . ."

Bern held the phone away after that, preferring to listen to the ringing inside his own head as he slid the photo of the glamorous woman in front of him. After last night, he no longer had an interest in tracking down some old lady, no matter how good she looked umpteen years ago. He had more important things to do now. The most pressing: Figure out how to escape this nightmare if things began to unravel.

They were unraveling fast.

The photo, at least, gave him something to look at while Shirley yammered on and on. Stare at the beautiful woman's picture too long, though, and something weird happened: the faces of the two dead girls were superimposed, one and then the other, beneath the glamorous, glossy hair and atop that pear-ripe body. Which got worse when the gorgeous woman's face became his wife's face . . .

Bern blinked and shook himself, then pushed the photo away. But the image lingered: his wife, Shirley, with her pudgy white cheeks, her mouth always moving, hair smelling of the beauty parlor where all her friends went—their church group, and her book club—always lots to gossip.

Which is why it had been heaven for him, moving to Florida and away from her—for the first few months, anyway. Whole different world than what he was used to.

His grandfather had entrusted him with a completely different sort of job.

Bern was suspicious then. Still was.

Bern had spent eleven years at Gimpel Cadillac, Madison, selling new and pre-owned vehicles, enjoying the long microbrewery lunches, and shaking hands with adoring Packers fan buyers, saying things like, "No finer man ever lived than Mr. Vince Lombardi." Or: "The quarterback position, which is *probably* the toughest job in all sports, I can sum up the definition in two words: Bart and Brett." Or, if it was a guy buyer, his wife not around: "When they blocked that little Polack's kick and I saw him pick up the ball? I thought, geez, he won't even know which way to run. I was tempted to stick the guy under my arm and run her in myself!"

It was a fun job. Easy; something he was used to. But he didn't enjoy going home to Shirley, with her perfume and sprayed hair, and a mouth that never stopped moving. His only escape was the occasional sales meeting in Green Bay, or Chicago, or Milwaukee, which was his favorite city because of the nice nudie bars where the girls were so normal acting, especially the one in the strip mall with the store that pretended to be a museum but actually sold retail. He'd bought the German Luger there, which worked like a real one but was made in Taiwan.

Bern had considered using the Luger last night to shoot the Cuban. Instead, Moe didn't bat an eye when he'd asked, "Hey, Moe, do I remember you saying something about carrying a gun in your truck? If I keep my knee on this guy's neck much longer, he's not gonna be able to try and run again."

Moe answered, "You betcha I got a gun. I know how to use it, too." Then returned with a chrome .357 revolver in a fancy holster, which the Hoosier didn't strap on but wanted to, Bern could tell by the way he kept straightening his cowboy hat.

The Cuban's eyes got very wide when Moe pulled the revolver out to show what an expert he was with the thing. Cocking it and releasing the hammer, popping the cylinder to count the six pinky-sized hollow-point bullets inside. Acting like a gunfighter until the damn gun went off accidentally, the bullet passing so close to Bern's ear that his legs buckled, certain he'd been shot through the head because of the ringing pain.

Fucking Moe. Who kept apologizing over and over, repeating the exact same thing because he was too stupid to realize that Bern was deaf, temporarily, and why he was squinting at the cowboy's ugly, moving mouth, asking, "What? . . . What? . . . *What?*"

What a night.

Nightmare, more like it . . .

Wisconsin wasn't so bad, all things considered. The boats up home were mostly aluminum, and the weather could be bad eight or nine months of the year. But he still got out. He'd had some fun on the road. Sometimes the girls wanted to, sometimes they didn't—quite a few had done a little kicking and scratching, but nothing that had caused him to get carried away.

Not like Florida. Jesus. He regretted ever coming here.

Why had he?

It still didn't make any sense what his grandfather did. Not to anyone. Grandy had shocked the whole family when he telephoned Bern out of the blue and offered him the CEO job, Indian Harbor, and two similar developments, one near Bradenton, the other near Marco. They hadn't exchanged a word in years, even at the family reunion in Appleton. Everyone knew that Grandy and Bern hated each other. They still whispered about the unfortunate incident when Bern, age thirteen, got so angry at Grandy that he snuck up behind the old man and brained him with a hammer. Those two had been back and forth at each other's throats ever since.

"It's 'cause they're two peas in a pod," relatives would say.

Maybe so, but it still didn't explain why the old man offered him the job at a salary three times what he was making at Gimpel's, and a contractual guarantee that Bern would inherit fifty-one percent of all the Florida landholding company's property and assets.

There were only two stipulations: Bern had to sign over all his personal assets to the company so that he had a vested interest.

"You're going to inherit it all back, anyway," his wife had told him after reading the contract. "That's not a gamble, it's a guarantee."

The other stipulation was that he had to fulfill the obligations of his current position for at least two years after the old man's death.

"That means showing up on time," his wife said, her tone asking: *How easy can it get?* "Your developments don't even have to make a profit. As long as the company remains solvent, we own half. It's too good to pass up!"

Exactly. Which was maybe what Grandy had in mind: luring Bern down here to a job that had come to seem more like the old bastard's way of getting even.

No, it was worse than that. Coming to Florida was more like a curse.

30 Moe's Dodge Ram pickup, with the big tires and the gun rack, came skidding into the marina parking lot as Bern sat at the office computer having some quiet time on the Internet. It was late Saturday afternoon, around 6 P.M. Augie still hadn't returned with the Viking, but Bern's anxiety had calmed on this calm day with the salvage crew off, no employees around to upset him, and no recently discovered bodies to deal with that he knew of.

That was about to change.

When Bern saw the Hoosier's vehicle, he felt a sickening tension in his stomach. His hearing was back to normal, but not his nerves.

Redneck Indiana trailer toad.

His day was coming. Augie's, too. Bern's list was growing, and why not, if he had to disappear? Go out with a bang. Like the old man used to say: Forgiveness is for people who don't have the balls for revenge.

Bern would have his balls with him if he had to run away to a foreign country. Might as well even some scores.

From the Internet, he'd printed information on remote islands off Mexico and Central America that were more or less connected to Florida by shoreline—if a boater was willing to follow the contour of the Gulf of Mexico, stay close to the beach along Louisiana and Texas. Which he was.

He'd also read and printed out an article titled "How to Change Your Identity and Disappear Forever."

Interesting. Nearly twenty thousand Americans disappeared each year by choice, the story said, and many of them went on to live happy, anonymous lives. Fake passports, driver's licenses, Social Security cards—all that stuff could be bought if you had the right connections. A better way to do it, though, was to steal the identity of a person who'd died recently. It was best if they were poor, or had only a small number of living relatives—fewer people to blow your cover, that way.

Of course, the article didn't give the actual details—you had to buy the guy's book to get the real scoop—but it had lifted Bern's spirits to read that it was possible to vanish and leave your old life behind.

That day might be coming for him very soon. All because of the hick from French Lick.

When Moe's .357 went off accidentally, exploding so close to Bern's ear that it caused his legs to buckle, a lot of things happened at once: Bern collapsed, screaming that he'd been shot. Moe backpedaled toward his truck, fearing that it was true, but also fearing that his boss might not die. And the Cuban, who actually had been shot, managed to get to his feet and stumble into the mangrove swamp.

They found a grapefruit-sized splash of blood where the man had been standing, then a blood trail. Bern and Moe had searched until 3 A.M., looking for the wounded Cuban. They didn't know where he'd been shot, or how seriously he'd been wounded, but he had enough life left to evade them.

As a preemptive measure, Bern telephoned the police and gave them an edited version of what had happened: They'd surprised Javier Castillo, who was attempting to steal a boat from marina property. Moe was carrying a gun because of the incident two days before. The lighting was poor, but Moe was certain the man was armed and he'd fired a warning shot. That's all. A warning shot and the Cuban had fled.

The cops kept them up until 5 A.M., taking their statements, the blood trail erased by bulldozer tracks before they arrived.

For all Bern knew, Javier Castillo was at the sheriff's office right now, a bandage around his arm, telling them about the dead girl in the fifty-gallon drum, available for viewing at Indian Harbor Marina.

Another preemptive measure: Bern told the deputies several times that the Cuban had acted crazy, hoping to sabotage his credibility. Coming to the marina with a gun—wasn't that evidence enough? Also, the Cuban had started the marina's bulldozer for some reason. Why?

Down the road, Bern might help the cops guess that the Cuban was using the dozer to bury a dead girl's body.

God Almighty, he'd give anything to be back selling Eldorados.

Sitting at the computer, Bern watched Moe swing down out of his truck. As he waited for the door to open, he reached into his grandfather's briefcase, removed the Luger, and placed it at his right, on the desk.

There was no telling what terrible dark cloud the redneck was dragging behind him this time.

Moe had a newspaper under his arm when he came into the office, saying, "Bern. *Bern.* You're not gonna believe what's happened." The man sounded winded, he was so nervous. "The cops are outside right now. In police boats—"

That's all he got out. Bern had stood as the man came into the room. Was waiting for him. As he said, "The cops are outside . . . ," Bern took a giant step, locked his hand under Moe's neck and chin, lifted him off the floor, and slammed him against the office wall. Held him there at eye level, feeling sick inside. Trapped.

Bern's voice was shaking as he said, "If the cops are here to arrest me, motherfucker, I'll cross you off my list before they get the cuffs out." He had the Luger. He touched it to the Hoosier's ear.

Moe couldn't respond because he couldn't breathe, his face turning purple around his bulging eyes. *List? What list was he talking about?*

Moe was newly aware that when his boss used profanity, it signaled that he was in a crazed and dangerous mood. Which had been happening a lot lately. If Heller had it in him to murder a girl and bury her in a barrel of oil, he could kill a man—a terrifying scenario to contemplate, being stuffed into a fifty-gallon drum. Moe knew he had to do something fast before he blacked out.

He managed to get the newspaper in Bern's face, and made a heron-like noise—*Awk! Awk!*—hoping the man would understand that Moe had information to share. It was good news, not bad.

Bern said, "Beg. Go ahead and beg. You think that bothers me?" *Wanting* to choke the life out of him.

A moment later, though, he said, "Cops? *Why* are they here?," as he lowered Moe to the floor, his eyes glassy, his voice a monotone, sounding like when you called a bank and got its automated phone system.

Oh yeah, this man was capable of stuffing him into a barrel of oil and burying him alive.

Moe gasped, "Everything's okay. I've got great news!" Getting that out before he took a full breath, hoping to buy himself some time.

Bern waited.

"This was in the paper yesterday, but I missed it. Maybe you did, too. You're not gonna believe how lucky we are." He held the newspaper out.

Bern was thinking: *In French Lick, you'd consider last night lucky? The town should be napalmed.*

"Read this, boss. Talk about perfect timing." Moe risked squatting to retrieve his straw hat. "And I'm saving the really good news for last."

Bern used reading glasses. He placed the Luger on the desk and put on his glasses. As he did, Moe moved around the desk to the computer, creating some distance between them. Trying to act nonchalant, as if he didn't care that the Luger was now within his reach.

If what the newspaper story said was true, Moe could shoot Bern and not spend a minute in jail. All he'd have to do is show cops the bruises on his neck from Bern's fingers.

FLORIDA ENACTS TOUGH SELF-DEFENSE LAW

(Tallahassee) Yesterday, the Florida Legislature, in special session, enacted a tough and controversial self-defense law that allows citizens to use deadly force, on public or private property, as long as they believe they are in imminent mortal danger.

The new "Stand Your Ground Law" vastly broadens the criteria under which a potential victim may shoot and kill a perceived attacker. The victim need not be in his or her own home, and the attacker need not be armed.

Under the old law, a person who killed someone in their home must prove that they were in fear for their safety. The new law, however, is based on the presumption that anyone who illegally enters private property is intent on threatening the lives of the people within, and deadly force is justified.

Under the old law, if assaulted in a public place, a person must first attempt to "flee to safety," and could use deadly force only if pursued by their attacker. The new law, however, accepts the legal premise that citizens have a right to "stand their ground" against a perceived attacker, no matter when or where, and deadly force is justified if the citizen feels in imminent danger.

Moe kept track of what his boss was doing. Used his peripheral vision to watch Bern standing there, the newspaper hiding his face—no telling how the man might react—while he sat at the computer, looking at the screen, seeing that Bern's personal folder was open, a list of documents he'd saved there.

Some interesting ones:

How to Change Your Identity and Disappear Forever.
Costa Rica: The New Promised Land
Live Like a King in Old Mexico

Hmm. Looked like Bern was thinking about getting out of Dodge, the trauma of last night clearly affecting the man. Which would leave an executive position open in the family corporation—something Moe would discuss with his good friend Augie when Augie returned with the Viking.

Moe could empathize with Bern. On the way home, he'd pulled over to the ditch and vomited, thinking about the Cuban's blood trail. He *liked*

Javier. They'd drunk coffee together. Moe didn't mean to shoot him; it had been accidental.

Moe had been a mess, but it had gotten worse when a drinking buddy of his called an hour ago and told him what the Marine Patrol had found floating only a hundred yards or so south of the marina docks. Moe had been reading the newspaper when he got the call. He'd just finished the story on the new Stand Your Ground Law, which had to be fate, because the timing was perfect, and it made him feel so much better.

Bern didn't get the connection, though. He rattled the newspaper and folded it. "Why should I care about this? I thought you said you had good news."

There was a document open on the computer. Looked like Bern had been copying and pasting fragments from sports articles, after having typed: "Dear Sir, Your All Time Greatest Team is missing a name."

Moe said, "It is good news, but I want to show you," as he skimmed what Bern had posted next:

Lyle Alzado, L.A. Raiders badass. Sid Gillman. Sid Luckman. Benny Friedman. Ron Mix, called "the greatest tackle who ever lived." Mike Rosenthal, star lineman at 6´7˝ 315 lbs. Hayden Epstein, Lennie Friedman, Sage Rosenfels, defensive end . . .

Bern said, "Show me what?," glancing at his watch: 6:15 P.M. *Where the hell's Augie with my boat?* Then asked, "Why do you have that idiotic smirk on your face?"

Moe said, "This list of football players? I've never heard of any of them—"

"They're great athletes, that's who they are, you racist asshole! You couldn't carry their jocks—as if it's any of your fucking business. *What* do you want to show me?"

Moe stood, went around the desk, moving faster as he passed his boss, then opened the door. "You don't have to worry about Javier no more, that's the good news. Me neither, 'cause what I did is okay. He could've had a gun. We didn't search him. Come on out, you can see it from the docks."

A fisherman had found Javier Castillo's body floating in the bay about three hundred yards south of the marina, Moe said.

From the docks, Bern and Moe watched EMTs and an investigator from the medical examiner's office bag the body. It was an hour before sunset— pretty, beyond the raft of law enforcement boats, where the sky was yellow streaked above mangrove islands. In the shallows, long-legged birds waded, some of them flamingo pink, on this falling tide.

Sounding nervous again, Moe said, "The cops are probably looking for me right now. They'll want to question me again. Jesus Christ, Bern. I *killed* a man. But I was afraid he was gonna shoot us, right?"

Bern was smiling for the first time in days. "Yeah."

When we got back to Sanibel, Mack had to call the police to escort Augie off marina property. The sight of Jeth and Tomlinson sitting on the Viking's flybridge, trying to back the monster into a Dinkin's Bay slip was too much for him.

"That's my boat. *Indian Harbor's* property. You can't just take what's mine!"

We'd gotten a rope on the Viking while she was adrift. First Jeth, then Tomlinson, used the line to pull themselves aboard, then fired the twin Detroit diesels. They swung the vessel off its collision course with Estero Island, toward deeper water, then contacted John MacNeal through the marine operator. From the trawler's pilothouse radio, we listened to them share the good news.

The boat was their custodial responsibility pending negotiations of a salvage fee, a date to be set sometime after the holidays. Until then, no Indian Harbor personnel were to be allowed aboard.

Augie had his uncle's mean streak, but he didn't have his self-control. As we turned into the marina basin, half an hour behind the much faster Viking, Augie was still pacing and fuming. "My personal belongings are on that fucking boat. Trippe's, too. Our clothes, our wallets. My *uncle* has a ton of shit on the Viking, man, he *loves* that boat—which is worth a half million, easy!

"You think he beat the shit out of you before? Wait 'til he hears about this. What you're doing is stealing!"

I hadn't said a word to Augie, but now I did. "A friend of mine named Javier's in the same situation. There ought to be a law, huh?"

Jeth had called ahead on the VHF, so there was a crowd of islanders waiting on the dock. It was an hour before sunset, so a lot of them would have been there anyway, but news of the Viking added a celebratory note. *Spoils of salvage*—it's a whimsical phrase when used around a marina because it's usually a pirate fantasy.

Not this time, though. The boat was real, islanders wanted to hear what they expected to be an interesting story, and were eager to have a look at this big-dollar craft with luxury appointments that included a sunken tub in the master stateroom, full kitchen, a wet bar, a sophisticated Bose entertainment system, even a central vacuum station.

Among those on the dock was Jeth's wife, Janet, who appeared healthy, ripening, and happy from my vantage point on the trawler's flybridge. Her man was back in business. She wouldn't have to return to Ohio as one more casualty of the hurricane.

It was a pleasant scene to watch, until Arlis launched into another one of his monologues.

"See there? Jeth can't get the boat docked because there's not enough water. I *told* him that boat draws too much for Dinkin's Bay. On this tide? You see herons standing on grass flats, that should tell you something!

"Take it to Ferry Boat Landing, down on Lighthouse Point, I said. Or South Seas Plantation. But would he listen to me? Hell, no. I've only lived around here seventy-some years. Only driven every kind of vessel except for the space shuttle and a submarine. So why should he listen to an expert when he can make a fool of himself showing how bullheaded he is . . ."

My impatience with Arlis now bordered on animosity. What had Hannah seen in this undersized man with his oversized ego? If he didn't have information I wanted, I would've kept a boat length between us.

But I still had lots of questions.

I had waited until we were off the beach that fronted Chestra's family home, Southwind, before asking about the escaped German prisoner of war. Maybe seeing the place would jog the old man's memory.

In reply, Arlis made a grunting sound of disinterest, and said, "Maybe what I need to do is put all my stories down in a book. If I do, I'll let you buy the first copy."

Ask the man to talk, he wouldn't. Ignore him and he wouldn't shut up. There seemed to be an old-time horse trader's dynamic at play: Information that I wanted was valuable. It went against his instincts to give it away. Information I didn't want, though, was worthless, so he could ramble all he liked.

Frustrating. I considered trying reverse psychology, but that only works when both parties want it to work and both think there's something to gain. Arlis was too smart. I didn't have the patience.

So I tried again. Took the straightforward approach. Asked what he meant when he implied that one of the Dorn girls had helped the German POW. There was also a snide inference about a man named Peter Jefferson.

Arlis loosened slightly. "There was no better family on the islands than Oscar Jefferson's people. They got along fine with everybody. The Dorns and Brusthoffs owned that house right there"—he swung his eyes to the beach, where Southwind was fading from sight off our stern—"but they were still tourists.

"Could be ol' Peter got sweet on one of those pretty Dorn girls—not a smart thing to do in those times, mess with a white girl, no matter how fine a people the Jeffersons were. Then someone found Peter walking like a zombie down the sand road, skin hanging off him he was burnt so bad. The Kraut did it. Though Peter didn't live long enough to say it was true."

If the murderer was a local, he said, the truth would have slipped out as the decades passed.

"The Krauts had been sneaking around the island for a couple of weeks by then. Someone was helping them, giving them food. We found lots of their tracks going back and forth to the house where the Dorn girls lived—"

I interrupted. "*Their* tracks?"

"How many sets of tracks do you expect two men to make?"

"I thought you said there was only one."

"No, I told you there was *three* escaped P-O-Ws from the Belle Glade camp. Not one. *Three.*" He exhaled noisily. Why did he bother?

"Okay. All three POWs found their way to the islands, and you captured one."

"I didn't say that, neither! How the hell am I supposed to know if all three come here? There was tracks from two men, but we only caught the one. Maybe the third one didn't walk around much. Maybe he wasn't a Kraut. Or maybe he was a Kraut and went to Key West and opened a perfume store, how would I know? You think I'm a mind reader or something?"

Impossible to keep the man on topic. I said, "You think they got help at the Dorn house, though. Am I clear on that?"

"That's how we caught him. At night, waited outside the house. Which I thought had been torn down long ago. If Peter was sweet on one of them girls, he never got the chance to say good-bye."

I said, "Because he was burned so badly. He didn't live long enough."

Arlis gave me the look again: *Are you an idiot?* "Of course he *died.* What I'm telling you, if you'd *listen,* is that they had to leave the island. People around here will accept damn near anything. But helping a Nazi who pours moonshine on a good man and lights a match? We didn't want 'em here after that, and they knew it."

I had to risk it. "You're talking about all three families. The Dorns, Brusthoffs, and the—"

"Isn't that what I just said!"

"Then why didn't they sell the house?"

"The house we just passed? Them people *did* sell it. That's why I thought it was long ago torn down." Arlis shook his head, then rolled his eyes. "What else you gonna do when you leave an island and you can't come back?"

I wanted to call Chestra but realized I didn't have a number. Had I even seen a phone in the house? If the family estate had been sold years ago, what was she doing there? Why were old family photos still on the wall?

Arlis had to be wrong. There was no reason for him to lie, but he'd already demonstrated that his memory was faulty.

Chestra, on the other hand, *had* lied—I felt certain of it. But she was much too smart to base an elaborate charade on such a flimsy deceit. Her reasons would become known to me. Lies are the DNA of diplomacy and good manners. I assumed her reasons were altruistic at best, self-serving at least. If they weren't, I'd know soon enough.

I much prefer lies to inaccuracies. Lies reveal themselves.

It was nearly sunset by the time we got the trawler docked. Low tide was a little before 8 P.M., in synch with the rising moon. It was a spring low—all new and full moon tides are called spring tides—which meant water was lower than normal.

It peeved me to acknowledge that Arlis was right, but Jeth couldn't get the Viking into a slip. He churned up a lot of mud trying, but there's a limestone base beneath the muck and it wasn't worth bending a propeller.

Jeth was still smiling, though, when he bowed up to the fuel dock and let Tomlinson scamper monkeylike off the pulpit railing, then backed away. He used the PA system to show off a little, saying, "You can find me with the other millionaires tying up at Ferry Boat Landing."

Arlis—right again. He let me know it, too, with his ragged smile.

A ugie kicked a trash can as we docked. Crumpled his plastic cup and lobbed it into the water, before snapping at Oswald, "Grab your shit and let's get out of here"—a couple of telling ticks of the bomb inside him. He was going to be trouble.

I wanted to get the wooden sign, ARK LIGHT, and other objects we'd found back to the lab and into salt water or sodium hydroxide as soon as possible. First, though, I made a quick detour to the docks, looking for

Mack. The Sanibel Police Department is efficient and professional. If Augie made a scene—I felt certain he would—they would deal with him in the whisper-quiet way of experts.

Mack kept the department's phone number above the cash register. A marina that rents boats is guaranteed to have the occasional outraged customer, and Mack had seven jon boats and two runabouts that he rented throughout the year—barring hurricanes. The police were no strangers to Dinkin's Bay.

As I stepped off the boat, the moon was ghostly silver to the east; the sun was westward, in slow, incendiary descent. Dinkin's Bay, our small marina, was suspended in balance: a mangrove clearing, boats, buildings, and people.

I was carrying our sopping dive bags, smiling hello at friends, asking them to wait until I returned from the lab to help Tomlinson tell our story of high seas salvage. There was also the not-so-small matter of refueling, unloading, and cleaning the Island Gypsy, then discussing a suitable present for owner Bill Gutek.

The rules are unwritten: If you borrow a boat, replace anything you use or damage, leave it cleaner than you found it, with tanks topped off, and reward the owner for his generosity with a gift.

Before I found Mack, though, I was intercepted by Rhonda Lister, who lives aboard the venerable old Chris-Craft cabin cruiser, *Tiger Lilly.* She and her longtime partner, JoAnn Smallwood, had arrived on Sanibel years ago, both of them broke, and on the run from abusive husbands. They'd pooled their meager funds and started an advertising sheet they called the *Heat Islands Shopping Guide.*

The shopping guide is now a full-color weekly newspaper worth a ton of money. The women have demonstrated their entrepreneurial genius by expanding into real estate, and also investing in a couple of restaurants, including a gourmet sports bar that was Tomlinson's brainchild: Dinkin's Bay Rum Bar and Grille, located only a few miles away on the road to Captiva, near the wildlife sanctuary.

The women own a beachfront condo, and a home near Asheville, but they prefer to live where they have always lived: on their roomy old hulk of a boat, Dinkin's Bay Marina, where they have become maternal icons in our small community's hierarchy.

Rhonda sounded motherly now as she took my arm, stood on tippy-toes to inspect my face, and said, "One more scar on that mug of yours, you're gonna look like a Japanese haiku. That hack job someone did on your forehead, those stitches should have been removed a week ago."

The hack job had been done in the field, with monofilament fishing line, by the wife of a man who had an unpronounceable name.

Rhonda was right. I should have removed the stitches myself days ago.

She touched her finger near where I'd been head-butted, then where the driveshaft had caught me. The cut wasn't as deep or long as the one on my forehead, but it needed attention.

"If you're not going to take care of yourself," she said, "I will. I tried to corner you last night, but you disappeared. Why'd you leave the party so early?"

"We dove today. I didn't want to stay out too late."

She gave me a knowing, concerned look. "That's the same sort of baloney Tomlinson tells us when he was sneaks off to see his mystery women. She has you on the hook now, too?"

In a marina community, well-kept secrets are as common as well-kept fences.

"Her name's Mildred Engle. She doesn't have me on the hook, and there's nothing mysterious about her. She's going to finance our salvage project—which means Jeth has a job."

Women are as territorial as men but more subtle. "No kidding? Then we'll finally meet her. She'll come to the marina and say hello to the friends of the men she's dating, just like any woman would do if she's got nothing to hide."

I was smiling, surprised by the heat of her disapproval. I said, "We're not dating. And I'm sure Ms. Engle will make an appearance some evening, eager for the Dinkin's Bay ladies to vote on whether—"

I stopped and turned, because I heard men arguing. Augie was standing nose to nose with Arlis, yelling at the old man. Arlis looked to be enjoying himself—maybe because a half-dozen fishing guides formed a semi-circle behind him.

I told Rhonda, "Mack should call the cops, and I need to get back to the lab."

The woman said, "Meet me aboard *Tiger Lilly* in an hour so I can take care of those cuts. I mean it. Or I'll come looking for you. Seriously, we need to talk."

Through the marina's office window, I could see Mack on the phone, already aware of what was going on. The fishing guides could look after Oswald and Augie until the police arrived.

I put my hand on Rhonda's shoulder and squeezed. "Make it half an hour."

It was nearly 8:30, and I was eager to knock on Chestra's door, tell her what we'd found, and say, "Okay, it's time for the truth. What happened the night of October 19, 1944? *Really.*"

32 I told Rhonda, "I don't know how old the woman is. And I don't understand why you're so concerned."

Rhonda had my head in her lap, a washcloth in her hand. She'd already snipped the stitches and pulled them out with tweezers. Now she was using the cloth to scrub the cut beneath my eye with Betadine, the two of us on a settee in the main salon of *Tiger Lilly*.

She replied, "JoAnn thinks she met her one night, walking on the beach. The big gray house that you couldn't see until the storm knocked the trees down? With the gray gables?"

I tried to nod, but she was holding my head tight.

"JoAnn said she tried to talk to her—this was right after the hurricane when everyone was chatty. JoAnn said the woman was pleasant enough until she found out Tomlinson was a friend. After that, it was like a curtain dropped. An *ice curtain*—JoAnn's words."

As I began to reply, she muttered, "This thing's not as long as the cut on your forehead, but it's deep. Almost to the bone and only an inch from your eye. Gad. The guy who beat you up did this?"

"He didn't exactly beat me up—"

"You don't have to lie to me. The story's all over the island. Then you got another knock on the head while you were diving?"

I said, "Minor. It doesn't hurt."

"Three severe blows to the head. A guy like you who uses his brains for a living. Minor?" She expected a response. Began to scrub harder when she didn't get it.

"Does *this* hurt?"

I said, "Yes! You could take varnish off wood, the way you're digging. It burns like hell."

"Good! Serves you right for behaving like a damn schoolkid. No"—she pushed my shoulders back when I tried to sit—"you're not going anywhere until I get you patched up. Afterward, you can help me decorate for tomorrow's party—out of gratitude."

"A party?" Friday was the traditional night for marina parties. Tomorrow was Sunday.

"Why not? We're making up for lost time."

A marina party hosted by the ladies of the *Tiger Lilly*. The first since the hurricane. Also the first I'd heard of it.

Tiger Lilly is a forty-one-foot Chris-Craft Continental, a wallowing, teak-and-mahogany hulk, party-sized and homey, which is how she's decorated: potted plants and Japanese lanterns strung along the weather bridge, full bath, staterooms fore and aft, stereo speakers all around. A boat that's rigged for socializing, not open sea.

A few years back, after a run of bad luck, the ladies had had a ceremony and changed the boat's name to *Satin Doll*. Things kept getting worse, however, until they reversed the ceremony, and it's been *Tiger Lilly* ever since. It's moored at the deepwater docks, Dinkin's Bay Marina, neighbor to a dozen or so other live-aboard vessels—houseboats, sailboats, and trawlers.

Four weeks earlier, there'd been twice that number.

Lucky.

Aside from a Danforth compass, the only navigational equipment aboard *Tiger Lilly* is a brass plate that points toward the ship's toilet. The ladies installed it as a precaution against confused and desperate drunks.

"Doc," Rhonda continued, her tone severe, "we worry about you. That's why I asked about your new lady."

I repeated myself patiently. "Mildred Engle is not my new lady," I said, and fought the urge to check my watch. I didn't want Rhonda to know that I was eager to get to Chestra's house.

She said, "It doesn't matter what you think. It matters what the woman thinks. You're a dear, sweet guy, Doc, but forgive me for saying this—you're pretty damn dense when it comes to women."

I wasn't going to argue.

"Same when it comes to fighting. That's just dumb. Especially with some low-life marina punk—we heard about the fight so don't even bother to deny it. Some freak named Heller? You don't think a jerk like that can't take one look and know you're the scientific type, not a fighter? That's what I'm trying to get through your head. You're an easy target for a punk like that to show off. And also for a certain type of woman."

Rhonda's hair was colored Irish copper instead of the usual brown . . . a stylish new wig. She was wearing shorts and a dark blue blouse that was buttoned one notch higher than normal. She's tall, heavy-hipped, and busty—busty until a recent illness, anyway.

She was one of the friends who'd been hospitalized.

Rhonda had been scolding me about the fight, fussing about Mildred Engle, but something else was on her mind.

Her encounter with cancer and the black void was recent. She deserved my patience.

Rhonda said, "You got about as many scars on your face as I got on my belly and boobs," She was done with the washcloth and opening a tube of antibacterial cream. "Get a few glasses of wine in me tonight, maybe we can compare."

"Tempting," I replied.

"I'd like to think you're serious. Since the operation, I'm worried you and other manly man types won't be interested. As if the hysterectomy didn't make me feel self-conscious enough."

Self-deprecating humor, typical of her. But it contained an underlying truth. A few months before, she'd found a lump on her breast. Her physician had removed the tumor after assuring her that the biopsy report could have been a lot worse. Rhonda had finished her last week of chemotherapy just before the hurricane.

"If you're serious," I replied, "I'll return with a long line of the manliest men who'd love to get a look at that body of yours. Dozens, probably hundreds. Me included."

"Hah!"

"Don't offer unless you mean it. There're guys on these islands who've been lusting after you for years."

"Really? That's a shock, because I've been lusting after a few of them, too."

I told her if that information got out, we'd have to build a new marina parking lot.

It's understood that the partnership between Rhonda and JoAnn is more than business. They've been dedicated to one another for years; confident in the way strong couples are confident. Which is maybe why they seem to get a kick out of discussing their occasional bawdy interest in men.

That interest wasn't always a ruse, either. As I knew.

Rhonda was laughing. "Good ol' Doc. You always know the right thing to say to a woman." She reached and opened a box of bandages. Began to sort through them. "That's another reason you've gotta take care of yourself. The summer's been shitty enough, we can't afford to lose you. Fighting like some teenager." She made an introspective noise of disgust. "After the storm, before the cops finally let us back on the island, JoAnn and me about got sick when we heard you'd stayed here, rode the damn thing out. Didn't know if you were alive or dead. Tomlinson, too—there's another man who'll never grow up. Crazy coconut-headed fools, the both of you."

Not quite accurate. Tomlinson hadn't been at the marina when the winds began to build. He'd used the flood tide to pole and wade his sailboat into the same tidal river where the fishing guides had moored several of Dinkin's Bay's larger vessels, *Tiger Lilly* included. He'd tied a spiderweb of lines to the mangroves, burned incense, then roped himself to the ship's helm and was meditating naked, he told me, when the eye passed over.

I was the only one watching as he sailed back into Dinkin's Bay under full canvas, the sunset an eerie green as the hurricane pulled the last of its funnel clouds northward. No other vessel under way for a hundred miles. Few human beings on the island, none at Dinkin's Bay. Standing on the broken decking of my roofless home, I considered the possibility that I might be hallucinating because of the recent concussion. Quite a vision; quite a night.

"You have a son to think about," Rhonda reminded me primly. "A new daughter, too. People who care about you, and rely on you to stick around. Who worry about some of stupid things you do."

As she said that, into my mind appeared the image of an adolescent boy, playing baseball in the jungle. Then a infant bundled in pink, her face an undefined space. It was the daughter I'd never seen.

Rhonda had unwrapped a butterfly bandage and leaned in to apply it. I took her wrist, stopping her. "Why is it I get the impression you've practiced this little speech? And you're not only talking about the fight. You're putting a whole lot of mysterious implications between the lines—"

I paused when the cabin door opened and we watched JoAnn Smallwood step into the salon.

JoAnn is a shorter, bustier version of Rhonda; she looked businesslike in stockings, dark skirt, and blazer. She was carrying a sack of groceries in one arm and the marina's resident cat, Crunch & Des, in the other. JoAnn and Rhonda exchanged looks as we exchanged greetings, and then JoAnn said, "You're having that little talk with him?" Expecting it.

"Just getting started," Rhonda said. She pushed my hand away and leaned toward me with the bandage.

Sounding like a tattletale sister, Rhonda said to JoAnn, "Guess who got into a fistfight? Got himself beat up. Look at how deep this gash is—thing needs stitches. Then he got clunked on the head today while they were diving that wreck—"

JoAnn said, "I heard. I heard," letting the cat drop pad soft on the deck and taking groceries to the galley. Began to sort items on the teak cupboard. Cheese, tortillas, coffee, toilet paper, party hats, candles, tonic water, wine. Cat food, too. The expensive kind in caviar-sized tins.

Which explained why Crunch & Des hadn't visited me at my stilt house for a while. A burly black cat with ragged ears and a white patch. It wasn't the first time he'd been lured away by better food.

"I told him what you said about the woman you met on the beach."

JoAnn replied to me, saying, "I hope it doesn't seem like we're being nosy, but—"

I interrupted, "Of course you're being nosy. But it's okay. Being nosy's one of the perks of friendship."

"Then I'll tell you what I think. I think there's something strange about that woman, if it's the same one. Slender, very elegant—even at night on a beach—but something . . . dated about the way she dresses. Even the way she talked. Some of the phrases she used. I'd guess her to be in her late sixties, so maybe that explains—"

I said, "Mildred Engle isn't that old. It must have been someone else," but knew she was talking about Chestra.

It allowed JoAnn to be less guarded. "I hope so. A woman who won't risk meeting a man's female friends? That's a danger signal. Always trust a woman's instincts when it comes to other women. The one I met is cold. The kind of coldness that's hiding something. So I'm glad it wasn't the same woman."

Her tone said she suspected it was.

They still weren't done with me. This wasn't just about Chestra, or the fight. What was on their minds?

I listened to JoAnn talk about how hot it was and that they needed to get a new air conditioner, the old one was so noisy, before she finally started getting to it. "Maybe we shoulda tried to talk some sense into him earlier, huh? Maybe he'd a thought twice before getting mixed up in a brawl."

"Probably should've," Rhonda said. "Someone needs to find out why our old buddy seems to have a death wish."

I removed the washcloth from my forehead and sat up. "Death wish? Okay, ladies, what's this about?"

Rhonda said, "It's about you staying in that rickety old piling house of yours when everyone else in their right mind evacuated the island. And it's about—"

"Hold it," I said, and began to explain that I'd been on a trip, returned late, didn't realize how bad the storm would be. But she cut me off, saying, "It's not just the hurricane, Doc. And it's not just you getting into a brawl—"

"It was worse than just a brawl," JoAnn put in, "a lot worse," her tone saying she had additional information.

"It's about the risks you've been taking," Rhonda continued. "At least, risks that some of us around the marina think you're taking. We're not stupid. We pay attention to what goes on in this weird little fishbowl of ours and some of us are worried. Worried about you."

I became more focused. Uneasy. Wasn't certain that I needed to respond cautiously but did. "Risks?" I said. "I don't know what you mean."

The women exchanged looks again, Rhonda's expression telling JoAnn to take over.

"Let me go down the list," JoAnn said. "A couple months back, you went for a cruise on the *Queen Elizabeth*. A guy like you on a cruise ship. Wearing a tuxedo, shopping in tourist dumps like Jamaica? No way. Then you come back with a big bruise on your neck like someone smacked you with a sledgehammer—"

"The *Queen Mary 2*," I corrected her. "There's nothing risky about that because she didn't stop in Jamaica. No one in their right mind intentionally visits Jamaica. Not me, not the *Queen Mary*. I took Ransom because she needed a break. Ask her, she'll tell you."

My Bahamian cousin, Ransom Gatrell.

"That's my point," JoAnn said. "We *did* ask her and she *didn't* tell us. Hardly said a word. You didn't, either, the both of you hush-hush, like you didn't want to talk about it. That woman, you're closer than brother and sister. She'll say whatever you tell her to say. But wait. I'm not done.

"A month or so before that, you took off to God knows where. South America, you said. But your tan was nearly gone when you got home, so I don't know where in the tropics that would be.

"A few months before, you came back from a trip with a big gauze bandage taped over the meaty part of your right side." She raised her voice when I tried to interrupt. "Don't deny it, I saw the dang thing. I was out for a walk and watched you taking a shower."

My outdoor shower has no curtain, but it's located at the back of my stilt house, out of sight unless someone's willing to stand in the mangroves off Tarpon Bay Road. Or arrive by boat, like Arlis.

"You watched me shower?"

"Only five minutes or so, yeah." In reply to my expression, she added, "Doc, almost every woman on this island has seen you showering at one time or another. Some nights, we could sell popcorn. As if you didn't know—but don't change the subject. Point is, you came back injured. Again. Maybe a gunshot wound, that was one of the rumors."

"A gunshot?" I was shaking my head, smiling. "Unbelievable. I didn't realize my pals had such good imaginations. No . . . I was diving off St. Martin. A biologist friend wanted my opinion on something, and I got sliced up by a chunk of coral. You can see the scar, if you want."

Which was close to the truth. I'd been cut—but not by coral. A knife.

I said it again, "A gunshot wound? Boy oh boy," then waited. Made an effort to appear relaxed, indifferent. I was worried that JoAnn and Rhonda had correlated the dates: When I left. When I returned. And that they had associated my visit to St. Martin with an incident that occurred while I was there. A small item in the national news: the unexplained disappearance of Omar Muhammad, prospective head of Abu Nidal, a fundamentalist terrorist organization.

Muhammad had vanished while snorkeling on a shallow reef off St. Martin. His body was never found.

I relaxed a little when JoAnn pressed ahead, saying, "Then there was the time you said you had to go to Key West for a few weeks, but I know damn well you went to Colombia or someplace like that, because Sandy Phillips mentioned she saw you at Miami International, the TACA gate, and . . ."

"We also know how Tomlinson makes his living," Rhonda cut in severely. "That's what we're getting at. I don't know why he didn't stick with his Internet meditation school, Ransom did such a great job setting that up. He was making plenty of money. Bought the Harley, and the cool minivan. But now he's back to importing and selling what everyone knows he's always imported and sold, and, well . . . Doc—"

"Doc," JoAnn said, "we love Tomlinson. You know that. But if that crazy old hippie has somehow talked you into helping him smuggle marijuana and God knows what else . . . sending you off to foreign countries to do the dangerous stuff while he hangs out here getting stoned and working on his tan—" The woman paused and looked at me. "Why are you laughing, Doc? What's so damn funny?"

After several more seconds, Rhonda said, "Doc. Stop it. We're not joking. Today, you show up with a fancy new yacht you say you got as salvage. We're not dumb. That's the sort of thing men buy with drug money. Now you've got Jeth involved?"

JoAnn said, "We know a lot of people are hurting since the hurricane. If you need cash, we can turn you on to some good investments. But smuggling is poison, and it's bad for Dinkin's Bay—"

Thin-lipped, Rhonda said, "He's not listening. I don't know why we're bothering."

I couldn't talk. I was laughing that hard.

33 I knocked on Chestra's door. No answer. Placed my ear near the window and heard music, the piano. I tested the knob. Unlocked. Considered sticking my head in and calling her name but decided I didn't know the woman well enough.

Instead, I took a business card from my billfold, and wrote, "We're in the salvage business. Back at 9. MDF," and wedged it at eye level inside the doorjamb.

I'd ridden Tomlinson's gaudy beach bike, which was now propped against a gumbo-limbo tree. From the basket, I took my foul-weather jacket and walked to the beach.

I'd spent the day on the water, but weather changes quickly in the subtropics and I wanted to have a look at the Gulf. At the lab, I'd listened to NOAA weather while connecting the flask-sized object and the gun-sized object to the electrolytic reduction circuit. The other artifacts—the German coins and the diamond swastika—were already cleaner, more detailed. The cigarette lighter wasn't much improved—the engraving only slightly more legible. Yes, the first letter was an M.

Marlissa?

As I worked, the computerized voice of NOAA told me that hurricanes near Grand Cayman and Cuba were gaining mass, moving slowly toward the Gulf. The low-pressure system off Nicaragua was spinning eastward toward open ocean.

The hurricane most likely to effect Sanibel had formed a week earlier near the Windward Islands as an unnamed tropical depression. It moved southeast near Grenada, then arched to the west-northwest toward Jamaica with maximum winds of forty m.p.h., vacuuming heat off the Caribbean Sea. The storm was now approaching the western tip of Cuba with sustained winds of more than one hundred m.p.h., and would gain strength once over water.

Only a month after being cross-haired by a category 4 hurricane, Southwest Florida residents were still panicky. The storm that hit us had had steady winds of 145 m.p.h., with gusts of more than 170 m.p.h. This new hurricane was following a similar path, and I knew that lines at supermarkets and gas pumps would be long tonight. By tomorrow afternoon, northbound lanes would be clogged with vehicles evacuating to Georgia and the Carolinas.

Panic triggers herd instincts. Government agencies, fearing post-storm criticism, are quick to overreact. It was a statistical improbability that another hurricane would make landfall near Sanibel. There was no reason to evacuate yet thousands would flee. It was more dangerous, in fact, on the road than to be battened down at home.

The dynamics of wind, heat, and water are indifferent to human thought, irrational or otherwise. But this storm now had a name. It was an entity that evoked fear. The instinct to appease by sacrifice, hording, or flight is ancient.

Traffic was already backed up on the island—which is why I'd come by bicycle. The causeway that connects Sanibel to the mainland had been damaged by the hurricane, so the Department of Transportation was closing it every other hour for repairs. Only emergency vehicles were allowed to cross between midnight and 6 A.M.

Islanders were running in advance.

Not Mildred Engle, though. She was unconcerned, content to play the piano while the world panicked around her.

A woman who loved storms.

I walked to the beach, feeling the thunderous resonance of waves. A tropical cyclone was breathing out there, siphoning heat, and exhaling a water-dense southwest wind.

As I walked, I reviewed details of our dive. What remained among the wreckage of the motor yacht *Dark Light*? Gold? I'd convinced myself I was imagining things. Gold on a family-owned boat that was being used by Civil Defense for coastal patrols? That was as improbable as . . . well, as finding a diamond-studded swastika and death's-head.

Maybe there *was* gold out there.

Something strange happened that long-ago autumn night, in 1944. *What?* Key parts of the puzzle were missing.

I stepped into the tree line, sand pliant beneath my jogging shoes, and stopped at the edge of the Southwind estate. The upstairs light was on, balcony doors open. Curtains moved in the wind like shadows dancing. I continued toward the house until I could hear Chestra at the piano. I recognized "In the Still of the Night."

I turned toward the horizon. The moon was masked by turquoise clouds. The sea was Arctic silver; ice ridges on an oleaginous plain. Inside me, music found tempo in waves as I tried to imagine what had happened the night *Dark Light* went down. I needed plausible data to assemble workable scenarios.

I thought the whole thing through; tried to keep it orderly.

Supposition: Unaware of an approaching hurricane, two people boarded a thirty-eight-foot Matthews, and ran a 240-degree course off Sanibel Lighthouse. They were investigating a report of suspicious lights sighted offshore, possibly a German U-boat. Coincidentally, there was also one or more boats in the area containing Cuban fishermen—several of their bodies washed ashore the next morning.

Conclusion: If lights were spotted, they belonged to Cuban fishing boats, or an unidentified vessel, a U-boat, or a combination of the three.

Supposition 2: *Dark Light* sank during the storm.

Observation: The boat went down quickly. Its remains were only a degree or two off the original heading. A vessel floundering in a storm commonly drifts miles before sinking.

Probability: *Dark Light* sank because of a circumstance or event that was abrupt, not cumulative.

Supposition 3: Aboard *Dark Light* were Marlissa Dorn and Frederick Roth, secret lovers. They also had at least minor business dealings. Dorn loaned Roth money to buy real estate. Both emigrated from Nazi Germany, so may have come into possession of Nazis medals that were: 1) awards for government service, or 2) acquired independently, perhaps because of their monetary value.

Probabilities: 1) Dorn and/or Roth were awarded, or acquired, the medals found at the wreck site. 2) The medals were placed on board by someone else. 3) Another person or persons came aboard *Dark Light* that night.

Supposition 4: The body of Marlissa Dorn washed ashore the day after the storm. Roth's body was never found.

Conclusion: Dorn died during the storm. Roth may or may not have died during the storm. If he did not die, he wasn't aboard *Dark Light* when it sank, or he found refuge aboard a vessel capable of surviving 140 m.p.h. winds in open sea.

Probability: A submarine.

Valid so far?

No.

The data was flawed; at least one of the conclusions implausible.

I stretched, and looked toward the house. Chestra was now playing the poignant melody that I recognized but still couldn't match with a title. I reminded myself to ask again. I also had a more important question: Was she sure her godmother's body was found on the beach near Lighthouse Point?

It had been bothering me on a subconscious level for a while. I now understood why.

Five hours earlier, when Augie and Oswald had been set adrift, they had been precisely where *Dark Light* had spent her last minutes afloat. By the time we'd found the two men, half an hour later, they had drifted more than a mile *away* from Sanibel Island, not toward it. If allowed to drift all night, I'd calculated they would've come ashore near Naples—forty miles to the south—or, more likely, they would have been swept out to sea, into the Gulf Stream.

Currents in the Gulf of Mexico are complex but tend to flow either northward or southward, interrupted by circular eddies that rotate like slow, underwater tornadoes.

Even driven by dissimilar weather conditions, the body of a dead woman would not have drifted directly east. She would not have come ashore near Sanibel Lighthouse.

If Marlissa Dorn's body had washed up on the beach on the morning of 20 October 1944, she'd either gone overboard when the thirty-eight-foot Matthews was only a mile or two off Sanibel—long before it sank— or she'd entered the water from land.

That presented a very different, and darker, scenario.

If Marlissa had fallen overboard, would her lover have continued his westward course?

No. Not if he wanted her to live.

Do rational people walk the beach, or swim, during a hurricane and risk being swept away?

No. Not if they value their lives.

Conclusion: Marlissa Dorn had either been murdered, or she'd died of misadventure that may have been storm-borne and accidental, or may have been invited by her own recklessness—a form of suicide.

I pictured Chestra energized by storm wind, indifferent to lightning strikes.

The music was still playing.

I turned toward the house and followed the path of silver sand.

Chestra was singing lyrics unfamiliar to me; lyrics that she'd written.

> *. . . the sun is on the sea*
> *In my mind, waves wash over me*

We'll never know
All that we possess
'Til the end of time
We can only guess

I stood near the piano, listening, the photograph of Marlissa Dorn on the table nearby. Chestra had yet to reply to the first of my pointed questions, but I couldn't bring myself to interrupt. She had a remarkable alto voice. Her interpretation was soulful, smoky, but understated; her lyrics, articulate. Tomlinson had described her music accurately: The effect was more than auditory, it was chemical.

Once again, I wondered: How could someone with her talent have slipped through life unknown?

Down a haunted highway
Wind in my hair
And the night is laced
With moonlight everywhere

Then I heard you whisper
Right in my ear
You have come this far
You can go from here

She tried to keep the last chord alive, her foot on the sustain pedal.

"Do you mind, Doc, if I play just one more? Music—I get carried away. It's my favorite mode of travel."

I said, "For now, let's stay where we are, okay? I'd like to talk." As she sighed, registering disappointment, I added, "Later, I'd enjoy hearing you play. It's still early"—I checked my watch—"not even nine-thirty. I thought you'd *want* to talk. That you'd be more excited we found your wreck."

"I'm thrilled. It seems too good to be true. I guess I'm still in shock."

She didn't act thrilled when I told her. She looked troubled. Something had changed in the last twenty-four hours, that was my impression. Something else: She became flustered when I said I'd heard a rumor about the Dorn family and a German POW.

"All families have their skeletons," she'd laughed, making light of it. But she escaped immediately to the piano after adding, "Guilt. It's the gift that never stops giving. Some legacy, huh, kiddo?"

When I said, "Then it's true?," she began to play, her furtive shrug saying: *It's a long story.*

Obviously, she hadn't told me everything.

She'd played a medley of her own work—impressive. But I was determined to get answers. "Chessie, tell me what you know about the night the boat went down. Everything." I held Marlissa's photograph up as if it might freshen her memory. "It was so long ago, no one cares anymore. What do you *think* we'll find on that wreck? You're investing thousands of dollars. *Why?* There's no need to edit your story."

Her fingers were long, and as elegant as her legs. They moved with a surgical certainty on the piano keys, independent of her body. As if reading my mind, she said, "I don't tell stories, my hands do. Fairy tales. Tragedies. I'm always a little surprised by their confidence." She lifted her eyes to mine without moving her head. "Does that seem strange?"

"I don't know. My hands aren't skilled."

"I'm astonished. Maybe you haven't found the right instrument yet. The truth"—chords she played transitioned to the melody I thought I knew but couldn't name—"you say that word like it's something final. *Truth.* It's the same when you ask questions. You're . . . so definite. So straightforward."

I replied, "The truth often is."

"I'm not so certain. I don't have anything against people who say they're searching for the truth. It's the ones who claim they've found it, I don't trust. There are people who go around trying to neaten up a disorderly world. Are you one of those men?"

"No. I'm one of those men who bumbles less when I know the facts."

She dipped her head toward the piano's music stand, where there was no sheet music. "Just the facts, ma'am. Okay. Musical notes are facts—

professional piano tuners adjust each note mathematically, did you know that? You don't believe facts lie?" She smiled. "Then we haven't been riding in the same elevators. And you've never heard karaoke."

It was impossible not to like the woman. It was also impossible to pressure her.

I said, "The title of the song you're playing. I've asked before, what's the name—" but she interrupted my question with a lyrical flurry, an introduction. As she sang, I listened attentively, expecting the lyrics to jog my memory.

They didn't.

> *Morning is breaking in New York*
> *Silver horns and a golden sky*
> *I see you, I need you*
> *Don't you ever say good-bye*
> *You're so tender and you're mine*
> *So I'll draw the dusty blind*
> *You are mercy*
> *And holy to me . . .*

> *Roof by roof*
> *Through corridor and street*
> *Room by room*
> *The chain of memory*
> *Make another face*
> *Another joke*
> *Another scheme*
> *'Til we are gone forever*
> *And free . . .*

When she'd finished, I didn't speak for many seconds. "That's lovely."

"Thank you."

"You wrote it?" I was contemplating the lines: "You are mercy/And holy to me." Pained but adoring. At one time in her life, Chestra had been in love with an extraordinary man.

She surprised me, replying, "Yes. I wrote that many, many years ago. It's about my first love—Manhattan." Her fingers found the keys again, softly. "I enjoy the anonymity of crowds, the sanctuary of strangers. Like a lot of people, I cling to the silly notion I'm having a love affair with that great big wonderful city because I wake up with it most mornings. *One* of us is a harlot, and that's all I'm going to tell you." Laughter.

"The song was never recorded?"

"No. I write for myself. And a few others."

"I was sure I'd heard it. That I knew the title but couldn't remember." I didn't add that it was more mystifying because the melody didn't resemble any well-known song.

"My uncle Clarence Brusthoff—he was the grandson of Victor Dorn, who built this house—my uncle Clarence liked to quote Thomas Edison about strange things like that. Knowing a person you've never met before. Recognizing a tune you've never heard."

I looked at the wall of photographs as she continued. "Edison and Henry Ford were both closet mystics. They believed the air was full of microscopic bits of knowledge. 'Entities,' they called them. Or 'little people,' left over from previous lives; other worlds.

" 'Ideas are in the air,' Mr. Edison told one of my uncles. Everything already exists; every idea, every event. It's all available to us if we're persistent, and allow it to happen. My uncle had asked Mr. Edison how he happened to invent both the phonograph and moving pictures. No human being had even contemplated such marvels."

It was a conversation that Tomlinson would enjoy.

I tried to get her back on the subject. "I don't know much about the entertainment business, but someone had to offer you contracts. Anyone who's ever heard you perform has to wonder why your name, your music, aren't well known."

She laughed again, swaying as her fingers pulled her along the keyboard. "I had a few offers, sure. Records, films. I wasn't a bad-looking gal, and I used my looks like a proper New York woman—which means I *never* exposed my breasts unintentionally. Recording my music, though, would have been like walking down Broadway naked. Same with Hollywood. No thanks." She laughed again. "Especially at this stage of life."

"Marlissa Dorn would've envied you." My eyes were moving from Dorn's photograph to Chestra's face, gauging the size of the earlobes, the nose, the full and swollen lips. "You turned them down. Marlissa never got her chance to accept."

The woman was thoughtful for a moment. Her music slowed, then stopped. She stood, closed the keyboard lid, and came around the piano, her hand out. She'd made a highball for me, a chartreuse and soda for herself. I put the drink in her hand.

"You're right, Doc."

"About Marlissa envying you?"

"No. About me leveling. There are parts of the story you don't know. It's time I came clean."

 "There are no photos of me on the wall because our families closed this house shortly after the war. Marlissa was involved in a scandal that caused quite a stink at the time. Made it awkward for them to remain in the area, so they boarded up the place, and seldom returned. Never again for a vacation.

"I have a few memories—the sound of waves, the weight of the air. That's all. I was a toddler, not old enough to make Southwind's photo museum."

I said, "They closed the house because of the scandal? Or because of your godmother's death?"

It seemed odd she didn't automatically mention the latter.

"Both," Chestra said, "of course. It was painful. The family was deeply upset by her death *and* the incident I'm talking about. That's why I didn't come straight out and tell you. My uncle Clarence is the only one still alive who's old enough to remember, but it's something even we don't discuss."

Chestra was wearing a black cardigan jacket tonight, pleated pants, and a white blouse with an antique emerald necklace. The bracelet was sterling silver; her watch gold, very thin. She'd closed the balcony doors—too windy—and we were sitting in the candle-dim dining room. On the table, she'd placed a Federal Express envelope and a leather-bound book, its gilded pages darkened with age.

The FedEx envelope, I noticed, was from a Wisconsin law firm. An attorney named Jason Goddard.

The book was Marlissa Dorn's diary.

I was eager to get a look inside the diary but let Chestra move at her own speed.

I was right, she said. The incident involved at least one German, maybe two. "I wasn't aware they were POWs," she said, "but that solves at least part of the mystery, if it's true."

A local man was also a tragic victim of events, she added.

She wasn't aware that Arlis had already told me the man's name: Peter Jefferson.

"There's something else I left out of the story," she said. "I didn't think you needed all the details until we were certain that you'd found the boat's wreckage." She took a few moments to wipe the condensation from the outside of her glass, staring into my eyes. She took a sip. "You *are* sure?"

I told her for the second time: "We found a wooden nameplate, one of the letters broken off—ARK LIGHT, it says. That and some bottles from the same era." I hadn't mentioned the flask-sized metallic object that Jeth had found but did now. The woman wanted to be convinced before entrusting me with family secrets. "The cigarette case that Marlissa's holding in the photograph, the one you told me you'd like to have? It's the right size. It could be silver, judging from the black patina. But don't get your hopes up."

She did. Her expression was intense for a moment, then became more guarded.

What was so special about a cigarette case?

I waited.

Chestra said, "What I haven't told you is, there may have been more than two people aboard *Dark Light,* the night she went down. There was Marlissa, Frederick, plus one or both of the Germans. My family never knew. No one did. Only someone who's read Marlissa's diary would suspect."

Chestra slid the book in front of me, the expression on her face expectant. I'd asked for the diary, now here it was.

"May I read it?"

The woman said, "You're welcome to try."

I opened the book. Leafed through the first few pages before opening to the middle, then skimming pages toward the back.

It was in German.

"She wrote wonderfully in English, but German added another layer of privacy. Beautiful women learn how to hide their secrets very early in life."

"You sound experienced. And cynical."

"I was never in her league. But I've walked into rooms of men where I felt like I was the bull's-eye behind every lie. An example of how men and women are different? My first husband worried that I'd embarrass him in public, or laugh at him. I worried that he'd hire someone to murder me. The dark side of beauty isn't balanced by the bright—people don't realize."

I was still leafing through the diary. The first entry was January 1939—her new life in America. The last entry was dated 19 October 1944—the last day of her life.

"Tomlinson speaks some German. And there's a retired German psychiatrist at the marina, Dieter Rasmussen." I remembered what JoAnn said about women who avoid a man's friends. "I can come back in my truck, if you'd like to say hello. You can visit my lab and see the nameplate, and the other stuff we found."

"And bring Marlissa's diary? No. I'll share it with you but no one else. It's my godmother's private life, Doc. Even though the woman is dead."

She reached. I handed her the book.

"I'll tell you the story as I know it. If you have questions, I can translate passages as I read."

On a night in late September 1944, Marlissa Dorn was walking near Sanibel Lighthouse when she realized she was being followed by two men. She began to walk faster, returning to Southwind, but stopped when one of the men hailed her by name.

Chestra had the diary open and began to read, sometimes haltingly as she translated Marlissa's own words. "I nearly fainted when I realize the man was H.G., whom I last saw more than six years ago. I met him at a dinner party hosted by [blank] at the [blank] several months prior to my ocean voyage.

"H. was infatuated with me. He pestered for weeks before I agreed to a social outing. It was to a film; a private viewing for a group of high-ranking officials, all much older than we. Later, he tried to touch my breasts. When I refused, he ripped my blouse. I think he would have raped me if I hadn't scratched his face and screamed.

"It was terrifying to see H. He's disgusting, and scares me. I hate it that he's in America and knows where I live."

Chestra lifted her eyes from the diary. She'd become emotional as she read, but now calmed herself by explaining, "I'm reading the code words as blanks. They would only confuse you. Marlissa has been my hobby for years, but there're still abbreviations and codes I don't know."

Marlissa met H.G. at a restaurant in Berlin, Chestra said. Her "ocean voyage" was code for sailing on the *Normandie.*

"She never identifies the second man, other than to say he was also German. They told her they'd escape the Reich, and needed food and a place to stay for a few nights while they waited on a boat to pick them up. They were on their way to South America to join other Germans who had turned against Hitler and were forming a government in exile. They said they were afraid U.S. authorities would mistake them for spies, so that's why they were in hiding."

"Your godmother believed that?"

"I doubt it. I wouldn't have believed it. The story would've made sense, though, if the men were escaped POWs. They had to explain themselves somehow."

Chestra said that Marlissa was staying at Southwind alone at the time, except for occasional visits from Frederick. She gave the Germans food and supplies but refused to hide them in the house.

I said, "If they were POWs, how did they find out where your god-mother lived? Six years without contact, in a different country, they meet

coincidentally? Even if that's what happened, why would she help a man who tried to rape her?"

I was getting that feeling again—Chestra wasn't telling me everything.

I added, "They were waiting on a boat that was going to take them to South America? If what the diary says is true, the night of the storm, they didn't go offshore looking for a submarine. They went to *meet* a submarine. The Germans had to have leverage to get that kind of cooperation from Marlissa and her boyfriend."

I was thinking: If Frederick was a Nazi spy, maybe they'd threatened to expose him. I was aware that, during WW II, every foreign spy caught on U.S. soil had faced a firing squad. The sentencing process was not lengthy.

The woman's eyes were glassy, alone in some distant place. After a moment, she said, "The answer is here in the diary. Yes, they had a tremendous amount of leverage. They also had a gun."

The Germans had been watching this house, Chestra said. Secretly. They knew that Frederick sometimes visited late at night. They also witnessed something that Marlissa didn't want anyone to know. Especially Frederick."

Marlissa had been experimenting with other men.

Chestra stood and motioned me to follow. There were more photos to see.

Marlissa Dorn wasn't made for the 1940s. She was a freethinker, outspoken, uninhibited.

"In those days, women had to pretend to follow the rules or they were ostracized. Sometimes crucified. Marlissa lived a secret life. A lot of strong women did."

Frederick was one of her secrets. Her friend Vincent was another.

Once again, we were standing at a wall covered with photographs. I was looking at a shot of Edison and Ford, the two surprising mystics, as Chestra said, "It was only a few years ago—I was reading some book about the history of Sanibel—that I realized who Vincent was. Marlissa mentioned the name so often in her diary. 'Vincent has composed a hilarious poem. Vincent has such brilliant ideas about politics, and social reform.'

"My godmother was very impressed. Vincent influenced much of her thinking about women's rights, racial equality. Morality, too. Vincent was . . . open-minded. Marlissa was already too opinionated and free-spirited for women of that time. Vincent encouraged her."

Chestra pointed to a photo. Vincent was Edna St. Vincent Millay, the internationally admired poet and Pulitzer Prize winner. It was the photo with Frederick in the background, holding a towel. The poet was wearing the flapper's hat, smoking a cigarette, staring into the camera with her fierce, intelligent eyes.

"Vincent's husband, from what I've read, was as open-minded as his brilliant wife. All that puritanical nonsense about sex being sinful, dirty, and about women being subservient to men. Vincent lived the way she wanted to live. Sanibel was her escape."

According to Chestra, the diary contained no hint the women had a physical relationship, but Millay's opinions and open lifestyle validated Marlissa's own instincts.

Marlissa's sensuality was more than skin-deep, Chestra told me. "She was never promiscuous, but she did experiment once or twice with other men—what could be more natural for someone like her? A young, healthy woman alone in this house, with the beach, the moonlight? What is it about the tropics, Doc, that makes sin so delicious?"

I said, "Maybe it's the baggage people leave behind," before asking if Frederick was as open-minded as Millay's husband.

"She never told Frederick. She couldn't. Besides, it wasn't another man she wanted. It was the experience; the fun of it. Sex is healthy, we know that now. Marlissa believed it then. You're the scientist—sexual activity changes our brain chemistry somehow. It keeps us young. She was decades ahead of her time."

Marlissa also experimented, Chestra said, because it was a freedom she'd never experienced.

"Imagine what it's like to be pursued relentlessly. Your every move watched by men who want more than your body, they want to possess you, even your most private thoughts. No woman can live up to the expectations of that kind of beauty. To chose a partner on her terms? That was freedom. Enjoy sex because *she* wanted it, that was the allure. But it had a price."

Chestra read from the diary. "Tonight, H.G. threatened me. *Blackmail* is the word in English. He saw P.J. enter the house three nights ago. It was an innocent visit; he's an old friend of the family, and often does yard work at Southwind. No matter. H. somehow knows I've strayed, and is threatening to inform. I would rather die than hurt my dear Freddy."

On the wall was a photo of two of Chestra's great-uncles posing with an alligator they'd apparently killed. In the background was a good-looking man with shoulders, and a saddle brown face. He wore bib overalls; looked to be in his midthirties. It was Peter Jefferson, Chestra said.

The next entry in Marlissa's diary contained the news that someone had gone to Jefferson's moonshine still, poured liquor on the man, and set him afire.

Once again, Chestra read. "I know it was H.G. I rejected him. He despises me because of it. Only he has that much hatred and evil inside. I am lost as long as he is here. Maybe lost, now, forever. Poor, poor, dear Peter."

Chestra closed the diary. "For years, I assumed everyone aboard died the night *Dark Light* sank. I was wrong."

A year and a half ago, she said, her uncle Clarence Brusthoff's office received a letter from a Wisconsin attorney, saying he represented an admirer of Marlissa Dorn.

"It was from the same law firm that sent this"—she indicated the FedEx envelope—"but it was from a different attorney. Not an attorney named Goddard."

I didn't understand why that was significant but let her talk.

In the first letter, the attorney wrote that his client was terminally ill, and wished to include Marlissa in his will. If Marlissa was no longer alive, the bequest was to go to Marlissa's oldest living female heir—provided she meet certain terms.

I said, "You?"

"That's right. This house was deeded to my uncle's company after our families stopped vacationing on Sanibel. It paid for itself many times over as a rental. My second husband died ten years ago, and I began coming here, always in October, and always alone. It's like heaven to me. A little less than two years ago, though, when Uncle Clarence's business was in trouble, and it seemed real estate couldn't go any higher, the house was sold to a Florida land company."

Marlissa's anonymous benefactor bought the estate. There were conditions to the man's bequest.

"If I lived in Southwind for six months," Chestra said, "the house would be available to me for the rest of my life. I wouldn't own it. The estate would remain deeded to my benefactor's company, which was responsible for taxes and normal maintenance. So it was better than owning it, in a way.

"It was a gift of time, not property. Those were the terms. My uncle thought it was some kind of horrible con. I was suspicious, but I can't resist adventure. I adore this place, plus I had to find out who my godmother's secret admirer was. It was a mystery! What did I have to lose?"

I said, "It's an unusual gift."

Women employ delicate understatement when dealing with topics they believe men are too naïve or insecure to handle. It's part survival mechanism, part kindness. "Doc, it might surprise you some of the gifts I've been offered during my lifetime. Some of them from men who were supposedly friends of my husband.

"I was offered the deed to a villa in Majorca if I agreed to spend a month there each winter. I've been offered the use of private planes and apartments. A gentleman once showed me a magnificent eighteen-carat emerald pendant on a chain of Mayan gold. He said it was mine if I would spend the weekend with him in Paris. Instead, I spent the weekend with his wife, helping her shop for his anniversary present.

"In comparison, the only thing unusual about this gift was that I couldn't keep it. But at least there were no strings attached."

Through her uncle's attorney, Chestra accepted. A Sanibel real estate agency that specialized in rentals opened the house to her and gave her the keys.

"Uncle Clarence brought boxes of family pictures; put them up personally to make this old gal seem like home again. The poor man wept as he hammered away. That was in March. I returned here last month, after the hurricane."

Her benefactor died around the same time, and his name was finally revealed.

"It was Frederick Roth," Chestra said. "I couldn't believe it. That's why I want to find out what's among the boat's wreckage. If there are no human remains, it tells me that maybe my godmother's lover really did survive. I'm not being made a fool by some elaborate hoax.

"But it also leaves a terrible hole in what I've always thought of as a beautiful, romantic story. If Frederick loved my godmother, why did he leave her? The first letter was addressed to Marlissa—he didn't know she was dead. Why did he never return? It was such cold behavior for a man who was so gentle and decent.

"Yesterday, this arrived, addressed to me. From the same law firm, but signed by Jason Goddard." Chestra touched the open FedEx envelope. "They know I'm her only heir; we had to get that straight before I moved in. Have a gander. I'm still in shock."

> *Ms. Mildred Engle, As executor for the estate of the late Frederick Roth, and acting on Mr. Roth's wishes, I write to make amends for a regrettable oversight. Many years ago, Mr. Roth borrowed money from Ms. Marlissa Dorn and purchased several hundred hectares of Florida real estate, much of it waterfront. In good faith, Mr. Roth signed promissory notes, using properties he'd acquired as collateral. Due to circumstances, my client never satisfied these debts, nor paid interest on monies due.*
>
> *Many of these properties are still titled to Mr. Roth's Florida land holding company. It was my client's desire to leave this world with a clear conscience, and so I write to inform you, as Ms. Dorn's heir, you may be due reasonable compensation. You may have claim to some assets associated with the company which owns real estate worth in excess of nine hundred million dollars.*

The wording of the promissory notes, signed by Mr. Roth, is important, as well as date stipulations, if any. It's my understanding that you are in possession of these documents. Please notify me when and if you have them available. You will then be contacted at this address by a company representative.

This representative is a trusted family member, personally selected by Mr. Roth. It was my client's hope that you two will engage in private negotiations, on behalf of a man and woman who were once friends, and thus avoid the complex legalities and expenses involved.

The letter was signed: Jason Goddard, Executive Assistant to Frederick Roth.

I asked, "Do you have the promissory notes?"

Chestra had been pacing nervously, using her scarf to carve the air. "Yes. I'm sure I do. But not here. They're in New York, although I can have a friend ship them down. I'm not so sure I should, though."

"Why?"

"Do you see how the letter's signed?"

"Yes." I still didn't understand the significance.

"The man Marlissa writes about in her diary, H. G. Goddard, begins with a G. Don't you see? His name *could* have been Goddard. Don't you find it frightening? Frederick Roth and H.G. on the same boat that night. Now both names reappear so many years later . . ."

I watched her twirl the scarf, aware that she was omitting information. Was she being unreasonably fearful, or did she somehow know H.G.'s last name?

Her expression became hopeful when I said, "Goddard and Roth are both common names. It can't be the same man. A Wisconsin attorney? There's no way—" I was interrupted by a determined knocking on the door below.

I waited as she descended the stairs, then heard her call, "Doc!"

It was Tomlinson. The instant I saw the stricken look on his face, I knew something was wrong.

Javier Castillo, he told me, had been shot and killed. His body found floating near Indian Harbor Marina.

35 The EMTs and medical examiner's people didn't leave with the Cuban's body until after sunset, and it was nearly eight by the time the cops finished questioning Moe and Bern. They'd kept the men separated, interviewing them in unmarked detective cars that smelled of plastic and electronics.

The cops wouldn't tell them, but a local fisherman said the Cuban had been shot in the meaty area just under the arm near the armpit. Not a bad place, if there's help around, but the Cuban had headed for the water for some reason, trying to escape through the mangroves, and bled to death because the bullet nicked an artery.

Before the cops had arrived, Bern had said to Moe, "Tell the story *exactly* as it happened. Only difference is, when the black guy jumped out of the boat you thought he had a gun, so did I. You fired a warning shot, the guy maybe stumbled and fell. We're not sure. It was dark. He ran off. We searched for a while before I called the cops."

Moe was feeling better about things after reading the newspaper article four or five times. He said, "We thought Javier had a gun, and we were standing our ground."

"Damn right we thought he had a gun. The asshole already threatened to shoot somebody if he didn't get his boat."

"The warning shot—did I fire it into the ground or up into the air?"

Jesus Christ, Bern knew running backs who were smarter than this guy.

"You hit him and *killed* him. So why don't you say you shot in his *direction*. At his feet, maybe, wanting to scare him. You shoot up in the air, and what? The bullet comes straight down, hits the guy on top of the head, and comes out his armpit? Back there in French Lick, I'm thinkin' babies get dropped a lot. Your doctors must be missing fingers; some kind of genetic deal."

It was eight-thirty now as Bern walked into his condo and noticed the FedEx package from the old man's assistant, Jason Goddard, on the desk. He still hadn't opened it, and thought: *Why not?* His luck was improving— one witness dead, one witness to go, and a new self-defense law that seemed custom made for Bern, considering how many times Moe had nearly killed him.

The Hoosier's time was nearing.

He found scissors and sat.

Inside the FedEx package, there was a cover letter that stank of mothballs, just like the tight-assed attorney who'd sent it. Bern didn't bother to read the thing. He went right to the contents, two more legal-sized envelopes, which he ripped open, staring out the window at the sky, which was graphite streaked with orange and pearl.

He stopped for a moment. He could see darkness beyond pools of security lights—empty docks, the canal, and a hollow-looking space that he knew was the bay. Something was missing from the deepwater seawall.

Where the hell's my boat?

He'd been so busy dealing with cops, he'd forgotten about Augie and his butt-buddy taking the Viking out to go scuba diving. They should've been back a couple of hours ago. Unless Augie had decided to stop somewhere for a drink, brag about what a hotshit he was in the fancy boat that he didn't own, and that—Bern was just deciding this—Augie would never ever use again in his life.

Bern needed that boat in case his luck hadn't changed, although he was pretty sure it had.

A moment later, though, after he'd leafed through the contents of the first envelope, he whispered, *"Shit,"* and dropped the papers on the desk.

Maybe his luck was the same. Still bad, getting worse.

Written in his grandfather's shaky hand: "Bernie, I kept a file on your recreational activities. I recommend you cooperate with Jason."

Bernie. Jesus Christ, he hated that name.

Attached to the note were copies of dozens of newspaper clippings: the *Milwaukee Journal,* the Madison *State Journal,* the *Baraboo News Republic,* and several weekly papers.

The clippings dated back to Bern's troubled adolescence, one headlined:

BARABOO TEEN EVALUATED
AFTER ASSAULT WITH HAMMER

It was not surprising the old man had kept the article. He held grudges for a lifetime, so why not keep them in a scrapbook like scalps?

The other clippings were more troubling:

ASSAULTS PLAGUE BARABOO PARK.
COPS HUNT RAPIST DUO

These were from his high school and college days; a time when he was first experimenting with a game a buddy of his called Caveman. They'd walk in from the backside of Devil's Lake State Park—a popular place for campers; neckers, too—and hang out along the Ice Age Trail, a famous Wisconsin nature path where granola munchers loved to hike. Around sunset was the best time: pretty, with the lake in the distance, trees on rock ledges above. Wait for some doper girls to come jiggling along and introduce themselves.

If the doper girls were friendly, he and his buddy would have fun. If they weren't, they still had fun. Grab them by the hair—like cavemen— and pull them down the hill to a place where they already had a blanket laid out and a couple of six-packs of beer.

How did the old man know it was him?

Spooky.

One clipping was headlined: LOCAL AUTHORITIES SEEK OUTSIDE ADVICE. It said an FBI expert on criminal profiling had been invited to Baraboo to help decipher a pattern in the timing of the assaults. Bern remembered reading this story, and thinking: *Uh-oh. Time for the Cavemen to hit the showers.*

His grandfather had circled the headline in red, and scribbled: "Idiots never checked local football schedule!"

Bern thought about that for a moment. What did playing Caveman have to do with football? Well . . . maybe the old man had something. They'd started grabbing girls when summer two-a-day practices ended, and went to the park only on weekend nights they didn't have a game.

By then, he and his buddy were being referred to as "the Devil's Lake Stalkers." Funny. All fired up on steroids, with no practice, no game, and tons of boyish energy to burn.

Once, a couple of local cops stepped out of the bushes as they entered the park; said they were staked out, waiting for the rapists, and wanted to ask a few questions. Bern's buddy—a defensive end who later started all four years at Grinnell—told the cops, "This is quite a coincidence, officers, we looking for those bad boys ourselves. If they're lucky, you'll catch 'em before me and my man Bernard get our hands on 'em," speaking in the funny way black guys did.

They spent the next hour with the cops, talking football, telling them Baraboo could beat any high school team in Milwaukee or Madison, bring them on.

That was their last visit to the park.

Bern took the time to read one of the articles and nearly smiled. "Descriptions of the stalkers are consistent in that both men are described as 'huge,' but otherwise vary greatly. Victims have described both as 'white, Hispanic, Afro–American, and Asian.' "

Bern was thinking, *Not even close,* as he tossed the article aside.

There was another packet of Xeroxed clippings, these more recent.

MILWAUKEE POLICE SEEK SERIAL RAPIST

There were several like that. But there were also stories about assaults that took place in Appleton . . . Sauk City . . . Prairie du Chien . . . that Bern wasn't involved with. No association whatsoever.

Just like the old bastard to blame him for crap he didn't do.

Bern couldn't say the same about stories in the *Miami Herald* and the *Tampa Tribune.*

HOPE FADES FOR MISSING GAINESVILLE COED.
MOTHER OF TWO DISAPPEARS FROM MALL

They gave him a chill. He'd never meant it to go that way. But sometimes shit *happened.*

The old man had circled a paragraph that read, "A witness who encountered the suspect prior to the student's abduction described the man as 'gigantic' and said he had a distinctive regional accent. Police believe the suspect left so many clues, they will be able to identify him soon."

On the clipping, his grandfather had written: "Stupid amateur!"

What did that mean?

Bern opened the second envelope, thinking: *She's been in that oil drum nearly a year and not a soul's come snooping. What's so stupid about that?*

Inside the second envelope, sent by the old man's personal assistant, were copies of handwritten bills of sale that were similar to the ones Bern had found in the foul-smelling briefcase. All dated between 1939 and October 1944, and attached to legal descriptions of land his grandfather had bought.

Stole, more like it, judging from some of the prices.

Wait . . . that wasn't fair. The old man was a sadistic bully, sure, but his business skills were hall of fame. He was tough, foresighted, shrewd—qualities Bern had yet to demonstrate, but hoped they were lying dormant somewhere inside.

He read a few of the bills of sale.

For a parcel of land, 22 acres more or less, running from the bayside of Marco Island to the beach, legal description attached, sale is hereby consummated in consideration of payment of $1,750 cash . . .

How much would an acre of Marco Island beachfront sell for today? Millions.

There was a bill of sale for three acres, "bay to beach," on Captiva Island—$600. Seven acres on Siesta Key—$350. Ten acres Clearwater Beach—$1,300.

Today, these three properties alone would be worth sixty, seventy million dollars. There were more receipts for acreage he'd purchased, fifteen . . . no, twenty-three more bills of sale. All beach or bayfront, with the exception of twenty-six acres he bought in Orlando—June 1943—lakefront acreage, cost: $2,145.

The company still owned the parcel, had yet to develop it.

The old man had sold some of his holdings to capitalize his developments. But there was still a lot of raw land in the portfolio. Bern made a mental note to look next time he was at the home office in Appleton. He had every right to do it. In fact, the bozos at the home office might as well get used to him poking around. As long as the company remained solvent for two years—actually, twenty-three months and counting—fifty-one percent of the Florida land company would belong to Bern. Plus, he'd get back his personal assets, which he'd signed over, so he had a vested interest.

Which was no big deal. He hadn't played long enough in the NFL to get part of that rich profit-sharing pension. His little piss-poor retirement savings from Gimpel's, some Cadillac stock, combined, worth around fifteen thousand dollars. Shirley had a collection of Hummel figurines she claimed was worth fifty or sixty thousand—maybe true, if God dropped everything else and zapped Michael Jackson knickknack crazy—and they still had ten years left on their home mortgage.

Before moving to Florida, Bern wasn't worth much. Stick it out another year, though, stay out of the Hoosier's line of fire, and he'd be wealthier than a lot of quarterbacks who owned car dealerships and restaurants.

Nothing too hard about that. Right?

Bern picked up Mr. Mothball's letter, the one enclosed with the bills of sale, not the cover letter. He knew right away it was trouble from the way it started.

Jesus, now what . . .

Bernard, This is confidential. If you can't honor that, please review the enclosed envelope containing newspaper clippings which are representative of a file your grandfather kept . . .

Here we go.

I have disturbing news regarding the corporation's Florida land company, your contractual employer. A woman claims to have promissory notes signed by your grandfather dating back to 1939. If authentic, they may cloud titles of real estate holdings worth many millions. Copies of bills of sale are enclosed . . .

Shit!

Bern threw the letter down, went to the fridge and got a Grolsch beer, green bottle, porcelain stopper. He opened the beer, poured it into a quart glass, and drank half of it, getting that cold hops taste from the bubbles.

He scowled at the letter as he finished the beer—*Sonuvabitch!*—then went to the fridge for another before returning to the desk.

> *. . . the woman's name is Mildred C. Engle. She is the heir of Marlissa Dorn, who was an actress, and said to be one of the great beauties of her time. I received your phone message inquiring about a photo in your possession. It was taken of Ms. Dorn in 1938, prior to her arrival in the United States . . .*

Perfect. He finds out the old bag's name now, when he's too upset to think about sex even with a *young* woman. Bern reached, retrieved the photo from a stack of papers, and looked at the woman's face again, her smoldering eyes.

Marlissa Dorn, huh? She couldn't have been much of an actress. He'd never heard of her. Which was probably why she was screwing the old man. Money.

He dropped the photo and continued reading.

No. Just the opposite was true . . .

> *From 1939 to 1944, while living in Florida, your grandfather and Ms. Dorn were friends, and hoped to marry. During this period, Ms. Dorn loaned your grandfather small sums of money to purchase real estate that only he, at the time, recognized as valuable. In the autumn of 1944, however, your grandfather discovered Ms. Dorn had been unfaithful, and he left Florida soon thereafter. He did not attempt to contact her until he returned to the United States in 1955, by then happily married to your grandmother . . .*

So, the old man *was* screwing the movie queen—until he caught her screwing someone else. That, at least, was interesting. But did Jason have to lay out his grandfather's life story before telling Bern how, exactly, he was getting it up the butt again, compliments of the old man?

Bern chugged the beer, slammed the glass down, and skipped ahead to the second page, skimming key passages.

. . . unaware of Ms. Dorn's death, and we could find no record . . . most prom-issory notes contain a payoff date, but these were "interest only" notes, a kindness to your grandfather, it seemed at the time . . .

. . . statutes of limitations do not apply to undated notes . . . even without con-siderations of interest due, attorney fees in a case that will go on for years . . . Our company losses could be in the millions . . .

Sadly, we wouldn't be in this position if your grandfather had not attempted to make amends for the unpaid debt prior to his death, and do what was just and ethical . . .

Okay, finally, Jason was getting to the important part. The little twerp always started with some outrageous lie before kicking you in the teeth— probably hoping to get a smile. The old man had never done anything just or ethical in his life.

. . . when your grandfather realized our acquisitions department had, coinciden-tally, purchased the estate where Ms. Dorn had once resided, he contacted her fam-ily anonymously, through this office. He offered her heirs free use of the beach home until the company sold or developed the property. It was a magnanimous gesture, made by a dying man who wanted to do the right thing . . .

Bought the property "coincidentally"?

That was a laugh. The acquisitions department consisted of only one per-son who had any say: Frederick Roth. If he bought the movie queen's house, it was the gesture of a dying man who wanted to fuck her over because she'd fucked him over. Screwing her heirs was close enough—the old man's way of tidying up accounts prior to moving along to his own corner of Hell, where he'd probably already been promoted to an executive position.

But how was he screwing them over, letting the movie queen's family use the place for free? Bern continued reading.

A few weeks ago, Ms. Dorn's heir, Mildred Engle, upon learning your grandfa-ther's identity, contacted me about the promissory notes. Instead of being grateful for his generosity, she threatened legal action. Ms. Engle wants compensation equal to the current value of properties purchased with Ms. Dorn's money.

If Ms. Engle can produce the original promissory notes, many of the company's titled assets will be clouded. I feel we should consider dissolving the company in advance, and thereby making our assets less vulnerable . . .

Dissolve the company.

Fuck!

Bern's was hyperventilating, his heart pounding. Dissolve the company and he would lose his job, his inheritance, his savings, his car, his home in Wisconsin. Everything.

That ruthless, miserable bastard.

Forgiveness is for people who don't have the balls for revenge—one of his grandfather's favorite sayings. But Bern, hounded by his slob of a wife, had gone ahead and signed the contract anyway.

How could I be so goddamn dumb?

36 Bern spent a moment punishing himself by revisiting the old man's traps in orderly succession: the offer of a job, a big salary, the contractual guarantee that he'd inherit fifty-one percent of the company if it remained solvent for two years after his grandfather's death. The requirement that he and Shirley sign over their piss-poor savings to a company worth several hundred million dollars . . .

Now this.

Bern balled his fist and hit himself on the side of the head. Really fucking dumb, that's how dumb he could be. He'd been suspicious of his grandfather's generosity from the first. The grandfather who Bern, at the age of thirteen, had tried to kill by sneaking up from behind with a ball-peen hammer. The grandfather who, more than once, referred to him as "a failed experiment," and "an embarrassment to the race." But he'd gone ahead and accepted the deal anyway.

Bern was thinking: I am fucked. I *am* an embarrassment to the race.

He'd probably been adopted from some half-wit floozy, courtesy of a little town in southern Indiana where he was related to a whole population of village idiots, including his long-lost retard brother, Moe.

Bern turned his face to the ceiling and screamed, "Why are you doing this to me?!"

He stood, knocking over the chair, lifted the beer mug and shattered it against the wall. Marlissa Dorn stared at him from the table. He was about to lose everything because of this woman's relative, some lawsuit-happy bitch named Mildred Engle. Bern grabbed the photo, balled it into a wad—*You whore!*—and hurled it at the window.

His hands were sweating.

He felt a roaring pain in his head. Bern paced for a few minutes, and got another beer, before he took the letter and finished reading.

Jason wanted him to contact the lawsuit-happy bitch and attempt to negotiate a settlement. "Treat her with respect, charm her if you can," the twerp suggested. Bern had until the family's Appleton Christmas reunion. That would give the board time to agree on the best method of dissolving the company.

> We must have the original promissory notes. Without them, Ms. Engle has no claim. She lives on Sanibel Island, Gulf Drive, at an estate named Southwind . . .

Bern crumpled the letter and punted it like a football—and damn near fell on his ass, he was so furious.

Perfect.

Oh, he'd charm the bitch, all right. She was threatening to ruin his life with some damn old pieces of paper? An introduction to a game named Caveman, that's what the woman needed. Have an oil drum open and ready, the Viking packed, waiting to cruise to his own private island. Get the woman naked, all worked up, then jam her in the barrel while she was still alive . . .

Bern stopped, head cocked, then looked out the condo's front window. A small boat was coming down the canal, no lights. Looked like a mullet boat.

The mood he was in, he *hoped* it was somebody coming to rob the place. He got his Luger, checked to see if it was loaded, and rushed outside ready to shoot the shit out of whoever it was. Say the wrong word, give him any lip at all, and *bang.*

Turned out to be Arlis what's his name, the old man they'd just fired, bringing Augie and his worthless butt-buddy, Oswald, home from Dinkin's Bay.

The Viking must have broken down or run out of fuel.
Why else would the little shit need a ride from Sanibel?

Arlis Futch was a perfect example of someone who got his rocks off being negative. The old man sat by the seawall in his shitty-looking mullet boat, laughing like a loon, while Augie told Bern that the nerd biologist, Ford, and his Dinkin's Bay buddies had stolen the Viking from them.

"Did you call the cops?" Bern asked.

Augie was in a smart-ass mood after a long day on the water, almost drowning, and also aware he was being laughed at. Old man Futch had been riding his ass relentlessly for the last hour. "Call the cops and tell them what?" he asked Bern. "Tell them that they salvaged the same boat legally that we salvaged *illegally*? Fuck 'em. They stole the Viking from us, I'll steal it back. I've got a spare set of keys in my condo."

Bern didn't grab the snotty little brat, or slap him as he had before. He stepped and raised his left hand, causing Augie to flinch, then hit him in the face with his fist, a crushing overhand right that busted the kid's nose flat, opening flesh cheek to eye.

"You oversized bully. You son of a bitch, you hurt him!" Trippe Oswald, the bubble-butted twerp, showed some spunk for once, kneeling beside Augie, who hadn't moved except for a muscle spasm that was causing his right foot to twitch.

Bern was still furious, having just learned that everything he owned was about to go down the shitter because of promissory notes in the possession of some old lady. Now Augie was telling him his last hope of escape, the Viking, was gone?

"Where's the key to Augie's condo? Don't lie to me, you little fairy, where's he keep it?"

Oswald didn't answer, he was so scared.

"Goddamn you, I am about at the end of my rope. *Where?*"

Bern grabbed Oswald by the T-shirt, the German Luger in his hand now, the gun he'd grabbed thinking the boat with no lights coming down the canal was a robber, wanting to shoot somebody. Anybody.

Oswald formed words. "All our shit's on the Viking, man. Keys, wallets, everything. It wasn't our fault!" Bern drew back the Luger as if to pistol-whip him. "But there's another key! At Augie's condo, the key to the door's hidden under a flowerpot! The boat key is somewhere in his room."

Bern wanted to shoot the disgusting little snitch. But old man Arlis Futch was there, still watching and laughing. Probably for the best, too. Knocking Augie unconscious would be tough enough to explain at the Christmas reunion in Appleton. But then killing his boyfriend?

That kind of talk, an ex–professional football player didn't need.

Instead, Bern smacked Oswald aside the head with the pistol. Not hard, but the snitch went down like he'd been poleaxed, looking like he was unconscious but was faking it.

The old man thought that was hilarious.

Bern swung the pistol at Futch and held it there, taking aim. The old man saw it but continued to laugh. *Forced* himself to laugh for a while longer so Bern could see that if he stopped, it was only because he wanted to.

Arlis Futch stopped laughing a moment later, and said in a low voice, "Go ahead and shoot, you fat fuck. Being old's a lot scarier than dying. You'd be doing me a favor." And meant it. Sounding like he had been a serious hard-ass in his younger years.

Then said, looking at the marina docks, all the boats sitting near the collapsed barn, "You shot and murdered Javier? I heard about it on the VHF. *Did you,* you fat asshole?"

Bern was thinking: *I squeeze the trigger, then tell the cops the old bastard was attacking me.*

But two corpses in one day?

That would only produce more trouble, more bad luck, which was typical of all the negative crap he'd been dealing with lately.

The old man wouldn't shut up. "If it turns out you murdered a fisherman, what you better do, *boy,* is pack your shit and run back to whatever hole you crawled out of. Don't be surprised if someone torches this place in the next few days. The way I picture it, you'll be tied up inside one of the buildings when we light the match. All that fat you got, I bet you sputter!"

A very negative guy, this Cracker fisherman. Scary, too, for an old man.

Bern left Arlis Futch in the boat, and Oswald to tend to Augie, while he drove his Beamer to Augie's condo. The place was a mess: crushed beer cans, ashtrays, porno DVDs. Bern found the keys to the Viking in Augie's room. He looked around: a king-sized water bed, half the closet filled with Oswald's clothes, some weird-looking stuff in a jar by the night-stand.

He also found several FedEx envelopes, addressed to Augie from Jason Goddard. It appeared that Augie received a package every time Bern did—but different stuff inside, cover letters included.

An example:

> . . . *confidentially, your great-grandfather asked me to send his personal effects, along with his reassurance that your inheritance will be substantially increased once your uncle, Bernard Heller, is proven incompetent. Once our board is convinced . . .*

So . . . the little bastard had been sabotaging him all along; Jason, too—which explained a lot.

The promissory notes were mentioned. They were real, not bullshit. Soon to be in the possession of the old lady who was living on Sanibel. None of this too surprising.

In another FedEx envelope, though, was a major shocker—as shocking as the passport that verified his grandfather was a Jew.

The envelope contained yet another passport, plus a letter. They confirmed his grandfather *wasn't* a Jew.

Bern took the passport, and all the papers—screw Augie, screw Jason Goddard. Let the whole family know the truth. Spring it on them at the Appleton reunion and watch their faces. See how many would be surprised.

Bern's guess: Zero.

The next morning, Sunday, Bern went to church before kicking back to watch the Packers play Cleveland, mostly so Shirley wouldn't call and have a reason to bitch at him, but also because he decided it wouldn't hurt to try to change his life by being more positive.

This run of bad luck was getting scary. He'd awoken in the middle of the night, his heart pounding, feeling as if he was suffocating. His world was collapsing around him, so maybe thinking positive would help.

His football coaches had often said that: Think positive. *Visualize.* Surround yourself with positive people.

There. That was another possible cause for all this trouble. He was surrounded by negative people.

Moe, being an uneducated redneck, was not a positive thinker, even though he knew it was a role business types were supposed to play. Augie, his own nephew, had been stabbing him in the back all along. His grandfather? Whatever the opposite of positive was (negative wasn't strong enough), he was that to the umpteenth degree.

Evil. That came closer.

Bern went to the Lutheran church in Cape Coral, the one on Chiquita, although he actually wanted to attend Temple Beth Shalom, which was closer, in fact, because it was off Del Prado.

Wanted to attend Temple despite finding out the truth about his grandfather: He not only wasn't Jewish, he had been a card-carrying Nazi, one of the elite. A Nazi medical student and research assistant who, in 1944, saved his own skin by catching a Swiss freighter to Miami.

Finally, something that *really* did explain why the old man was such a world-class asshole.

Good to know. But also kind of disappointing.

The last few days, Bern had gotten into it—the idea of being Jewish. Reading the history, finding out they had some famous athletes—even an all-time great list that he, as a former All Big Ten lineman, might have had a shot at. So he thought, screw it, he'd go to Temple anyway, no one else knew the truth, plus it was yet another way to get back at his grandfather.

Temple Beth Shalom, however, was closed on Sundays, according to the nice Jewish ladies who were there setting up for a charity bake sale. Quite a surprise, but it made the religion even more attractive, Saturday being a more logical day to worship because Sunday, of course, was when the NFL played.

It was a positive start to the day.

All that week, Bern worked at it. Staying positive. Visualizing. He even wrote down a list of goals. The promissory notes—he *had* to get those. They were his only protection. Jason Goddard and the corporate directors could fire him, dissolve the land company, but it wouldn't matter if Bern had the loan promissories in his possession.

Those old loan contracts were all the leverage he needed.

That meant several trips to Sanibel Island to check out the lady's residence, Southwind. Which he did, and got his first look at Mildred Engle. Goddamn, she was better looking than he expected. A *lot* better looking.

Sanibel—that's where the Viking was, too. Handy. More positive visualization: him on the Viking, water nice and calm, sailing off to an island where there wasn't so much pressure he woke up at night, gagging for air, thinking he was having a heart attack.

Staying positive meant waiting patiently until the Sanibel lady had the papers in her possession—they were being shipped down from New York, according to Jason. It meant visiting Augie in the hospital, acting like he was sorry he'd busted the asshole's jaw. Which he wasn't, but it gave Bern an opportunity to inform Augie that if he squealed to Jason, he, Bern, would tell the family about Oswald and the sleeping arrangements at Augie's condo.

Staying positive also meant keeping an eye on Moe. Not only was Moe a very negative person, even for a redneck, he was also a very *weak* person.

On Monday and Tuesday, cops showed up unexpectedly at the marina, saying they wanted to ask the Hoosier "just a few more questions." Moe was so scared his hands shook when he tried to light a cigarette.

Moe left work early those days, Bern noted, probably so he could find a good parking spot at the Sandy Hook and start drinking early.

On Thursday, cops arrived at the marina once again, but this time didn't ask to speak to Moe, who wasn't around, anyway. Plainclothes cops. Bern watched them stroll around the marina property, pausing an uncomfortably long time near the hill where Bern had seeded grass after burying two fifty-gallon drums containing women who hadn't been worth the little bit of fun he got out of them.

Shit.

Talk about scary.

On Saturday, Moe called and asked Bern, "Did you hear about the hurricane warning? I'm gonna stay home today and help the girlfriend board up her windows because of the storm. Trailers don't do good in storms, and she's nervous. It's supposed to be here Monday night or Tuesday."

Using his friendly voice, showing a smile, Bern had replied, "Your fiancée's residence? You do whatever it takes to make sure that young lady's safe. We want our administrative people happy, meaning *you,* mister." But thinking that Moe was lying again. It had been storming nonstop for nearly ten days, so what was the big deal?

They call this place the Sunshine State?

All it ever did in Florida was rain and blow until about noon, which is when the ground heated up like a sauna bath.

Bern reminded Moe that commercial fishermen were saying the storm wasn't going to be bad; that TV stations were full of baloney, telling people to evacuate when there was no reason.

Moe said he wanted to board windows, anyway—sounding more nervous than his trailer-trash girlfriend could have possibly been.

The Hoosier was telling the cops stuff, that's what Bern was afraid of. Maybe the truth about the Cuban. Maybe the truth about what was to be found packed in oil if authorities dug in the right place.

Bern tried to stay positive, though. Went to church the next day, Sunday, second week in a row.

On Monday, the last week of September, Bern decided there was yet another positive step he should take. Something that might give him peace of mind. He'd get Moe alone and find out the truth.

27 September, Monday
Sunset 7:20 P.M.
Full Moon +1 rises 7:25 P.M.
Low tide 6:47 A.M.
    Tropical storm headed our way, but weakening.
Maximum winds, 40–50 . . .

Chestra told me, "For the last week, I've had the feeling I'm being watched. Have you ever had that feeling, Doc?"

I said, "Yeah. When someone's watching me."

She laughed, sitting at the piano, and continued to play. We were settling into caricatured roles, as new friends do, our differences providing safe avenues of familiarity. I was the intractable realist, she was the urbane dame, expert at the social arts, but also an artist.

"I'm serious. It's that eerie sort of feeling, like there are eyes floating around behind you in the darkness. I went for a walk on the beach last night and I would've sworn someone was watching me from the trees." She was making light of it but serious. One of the maxims of recognizing danger is that, when instinct tells us something about a person or situation feels wrong, it is.

Maybe something *was* wrong. The night before, I'd noticed a big BMW sedan pass her drive slowly once, then again. I hadn't mentioned it.

Now this.

"If you want, I can go out and have a look. Any idea why someone would be watching you?"

"Ten years ago, *sure*. These days, though . . ." She shrugged, still having fun with it but troubled.

"I'll start keeping an eye on your house. Most nights, I go for a run, anyway, or ride the bike. I won't bother you; no need for me to stop. If it'll make you feel better, that's what I'll do. Oh—and start locking your doors when you go out. As a precaution."

I was already making nightly visits to the dock where the Viking was moored—Jeth believed someone had snuck aboard, went through ships papers, and possibly stole some things. The boat was nearby, close to the lighthouse. Adding Chestra's house to the list was no trouble.

The woman said, "Knowing that you're keeping watch. Yes. Yes, I *would* feel safer," not smiling now. "But, Doc? You are welcome to stop. Any night. Or every night." There was a candelabra on the piano, six flickering candles. Her eyes locked onto mine briefly, gazing through the light with a smoldering focus. It had been happening more often during the last week—an abdominal sexual awareness, even though, intellectually, I knew it was absurd.

It was true the woman looked taunt and fit. It was true, as Tomlinson said, she seemed younger as I got to know her. When the light was right, the age difference was more than manageable—she was lovely. But I had done some reading about the aging process. One of the papers was titled "Multidisciplinary Approach to Perceptions of Beauty and Facial Aging." It was written by a plastic surgeon, and it presented a mathematical graph model for aging. The shapes and sizes of our faces change, but some facial elements do not. I was confident I could guess Chestra's age within three or four years.

No. The age difference was not manageable even if she were interested—a signal that, if sent, was too subtle for me to be certain.

Still . . . there were times the woman exuded sensuality that was as tangible as a low, vibratory tone. Especially when she was at the piano. Years ago, she'd been offered a Spanish villa in exchange for the intimacy of her body? I didn't doubt it. I knew I had to maintain a distance or risk doing something impulsive that would embarrass us both.

It surprised me that, at times, it took a conscious effort.

D o you mind waiting just a few more minutes? I've got one little chord difficulty I've got to iron out, then I'll sing the first verse for you, if you like."

I was sitting at a desk opposite the balcony, reading while she worked on a new song. From the Sanibel Library, I'd gotten a book on military war medals, and also a couple of books about Nazi Germany, 1944, and the federal bank, or Reichsbank, in Berlin. I told Chestra I had seen something golden in the bowels of the wreck and asked if there was any mention in Marlissa's diary about valuables carried aboard *Dark Light*.

There wasn't, but Chestra offered to help with research. She was also helping with the legalities of salvaging the boat. Her family owned the vessel, according to maritime law, but there were still papers to file and an insurance company to contact. That's why we'd been spending evenings together—six of the last eight nights. It also gave me a chance to update her on items we'd recovered from the wreck, which she enjoyed.

The electrolytic cleaning process was slow, but it was working. The gunshaped object I'd found was in terrible condition, but enough remained to identify it as a German Luger.

The initials on the cigarette lighter looked like MC, followed by a letter that would possibly never be readable. Even so, Chestra was visibly moved when I brought the lighter for her to see, carrying it in a Plexiglas container of sodium hydroxide.

She was convinced it had been Marlissa Dorn's.

Because I didn't want to risk disappointing her, I hadn't yet told Chestra that the flask-sized object Jeth found was silver. It appeared to be an ornate cigarette case, similar in size to the one Marlissa held in the photograph. Much of it was still covered by a sulfide patina. However, there was already a design visible on the case, and a portion of an engraved initial, too. I had Tomlinson take a look, and he said the design resembled a medieval cross.

That didn't sound like something an aspiring actress would carry. But the initial might be an M—I would soon know.

"The lyrics aren't quite right yet, and it may sound a little rough in parts. Are you sure you don't mind?"

Glancing up from my book, I told Chestra, "Sure. I'd like to hear anything you've written. Take your time."

She brightened, began to play louder. I continued reading. We had followed the same routine for the last several nights.

Pleasant. A relief, too, because of a growing tension at Dinkin's Bay, and other marinas in the area.

It had been six days since Javier Castillo's funeral.

J avier's funeral had been a miserable day of rain and weighted gray inferences. The sound of a storm wind is not dissimilar to the sound of fatherless children weeping.

The hurricane that had caused thousands to evacuate the area had stalled for days over Cuba, sopping the Pinar del Río region. It'd waited until most of the evacuees returned home before rolling down the middle of the Gulf of Mexico, sweeping the Sanibel area with heavy winds and more rain.

On the day of the funeral, we learned there was yet another tropical cyclone gathering strength off the Yucatán. The news added a sense of foreboding to an already dismal day. The relentless storms had come to feel like retribution.

They also made it impossible to make our second dive on *Dark Light*.

At the cemetery, there was a big turnout, close to a hundred people. The rage Mack had mentioned was in attendance, too. Javier had been one of fewer than two dozen full-time fishing guides on the islands, employed by a half-dozen marinas. Unlike some areas of Florida, the guides here are a brotherhood, ready to help when one of their members is in need. The same was true when it came time to bury a colleague.

During the service, the guides gravitated into a tight little group, Jeth and Nels among them, sun-hardened men, their dark faces hollow-eyed in the rain. They were out of work. Out of money; some still homeless. The storm had exposed institutions they'd trusted—insurance agencies,

FEMA, banks—as cold-blooded adversaries, indifferent to what was equitable. Now one of their favorite members had been killed trying to claim what was his, a symbol of their trade, a workman's boat.

Rage was in them. It radiated from a casket epicenter.

The man who'd shot Javier had not been arrested. In fact, he was being congratulated in local letters to the editor. The marina that had stolen Javier's boat still had his boat, plus a couple hundred others. Law enforcement did nothing. Government did nothing.

Arlis was at the funeral, and I heard him mutter, "Forty years ago, that marina would of burnt to the ground, accidental-like. A man who murdered a fisherman trying make a living? He'd have burnt up with it. Who's the law when there ain't no law? Some damn storm? And we got another hurricane coming!"

Tomlinson and I had exchanged looks. Burn the guilty, sacrifice the unfaithful. It was a subject we'd been discussing. More than a month before, he'd described an epic storm as cleansing. Like celestial light. On recent nights, over beer, we'd debated his claim's validity or silliness. There was so much conflicting stuff in the news. Some religious groups said the relentless weather was Florida's punishment for attracting fun-loving sinners. Political groups blamed the storms on the indifference of their political opposition. There were academics who believed we've screwed up the biosphere so badly we were finally paying the price. Radio talk show hosts said the weather had nothing to do with global warming, and, in fact, proved there was no such phenomenon.

When destructive events occur in series, instinct demands that we assign blame, and the standard is always human based. After a season of famine or storms, mountain gorillas and dolphins do not instinctively make blood sacrifices to mitigate fear or guilt. We do.

I told Tomlinson that we blame ourselves because we're terrified of the truth: Life is random. There is cause, but there is no design.

Tomlinson stood fast. "There's *always* a reason. By assigning blame, we actually *accept* blame." It was a form of sacrifice, he said.

Usually, that's about as close as we come to agreeing.

I was reading about Nazi gold as Chestra worked on her new song. She would play a few slow chords, humming softly, then stop, make a notation on a yellow legal pad, then return to the keys. It gave the impression that creating music was a combination of architecture and artistry.

The music was backdropped by wind gusts and surf. The moon was full, and through balcony windows I could see trees wild in the wind, branches writhing.

Another bright and stormy night.

The tropical depression that had formed off Yucatán had drifted northwest, vacillating between a category 1 hurricane and a tropical storm. In the Caribbean Basin, a far more dangerous cyclone—the twelfth of the season—was already hurricane strength, with a well-formed eye. It probably wouldn't be a threat, but we wouldn't know for a week or two.

The tropical storm, though, was headed right for us, but it hadn't rallied mass or intensity. Now only a day or two away, maximum winds were fifty m.p.h., and the system was weakening. Even so, people were evacuating, lining up to buy gas they didn't need and canned foods they'd probably never eat. The reverse was also true: There were people who would do nothing no matter how much warning they were given and no matter how violent the storm.

Chestra, as usual, was unconcerned. She left her shutters open, as if inviting the storm inside. My home and lab were still boarded up from the previous hurricane, my generator fueled and ready. I was content to sit and read.

> . . . as German troops stormed Europe they looted bank reserves and took the gold to Berlin. Victims of the Holocaust were robbed of gold jewelry, even gold tooth fillings. All gold was melted, then recast into bars imprinted with the mark of the German central bank: an eagle clutching a swastika in its talons, and the words *Deutsche Reichsbank*.
>
> By 1944, high-ranking Germans realized the war was lost. The president of the Reichsbank ordered the country's massive gold reserves to be

secreted to the village of Merkers, south of Berlin, and concealed underground in a potassium mine. The mine was also used to store art treasures looted from conquered nations.

The village was captured by the U.S. Third Army commanded by General George Patton, and the door to the mine was blasted open. Inside, troops found 8,198 bars of gold bullion, plus gold coins and silver bars. The total value today would exceed a billion dollars.

Also, at least nine tons of gold were sent to Oberbayern, including 730 gold bars, thought to be hidden around Lake Walchensee. Some fell into the hands of U.S. GIs.

Few realize that the United States plundered Germany's assets as an official strategy of the war effort. Today, several thousand paintings from Germany are stored in a vault at the U.S. Center of Military History. Joseph Goebbels's 7,000-page diary resides in the Herbert Hoover Library . . .

On a smaller scale, many U.S. enlisted men—particularly those in supply and procurement units—figured out that it was easy to box up treasure they plundered and simply mail in back to loved ones via U.S. transport ships. Or carry it with them in their liberty bags. It's estimated that Nazi gold and artifacts worth many millions left Germany in this way. Little of it has been accounted for . . .

"Doc? Do you mind? I'd like to play this for you now. It's the first song I've written in . . . well, forever, it's been so many years. It's only the first verse and refrain, and it still needs work, so don't expect too much."

I closed the book. "I'm an easy audience because I'm already a fan. But can I ask a question before I forget? Did Marlissa have any friends or family who were U.S. servicemen during the war? Men who were close enough they'd trust Marlissa to keep a secret."

"Well . . . I suppose so. I'm not sure. Nearly every able man served in the military."

"What about your uncles?" I had seen photos on the walls of men in uniform.

"Yes. They were all Navy men, except for Uncle Clarence. He was in the Army. That's why Marlissa lived here alone during the war years. They were all active duty, but I don't think any of them served overseas. Of course, there were lots of soldiers and airmen stationed at bases around the area. Marlissa did USO volunteer work—she had no shortage of admirers among the troops, I'm sure."

I was thinking it through. Even if a GI had mailed Nazi plunder to Florida, what was it doing aboard the boat that night?

"Why do you ask?"

"I'm still trying to account for the diamond insignia we found. Unless Roth or your godmother bought it, how did it get aboard? Gold, though, that might be easier to explain, if it's there." I tapped the book. "According to this, small-scale smuggling was common in 1944. If soldiers found something they wanted, they boxed it and shipped it back to the States."

"Kiddo, I'm no expert on the war years in this area. The person who'd know more is Arlis Futch. You should ask him."

I said, "Yeah, Arlis, he's quite the talker." Then added softly, "How do you know him?"

Chestra laughed and shook her head, scolding me because of my tone. "You silly man—you are so suspicious. You told me about the old guy who ran the boat when you found *Dark Light*. That's the name you mentioned, Arlis Futch. Remember? You *don't* remember. Doc? Are you having one of your bad headaches again?"

The night before, I'd asked her for aspirin, and told her why. My head was pounding, but I said, "No, I'm fine." I was looking at her, still thinking about it. Tonight she was wearing a blue sequined vest over an ankle-length gown of paler blue. Her blond hair was down, framing the symmetry of cheeks and chin. It made her look younger.

I changed the subject. "Why don't you play? The first song you've written in years? I'd be honored."

"All right, I will. It's not finished, so be gentle."

She had made a drink for me, rum and soda, with juice from a whole fresh lime and lots of ice, in a large tumbler. I sat back comfortably, hearing the wind outside. When she began to play and sing, though, I heard only her.

Sit here next to me
Tell me what is real
Part of you I see
You try to conceal.
Do you have a secret place
Too dangerous to touch?
Still my beating heart
Loves you so much.

Through the world we spin
To come back again
The seagulls glide
The endless tide
And my body's yours
Safe and warm
In my dreams.
Still my beating heart
Loves you . . .

When she ran out of lyrics, she continued to play for a while before saying, "I finished only the first verse and the refrain. What do you think?"

I said, "Play it again, would you mind? Please." I was aware that I'd spoken so softly it was almost a whisper.

As she began to play and sing once more, I stood, left my drink on the table, and walked to the piano. It was not a conscious movement. Tomlinson was correct. Her music was hypnotic.

I waited several long breaths after she'd finished before I spoke. I had no idea why I was standing so close to her. "The lyrics. Is there a person . . . a man? Was there a man you're writing about—?"

She turned. Her shoulder brushed my thigh as she looked up into my eyes. Her right hand knew the keys and continued playing only the melody as she half sang, half spoke the words. "Do you have a secret place/Too dangerous to touch?/Still my beating heart/Loves you so much." The music stopped. Her shoulder was a weighted warmth. "Yes. There is a man. It's you, Doc. Of course it's you. You must know that. Are you offended?"

"No. But the meaning of the lyrics—"

"It's what I see in you. It's what I feel. There's something in you that's dangerous. Not mean, not vicious. But dangerous. Am I wrong?"

I didn't reply.

Her hand moved from the keyboard to my lower back. Her cheek made brief contact with my trousers just above the thigh, close enough to feel her breath as she spoke. "You're not the only one who looks for the truth inside people. You've been so busy trying to figure out what's real, what isn't, you didn't realize I was taking a look inside you, too. When a person's heart is bigger and stronger than most, it's usually because their secrets require so much space."

My hand had found the back of her head; my fingers already seeking, then massaging, her neck. Her fingers moved to the muscles in my lower back, each fingertip alive, intuitive.

Silence can imply a question; it can also refuse an answer.

I removed my hand from her neck abruptly, and said, "Chestra, I've got to get going. I . . . I have to see Tomlinson. See Tomlinson about a business matter. I want to hear the rest of your song next visit. Okay? But I've got to go now."

"I've upset you. I hoped you'd be flattered. I'm sorry; forgive me."

I was moving away, motioning for her to stay seated. I knew my way to the stairs. "Forgive you? There's nothing to forgive. Really."

There was an undertone of loss, but also resignation, when she replied, "Of course. We're friends, it's not necessary." She tried but failed to be the glib hostess as she added, "I'd forgotten. There are only two sins that women are never forgiven: infidelity, and aging. Anything else, there's no need to ask."

She laughed.

I hurried to the door.

38 I stepped outside into wind and shadows, immersed in salt-dense air as I walked the bicycle toward the road— then stopped. There was a truck parked at the drive-way entrance, no lights.

I stood for a moment, watching beneath a moon that was cloud-shaded. Moonlight flickered as if through a ceiling fan. The pickup truck had oversized tires, and chrome vertical exhaust pipes. Paint, dark. Windshield, tinted. When a car passed behind it, though, I could see a large person sitting at the wheel. Big, block-shaped head. A man.

I took out the palm-sized tactical light I carry when running or biking at night. It's a Surefire, military design, special-ops issue. Shine it in someone's eyes, it's as blinding as a flashbulb. I was about to point it at the car when the porch light came on behind me. Chestra—being thoughtful.

Maybe the driver finished his phone call, or maybe he was watching the woman's house and the light spooked him. Whatever the reason, the truck started and spun away, its engine making a distinctive NASCAR rumble. It was one of the expensive pickup trucks, all the options, I guessed.

A BMW doing slow drive-bys, then an expensive pickup truck tonight.

If Chestra's house was under observation, it wasn't by petty thieves. It was someone with money.

It caused me to think about the old promissory notes. She'd kept them in what she called "Marlissa's trunk," at her Manhattan apartment. A neighbor had shipped them. They'd arrived today in a box. Chestra had yet to hear from Frederick Roth's family representative, and mentioned that she had left a message for the attorney letting him know she'd done what he had asked.

Potentially, the notes were valuable.

She felt as if she was being watched? Now a vehicle in her drive, sitting in darkness.

I didn't like it.

I considered going back and telling her about the truck. Decided it would only scare the lady. And, frankly, I didn't trust myself. The axiom that it's painful for men to go without sex is an adolescent gambit. I hadn't dated for several months, but that wasn't the reason. I didn't trust myself because the pheromone wave I'd just experienced was unsettling. The woman's voice was mesmerizing, true, but how could someone her age have that effect on me?

No, I wasn't going to risk it.

Instead, I pulled the bicycle into the shadows and waited. Maybe the truck would return. Or do a drive-by. The big moon was behind clouds, so it took me a moment to realize that I was in the family cemetery. I had leaned the bike against a crypt. The leading edge of the Yucatán storm was miles behind me, the faint flare of lightning too dim for reading.

I waited for nearly ten minutes for the vehicle to return before using my little flashlight.

The crypt on which I'd rested the bicycle was inscribed:

NELLIE KAY DORN
CAME INTO THIS WORLD JUNE 9, 1868
WENT TO HER LORD JUNE 7, 1935
A BEAUTIFUL WOMAN AND RIGHTEOUS

I lingered as I studied the vault next to it. Placed my hand on the cold marble and leaned with the flashlight:

MARLISSA ARKHAM DORN
BORN FEBRUARY 7, 1923, VARGUS, AUSTRIA
DIED OCTOBER 19, 1944, SANIBEL ISLAND, FLORIDA
WHOM THE SEA GIVES UP, GOD EMBRACES

I'd seen photos of these women when they were young, stunning, full of life. Strange to be standing so near yet eternally removed. I remembered Chestra saying, "No woman can live up to the expectations of Marlissa's kind of beauty."

It was a touching observation; also, a telling insight. Beauty is a genetic device: trickery that instigates competition. All illusions are temporal, and death is as indifferent as life. What Chestra said was indisputable.

Someone had placed fresh flowers at the feet of both vaults. The man in the truck?

More likely, it was Chessie.

I was restless, my head was pounding, streets were empty because so many islanders had evacuated, and even the University Grille was closed.

Ten o'clock on an autumn Monday, full moon glowing, and Sanibel was like a ghost ship—moored, but felt as if it might break anchor in the wind.

I wasn't ready to go home to the lab, and I wasn't ready for bed. The Shop'n Go on the corner was an inviting fluorescence, but the idea of stopping at a convenience store because I wanted companionship was deflating. Instead, I pedaled hard along the bike path, Tarpon Bay Road behind me, the flower power beach bike creaking beneath my weight. I headed toward Captiva, mangroves to my right, then passed the dump created to burn storm debris, smoke and ash swirling. The wind freshened. I rode through pockets of sulfur-heated air, beneath trees; spooked a mother raccoon, a line of hunchbacked babies trailing.

Tomlinson's Dinkin's Bay Rum Bar and Grille was a mile ahead, on the left, at the intersection of Rabbit Road. A big tiki-shaped stucco building, the outside painted with tropic foliage, a parking area of brick pavers. There were lights on, silhouettes of people inside.

Normally, I'm happy to be alone. Tonight, I was elated to see a fellow human being. No luck, though. It was Big Dan, Raynauld, and Greg just closing the place, in a hurry to get to their homes so they could finish boarding windows.

Tomlinson had left an hour ago, they told me. They hadn't exactly asked him to leave, but they were glad he had. He'd been going from table to crowded table, wearing his weird goggles, and prescribing various drinks depending on the customer's aura. Sounded like Tomlinson was having a restless night, too.

I rode on. Over a wooden bridge, then passed the elementary school, its playground and ball diamond more silent because of the implicit laughter of children. I stopped for a moment to look at the moon through clouds. Blue light in the moonlight.

I turned, and returned to Dinkin's Bay. No one stirring at the marina, either. The approaching storm had chased most of the residents to the mainland. Boats with dark windows creaked on their lines; bait tanks hissed; halyards tapped in the wind. The bay was black but for the twin yellow eyes of lighted portholes on an old Morgan sailboat.

No Mas.

Tomlinson was awake.

I rode home, got a six-pack of beer, and started my skiff.

Aboard his boat, without an audience, Tomlinson is Tomlinson, not the ever-happy hipster people have come to expect. Tonight, he was more staid than usual, sitting at the settee berth, brass oil lamps and patchouli sticks burning, reading a book on the history of Islam.

I suspected it was the book that put him in a restrained, thoughtful mood, although he told me, "I was at the rum bar tonight and got weirded out, man, because I realized that just being who I am weirds out a lot more people than it used to. No matter how straight I get, the world manages to stay a little straighter."

"Maybe you're so far ahead, it just seems like you're behind," I offered.

"Um-huh. Wouldn't we all like to think that."

I ducked going down the three companionway steps, put the beer atop the icebox, starboard side, and told him, "I have a mystic-mental image of you going from table to table, wearing your Kilner goggles, telling customers to drink rum if they have green auras but stick to beer if they're red. A kind of vision. It just came to me."

He smiled and played along. "Very perceptive. Accurate, too. You're definitely into a whole new sensitivity trip. Soon, you'll be feeling actual emotions, Doc. *Human* emotions. The real test? That classic film, *Old Yeller.* I predict it'll get a sniffle out of you yet."

I was wearing my foul-weather jacket. It had begun to sprinkle while I was in my skiff. Light rain in a gusting wind. I hung the jacket near the aft quarter bunk, then adjusted the cockpit door, kerosene lamps fluttering, as I replied, "Nope. I always pull for the wolf. The one that's got rabies and wants to bite the nice-looking kids."

"You stopped by the bar?"

"Yeah. Dan and Raynauld told me about you prescribing drinks. Sounded like a good idea to me."

"Yeah, well . . . I think it scared some people, and everyone's already nervous because of the weather. I was surprised the restaurant was busy, so many people have split."

He sighed, irritated.

Occasionally, irrational behavior troubles the man. He was troubled now.

"Folks are packing their cars and running. Why? We'll get thunderstorms tonight. Wind's supposed to be fifty knots tops. Tuesday, it'll be a little worse, but so what? That's no reason to leave homes, shut down businesses. I put out a couple of extra hooks and laid in some emergency bags of weed. *That's* preparation, man. Everything else is just hysteria."

The news media had gone hurricane insane, he added, intentionally exaggerating information. I took a seat as he talked about it, finishing, "Fear sells. Every news story is a variation on journalism's favorite cliché: the apocalypse. But they're screwing up the economies of whole cities, and I'm not even a capitalist, man. They're screwing with people's lives!"

Was that tea he was drinking?

Yes. Green tea in a ship's mug. Something else added, possibly, but maybe not. He was uncharacteristically cogent for this time of evening. Yes, getting straighter and straighter while I, as he claimed, was becoming more in tune with . . . something. I have learned not to ask.

Tonight, though, I did not feel like the reasonable, rational man I attempt to portray. So maybe he had a point.

Tomlinson stood, took a can of beer and offered it to me. "No. Tea's fine. Or nothing."

"Your head's killing you, man. I can tell. Your eyes get glassy. A CAT scan is what you need, amigo."

"Do you have one aboard? If not, please drop it."

"No. But I can get you something that'll help."

I said, "I'll take it." I thought he meant aspirin. Instead, he shrugged— *Okay, if that's what the man wants*—and removed the teak cover from the icebox.

I watched him stick a bony arm into the icebox, and retrieve a plastic bag bulging with what looked like oregano but wasn't. I'd seen this ceremony many times. When he lit up, I would go outside. Or we both would.

I never smoke. Not even cigars.

As he took out rolling papers, I said, "I've always honored the unspoken agreement you and I have about women we date. We don't risk embarrassing them by sharing details."

"We have an agreement about that? I thought we were both just being sly."

"It's a small island."

"That's true," Tomlinson said. "The only drawback of living on an island is that resources are limited. Particularly around bar-closing time. Men's paths are bound to cross. That's the crass version, anyway." He had separated two papers, now somehow joined into one. "The way we honor the ladyfriend deal, yeah. It's very cool."

"I'm talking about Chestra."

"I'm aware of that. Are you asking me if we made the beast with two backs?"

"Maybe, but don't answer yet. The effect she has on me when we're alone is abnormal. Even if she's fifteen years younger than I think she is, it's still not normal. I'm trying to figure it out."

"The age thing, yeah, man. It's one of your hang-ups, I know. When you found out Hannah Smith sometimes treated old Arlis to the lady's Triple Crown, you said it was disgusting. So maybe karma's taking you down this road for a reason."

"Distasteful" is what I'd said, but I didn't correct him. "The dynamic is entirely different. Did you feel it, when you were alone with Chestra? The attraction? I saw you lose your temper, first time ever. I saw you choke a man. Testosterone. Rage, the murderous variety. Territorial displays of aggression. All at about the same time you were spending time with her."

Tomlinson licked the paper again, poured in dried leaves, then rolled it into a fat cigarette, pointed at both ends. "When you put it that way, it *does* sound like I was being a romantic fool, head over heels in love with the woman. The attraction? Yes, I felt it. Powerful, too. Not at first, though. Every time I saw her, it got stronger." He focused his sad blue eyes on me, being serious for once. "I'd get the shakes if I felt her breath on my cheek. When she sang, I wanted to *possess* her. I wanted to take her from behind, naked, and watch our reflections on the piano's surface. Oh yeah, compadre, there was attraction."

I felt a flash of anger, a territorial response, but recognized it for what it was.

"To possess someone. That's out of character."

"Man, it's against everything I stand for. But you're asking me for the truth."

"Why did you stop seeing her?"

"Because she scared me, man. Chessie's a rare being. One of the world's coolest creatures, but she scared me. No colors in her aura, I already told you about that. Plus, she was immediately into you. More than attraction, it was a history kind of deal. There's no fighting a connection like that."

I watched Tomlinson light the cigarette, inhale sharply three times in quick succession, then hold his breath, his attention abruptly inward, gauging the potency.

I said, "We both have the same question about her music: How could someone with her talent slip through life unknown? I think I know the answer."

He looked at me.

"You saw the photograph of Marlissa Dorn."

He nodded.

"Chessie said you commented on how much she looked like Marlissa."

Tomlinson nodded again, still holding his breath but paying attention.

"I think there's more than just a similarity. Study her nose, the eye spacing, some other details. I don't think Marlissa Dorn drowned in a hurricane. I think Chestra *is* Marlissa Dorn. She slipped through the world unnoticed because that's what she wanted. Somehow, she got a chance to disappear. She took it."

Tomlinson nodded emphatically, as he exhaled. "I've believed exactly that for a while. No way I could tell you. You'd of thought I was just being weird again."

I said, "The problem is . . ." I had pondered this without explanation. "How can she be the age she *must* be and still look the way she looks? And her sensuality—it's behavioral, but it's also chemical. You noticed it before I did. If Marlissa Dorn is still alive, she's also still extraordinarily attractive. Can it be possible?"

"One of the world's great beauties, man." He shrugged. "Sunlight on the skin; ultraviolet rays, that's the principal cause of aging. The skin condition she says she has, why she only goes out at night—"

"Xeroderma," I said. "It's in the medical literature."

"I know, I read about it. People who have it, are called Children of the Moon."

I was unaware of that. "Children of the Moon. Interesting. Even so—"

"Did she tell you the story about Hitler touching her shoulder? Like a curse."

I said, "That can't have anything to do with it."

"That's not what I'm saying. There's something I didn't mention. When she realized I believed she was Marlissa Dorn, the woman Hitler had put his mark on, it was like a door slamming. That's what really ended it between us. *Think* about it." He held the cigarette out to me.

I shook my head, as I always did—and my temples throbbed with the movement.

"This'll help, Doc. Medicinal use, man. And not a bad way to spend a stormy night."

I was about to open a beer, but thought, *Why not . . . ?*

39 "Her age changes. The way she looks. It's because she's a ghost."

Chestra, Tomlinson meant.

I replied, "You keep saying that."

I had taken two puffs on the joint, then refused when he offered again. Felt no effect, zero, and it tasted like an ashtray. Tomlinson smoked the rest as we sat in the boat's cabin, him inhaling deeply, making hissing inhalations, savoring marijuana he called Seven Mile Bridge because it was from the Keys.

Already high, too. He got on the subject of ghosts and wouldn't let it go.

"Ghosts aren't like the ones in cartoons. They have bodies, they eat food, make love. But they're empty people because they're just visiting. Trying to finish unfinished business. Most of them died too early. I meet ghosts all the time. Everyone does."

I said, "I don't doubt it," aware I had to be patient.

There were things I wanted to discuss: POWs with enough clout to summon a submarine. A diamond death's-head, and German expats on an island interacting with some of America's most powerful figures. Ford, Firestone, and Thomas Edison's search for synthetic rubber. A black man drenched with his own moonshine, and set ablaze. An old woman who radiated sexuality.

There were powerful dynamics at play on that long ago October night. How had the story remained a secret?

I listened to Tomlinson tell me, "Some of the lonely-looking people you see in train stations? They're ghosts. A lot of hitchhikers; pilots in small planes. Certain areas of the country attract them. Louisville—loaded. Same with your New England states, the Carolinas. Hollywood and Manhattan, the old hotels are full. Sometimes ghosts don't even know they're not real."

I said, "Unreal reality. I've had that feeling. Actually, I've come to associate it with this boat."

"*No Mas*? Ghost ships, oh yeah. There are lots of those. When you see a boat at night and there's only one person aboard?"

"He's a ghost?" I guessed, playing along. "Spirits come back to earth."

"Now you're catching on. But ghosts and spirits are very different manifestation. Spirits are energy. Ghosts are empty. Unfulfilled lives, man, and they've returned in search of whatever it is they missed. *Searchers.* They're everywhere.

"You want an example of spirits? The difference, I mean. When we were diving the wreck in the murk. There were spirits down there, man. Dark spirits; a very heavy mojo. One of them banged into me. Like a warning."

I leaned toward him. "You got bumped? I got bumped twice."

"I'm not surprised. It scared the hell out of me, man. At first. Then I just figured, Hey, stay cool. It wasn't the first time evil spirits have blindsided me. You know, follow the drunk tank's safety rules: Keep your mouth shut and your butt cheeks closed."

I said, "I think it was a shark. Or sharks. Not evil. Just big fish doing what they're coded to do. Probing, deciding if we were protein."

"No. It wasn't a shark. Not the thing that hit me. I would've known. It was a spirit. Darkness. The real deal. Which is a very different thing than a ghost. As I was saying, talking about empty souls. Searchers . . ."

Yes. The man was stoned, getting higher. Fixated on the subject.

I sat listening for a while longer before I stood, careful to duck my head. This was going noplace. In fact, the more Tomlinson talked, the more I became convinced that I was mistaken about Chestra. She wasn't Marlissa Dorn. It was as implausible for her to be Marlissa's age as it was for Chestra to be a ghost.

It was a valid analogy. When I thought of it that way, my suspicions seemed ridiculous.

Genetic facial similarities. That had to explain it.

I continued to listen to Tomlinson, though, as I stood at the top of the companionway steps. My headache, mysteriously, was gone, I realized. Nice up there in the fresh air, feeling the breeze, gazing out: small marina in moonlight, parking lot empty, clouds wind-driven above dark trees, yellow windows of my stilt house and lab shimmering on the bay. Storm clouds over the Gulf, glowing like Japanese lanterns with each lightning blast.

It would be raining soon.

My eyes came to rest on my new skiff, which was tied off the stern. The deck was white, a slight incline aft to bow, all hatches flush. The deck seemed to glow in contrast to the black water. The hull, gray-blue, floated buoyant as a bubble.

I heard Tomlinson say, "I've been wanting to tell you about ghosts. But the time had to be right. Now, here we are, so I guess it's time to lay the cards on the table. There are a couple of ghosts who live at the marina, you know. For years. I didn't want you to be shocked."

I said, "Ghosts living at Dinkin's Bay? That explains all the trick-or-treaters at Halloween." I continued to gaze at the boat.

It was my third twenty-one-footer built by the same manufacturer, but I had never paused to appreciate the skiff's symmetry. Its lines were as elegant as an aspen leaf but functional. So simple in appearance that only an expert would recognize the engineered complexities. No cabin, no windshield. Cut a surfboard in half, sink a rectangular space for a console, steering wheel, and throttle. Add three swivel seats mounted low, and an oversized outboard that ensures velocity.

Clean. Efficient. Just looking at it gave me pleasure.

"Doc? Are you listening to me?"

"Oh sure."

"Are you okay? You've been standing there for, like, ten solid minutes, man. Hey. How about some music? When's the last time you listened to Buffalo Springfield? No. America! 'Ventura Highway,' 'Sister Golden Hair'—the classics, man. But close the hatch. It's gonna be pouring rain here, like, in two minutes."

I felt the walls of the boat move as Tomlinson went to the stereo.

I said, "Tomlinson? Have you ever noticed how . . . *exacting* my skiff is made? Seriously. Minimalism. It's an art form. The way it's designed, I mean. Clean."

"It's gorgeous, man. Yeah, and you keep it spotless."

"The color, too. Gray-blue. I really like the color."

"Gray-blue is not a color, Doc. It's camouflage—your boat's invisible on the water. Which . . . now that I think about it, makes gray-blue the perfect color for you. Like your birthstone, or something. Boats, man"—he was now calling to be heard from the sailboat's cabin—"don't let yourself get lured off on a boat tangent, man. You'll sit there catatonic for hours. I look at *No Mas* sometimes, I start bawling. Doc? Doc! Where're you going?"

I was aboard my skiff, starting the motor. Beneath me, through fiberglass skin, I felt a familiar vibration, similar to riding bareback on a horse, the rippling muscularity.

I let go the line, touched the throttle—a slight nudge of the knees was all it took to get the animal moving. I idled into the night, toward my home. A man alone in his boat.

Yes, it was a cigarette case. That was evident, now . . .

I didn't have the photo of Marlissa Dorn, but the cigarette case was similar. Silver, ornately embossed. On one side, a small medieval-looking cross, but with double horizontal arms, the upper arm longer than the lower. On the case's other side were initials. The first letter now visible: M.

Marlissa.

I didn't know the significance of a doubled cross. Tomlinson would.

I was standing in my lab, staring into trays of sodium hydroxide. The cigarette case was in the middle tray of three. The diamond death's-head, and the bronze eagle were in the tray to my left. The table was too small to push that tray out of my peripheral vision and so I finally covered it with a towel.

Much better.

The death's-head was impossible to ignore. Drew my eyes as if transmitting an invisible tractor beam. Light discharged by the diamonds was so penetrating it made me wince. The laughing skull was like ice on a bad tooth.

I concentrated on the cigarette case.

More of the black patina was gone. The double-bladed cross was unmistakable, but there was something at the bottom that required more cleaning. The base of the cross tapered into a dagger's point, touching something—a symbol? Couldn't tell. It was undecipherable.

Same with the other side of the silver case. An initial: м. Black sulfide covered the rest.

I was concentrating on the cigarette case because . . . ? Well, for no particular reason. The case was there. It meant something . . . what?

A woman.

Yes. But which one? That was the question.

I continued to stare, seldom blinking.

The first squall edge of tropical storm was over Sanibel. Outside, wind was gusting; rain pellets rattled at the windows. My laboratory lights flickered with each blast of lightning. Power outages were common of late. I might have to start the generator soon . . .

It was unpleasant, the prospect of starting the generator. The effort it required: rechecking oil and gas, priming the carburetor, then pulling the cord. Made me tired to think of it . . .

What's wrong with sitting in the dark? Nothing! Big moon. Sit inside and . . . do what?

Nothing.

No, having light was better. I would rally. I would find the energy. Start the generator, fill oil lamps if needed. Make tea. Read. Listen to shortwave radio; find out what was happening in small places on the far side of the earth.

I liked that idea. It made me smile.

My head moved, eyes searching until they found my left arm, then my wrist watch: 11:15 P.M.

Had I been standing, looking at the cigarette case, for ten minutes? Impossible.

My eyes moved around the room until I found my wrist watch again. 11:16 P.M. No, it was possible.

Listen to shortwave radio, that's what I would do. Delicious, the prospect of that. Make tea. Get some food—did I have potato chips? Sit and listen to radio broadcasts—Radio Singapore, perhaps—the storm outside, isolated on this island by the weather and . . . something else.

I found my watch again: 11:17.

Oh yeah. They closed the bridge at 10:30 because of the storm instead of midnight as usual. Mack had told me, not that I cared. That's another way I was isolated. No car traffic, so Sanibel was cut off. Like being on a ship at sea, riding out a big blow. I would stay alone in my cabin, because no person in their right mind would be out in a storm on a night like this . . .

At the north window, there was a dazzling explosion of light, then another. Wind sounded passages through my windows that were reed-sized, a moaning pitch, warbling variations of oboes and flutes. My eyes, once again, were locked on the cigarette case.

Chestra.

The woman's name was important for some reason. Why?

I thought about it.

She loved storms.

She could be out in a storm like this.

Yes, it was a possibility.

There was another lightning blast; wind screamed. Chestra's voice came into my head. "I adore storms. Never miss one. I take energy from them!"

My mood changed from lethargy to slow panic.

Chestra *would* be out in this storm. Of course she would. She lived for this sort of thing. Insane. Fifty-knot winds were no reason to evacuate an island, but they were much too strong to risk a walk outside. A woman who didn't weigh much more than a hundred pounds? She would blow away like a palm frond . . . or be hit by a palm frond and killed.

I had to go get her.

I began to pace the room, searching for something—what?

My foul-weather jacket. I found it. The keys to my truck. I found those, too. And a flashlight—proof my brain was beginning to work again.

Panic had become fear; fear was becoming concern. My head was clearing, forced to focus . . .

The woman was probably on her way to the beach right now, indifferent to the danger. Fifty-knot winds from the southwest. What did that mean?

I processed it carefully: Water on the bay side of the island would appear calm because it was in the lee. Little wind ripples but no waves. The beach, though, could be fatal. Rogue breakers; tidal surges . . .

Yes. I had to find Chestra, then talk her into returning home.

Before I shut off the lights, the cigarette case caught my attention—something that would make her happy. I could use it to lure her back to her house. I'd planned on making a gift of it to her in a few days, anyway.

I wrapped the cigarette case in a towel, put it in my jacket pocket, and hurried out into the storm.

The storm moved across Sanibel in bands, wind howling, calming for a few minutes, then howling again. The wipers on my old Chevy couldn't handle the volume of sluicing rain as I drove Tarpon Bay Road toward the Gulf of Mexico. My headlights were feeble yellow cones. Lightning bursts illuminated the way. Trees wrestled in an agony of wind; debris tumbled. I passed a vehicle coming from the opposite direction. Then another. Water wakes battered my windshield.

Amazing that anyone was out tonight. Cops, probably, keeping an eye on the island.

I leaned to see through my windshield. Squinted to glance through side windows. A tree was down . . . a garbage can rolled randomly along the road's shoulder. Was that a car in the public beach parking area?

Lightning flared.

No. It was a big pickup truck. Or SUV.

Yes. Amazing that people were out.

I turned on Gulf Drive, then turned into Chestra's estate, my headlights a vague illumination: Southwind, mailbox swaying; family cemetery, a garden of stone beneath bare trees; gazebo, a darkened sanctuary to the left; house of gray shingles ahead, upstairs windows bright.

I swung out of the truck, splashed my way to the door. Rang the bell, then knocked.

No answer.

I rang the bell again, then used my fist.

Door was locked.

I remembered telling Chestra to lock her doors when she went out as a precaution. Did this mean she was outside?

I wore my foul-weather jacket, but was already soaked, the ocean-heated rain helping me sober. No, the locked door didn't mean she was outside. She *could* be outside, but she could also be inside playing the piano, listening to music.

I banged on the door again. No response.

If she was inside, she was safe. But if she wasn't outside . . . ?

I looked toward the beach. Saw a lightning bolt touch sand, the explosion instantaneous.

I rang the bell again. Nothing.

I turned the knob and threw my shoulder against the door, a last attempt . . .

 **40** When a vehicle turned into Mildred Engle's driveway, Bern Heller was inside the house. He saw car lights pan across the woman's bedroom ceiling, and thought: *Damn. It's gotta be cops. Nobody else would be out in this storm.*

Cops, or someone desperate. Someone on the run—like Bern. It was because of something that had happened just after sunset, only a few hours ago. What a day.

It seemed longer.

Bern looked at the clock on the woman's nightstand: 11:28. He'd been in the house for less than ten minutes. Yeah, about that. The front door was locked, but the downstairs sliding doors weren't, so he had come in silently, hearing the wind whistle . . . then music coming from somewhere. Upstairs. Longhair kind of music. Fancy piano.

That's where Bern headed. No one there, just the stereo playing.

Five minutes later, he was downstairs again. In Mildred Engle's bedroom, going through drawers, and about to open her closet when the car lights stopped him.

Shit!

Bern ducked, went to the window, and peeked out: It looked like a pickup truck coming down the shell driveway, headlights yellow in the rain, the vehicle was so old.

Not like Moe's fancy Dodge pickup with the big tires and gun rack, which was parked in a public access lot nearby. Bern had learned that tourist cars often sat for hours there without drawing attention from island police.

He watched as a man stepped out of the old truck, his head down in the angling rain. A big man, wide shoulders, about the size of the guy he'd seen exit the house a few hours earlier. The man he'd seen a few times last week. He came and went from the old lady's house on a bicycle. Linebacker-sized, that's the way he thought of the guy. Not by pro standards, of course. Small college.

It was a relief seeing it was the bicycle guy, not the cops.

The bicycle guy Bern could deal with, but it was still a serious matter because it was unexpected. One more surprise that caused things not to go according to plan.

Bern had been doing drive-bys for the last several days, checking out Mildred Engle's house, planning how to work it. Staying *positive,* as he was determined to do. A plan was important, or else bad things happened . . . as he knew too well.

The first time, he'd driven by Southwind was in his BMW sedan, which didn't attract a look on an island with so many rich people. Tonight, he had the truck.

Changing vehicles—smart.

The last few nights, he had watched the woman move across the lighted windows. He'd watched the man come and go.

Irritating, they were together so much.

Bern hadn't gotten close enough to bicycle guy to see his face. No need to. Who cared? It didn't matter because Bern had seen the *woman's* face. What a face, too. Quite a surprise! A nice surprise.

A couple of days ago, after dark, he'd crept up to her bedroom window—this window—and watched her get undressed by candlelight.

It was good timing because, for once, bicycle guy wasn't around.

Oil lamps and candles, that's about all the woman used for light.

Bern watched her pin her hair up, then peel a gold lamé gown over her head as she turned toward the window in bra, garter belts, panties, and stockings, her face illuminated for the first time by the candle on her dresser . . .

Jesus Christ . . . and there she was: the glamorous woman in the photograph. The cheekbones, her full lips, the smoky eyes dreamy looking, as if she was thinking about something sexy as she got naked. A man, maybe, the expression on her face naughty; enjoying something, it looked like, that women weren't expected to enjoy.

She was a lot older than the picture, of course. But it was the same woman. Had to be. She hadn't turned into an old hag, either, unless . . . wait a minute . . .

Something didn't make sense.

If the woman he was watching undress was the glamorous woman in the photo, why had Jason Goddard said her name was Mildred Engle? The woman in the photo was Marlissa Dorn. The lawsuit-happy bitch, Mildred Engle, was supposedly the movie queen's heir. Which meant the movie queen was dead. Right?

Could women relatives look that much alike?

Bern wondered about that, but not for long, because the woman leaned toward him and began taking off the garter belts, the tops of her breasts vanilla white in the bra's half cups. Then she sat and stripped off her stockings.

It was a night of firsts: He had never seen a woman wearing stockings. Real stockings, not the panty hose things. And he had never seen an older woman naked.

It wasn't like watching the neighborhood girls strip at the nudie bars south of Milwaukee. Her body was skin over bone, stomach firm, breasts flat but real, nipples as long and pale as they probably were when she was sixteen.

Damn. It didn't matter what the woman's name was, or how old. She was sexy. The old man had screwed her . . . or screwed her dead relative, the movie queen, which was close enough. That's what mattered. Like visiting a museum. That's the way Bern decided to approach it. Get her naked again and make the old girl bounce.

Then sit back and wait for the earth to rumble. It would be the sound of his grandfather rolling over in his grave.

Be positive, stay focused. In football, it was the only way to change momentum . . .

Was that true? A lot of stuff coaches said was crap, although Bern would only share that information with fellow athletes. It was not the sort of thing a man purchasing a Cadillac or a Florida condo wanted to hear.

Make a game plan, then follow it: That's why Bern had been on Sanibel every free evening for the last week, getting to know the area. Which was convenient, in a way. Killing two birds with one stone because the beautiful yacht his idiot nephew had lost, the Viking, was tied up at a dock less than two miles away, near Sanibel Lighthouse.

Bern had his own set of keys to the Viking, having taken them from Augie's condo. It'd been no problem at all getting aboard the boat, either, especially with the island almost empty.

Bern had boarded the Viking, but only for a few minutes, just to start the engines, make sure everything was working, and to transfer three suitcases he had packed before leaving Indian Harbor.

He'd carried the suitcases down to the dock, stepped aboard like he owned the place. No one around to say a word.

He had to do it because of another surprise: Tonight, they'd closed the bridge to the mainland at ten-thirty, due to the storm. Not midnight, as the previous week. Bern had discovered this after almost being spotted by bicycle guy earlier when parked, lights out, in the woman's driveway.

Not good news.

The bridge being closed was an extremely shitty surprise because it meant there was only one way off the island—by boat—unless Bern wanted to wait around in Moe's pickup truck until morning.

No, thanks.

Bern would be taking the Viking tonight, even though he hadn't planned to do it until later in the week.

What he had *planned* to do was grab the loan documents and Mildred

Engle tonight, drive her to Indian Harbor, have some fun, then tuck the lady into a fifty-gallon drum that was already waiting.

By midnight tonight, he wanted to be halfway to Miami. The beginning of a four- or five-day road trip that included a visit to a man who specialized in fake IDs and passports. Also visits to a couple of banks. He'd cleaned out the marina's safe, and had twelve thousand dollars cash on him, which he wanted to change into traveler's checks. Isn't that what they used in foreign countries?

Friday or Saturday night, when the weather was better, that's when he'd *planned* to return to Sanibel and take the boat. Good-bye, Florida, which had been like a curse to him. Hello, new life.

But that wasn't the way things were shaking out.

Bern would have to leave tonight—crappy weather for boating. Which worried him. Big storm, lots of wind . . . but the bay was amazingly calm when he went to take a look. Big moon, too, with clouds streaming by. And the boat was close to the woman's house.

Maybe his luck was changing.

This Monday morning had *started* in a unusually positive way. Jason had left a phone message saying the promissory notes had finally arrived on Sanibel. Ms. Engle was ready and waiting.

Well, Bern was waiting, too, ready to introduce himself to the old woman with the beautiful face. He'd been looking forward to it a *bunch* since the night he'd watched her strip naked. The glamorous photo, which he had crumpled, was now taped to his bedroom mirror. From a distance, the woman was as beautiful as before.

A new detail Bern noticed: The woman's eyes followed him around the room no matter where he went.

That afternoon, though, Moe came to visit, the hick from South Lick, and instantly, Bern's life began to change from good to bad, then from bad to worse.

So what else was new?

When Moe arrived, Bern was in the marina office, using the Internet, following steps as listed in the document <u>How to Change Your Identity and Disappear Forever,</u> planning his escape, just in case the Hoosier turned out to be the spineless bohunk Bern feared.

Which, of course, he was.

Identity theft was the key to disappearing. Find information on a person who had died recently. Ideally, someone with many assets but few relatives. Use their Social Security number to obtain a copy of their birth certificate, to get a new passport, and take control of whatever assets they had.

His grandfather had done it successfully in 1944. Why couldn't Bern?

In truth, it had been easier for the old man—the old man being, essentially, a ruthless Nazi murderer, Bern had decided.

At Bern's elbow, near the computer, was his grandfather's passport. His *real* passport. A German passport, green, with a Nazi eagle embossed on the front cover, many, many swastika stamps but no big red *J* inside.

He had gone through the passport enough to have the information memorized: Issued 1938, Berlin, his grandfather's precise signature legible beneath the photo: Heinrich Bernard Goddard.

Heinrich Goddard. Jesus, the perfect name for a proctologist.

Vicious son of a bitch. His whole life was a lie.

Bernard?

Fuck you, old man.

Even at nineteen, his grandfather's piggish face and brutal eyes were unmistakable. He looked nothing at all like the blond guy whose identity he had swiped, along with the guy's assets—a box full of real estate deeds—before catching a boat to Colombia, then Brazil, then home to Germany.

Bern knew this because, along with the passport, he had also taken several letters, Jason Goddard writing to Augie. Confidential, of course. Typically, you had to skip to the last pages to avoid Jason's bullshit.

An example: "... our great-grandfather did what was necessary to survive in tough political times. He was a brilliant medical student, personal assistant to Dr. Carl Clauberg, world authority on genetics. However, he knew ridiculous charges awaited after the war, so he fled to Florida, where a German agent provided assistance in return for ..."

In return for a couple of bars of gold bullion, that's what.

Bern found that tidbit in yet another personal note to Augie—Augie and Jason being the only two Wisconsinites named in the late Heinrich Goddard's primary will, clearly favoring his firstborn son in Germany, and the son's family.

The old man had stolen a bunch of it. Gold bullion.

". . . he liberated a significant amount while U.S. troops advanced."

What else could that mean? Sometimes, you had to read between the lines.

Another for instance: ". . . tragically, the agent who transported grandfather out of Florida waters was piloting a U.S. vessel, enemy of the Reich, so was fired upon and sunk, as duty required . . ."

". . . grandfather used Frederick Roth's passport to ensure his own freedom, which he viewed as tribute to Mr. Roth's bravery. He continued to use the name out of respect . . ."

Translation: The old man stole the blond guy's identity, stole his real estate deeds, then made sure the guy was dead.

Which was the smart thing to do, Bern had to admit. He had been reading a lot about identity theft lately and it was the best way.

But what about the gold bullion? Had the old man paid the German agent first? Maybe that's why the nautical map was in the briefcase. Bern *knew* where the wreck was. If he got the Viking back, got this other bullshit settled, and there was a nice calm day . . . ?

Bern was wondering about the gold when the office door opened, and in walked Moe, ducking his head into his cowboy hat, already sweating on this storm-cool Monday afternoon. Nervous. A little drunk, too.

Hmm-m-m-m. Suspicious.

Right away, Moe started talking loud. Too loud. Enunciating his words, as he probably had in class while reading aloud prior to dropping out of the third grade. Asking dumbass, transparent questions, too, such as, "Bern, I'm trying to remember. What was it you said poured out of that barrel the other night? The fifty-gallon drum. A *girl*?"

Uhh-oh. Time to think fast.

Bern was on his feet immediately, big salesman's grin in place. "Great to see you, Moe, just the man I want to talk to! A girl? I don't remember anything about a girl—unless it was the one you were joking about."

"Huh?" Moe couldn't talk, he was so taken aback.

"The college girl you said you murdered 'cause she expected you to have two dicks—your IQ being half the male average. Funny. Man, how do you come up with that stuff?"

The look on Moe's face. *That* was funny.

Bern placed his hand on the back on the Hoosier's Wrangler jacket, feeling for the tape recorder or microphone that had to be hidden somewhere.

As he did, he steered the man outside to see if there were cops around in unmarked cars listening.

No cops. No unmarked cars for half a mile down the road either direction.

Bern said, "Moe, let's go for a walk," and led the redneck past the collapsed barn, boats sitting in rows, to the little hill where the dumbass had dug up the barrel. But there were a couple of guys fishing near the boat ramp. Witnesses.

Shit.

So Bern said, "Moe, let's go for a ride."

They took the redneck's Dodge pickup, Bern at the wheel, and turned down a sand road bordered by mangroves. Moe started crying when Bern found the tape recorder in his jacket pocket.

To get the truth, Bern had to slap and kick the shit out of the Hoosier, who was tougher than expected. But he finally talked. The tape recorder was Moe's idea, because he wanted to cover his ass, no cops involved. And, yes, he had told them about the dead girl in the barrel.

Moe was sobbing. "I hope this doesn't mean my job here's been terminated. My old lady would break off our engagement."

Jesus, the guy's IQ took a nosedive every time he opened his mouth. Maybe air was leaking into his brain through a bad tooth.

Bern replied, "Well, Moe, it does kind of create a *trust* issue."

He used the Luger.

Bern was still at Mildred Engle's bedroom window, peeking from behind the curtain, watching as the man from the pickup truck approached the house. He watched the man pause, standing like an idiot out there in the rain, looking at something. What?

The moon.

It wasn't raining as hard now—the storm came in waves—but even so. Bicycle guy was a dumbass to stand there and get soaked.

Bern watched the man approach the house, then he heard the doorbell ring. Heard it ring again. Now the man was pounding on the door.

Bern stepped away from the window and walked toward the door, a pistol in his hand. It wasn't his imitation German Luger. It was Moe's chrome-plated cowboy pistol, the .357 revolver that the cops had recently returned after deciding, yes, the Hoosier had done society a favor shooting his attacker.

The cylinder was loaded with five pinky-sized bullets, hollow-points that expanded when they hit flesh. The missing slug had certainly done a job on the Cuban, hitting him in the arm, but killing the man, anyway.

Bern hoped the other five were just as lucky. Good omens in the heavy handgun that he now raised as he approached the door where the man, bicycle guy, was hammering away with his fists.

If the man opened the door, Bern would shoot him. He was sure of it. First, though, maybe he'd ask him where Mildred Engle was. Bern had been upstairs and downstairs; hadn't seen her. More important, he hadn't found the promissory notes that were supposed to be somewhere in the house.

Bern *had* to have those old loan documents. They were the main reason he had come to Sanibel. No, after what had happened this afternoon they were the only reason. The loan documents, signed by Frederick Roth—the *real* Frederick Roth—he needed them.

The promissory notes and the Viking. Without both, he was screwed. No way to pay for his new life in a country Bern had yet to choose—as if he'd had the time. And no way to escape.

All because of that trailer lizard Moe.

Outside, the man was still pounding on the door. Then, after a brief silence, the frame and brass lock both cracked when he tried to knock the door open with his shoulder.

The guy seemed determined. Did he somehow know the old lady had company?

Bern aimed the revolver, chest height, and pulled the hammer back . . .

**41** When I threw my shoulder against the door, I felt the wood frame and dead bolt screws give. I stepped back to ram the door again but caught myself.

A dead bolt. Didn't that tell me something? If the door was bolted, Chestra was inside.

No . . . she could have bolted the front door, then exited through the downstairs sliding doors, beach side.

My jacket had a hood. I held the hood tight as I splashed my way around the house to check, moon almost bright enough I didn't need my flashlight. The glass doors were open, curtains billowing.

Strange for her to leave doors open . . .

I stepped inside to have a look—a light showing down the hall, beneath her bedroom door. I called her name.

Chestra?

Called once more.

Should I go to her room and knock?

No. Decided that would be intrusive.

I turned to look at the beach. The wind and rain were abating. The cyclone's volatile bands traveled in incremental waves, the space of each lull shorter as the storm's center neared. In a few minutes, the gale would resume.

If she was out there, now was the time to find her.

I closed the doors, and started along the path to the beach.

During the last storm, she'd led me in the direction of Sanibel Light. I remembered that.

When I reached the beach, I took a chance and retraced our course, then began jogging toward the point. To my right, the sea was a deafening darkness. In the far distance, the lighthouse was awash in monstrous clouds, each frail starburst reflected skyward, then absorbed as if ingested.

Over the Gulf, there was a flash of lightning. Another. The horizon was briefly illuminated by random voltage, an electrical pattern as intricate as synaptic nerve fiber.

Ahead, the automated beacon revolved with indifferent synchrony: two one-second flashes followed by darkness, over and over; a metronome warning to mariners that was issued every ten seconds.

Light-light . . . dark. Light-light . . . dark. Light-light . . . dark.

Ahead of me, at the surf's edge, I saw movement . . .

What?

A person. Far down the beach. I saw the figure only for a moment as the beacon flared: a human silhouette tethered to its shadow.

A person, yes. Someone walking toward the lighthouse.

I jogged faster, leaning into a water-heavy wind. The storm was freshening. I knew it would rain soon.

It did. I heard the curtain of rain before I felt it: a xylophone patter backdropped by the drumming percussion of waves. Sand beneath my feet vibrated with each breaker's weight; soft rain became a torrent. Wind arrived, a tumid wall that made it a struggle to run.

I was close enough to see it was a woman: a solitary figure, head down, dressed in pale clothing that caught the wind like scarves.

I jogged for another minute.

"Chestra?"

The figure turned.

I was close enough to see. It was her.

"Doc . . . ? Doc!"

"Yeah."

She held her hands out. I took them. "My God, what are you doing on the beach? I'm so happy to see you, kiddo!"

We were closer to the lighthouse; moonlight was diffused by clouds. Rain was angling.

"I was worried. Storms, I know you love them. So I came looking. Chestra, this is crazy. I'm taking you home right now—"

I was silenced by a sizzling explosion. Lightning. A blue glare illuminated Chestra's face, her water-soaked hair. It was an incandescence so pure that I felt as if I were seeing her for the first time. Extraordinary. Had I once really thought she was old?

I found myself unable to speak. I had never been face-to-face with a woman as beautiful as Mildred Chestra Engle.

"What's wrong, Doc?"

We stood for a moment in the silence of storm and pounding surf.

"Doc?"

I touched my hands to her hips; felt her arms go around my neck. Her eyes stared into mine, their intensity rhythmic in the contrasting tempo of automated beacon and wild electricity. Both revealed a woman who was described to me as ageless.

Light-light . . . dark. Light-light . . . dark.

Her eyes, her lips . . . her flawless face.

Yes, she was. Ageless.

We kissed.

I touched the back of my hand to her lips—no, I had not imagined their heat. My fingers moved to her cheek, her throat, then stroked her hair as I slipped my right hand inside her jacket, cupping her ribs through sodden blouse.

We kissed again.

In a lightning burst, Chestra's eyes smoldered. They floated a question. I touched my lips to hers in reply.

"Your house?" I said.

"No. The gazebo. It's the way I've imagined it."

I felt my pocket to make certain the cigarette case was there. "I have something for you. A surprise."

Chestra put a fingernail to my abdomen, tracing downward. "I'm sure you do."

The gazebo was equipped for family barbecues. It was board-and-battened to waist level, then screened. There was a couch, a patio table, a couple of oil lamps, a little fireplace.

I was trying to get a fire lighted, using damp wood and damp matches.

Chestra was in the shadows, toweling her body, a blanket nearby.

When I broke another match, I said, "You're right, it's going to take charcoal lighter to get this thing going."

She lowered the towel enough so that I could see her breasts, nipples pale beneath the thin material of her camisole. "Kiddo, you're carrying the only fire starter I need. But I'll pop into the house. When I get back, I promise you'll have all the heat required."

Lighter fluid, some rolled-up newspapers, and towels—she said it wouldn't take a minute. A woman determined to make love beside a fire.

I smiled. It was around midnight, gale blowing. The gazebo was almost as good as being out in the storm, she said. Wind. Lightning.

We had not waited for the fire. Or dry towels. Or anything. I couldn't wait. She was as eager.

We had undressed each other quickly . . . all but a sheer camisole top which Chestra wouldn't remove. "Use your hands anywhere. Everywhere. But allow me this one conceit. Please, my love?"

I thought it was because of her age.

It was not.

Her body was alive beneath my fingers. She meant what she said. I could touch her. Anywhere. Everywhere. The camisole could be lifted for my mouth and eyes to enjoy.

Not her right shoulder, though. She would not bare it. There was scar tissue. Small indentations—several. Five? My fingers swept across them, counting. I felt the scars . . . but only for a moment before she pulled my hand away.

It created an uneasiness that, for her, vanished with our next kiss.

Incredible. Her body consumed mine. Astride me, she made low breathless sounds of craving, head back, eyes closed, her face a mask of shadow and light.

Her fingers knew male sensitivities as well as they knew keys on a piano. They understood where tiny collectives of neurons lay beneath skin and they played there delicately, then demanding.

In her hands, I disappeared. Within Chestra, I vanished. I felt a transcendent contentment, like a shadow released.

"Doc, you know what they say: A woman's only as old as the man she's feeling."

I laughed. Her bawdy side. Earlier, she had made a dreamy growl of satisfaction, and whispered, "American men. You just reminded me why I prefer domestic to imported."

I placed the damp matches on the table and stood. Chestra was wearing a robe now. I was naked—her eyes liked that. I said, "Your present. I haven't given it to you yet."

"You're kidding. Then one of us wasn't paying attention." She came to me, let me slip my hands inside the robe as we hugged, then kissed.

I found my jacket. Took the flashlight and unwrapped the cigarette case. More of the black patina had come off on the towel. I looked at the case in the light, before saying, "This is what I was talking about."

I handed it to Chestra as distant lightning flared behind her. "Is this . . . is this what I think?" I stood nearby and switched on the flashlight. "Oh my God! Doc, you *found* it. You actually found it!"

I expected her to be pleased. Instead, she was overwhelmed. Near tears. Holding the silver case, her hands began to shake. It was a reaction I would expect from a young woman who had just opened a box and seen an engagement ring.

"How could you have possibly found this and not told me immediately?"

Was she peeved? No. She stared at the case, hugged me, then hugged me again.

I got my first good look at it. On one side, the small engraving was visible: a doubled cross on a stiletto blade. The stiletto's tip was overset with the Star of David. On the other side of the cigarette case were Marlissa Dorn's initials: MD.

Chestra became animated. "Do you know what this means? Doc! I'm in shock. But, in a way . . . I've known it all along."

I put my hands on her shoulders, steadying her. "What are you talking about?"

"When I was contacted about the house . . . the promissory notes, I was told that it was a bequest from Frederick Roth. That he hadn't died in 1944. But all these years I thought he was *dead*. Lost in the storm. Then I'm told that he lived to a ripe old age, made a lot of money. Which meant that he left Marlissa and never came back. Freddy *abandoned* her, don't you understand? Abandoned the woman he said was his only true love. He went on to live his life without her."

I had never heard Chestra so excited. "Yeah?"

"This cigarette case was a present to Freddy from Marlissa. Don't you see?" She waited for the flashlight before pointing to the cross and Star of David. "This was a symbol used by the German underground. The cross—it's actually an *F. Freiheit,* it means 'freedom.'

"Freddy was living aboard *Dark Light* at the time. Most of his clothes, his papers, were there. Even if he chose not to return to Marlissa, he would have never left this case behind. A German Jew in 1944? It was better than a passport. At restaurants, in train stations, people who understood would see it and *know.* Yes, Marlissa had been unfaithful. Heinrich Goddard made certain he knew all the gory little details. But Freddy still wouldn't have left *this.*" I watched her pull the cigarette case to her bosom—an embrace. Why was she so happy to know that Roth had died the night of the storm?

"Heinrich Goddard?" I repeated softly.

"Yes. A Nazi. A terrible man. Evil. A medical researcher who worked at one of the camps. He had money, all the right connections. He was on the run. The night we read Marlissa's diary, I mentioned his name."

No, she had not mentioned his name. She used the initials H.G. It explained why a letter from an attorney named Goddard was upsetting.

"It was the night I suggested Roth was a Nazi agent. A spy on an island with so many powerful Americans? Threaten to expose him—take the Germans to their rendezvous or face a firing squad. There's no statute of limitations on espionage. It made sense. At the time."

Chestra turned. She began to retie her robe.

"But he wasn't a Nazi agent. Apparently, he was part of the German underground."

"Yes. That's my understanding. I'm sure he was."

"I wonder what they used to make him go out that night. Money . . . gold? Even if they offered, it wouldn't have been enough. Not twelve miles offshore in a hurricane. And he certainly wouldn't have taken a woman—even if she had been unfaithful." I waited a moment before adding, "Even if *Marlissa* was the spy. But to save her from a firing squad . . . maybe that's why he went out that night."

Chestra was looking at the floor, her voice soft. "It's possible, I suppose."

I was thinking about the diamond death's-head—it could have been a calling card. It could have also been a death sentence.

"Marlissa was very young. She wanted the world. If powerful men told her things . . . lies . . . she may have pretended to believe them. Even pretended to help them. But not for long.

"Frederick was an extraordinary man. A genius. Decent and good. Marlissa adored him. Loved him like she would never love another. Why else . . . why else would she drown herself when Frederick didn't return?"

I went to Chestra and made her face me. "Then she *wasn't* aboard the boat."

"No."

"Because she knew that Goddard was going to kill Roth?"

"No!"

"But Goddard *did* kill him. He must have."

The woman's eyes were teary in the moonlight. "I don't know. There's no way to ever know. But I so wish, after all these years . . . Doc?" She was looking beyond me, toward the beach.

"Yes?"

"The inscription on Marlissa's grave. Do you believe it? The old saw about the sea giving up its dead?" Her breath caught; a muffled sob.

I said gently, "I don't believe the sea takes anything. Or gives."

I watched two slow tears move down cheeks. "It's the worst sort of romantic nonsense, I suppose, thinking people have only one love. That they search for each other through the ages. I'm sure you don't believe that, either."

I didn't reply.

A gust of wind pushed rain through the screening. Her attention had turned inward. It brought her back. I felt a shiver go through the woman's body. She sniffed, touched a knuckle to her eye, then made a gutsy attempt to sound cheerful.

"Of course you don't believe it! You're a scientist and I'm just a sappy saloon singer. But what a fool I am talking about another man!" She pulled away from me and reached for her rain slicker. "I am alone in the tropics with a guy who is absolutely scrumptious. The storm is wonderful"—she was walking to the door—"and in two minutes I'll be back with a bottle of wine, which we will drink by a roaring fire. But *after* we make love again."

I had a towel knotted around my waist. I watched her duck into the wind and walk beneath trees, through pools of moon shadow, following the sand trail that led past the family cemetery to the house.

I don't know why I would risk something as indelicate but I did. I called after her, "Marlissa!"

The woman slowed, turned, waited.

I wanted to ask who was buried in the vault. One of the Cuban fisherman who washed up on the beach that October night in 1944? A fisherman's wife? Or was it empty?

"Don't forget to bring matches!"

She waved and was gone.

 **42** Was that someone coming in the back door . . . ?

Bern was upstairs, standing next to the piano in the room with the balcony. He hoped he'd heard the door. Hoped it was Mildred Engle, not bicycle guy. Just the woman, alone. Bern had wasted enough time on Sanibel, he didn't want to deal with some pissed-off boyfriend.

He paused . . . strained to listen: sliding doors opened, then closed. Footsteps on the stairs were light, like a dancer. Yes, the woman.

Good. If she'd come through the main entrance, she would have seen the trunk that he'd lugged down the front steps about thirty seconds earlier. It would have scared her. The trunk contained the loan documents. Big old steamer trunk like in the movies. Musty with leather straps. Bern put the thing next to the door so he could bring Moe's truck around and load it without busting a gut.

Christ, *now* she shows.

He'd spent nearly an hour inside the house. When bicycle guy had decided not to break the door down but hadn't started his truck and left either, Bern figured the woman must be at a neighbor's house and the guy knew where to find her. She certainly wasn't out in this storm. How crazy would that be?

He spent half an hour hunting for the promissory notes, looking

through desks and files—places *normal* people kept important papers—
hurrying like crazy. He wanted to be gone by the time they returned.

No luck.

So then Bern decided, screw it, he would wait until they came back and
make the woman give him the papers. Maybe have some fun with her
while he was at it . . . which would mean taking care of bicycle guy, something he didn't *want* to do. Enough shit had hit the fan today . . .

Bern pictured Moe's face, as he thought about what happened that afternoon . . . the way Moe's face looked *after* he'd been shot. Disgusting;
almost as bad as being seasick.

Just one more thing not in the game plan.

Well . . . he would play it by ear. If bicycle guy got snotty, what choice
did he have?

Bern went to the woman's bedroom and found a comfortable hiding
place next to what turned out to be a great big musty steamer trunk. He
waited ten minutes . . . twenty minutes, the illuminated clock on her night-
stand sitting right there.

Where the hell is she?

He stuck with the plan, but decided ten more minutes, no more.

After that, he would ransack the fucking house because he was *not*
leaving without those loan notes.

Bern got so bored he opened the trunk and started snooping through
the old photos, letters, and papers inside.

Bingo.

There it was, an envelope, *Loan Documents, Mr. Frederick Roth,* written
in ink, plus other loan documents scattered throughout the trunk.
Photos of Marlissa Dorn, too. The blond guy, Roth, was standing next to
her in a couple of them. The most interesting shot, though, was taken at
some fancy restaurant: the movie queen sitting at a table, men on both sides
of her, a couple of them wearing Nazi uniforms and gun belts, the handles of their German Lugers showing.

That was cool. Like his Luger, only these were real.

One of the guys was wearing a suit, not a uniform—*holy shit*—it was his grandfather, back when he was using his real name, no doubt, Heinrich Goddard. No mistaking the old man's piggish face, that sneering expression.

Amazing—but not because of his grandfather. His grandfather was sitting on the movie queen's right. To her left, at the head of the table, was *Adolf Hitler.*

Goddamn. Was there anybody famous that old bastard didn't know?

Bern decided to leave while the going was good and lugged the trunk to the front door, ready to load onto Moe's truck. The only reason he returned upstairs was to retrieve his reading glasses, which he'd forgotten, but then he also decided to grab a few mementos while he was at it. Couple of bottles of booze . . . and that's when he heard the sliding doors open and realized it was the woman.

A small woman . . . that big steamer trunk. Bern thought about it. Lots of room in the trunk; the woman couldn't weigh a hundred pounds.

Bern walked tiptoe soft to the balcony curtains, a good place to hide in a room where lights were dim.

Rumbling thunder; lightning struck nearby, dishes rattled. Standing behind the curtain, Bern heard the woman stop at the top of the stairs. He couldn't see her, but he heard her—a long silence. Maybe she was worried lightning had hit the house . . . or waiting for bicycle guy to follow.

He hoped not. *Shit.* He'd left Moe's chrome .357 downstairs on the trunk, thinking that he would grab his reading glasses, return a second later, and be *out of there.*

Didn't have his Luger, either. That was in the bay, Bern had tossed it off a bridge near Indian Harbor.

Bern expected her to turn on more lights. She didn't. Heard the woman begin to hum a little tune . . . then she was singing softly.

Nice voice. It gave him a funny feeling. Like soft thunder, vibrating inside his chest.

Bern listened while waiting to see if bicycle guy appeared. He heard the woman cross the floor near the piano . . . heard her voice grow softer as she entered a hallway where there was an office and a guest room.

He had searched both, left them neat.

Bern peeked. She wasn't there.

He peeked again a moment later and she *was* there. Standing right in front of him.

Jesus.

"Did I scare you, kiddo? Hello . . . I'm talking to *you,* dear, behind the curtain. Are we playing hide-and-seek? I *hope* so, because if you're playing hard to get, you've chosen the wrong playmate. And the wrong house. *Move.*"

Bern did, feeling stupid . . . and there she was, the movie queen, not an old woman as expected. The piano was behind her as if she had just stepped out of the glamorous photo, but wearing a white robe, not a sequined gown, hair up because it was wet, holding a pistol in her left hand.

Older . . . but those eyes, her lips, were the same . . .

"Why are you in my house?"

Bern didn't hear the question. He was staring at her face, feeling the heat of the woman's eyes, thinking, *It's really her.*

"My God, man, can't you talk? You look like something that should be saddled and fed apples. Stomp once for no, dear."

It was weird. All the nights he'd studied her photo, now here she was. *Different-looking,* for some reason, maybe because she was close enough to touch . . . or maybe because he'd heard her sing. Peculiar, the way her voice vibrated inside him.

Bern spoke. "I was . . . behind the curtain," then grimaced because it was the sort of dumb thing he always said to beautiful women, unless it was sneaking up behind them in a parking lot, in control.

"Yes, the curtain, dear, I know. But I'm not Dorothy, and this isn't Oz. Why *are* you here?"

He shook his head, trying to get rid of the spooky feeling. He focused on the gun she was holding. Goddamn, it was a German Luger. Not shiny like the one he'd used to kill Moe. The barrel showed some pitting. A real Luger. He was impressed.

Bern put on his smile. "Hey, I had a gun like that. Great little weapon, isn't it?" He took a step toward the woman but stopped when she clicked the safety off, a distinctive sound Bern recognized.

Sounding suspicious, she asked, "Have we met? I would *swear* I've seen your face before."

Bern shook his head slowly, not sure how she did that, made her voice sound spooky. "No." But he was remembering the photo he'd found in the trunk. Everyone said Bern looked like his grandfather. If that's what the woman was thinking, it probably wasn't a good thing . . .

The softer her voicer, the spookier. "Are you certain? You look just like a man I once knew named Goddard. A very *bad* man."

Bern thought about admitting it—yeah, you used to know my grandfather—but could see that would be dangerous, the way her eyes glittered.

She looked at him hard. "Are you here to rob me? Or have you already robbed me?"

The woman took a couple of slow steps backward, closer to the piano. It gave her time to glance to her left, then her right. Bern hadn't ransacked the place. It looked the same as when he arrived.

Except for . . . shit, except for the booze. He'd left it on the counter.

She noticed. "A man your age out in a tropical storm stealing whiskey? Do you realize how pathetic that is? If your name's not Goddard, then what is it?"

"Uh . . . Moe. My name is Moe."

"Charming. There's a meeting you should attend. Stand up and say, 'Hello, my name is Moe!' It may save you some doctor bills down the road."

Now she was getting irritating. "I don't need to go to AA meetings, lady. My health's just fine."

"Not after I shoot you." The movie queen raised the Luger slightly, now holding it in both hands. *Aiming* at him.

"Hey. Wait a minute." Bern began to back away.

She had one eye closed now, leaning as marksmen do just before they pull the trigger. "First offenders I generally just shoot in the stomach and let God decide. With you, though, Mr. Moe Goddard, I think I'll make an exception."

Jesus Christ! She meant it!

Bern was wondering just how much it was going to hurt, when lightning zapped the balcony railing. The movie queen's eyes flicked to the window for only a second.

It was all the time Bern needed . . .

**43** Chestra left during a lull in the storm, but a squall band was over the island now, lightning popping, and I could hear more rain rattling through trees toward the gazebo.

I also heard was a muffled *bang*. It sounded like a door slamming or the backfire of a car.

I checked my watch. Chestra had been gone nearly fifteen minutes. That seemed too long. I waited another five minutes before deciding it *was* too long. I should check on her.

My shirt and khaki slacks were hanging on a chair, still soaked. I dropped the towel and walked to the chair. I had one leg in my pants when I realized there was a vehicle sitting in the drive, headlights visible through the trees. They illuminated a section of Chestra's house, the cab of my old Chevy, and froze silver tracers of rain.

I hadn't heard it arrive, because of the storm.

As I zipped my pants, I opened the gazebo door for a better look. It was a pickup truck. Big tires, and vertical chrome exhaust pipes that would might make a NASCAR rumble, if I was near enough to hear.

It was the same truck I had seen earlier that evening, lights out, parked in the drive.

I felt a chilly spike of awareness move from spine to neck, and I rushed to get the rest of my clothes, watching. As I hurried through bare trees, I saw Chestra's front door open and a man appear. His shadow was massive on the house's gray shingles. He turned and pulled an object through the doorway. Something heavy. I watched him drag the thing across the sand, toward the waiting truck.

I was looking for my shoes. Where were my shoes? I decided, to hell with my shoes, and charged out. As I did, I saw the man squat and heft the thing onto his shoulder. A box, maybe . . . or a sack. He took a few steps, then dumped it into the truck's bed.

I yelled as I sprinted toward him.

There's an old fake film clip of a creature that woodsmen in the Pacific Northwest call Sasquatch. In the clip, a guy in a hairy costume turns to face the camera, pauses, then flees, taking long, deliberate strides. The man's reaction was similar: in a hurry but not scared.

He crossed in front of the truck's headlights, then gave me one last look before getting into the cab. No, he wasn't afraid. Not of me—although I doubt if he recognized me. It was Augie's NFL-sized uncle from Indian Harbor. The man who'd head-butted me, then kicked me with contempt. The big square face; jaw like a robot, the frozen smile. He owned the marina where Javier had been shot and killed. Bern something . . .

The name came to me despite the crazy unreality of seeing the man here. At Chestra's house. After midnight in a storm?

Bern Heller.

What was the connection?

He slammed the door, threw the truck into reverse, and backed out of the drive at an insane speed, tires squealing when they hit asphalt. The tires spun again when he sped away on Gulf Drive toward the lighthouse.

What the hell is going on?

The box . . . what was in the box? Old papers—my first thought. The promissory notes. Even if Heller knew about them, though, they couldn't be that heavy.

He had left the door to the house open. I stopped, and yelled toward the stairs. "Chestra? Chestra!"

Silence.

"Marlissa!"

I heard a door slam, simultaneous with a gust of wind.

I considered running upstairs to look for the woman but my instincts were fixated on the weight of the box. Why was it so heavy? Why was the man in such a hurry? He was running for a reason.

I had witnessed Bern Heller's secret craziness. I saw the vicious little boy who lived behind his eyes. If he had kidnapped Chestra . . . ?

I sprinted to my truck, shifted to reverse, floored the accelerator and turned onto Gulf Drive.

It was raining again. The old truck's wipers squeegeed brief snapshots of the road ahead. As I drove, my brain scanned for a connection.

Bern Heller . . . Sanibel . . . Javier . . . Indian Harbor . . . Chestra?

No meaningful linkage.

Gulf Drive turned sharply toward Casa Ybel Road. I nearly missed the curve. If my truck wasn't so old and slow, I probably would have skidded into trees.

It was the back way to the causeway bridge. A route well known to locals, but Heller wasn't local. If he wasn't aware the bridge was closed, I had him. There would be police at the intersection turning away traffic—if there was any traffic on this stormy night. I would pull in close behind his vehicle, block his retreat, and ask the cops to take a look: Find out what was in the box he stole from my friend's house.

I was torn. Had he kidnapped Chestra? Or was she still in the house, possibly badly hurt, unable to answer when I called her name But the box . . . its weight.

The thought of her stuffed into a box, riding through rain in the back of a truck, was sickening.

As I approached Beach Road, I saw taillights ahead. I couldn't tell if it was Heller, but the vehicle didn't turn toward the bridge. Nor did it turn on the next road, Lindgren Boulevard—the driver wasn't escaping to the mainland via the causeway. The vehicle was headed for a residential area, streets named after seashells, then East Gulf Drive.

East Gulf Drive was near a large rind of public beach, the lighthouse, and deepwater docks on the bay side, Ferry Boat Landing, where Jeth moored the Viking . . .

The Viking . . .

That's it.

The connection. I had it. Bern Heller and Sanibel. Jeth told me someone had snuck aboard the boat, stole some things—it was Heller. Which meant that he was no stranger to the area. But why was Chestra involved? I had no idea unless . . .

The wreck—*Dark Light*. Her family owned it. Heller had seen the Nazi artifacts. He wanted them, so did his nephew. Somehow, he had found her. The linkage was tenuous, but it was meaningful. It was all I had, and if I was right I knew where he was headed.

I was right.

When I skidded into the parking area at Ferry Boat landing, Heller's truck was there—a much faster truck than mine, because the big man already had the Viking's engines started. No cabin lights or navigational lights showing, but he was easy to spot. The docks were illuminated by shepherd's crook lamps, plus the lighthouse was only a few hundred yards away: a medieval-looking tower capped with crystal. Its revolving column of light was much brighter here, illuminating clouds above, and whitecaps breaking bayside.

With each revolution, the beacon exposed Heller as if he were on stage. He was dragging a bag toward the Viking. A very heavy bag, not a box as I had thought. When he got to the gangplank, he lifted the bag, swung it to get momentum, then tossed it aboard.

I was out of the truck, running, and close enough to hear the bag hit. It was a sickening bone-on-wood sound. Distinctive, even with the rumble of engines.

He hadn't noticed me pull in. I wanted to come up behind him and take him by surprise. He'd waved a semiautomatic at Jeth and me when he was seasick. Maybe he was carrying the gun now.

Maybe . . .

Behind me, headlights blinked from low beam to high. There was another vehicle in the parking lot. When Heller turned to look, he saw me. I watched his expression change from surprise to rage . . . then to recognition. He *knew* who I was. I was the Sanibel guy who'd taken the Viking from Augie. It registered on his face, a mixture of triumph and satisfaction.

His turn to steal the Viking.

Heller stepped aboard the boat and kicked the gangplank free. Before he turned to the controls and got under way, he showed me his vicious smile . . . along with his middle finger. Then he nudged both throttles forward.

It was like the day we'd found the wreck *Dark Light*. The day I watched his nephew make every mistake a novice could make, from bungling the anchor to losing this vessel.

Heller had already freed ropes at the front and back. But he hadn't noticed four additional lines that ran from the Viking's aft, middle, and forward cleats to outboard pilings—spring lines, they are called, because they absorb shock and limit a boat's movement.

Jeth had used good braided line, and done a professional job, anticipating the storm.

When Heller pushed the throttles forward, the diesels rumbled, propellers frothed the water, ropes and the pilings creaked . . . but the boat didn't move. He gunned it a couple of times . . . waited, then hit the throttles again before he shifted the engines to neutral.

I was sprinting full speed along the dock when Heller exited the cabin to see what the problem was. I didn't break stride. His eyes widened as I leaped onto the Viking and put my shoulder down, hitting him belly high like a linebacker.

The bag he'd tossed onto the deck was there. I nearly tripped over it. An oversized duffel bag, like a pro jock might use. I only got a glimpse as we struggled, but a glimpse was all I needed.

Fingers of a human hand were visible, protruding through the top. Long white fingers, frail looking in death.

Chestra.

My legs continued to drive Heller backward across the deck. I wanted to kill him. But not here. He was bigger, stronger, and quicker. He had proven it. I wouldn't give him another chance.

I used our momentum to back him up until he hit the guard railing. The man gave a woof of pain and surprise as we both tumbled overboard into black water.

I surfaced first, as a column of light panned the marina basin. The beam swept across me, then was gone. A moment later, Heller's massive head appeared. He was sputtering and blowing water from his nose—draconic.

He was within arm's reach, glaring at me. It must have surprised him when I submerged. I found his legs by feel and spun his back to me, as if I were a lifeguard making a rescue.

This was not a rescue.

I came up behind him and locked my arms around his neck, fingers burrowing into soft flesh beneath his jaw mandible. At the same time, I wound my legs through his legs from inside out. Like a grapevine.

He was immobile. The only thing keeping us on the surface was the air in his lungs, the air in my lungs.

From the parking lot, I heard a man yell. There was a sudden flurry of colored lights, red and blue mixing with the lighthouse's pale metronome—police. How had they found me? The difference between perfect and imperfect timing is sometimes only a few seconds. Their timing was not perfect.

Heller began to speak, shouting, "What the hell do you think you're doing, Ford—"

I silenced him, closing his throat with the edge of my forearm. An instant later, I ceased applying pressure. He inhaled mightily, then exhaled, making a guttural *woof*. Immediately, I ratcheted my forearm tight. His lungs were empty; mine, full. I exhaled as I readjusted my grip. I took the man under.

He struggled; I held. He became desperate—my arms and fingers were locked; his legs tied up by mine. Then he panicked, his strength freakish.

I anticipated the three stages. It is the way men die underwater. I had taken men better than Bern Heller beneath the surface. I knew.

Exhale and human lungs still retain a volume of air. Consciously, I relaxed all but those muscles required to control the man. He conserved nothing and therefore expended everything—his breath . . . his cold composure, once so intimidating. His life.

I waited. Patiently.

Underwater, the human eye fails, but pupils remain apertures sensitive to changes in darkness and light. My eyes moved to the surface where a radiant beam sped past . . . then another. The lighthouse's pulse became an exact gauge of Heller's slowing heartbeat.

Light-light . . . dark. Light-light . . . dark.

Unexpectedly, another light then appeared: a spear of incandescence that probed from the darkness above. Then there were several lights above us, much brighter. They were coming from the Viking, or the dock.

Heller's huge hand had tried to break my fingers free of his throat. His hand was still locked on mine, but now only tapped gently, as if keeping time to a fading melody.

Police were up there waiting, I knew. I wanted only a few more seconds . . .

They didn't allow it.

I felt a depth charge percussion, then another—the sound of men jumping into water. Their lights were beside me now. I felt frantic human hands grab my shirt. I pushed them away; they grabbed again. I surfaced, taking Heller with me.

Police, yes. Their lights were blinding . . . and their hurried questions, to my surprise, were based on a flawed assumption.

"Is he okay? Did he fall overboard?"

Talking about the unconscious man who was still alive: Bern Heller. The man they believed I had gone underwater to save.

The police wanted me to look at the body inside the duffel bag.

I told them, "I'd rather not."

They pressed.

EMTs were on scene. Heller was faceup on a gurney inside an ambulance. In the glare of lights and silver rain, efficient silhouettes moved around him working to bring him back.

I hoped they failed. I feared that if I saw Chestra's body inside the bag, I would lose control and try to fight my way to the ambulance; try to get my hands around his throat—damning behavior for a man being credited for a heroic rescue attempt.

I had told them I followed Heller because I saw him steal what I thought was a box from Mildred Engle's home on Gulf Drive. I'd ended up trying to save the man when I realized he couldn't swim.

"We know you've been through a lot," one of the officers now said to me. "But . . . we found a body aboard the boat. He may have been headed out to dump it when you saw him fall over. Do you mind taking a look it?"

I minded. But I followed the officer, anyway, feeling sick.

It was nearly 1 A.M. Storm winds gusted, no longer gale force. I had a towel around my shoulders. I felt exhausted.

Unreal reality. I wished I was aboard *No Mas,* discussing inanities with Tomlinson.

Instead, I stepped aboard the Viking. There were a half-dozen law enforcement people shielding the bag and the body from me. My presence, a civilian, caused them to lower their voices. The officer I was following held up a finger—it would be a minute or two before they were ready.

I turned my back to the group and waited. The lights inside the boat were on, cabin door open. No one stopped me when I stepped inside and took a look.

Three suitcases there, Heller's name and Wisconsin address on one of the tags.

Yes, he had been attempting to escape by water. But where?

I didn't give it much thought. I didn't care.

I had been aboard this vessel enough to notice that along with the suitcases, Heller had brought something else into the cabin. It was a trunk. The old steamship variety: wood and leather, with a brass lock.

The lock was sprung. I opened the trunk.

Inside were packets of letters, some sheet music and old photos. I looked at one. Marlissa Dorn. Not a glamour shot, but taken when she was about the same age.

A beautiful woman.

The promissory notes were there, too. Some were in an envelope, others scattered throughout the trunk—rectangles of fragile brown paper signed by Marlissa and Frederick Roth. It was the box I'd seen him take from Southwind.

I was confused. When had Heller loaded the bag containing Chestra's body into the truck?

I stepped outside. People standing around the body made room.

I forced myself to look at the bag. It wasn't Chestra.

It was a man, his face unrecognizable because he'd been shot execution style in the back of the head—grotesque.

I recognized the straw cowboy hat, though. Heller had called him Moe.

The officer asked, "Any idea who it is, Doc?"

I shook my head. If this was Moe, then Chestra was—oh God. I brushed past the cop, and sprinted toward my truck before he could ask anything else.

Several minutes later, I skidded to a stop in Southwind's driveway expecting the worst.

C hestra!"

The front door was closed but not bolted. I stepped inside, calling for her.

"Chestra!"

Behind me, the tree canopy flickered with light, bare limbs gray, black, bronze.

I sprinted up the steps, still calling for her . . . then stopped at the head of the stairs . . .

Chestra was at the piano, bent over the keyboard as if she'd fallen sleep. The piano's candelabra was a pyramid of lighted candles. The balcony doors were closed, but curtains allowed moonlight. A white lace shawl covered her head. She looked frail, like an October leaf about to blow away.

"Chestra."

She stirred. Slowly, then, the woman removed the shawl and looked at me. She had been holding a compress to her forehead, I realized.

"Doc? Doc, thank God you're not hurt. I was worried."

I walked to the piano. There was a bowl of ice and another cloth compress on the stand next to her. I knelt and put my hand on her shoulder. "Are you all right?"

She had been crying, and I could see a plum-sized lump above her left eye.

She used her hand to dismiss the subject. "Yes. But he did *surprise* me. I was terrified, of course, but I tried not to show it—remember my philosophy about men and wolves?"

Never show fear. I remembered.

"I inherited a little popgun of a pistol from Marlissa, and I managed to get it on him, but he wrestled it away before I could—"

Shoot him?

She didn't finish. She looked at me. "What about you? Did you catch him?"

"Yes."

Her tone became expectant, although she tried to mask it. "I hope you didn't do something crazy—like kill him?" She looked at me suddenly, searching my face.

I said, "Almost. But, no."

She nodded. "I don't know why the fool didn't shoot *me*. But it was the strangest thing, Doc. He had the gun, pointing right at me. Then there was a lightning flash, and . . . he got the queerest expression on his face. It was as if he'd been struck dumb." The woman touched a gentle finger to her forehead. "He just stood there, staring, then he must have hit me. When I came to, I heard your truck leave. That's why I called the police. I was worried you would follow him. And he was *monstrous*."

No wonder the cops reacted so quickly when they spotted my truck at the ferry landing.

There was a box of tissues on the piano and she took one. She dabbed at her eyes, then blew her nose delicately, before standing and walking past me. She was bundled in a white robe, hair frazzled from the storm. "If you don't mind, though, Doc, I'd prefer not to discuss it anymore. I'm not prepared for visitors, I'm afraid. And I have a lot to do."

Outside, lightning flared twice. It illuminated her face . . . abandoned it to shadows . . . then illuminated her face again. I took a step back, and shook my head, trying to clear what had to have been a hallucination.

"Doc? You're white as a ghost. Can I get you something?"

I said, "No. But I need to sit down a minute." I walked to the bar and poured soda water over ice, intentionally not looking at Chestra. In the strobing light, her face had changed . . . no, it had *appeared* to change. One moment she was old, an instant later she was young. Old . . . young . . . dark . . . light.

Heller had stared at her instead of killing her. Had he experienced the same dizzying hallucination?

"Men," I heard her say. "Hard on the outside, but so soft on the inside. Sit there and rest, dear."

I plopped down in the chair near the piano. She patted my shoulder as she past.

I felt distanced from reality.

Several hours had passed since I had sat aboard *No Mas* and taken a couple of puffs from a joint. I'd been in water that was dark and cold; I'd sobered. I was sober enough to realize the drug had affected me. But had it done this?

The drug had scrambled my sense of time. It had also intensified various fixations, and I'm tunnel-visioned to begin with, prone to what shrinks call OCB. So it had skewed my judgment, too.

Tomlinson covets varieties of cannabis that cause hallucinations. Could hallucinations be so emotionally authentic that they registered inside the brain as fact?

Was that why Chestra was behaving so distant now—as if our time together in the gazebo was something I'd dreamed? Or . . . was it because I had called her *Marlissa*?

I remembered Tomlinson telling me that she had ended their relationship when he'd done something similar . . . But, no, this was ridiculous. I was just tired and beat-up, that's all.

I noticed something for the first time. The hallway was a chaos of clothing, personal items and suitcases. Either Heller had made a mess of the place, or . . .

She saw my expression.

"Yes, dear, I am packing to leave."

"What?"

"That's right. It's *time*. Thanks to you and your friends, I found out the truth tonight about Frederick Roth. I had no idea it would be such an emotional experience. Marlissa has become more than a hobby, I've realized. In a way, I'm her . . . custodian. It broke my heart when I was told Freddy abandoned her. Doc"—the woman paused long enough to smile at me—"you made Marlissa's memory . . . her story . . . *romantic* again. Thank you for that."

I said, "You're welcome. But does that mean you have to leave, go back to Manhattan?"

"Let's just say I'm *going*. Leave it at that."

I stood. "Do you need help?"

She shook her head. "No, I want to be alone. With Freddy. I'm sure you understand."

No, I didn't. I put my drink on the table as she opened the balcony doors. I followed her outside. She was reaching for the light switch when I caught her. I placed my hands on her shoulders.

"Chestra. Why are you doing this?"

As I pivoted her, she reached for the switch again and turned on the lights. There were two flood lamps above the balcony doors, megawattage for security. They produced harsh, unfiltered beams that had a surgical sterility.

What she then did was intentional, like punishment. Chestra pulled me close, then tilted her face into the blinding rays, as if looking into the sun. She held the pose to make certain I had all the time I needed to see what she *really* looked like.

My reaction was involuntary: I stepped back.

This was not the woman I had lifted into my arms during the storm.

The woman smiled, still holding the pose, forcing me to look at her again. Something familiar was in her smile—the diamond glitter of her eyes? *Yes.*

"Don't you agree, Doc? It's time for me to be gone."

Chestra expected me to turn away. I didn't. I'd seen what she looked like in bright light, but I also knew how she felt and reacted when lights were dim. We had more in common than I had realized.

Instead, I put a finger to her chin and rotated her face toward mine. I held her there while my other hand found the wall, then the switch. The spotlights blinked off.

In the fresh darkness, the moon was huge, pale as a winter sun. She tried to pull away, but I wouldn't allow it. I touched my lips to hers.

She smiled, and placed her hand on the side of my face. "Good-bye, Doc."

Then she led me down the stairs to the front door.

After it closed behind me, I walked to the beach, alone. Wind pushed moonlight off the Gulf of Mexico, and I stood in the dark, listening, as the piano began, first tentative, then with more certainty, her voice matching the cadence of waves.

Never mind . . .
The sun is on the sea
In my mind
Waves wash over me
We'll never know
All that we possess
'Til the end of time
We can only guess . . .

EPILOGUE

By the first week of October, weather cleared, becoming typical of Florida autumns: tropic blue mornings, cool nights with stars, jasmine beneath a hunter's moon. Beaches were silver. At night, palms were moon-glazed.

After two weeks without wind, the Gulf of Mexico also began to clear. By October 15th, a Saturday, Jeth, Tomlinson, Arlis Futch, and I decided water visibility had sufficiently improved to make our second dive on the wreck *Dark Light*. Chestra was still funding the project, taking care of legalities through her uncle's lawyer. She had agreed that we were entitled to the majority of what we salvaged, minus all personal items that may have belonged to Frederick Roth.

In death, with Chestra standing sentinel, Marlissa Dorn remained faithful to her lover—something she'd been unable to manage in life. Penitence, perhaps, for a beautiful woman's imperfections.

The storm had blown away all but one of our marker buoys, so we began all over. Dropped a half-dozen new buoys to outline the wreck, then followed the same search plan as before, three divers swimming circles, an orderly pattern by use of a rope.

The visibility was poor. I could see only five or six feet before objects disappeared in the murk. But it was markedly better than before.

We found more interesting objects from a classic American era—a time of torch singers, inventors, immigrants, and industrial aristocrats. A time when common people lived heroic lives and battled epic evils.

We found bottles. Part of an Edison phonograph. A brass-handled walking stick.

We also found a couple of objects so valuable that Jeth howled underwater when he saw what I had dug from the sand: two gold bars. Small, about the size of miniature loaves of bread. Heavy.

Gold does not tarnish in salt water, so they looked as freshly made as the day they were struck with their mint ID:

DEUTSCHE REICHSBANK

I KILO

FEINGOLD 999.9

The bars were also stamped with a square-winged eagle, its talon clutching a swastika.

Later, we would calculate the value of a kilo of gold at current prices. Each bar was worth more than thirty thousand dollars. As historical objects, it was possible they were worth more. It was something to research.

Jeth and his pregnant wife, my dear friend Janet, were both ecstatic.

If, as Tomlinson said, there were dark spirits lingering among *Dark Light*'s ruins, they did not bump us. However, I did see a canoe-sized bull shark glide by, then vanish in the gloom. It was a male, easily identified because of the claspers near its anal fin. Bull sharks are responsible for more attacks on divers than great whites, so I called an end to the dive just to be on the safe side. Also, I had dealt with a shark of similar size in my past. Very similar. The resemblance frightened me.

Sharks do not track people over months, over years. Like storms, they are not energized by intent. There is cause but no design. My reaction proved I am not untainted by irrational thoughts and superstitions.

"You're starting to trust your intuition," Tomlinson said when I mentioned the shark. "You are opening up; beginning a very far-out, creative, reflective period of your life."

I told him I hoped not. There was too much work to do around the lab.

My reaction was the same when he offered me a lighted joint on the boat trip back to Dinkin's Bay. I refused, then told him to never bring the stuff aboard a working vessel that I was aboard.

He smiled, and said, "Lighten up, man. I can see you're undecided."

A joke, but I wasn't undecided. It was something I would not try again. The experience was powerfully linked with Mildred Chestra Engle. It had blurred the evening. Even now, I wasn't certain what was real, what wasn't. Like the appearance of a familiar shark, there were implications that frightened me.

One unambiguous reality was a note Chestra mailed to the marina, postmarked Manhattan. It arrived five days after she left.

> *Doc, dear man, I am embarrassed that I left so quickly, and also by my behavior. At my age, my God! I had more than my usual one chartreuse & soda that night, which is the only way I can explain it, plus there was that magnificent storm! I hope you will forgive me.*
>
> *Fondly, Chessie*
>
> *P.S. I shouldn't ask your forgiveness—I forgot your kind reminder: There are only two things women are never forgiven. Everything else, there's no need to ask. MCE*

On Tuesday, the eighteenth, we were readying the Viking for our third dive on the wreck when we got a phone call from Arlis saying he couldn't join us.

The previous night, someone had torched Indian Harbor Marina, its docks, fuel depot, and office. "It was one hell of a fire, lots of explosions, but nobody hurt," Arlis told me. Then added, after a pause. "That's what I heard, anyway."

Detectives wanted to question him, he said. He would be busy most of the day.

Indian Harbor had become well known to law enforcement types in the last few weeks. Javier had died there. His killer, a marina employee named Matthew "Moe" Klabundee, had been murdered there. Bernard

Heller was in jail without hope of a bond because two more bodies had been found on the property. Women who had been packed in drums, then buried. Investigators had found a lot of damning evidence in Heller's residence that indicated he might be responsible for other crimes around the country.

A vicious little boy lived behind the man's blue eyes.

When I read about Heller in the newspaper, I reflected on the night I held the struggling man beneath black water. Another few seconds was all I needed. A few seconds: the difference between perfect and imperfect timing.

We couldn't find a replacement for Arlis, but we made the dive, anyway.

Two more bars of gold. Same markings.

Frederick Roth, and *Dark Light,* had not been inexpensive.

Maybe there was more. We hoped. We hunted. There wasn't.

October 19th, a Wednesday, was too windy to dive—fine with me, because there was a decent collecting tide at 2:27 P.M. and that's how I spent the afternoon. Wading knee-deep water, searching sandbars, throwing the cast net.

By sunset, I was tired but felt great. Finally, a good working day on an island that was getting back to normal after one of the worst hurricanes in its history.

As I made notes in my log, and marked another day off the lab's calendar, I realized today was the anniversary of another terrible storm—the autumn storm of 1944. It seemed all the more reason to enjoy small, everyday niceties. So when Tomlinson invited me aboard *No Más* for a sunset beer, I accepted.

I had not mentioned Chestra for weeks. Nor had I discussed the scar tissue on her right shoulder. Had he seen it, or touched those small, distinctive marks?

It was not an easy decision. We had an unspoken rule about discussing women with whom we have been intimate. The agreement endorsed a code of chivalry that seems romantic—worse, irrational—to some, but I like it, anyway. I like it enough that it's become part of my personal scaffolding.

So I did not bring up the subject of the lady's shoulder. It was a relief to me, in a way. I knew that Tomlinson would insist on debating the tired old topic of good and evil—how could I not believe those two forces existed? Or not believe that a beautiful young woman could be forever scarred by the touch of an evil man named Adolf?

Even to discuss such a thing was absurd. It was as absurd, I had to remind myself, as my cannabis-induced fantasy that I had held Marlissa Dorn naked in my arms.

Instead, Tomlinson and I discussed familiar topics and exchanged local gossip. Inanities are fun, profundities are a pain in the butt.

But when he opened the icebox to roll a joint, I told him I was going for a run on the beach.

I did.

It was a night of wind and distant lightning. A waning moon was already over the Gulf by the time I got to the end of Tarpon Bay Road; surf was pumping, creating a waterfall roar. I jogged to the beach, then turned toward the lighthouse.

I had been working out hard of late, running every night, so my pace was strong, the route familiar. It took me past Southwind—nothing wistful or nostalgic involved, I told myself. It was a favorite route; one I had enjoyed for years.

A mild deceit.

I slowed, as usual, as I neared the estate. For the last two weeks, the house had been dark, shutters bolted. On this night, I expected it to be the same. It wasn't. The balcony doors were wide, curtains dancing, flickering candles bounced giant shadows among bare trees.

I stopped without realizing I had stopped. Stood with hands on hips, staring.

Was that music playing upstairs? It was difficult to hear because of the wind and rolling surf.

The path that led through trees, past the cemetery, to the house was ahead. I approached it cautiously—no reason to be cautious but it's the way I felt.

Was Chestra inside? It *had* to be Chestra.

Downstairs, I saw a flash of angular light, then darkness. Someone had exited through the sliding doors. Once again, I stopped. I waited, eager to see.

It was a woman, dressed in white. A lean, elegant figure, ghostly as she moved through shadows, hurrying along the path toward the beach, her perfume a vague intimacy dispersed by wind—vanilla and musk. *Familiar.* She passed without noticing me. The Gulf of Mexico was her focus . . . the surf line where waves sailed, then collapsed beneath their thunderous weight.

I took a few steps after her . . . then stopped. Took a few more, then called her name. She didn't hear. I called again. *Chestra!*

The woman was at the tidemark, where beach tilted downhill. I watched her strip off her robe, fold it over her arm, and walk mechanically toward the water.

Chestra swimming? On a night like this? The surf was booming. It was craziness—as crazy as her obsession with storms.

A question she had asked came into my mind. A question about the epitaph on Marlissa Dorn's crypt: WHOM THE SEA GIVES UP, GOD EMBRACES.

Did I believe it was true?

Of course not. But someone like Chestra might . . .

I called her name again. Then ran after her, still calling. Finally, the woman heard me. She turned.

"Hey, mister, what's the problem?"

The voice was eerily similar: a dense, smoky alto, but it wasn't Chestra. It was a young woman, lean, wearing a dark, one-piece swimsuit. The moon was not bright; the lighthouse was far down the beach. Even so, I could see she was remarkably fit. *Painfully fit,* Tomlinson might say.

"Mister? Is there something wrong?" The woman shifted her weight from one foot to another, communicating impatience.

I felt ridiculous. "No, I . . . I thought you were someone else. You looked familiar. I'm sorry."

Overhead, clouds moved. Moonlight brightened. I could see her in more detail: the symmetry of cheeks, pale hair piled up, eyes peering out from two shadowed caverns. I was facing the moon. It was easier for her to see me, I realized.

"The name you called me, what was it?"

I said, "Chestra. It's . . . an unusual name."

The woman's voice warmed slightly. "You don't have to tell me. That's my great-aunt's name. Do you know Chessie?"

It took me a moment to answer. "Yes. We were . . . we are . . . friends."

"Friends, with Aunt Chessie, huh? *Really.*"

The challenging inflection was familiar. *Really.* The woman's voice, even the way she stood, nose to nose, comfortable inside herself, at ease with her body in the one-piece swimsuit, her attitude saying: *Show me. Prove it.*

Intimidating. I felt as if I was being inspected and judged at the same time.

I said, "That's right. I enjoyed listening to her play the piano. She was working on a song when she was here. I liked it a lot. She wrote the song for—"

I stopped. That would have been going too far, saying she'd written the song for me. Indelicate.

As the woman patted at the pockets of her robe, she laughed—a purring sound, aloof as a cat. "My crazy old aunt Chess, yeah, I know the song you're talking about. Chessie left the sheet music here. I was upstairs practicing, but I needed a break. I love the stuff she writes, but she won't let me record anything. She's so damn private, I've never figured out why."

I had a guess but kept it to myself.

I said, "You're a musician?"

"An actress, but I sing, too. I know the song well enough, I could play it—"

It was her turn to stop; realized that she should complete her inspection before inviting a stranger upstairs.

The woman stared at me for a moment, eyes invisible in their two smoldering caverns, an implicit intensity. She said, "You were running. You're in pretty good shape—"

I didn't think she would say it but she did.

"—for a guy your age."

I said, "Thanks. I swim, too. There's a pool at the school, but I like the Gulf better."

That won her approval. The woman said, "Me, too. The ocean, it's *real*. I love to work out, swimming especially. Which will mean no more of these"—she leaned toward her cupped hands, lit a cigarette, but left the lighter burning so I could see her face as she lifted her eyes to mine—"I'll be here most the winter . . . if you need a partner?"